Brennan

Brennan

Bernard Knight

ROBERT HALE · LONDON

First published in Great Britain 2003

ISBN 0 7090 7334 8

Robert Hale Limited
Clerkenwell House
Clerkenwell Green
London EC1R 0HT

2 4 6 8 10 9 7 5 3 1

Typeset in 11/14pt Times
Derek Doyle & Associates, Liverpool.
Printed in Great Britain by
St Edmundsbury Press, Bury St Edmunds, Suffolk.
Bound by Woolnough Bookbinding Limited.

Acknowledgement

The author wishes to thank Mr Stuart McKay, Secretary of the de Havilland Moth Club, for generously providing information about the Tiger Moth biplane, though any errors in the story are due to my misunderstanding.

CHAPTER ONE

BRENNAN hunched over the wheel, his eyes aching from staring through the streaming windscreen in the grey light of an overcast morning. The Land-Rover was touching forty, its tyres whining on the cracked tarmac as they battled into the driving rain. Alongside him, Casey was crouched inside his bright blue anorak, his big nose resting against the muzzle of the shotgun clutched between his knees.

'Pushing it a bit, aren't you? The bridge is coming up.'

This was from the man sitting beyond Casey, squeezed against the nearside door. Now with grey unkempt hair and straggling beard, it was hard to believe that the querulous Mervyn James had once been a consultant physician to the Bristol Royal Infirmary. Brennan grunted and eased his foot from the pedal. The Doc was right, there was a nasty patch of road ahead.

'When Beverley came over last week, he said the bridge had lost a bit more.' Casey was a real Jonah, always relishing some titbit of doom.

The rain eased a little and Brennan leaned forward to peer through the glass, poorly cleaned by the worn wiper blades. Even after many journeys on this stretch of the motorway, he still found it disconcerting to be looking at the blank reverse sides of the big road signs, as they passed him on his offside. In the mirror, he dimly glimpsed the faded white letters which used to tell travellers to turn off for Chepstow and Monmouth. It was facing the wrong way because they were driving on the westbound carriageway of the M48, the other side being completely blocked by the wrecks of two articulated trucks which were rusting away across the whole width of the eastbound lanes.

'Did Bev say it was getting dangerous to cross now?' muttered Brennan, as he slowed to a cautious twenty-five.

'Still OK, he reckoned, but he was on a motorbike. Said the road-deck was beginning to sag in the middle.' Casey delivered the news with a kind of black satisfaction, his heavy features set in a permanent scowl. He had a lantern jaw and jutting brow-ridges and Mervyn had long ago privately diagnosed mild acromegaly, confirmed by the size of his huge hands.

'Another couple of years and the whole bloody lot will fall into the water, like the other one did,' grumbled the old doctor. A few miles further down, the second Severn Bridge had been destroyed by a drifting bulk carrier being driven into the supporting piers. Bound for Avonmouth, the last of its crew had died and the huge vessel had wallowed in the estuary until a ferocious gale on top of a spring tide had sent it smashing repeatedly against the central part of the bridge.

Brennan shrugged as he changed down into third gear. 'So what? We did without 'em for thousands of years.'

Mervyn snorted. 'That new one didn't last long! And this one's not much better!' He prodded a finger forwards, to where the original sixties bridge still clung to existence.

'We'll soon have to go around Gloucester way, like we used to in the old days,' muttered Casey, gloomily.

The mention of years past laid a silence on them, each occupied with their private memories. Brennan was sorry for them, they still weren't able to adjust fully, though they did much better than most. To the others, it would all come right one day. He knew it wouldn't, so it was easier for him to get on with what had to be done.

Slowing even more, he changed down again so that he could bump up over the central reservation, where a runaway truck had destroyed the now-rusted steel barriers between the lanes. Brennan straightened up the sturdy Defender on the proper side of the motorway and drove slowly up the long western approach to the great bridge. The twin towers of the huge structure still reached up to the low cloud and the graceful sweep of the road-deck still arched across the estuary. But through the drizzle, they could see that the bridge, built to last for centuries, was already doomed. As they crawled cautiously along, dodging the burnt-out wreckage of a coach hanging over the side-rail, they could see that many of the vertical steel hangers that slung the roadway from the huge suspension cables, were broken. There had been a great pile-up of vehicles and an intense fire near the centre of the bridge. The impact and heat had snapped some of the hangers and over the succeeding five years, rust, weather and the writhing of the bridge in winter storms, had stressed adjacent struts beyond their limit. Now part of the deck sagged alarmingly down towards the seaward side of the bridge.

More than a dozen cars, trucks and buses stood rusting between the towers and Brennan had to weave past several that all but blocked the lanes. As he edged past a huge Sainsbury's van, the empty eye-sockets of a skull stared blankly at him from the cab. By some quirk, it had remained in place after the driver had decayed across his wheel. The men in the Land-Rover hardly noticed, as death had become far more commonplace than life. Although the passage of more than half a decade had thankfully seen the end of the more offensive forms of corruption, the sight of the dead was still too common for even a casual comment.

Once across the bridge and through the desolate toll booths, Brennan put his foot down and made steady progress along the road on the English side. There were still plenty of wrecks and abandoned vehicles strewn along the M4 motorway, but except in a few places, they were not enough to present a serious obstacle. The three men sat in silence for most of the time, almost hypnotised by the swish of the tyres and a steady metronome beat of the wipers. There was little else to look at in the grey light of the April morning, save the unkempt fields and the rapidly-spreading scrub and saplings. Already much of the road was sprouting grass and weeds through cracks in the surface, especially on the hard shoulder, which was almost continuous with the overgrown verges. The rotting fences allowed wild cattle and horses to roam at will and once Brennan had to brake sharply to avoid half a dozen bedraggled sheep who were wandering about the road.

They drove through the deserted countryside of Wiltshire, but when it became Berkshire, they came upon a new obstruction on the top of the ridge where Membury service station still stood. The five-hundred foot television mast, its guide-wires slackened from lack of attention, had crashed down in the last gale and now lay right across the east-bound lanes.

'That'll take some shifting,' grunted Casey Wallace with morbid satisfaction, moving the gun barrel to the other side of his face.

'And who's going to do that?' demanded Mervyn dryly. The huge lattice-work would lay there until it rusted to nothing, perhaps a few centuries hence. As they drove up to the mast, they saw that the intact crash-barriers prevented them from crossing here to the other carriage-way to get around the obstruction. Cursing, Brennan stopped to wrestle with the transfer box to get into low-ratio and engaged four-wheel drive again. Turning hard left, he forced his way through the undergrowth and slowly bumped through the remains of the hedge and slithered over the wet ground of the field behind the base of the mast, to rejoin the slip road out into the service station.

With a last rattle of its diesel engine, the Land-Rover pulled up near the gutted restaurant, old habits making Brennan stop in the parking lot, though there was probably no other moving vehicle within forty miles.

The three travellers took the opportunity to eat and drink. There was nothing to be looted from the ruins of the service station – all that had gone years ago – but they had brought bread and meat with them, as well as a few bottles of home-brewed beer.

The rain had stopped for the moment, and they took a walk to stretch their legs and empty their bladders after the hard drive from South Wales. Brennan had stopped here several times in the past few years and knew there was nothing worth salvaging from the abandoned cars and remains of the buildings, but their feet still seemed to draw them across to the blackened shell of the restaurant and shops.

'Someone's been here recently,' pointed out Casey. In front of them was a Renault estate car with flat tyres. He jabbed a finger at the edges of the hatchback door, which was lifted up.

'No rust on those jemmy-marks, they're bright metal. Somebody's busted in during the last day or so.'

They looked inside, but whatever might have been worth taking had gone. When they walked on to the building, it was just the same desolate ruin, dripping in the rain. Inside the shattered glass doors could be seen some human bones, scattered by foxes and wild dogs. Incongruously, two electronic games machines still stood against the far wall, gaudy lettering inviting punters to Shoot the Bandits and try Grand Prix Driving. There was nothing worth going inside for, so they walked back, more wary now to watch for signs of living humanity after seeing the recent marks on the Renault. Casey wished that he had not left his gun in the Land-Rover, but all seemed as still as the grave – not that many Britons had graves.

As they started off again, Mervyn asked, 'Whose territory is this? I suppose Swindon or Oxford are nearest towns, but they're all burnt to the ground. No one's still living there.'

Brennan thought for a moment. 'Gloucester's patch comes up nearly as far as this – Jack's zone. I don't suppose the little group in Salisbury lay claim to anything here, they're pretty small-time. It's just a no man's land.'

As they drove around the bend of the exit road, past the ruined and forlorn petrol station, Brennan swore again at what was ahead. Across the road was a long Mercedes van, its once-white sides streaked with rust.

'Can't get around that. Not with that lorry lying there.'

Mervyn stabbed a finger at a big articulated truck lying on its side, just where the van blocked the remaining lane that led out to the motorway. It had obviously skidded and toppled over, lying with its cab towards them, the long canvas-covered trailer stretching away to within a couple of feet of the Mercedes. A brick wall ran almost to the front of the truck, preventing any exit over the verge.

'Sod's law again! Why did the flaming van have to conk out just there?' Casey sounded as miserable as he looked, as Brennan pulled up a few yards short of the double obstruction.

'It wasn't here a few months back, so someone else has been on the move around here. We'll have to push the bloody thing out of the way.' He switched the engine off.

'Come on, Doc – the exercise will do you good.'

He stepped out into the thin drizzle which had started again, pulling his leather car-coat closer around his powerful body. Mervyn James got down more slowly from the other side, his older joints protesting from the damp and the cramped front seat. Leaving Casey in the Rover, they walked together towards the Mercedes, but halfway there, a warning shout came from the Land-Rover.

'Brennan! Look at its tyre tracks!'

Casey, leaning out of the driver's door, was pointing at the ground under the back of the van. Their eyes shot to the wet surface behind the vehicle, where muddy tracks led back to the nearby grass verge. With all this heavy rain, they would have washed away within minutes, so this was no abandoned wreck.

'Back, Doc. Quickly!' Brennan crouched and turned for the Land-Rover, but even as he moved, there was the loud crack of a shot from behind the end of the overturned truck, followed by another from the corner of the brick wall.

'Run for it! Get behind the Rover!' roared Casey. As he spoke, he fired first one, then the other barrel of his twelve-bore over the top of the open door.

There was a yell of pain as the shot peppered whoever was hiding behind the rotting fabric end-flap of the articulated truck. Two more shots came from behind the wall, but thankfully the assailant was using a rifle, not a shotgun. His aim was bad and Mervyn and Brennan were safely behind the Land-Rover before he could fire again.

'Into the back – quick!' snapped Brennan. Casey had dropped down into the cab to reload, as Brennan scrambled over the tailboard and crouched low as he fumbled on the floor for a weapon. Another shot drilled a hole through the green canvas hood, thankfully well away from his head.

Grabbing a self-loading rifle, he passed it over the back to the doctor, then seized a machine pistol for himself. As he clambered out, he heard Casey blast off two more shells from his twelve-bore. Two more bullets ripped into the hood of the Land-Rover, as he tumbled over the tail on to the road.

'Cover me, Casey!' he yelled. The man in the front kicked open the driver's door and fired off a round through the wide crack between the window and the door-pillar. The shot showered the end of the brick wall and while the bandit was keeping his head down, Casey loosed off the other barrel at the long trailer. By then, Brennan had raced to the burnt-out cab of the big truck, which was only a few yards from the Rover.

Mervyn dropped to one knee on the wet road at the tail of their own vehicle and began firing rapid single shots at the end of the brick wall, to discourage the man from showing himself. Brennan suddenly jumped clear of the cab and swung around the back of the fallen truck. Standing with legs wide apart and with a two-handed grip on the machine pistol, he sprayed bullets along the length of the overturned trailer. The adrenaline squirted through his veins as he anticipated being met with a fusillade of shots, but his trigger-finger relaxed when he saw he was shooting at a dead man.

Leaning against the rear trailing-axle, a pair of wheels above his head, was a body, its neck a mass of blood from the impact of a shot from Casey's choke barrel. The blast had hit him as he had rashly come around the tail-end to fire his rifle. His weapon now lay on the ground and his limp body was slowly sliding down the under-surface of the trailer.

'All clear here!' yelled Brennan and he turned to join the other two, but they had done their work before he got back to them. With Casey blasting away as fast as he could reload, the doctor had run to the far end of the brick wall and was peering around its end. He was ready to shoot, but he saw it was unnecessary. A ragged figure was running as fast as his legs would carry him in the direction of the deserted motorway, heading for the other services building on the opposite side.

Mervyn thought of loosing off a couple of rounds after him, but the range was too great for snap shots – and anyway, his heart was not in killing if there was no longer any need to protect their own survival.

'Sure there's no more of the buggers?' Casey called, standing above the Land-Rover door, his gun still at the ready.

'Nobody here. Don't go shooting at me as I come out, OK?'

Brennan came cautiously from behind the overturned truck and saw that Mervyn was gingerly approaching the Mercedes van to make sure that no more thugs were hiding in it. All seemed deserted, but the three of them made a slow circuit of the wrecked vehicles to check that they were alone at last.

'Let's see who this joker was,' suggested Brennan, going back to the rear of the big trailer. They stood over the body, a victim of the latest crime wave. He was stone-dead, though blood was still draining from the gaping wound in his neck.

'What the hell did you load that cannon with, Casey? Elephant shot?' demanded Mervyn. In spite of having to live in a world replete with death, there was still a need to lighten the mood sometimes. Casey had already killed men, when many years before, he was in the Parachute Regiment before joining the Gwent police, but he gained no pleasure from it.

'A shotgun is better any day than those pop-guns,' he grunted.

The old doctor knelt by the man and almost absently checked that his heartbeat had stopped. The victim was a scruffy, black-bearded ruffian in a collection of old clothes that looked as if they had been looted from a scarecrow. He had a coarse, stubbled face and tangled, dirty hair. Even in death, he stank of whisky and when they searched his pockets, they found a half-empty bottle of Johnny Walker. There were no papers or any clue as to his origin, only an odd collection of jewellery, ammunition and few tattered bars of chocolate.

'The Merc must have been theirs – the tyres are good and hard. We should have spotted that before we got out.' Brennan was being too self-critical, but little slips like that could mean sudden death in these violent times. They walked to the white van and looked in the back. Lying on a sodden heap of old sacking was a hi-fi and a pair of speakers.

'Fat lot of good they are, these days, with no electricity,' grunted Casey. 'They must have been looting from force of habit.'

'Perhaps the poor devils were looking for food,' suggested Mervyn. 'Maybe they've got family tucked away in some hovel around here.'

The physician suddenly felt an aching pity for his fellow men, even those who had tried to kill him and he was glad that he hadn't shot the one who ran away.

Brennan hefted the gun in his hands. 'Come on, then. Let's shove this damned thing out of the way.' Releasing the handbrake, they strained to push the van to the verge to clear the road and walked back to their own vehicle, now quiet and subdued. There were too few

Britons left to have to kill any more, even though they had little choice on this occasion. Why did the others ambush them, wondered Brennan? Why attack just for a few sandwiches and their guns? He was bitter as well as sad about it, as there were ways to avoid these confrontations, if everyone cooperated. But these times made a man hard, if he wanted to survive.

The rain continued for several more hours as they drove on, the three of them sitting in almost complete silence, except when they stopped to top up with diesel from the jerrycans carried in the back. There was so much to remember and so little to look forward to. The present was so grim that most people spent their time living in the past. They all thought almost incessantly about their lost families and Brennan had additional worries about Gwen and Liz Peterson.

Though five years had blunted the immediacy of their sorrow, almost everyone that Brennan knew was a prisoner of their memories. They lived life on two levels: the daily round of tasks that was their only means of survival, and a silent vigil of recollection, replaying in their minds the life that they once had, which almost inevitably gravitated to the last awful weeks. Even Brennan himself, perhaps the best-adjusted man left in Britain, still had harrowing dreams and waking memories of the day he buried his wife and two children in a hole he had dug in their garden.

They were within twenty miles of Cambridge before conversation picked up again. The long journey had become more difficult as they turned north from the M4 motorway. Part of the M25 was completely impassable where an aircraft trying to make Heathrow had crashed across the road. With Casey now driving, they had to skirt the edge of London for ten miles, to get back on to the orbital motorway further north. The outer suburbs and the satellite towns were as desolate as the rest of the country, with thousands of burnt-out houses and shops. Roads were littered with rubble from collapsed, incinerated buildings and rusting vehicles were abandoned at all angles. Only the Land-Rover's capacity for taking to the pavements and fields allowed them to get through to the roads leading to the M11, which was relatively free from obstructions. As they neared the university city, Brennan relieved Casey at the wheel and Mervyn became more talkative again.

'This lot we're going to see, Brennan. Who are they exactly?'

The leader glanced across at the speaker and thought again how his alert blue eyes were so at variance with his unkempt appearance. The physician, now sixty-five years old, seemed all spiky grey hair and some flash of memory came into Brennan's mind as he recalled a television version of Robinson Crusoe, many years in the past. The shipwrecked mariner had looked remarkably like Mervyn James. In a way, he mused, that's what we all are now – shipwrecked on a desert island, grubbing amongst the wreckage for supplies. Maybe the whole planet is a desert island, for all he knew.

'Well, what about them?' snapped the doctor, jerking Brennan out of his reverie.

'The Cambridge group? I only know what Beverley told us last week and that letter the fellow brought us a month ago. Bev said they were well organised and had very good discipline.'

Mervyn grunted suspiciously.

'Discipline! Not another West Country set-up, I hope. With another Herr Adolph bloody Mellars!' His voice was heavy with sarcasm. Brennan shrugged, his eyes on the road as two scraggy ponies scurried across the cracking concrete, where lines of grass and weeds were flourishing.

'Bev estimated that they had at least three hundred people there, all in the city itself. They've had to pull in most of their outside folk from the farms, since the trouble began.'

Casey Wallace, his heavily lined face looking like a bloodhound, whistled through his teeth. 'Three hundred! Perhaps they'll want to take us over, not the other way round.'

Brennan sighed to himself, but said nothing. He was tired of trying to drum into the heads of people like Casey that he had not the slightest desire to 'take over' anyone. All he wanted was an alliance, some mutual agreement to work together and share resources and know-how. It was vital to have some degree of cooperation that might help one day to drag themselves back up the steep slope towards some sort of civilisation.

As far as he knew, the British mainland now had some twenty different groups, each with some semblance of leadership and organisation. These were slowly growing larger as they absorbed the remaining isolated survivors and bewildered wanderers, though there were still outlaws scattered in between, like those who had attacked them at Membury that morning. A vast no-man's-land lay between the various groups, as well as a few communities where tyranny and even slavery were the order of the day.

Some of the groups, mainly in Wales, the Marches and the Midlands, had formed a very loose federation. It was the largest unit in Britain, as far as they knew, given the lack of communications. They were now hoping to persuade the Cambridge community to join, to extend the 'Pax Brittanicum' eastwards across the country. It sounded as if the ancient university city had a fairly large and useful unit, measured by the pitiful standards of the day. They already knew from a visit last year, that its sister city Oxford was a deserted, burnt-out ruin and Brennan was intrigued to know why the other great centre of learning had survived so well. Cambridge had recently sent a rather tentative message, delivered to Gloucester by two intrepid men in a Nissan 4x4, asking about the present situation in South Wales and the West. Reading between the lines, it was a covert plea for help, in consequence of 'certain difficulties with immigrants'.

Beverley Truman, their own lowly equivalent of combined Public Relations Officer and Foreign Minister, had gone up to Cambridge on his motorcycle the previous week and brought back favourable reactions for an alliance.

Now the main diplomatic mission was bumping its battered ex-Army Land-Rover towards the city. At Duxford, which Brennan recognised from a visit to the Aircraft Museum long ago, they had to leave the motorway as the flyover of the interchange had completely collapsed, with the blackened wreckage of a large plane embedded in the debris, presumably another casualty trying to land at nearby Stanstead Airport. Brennan went back a short way and found a break in the crash barrier, then drove up the slip road on to the A505.

About six miles outside the ancient city, they saw the first signs of life. There was smoke rising from the chimney of a distant farmhouse and where a bridge over a stream had collapsed, the gap was filled with a rough but effective timber framework.

'Still a few folk living in the countryside. I thought Bev said they were now all holed up in the town?' asked Mervyn, looking out at a man herding cows in a field.

Brennan followed his gaze. 'I think he meant the other side, towards East Anglia proper. We're coming up from the south-west, but the boat people are pushing in from the east.'

He nudged Casey with his elbow. 'Better pull the canvas over that lot in the back. There's sure to be a checkpoint soon and we don't want them to think we've come to start a war.'

Casey twisted round and lowered his shotgun to the floor, next to a dismantled tripod-mounted machine gun, a box of grenades and an assortment of rifles and pistols. He dragged a thick plastic sheet over them and diplomatically scattered some coats and tins of food across the top.

A moment later, Brennan congratulated himself on his timing, as a few hundred yards ahead there was a barrier across the road, made of two farm gates, painted red and white. Beyond was a pair of old trailers, filled with rubble, placed so that they overlapped at the centre of the road to prevent any vehicle from making a dash through the gates.

'They're well organised, I'll say that for them,' exclaimed Mervyn. 'It's like Check-Point Charlie.' He used an expression from the divided Europe of decades ago, that was already ancient history.

At the side of the road, as they drew up at the barrier, was a small cottage, its windows partly bricked up. Brennan saw the muzzle of a large calibre machine gun poking out at them. A young man in a black raincoat came out of the cottage doorway. He had a red armband and carried a shotgun. In his other hand he had a small black box, which immediately caught Casey's eye.

'By damn, look at that! They've got mobile radio.'

Confident that his mate behind the cottage window had them covered, the guard came up to the Land-Rover. Staring at the occupants curiously, his gaze settled on the driver. He saw a large, craggy-looking man in his early forties. Well over six feet tall, Brennan had powerful shoulders and a heavily handsome face, with a square chin and deep-set eyes under thick eyebrows. His dark hair was streaked with grey at the temples and there was more grey at each side of his short, bristly beard.

Brennan returned his inspection calmly. 'Lovely day for ducks,' he observed lightly nodding at the rain.

The man looked at him suspiciously. People didn't comment about the weather these days – or bother to make jokes.

'You're not one of us. Where d'you come from, then?'

'I'm Brennan. The Federation man from South Wales. One of our chaps was through here last week, on a motorbike.'

The guard, a sallow young fellow with close-cropped yellow hair, dropped his radio into a pocket and rubbed the rain off his face with a hand.

'Can you prove it, mate?'

Brennan seldom smiled these days, but this was worth a grin. 'Try giving my bank manager a ring on that radio, sonny,' he suggested. 'I'm sure he'll give me a reference.'

The youth scowled, then sheepishly his face cracked into a reluctant smile.

'Fair enough, chum. But I'll have to call HQ before I can let you through.' He stepped back and spoke into his radio, his head turned away from them. Brennan and the others watched with interest and not a little envy. They'd not seen personal radios in action for a couple of years, since their batteries had given up holding the charge from their makeshift generators. Of course, all telephones, email and mobile phone systems had gone down at the beginning of the nation's collapse.

The young sentinel must have had a satisfactory response from somewhere, for he gave them a thumbs-up sign and went to pull aside one of the painted gates. As Brennan edged the Land-Rover through the gap, he called to the guard through the cab window.

'Where do you get the batteries for that thing?'

'They make 'em up at the factory. There's enough stuff there to last us a hundred years, the amount we need.'

He waved them away and Brennan dodged the vehicle between the blockade of trailers and on to the road beyond.

'Hear that!' exclaimed Casey, forgetting his pessimism for once. 'They've actually got a factory going. Be good allies, would this lot.

For God's sake let's swing a deal with them today.'

Brennan thought the same. The Cambridge Instrument Company, Pye Radio and many others had once been world-famous for electronics, before the Japanese scooped the pool. Even if the famous Cambridge technology was still functioning on only a miniscule scale, it could prove life-saving for their ailing equipment back home in South Wales. He looked forward all the more to talking to their leaders.

The spires and towers of the ancient city became just visible through the mist and another roadblock loomed up, but this time the sentries had been alerted by radio and were expecting them. One came across to give directions.

'You have to go to Addenbrooke's Hospital, chum. That's where it all happens now. The middle of the town's a mess.'

He pointed out the way and they drove through a mile of abandoned suburbs, following an obvious route that had been cleared of debris sufficiently to allow a vehicle to pass. Though a considerable number of houses had been gutted by fire, there was not the widespread destruction that had wiped out London and most of the big cities. But though mainly intact, the buildings here were all empty and most showed signs of rapid dissolution. The frequent violent storms of a changing climate had ripped off tiles and even whole roofs. Weeds and bushes were poking through broken windows and bared rafters, as nature hurried to reclaim her lost property. A pack of half-a-dozen feral dogs bounded across their path, snarling and snapping amongst themselves.

The route was fairly easy to drive along, most of the rubble having been shovelled or bulldozed on to the pavements. These heaps already had vegetation growing on them, especially the ubiquitous buddleia bushes, showing that the clean-up must have been at least a couple of years earlier.

They came to a roundabout, densely overgrown with bushes and small trees, on the other side of which was the entrance to an extensive campus, with large buildings visible beyond. A high chain-link fence had been built around it, with concrete-block defence posts at the corners. The main gate was heavily fortified, with machine gun posts at either side.

'Taking no chances here,' muttered Mervyn. 'Looks like Belfast in the old days.'

'With the Jerries on their doorstep, who can blame them?' grunted Brennan. 'Maybe we can pick up a few tips to help us with our own Irish problem back home.'

The gate guards sent them to a car park further inside the compound, where a few vehicles were coming and going, mostly small trucks and vans. Casey noticed that a number of them were electric-powered, like the old milk floats. There were a number of people hurrying about, wearing overalls or brown warehouse coats. A few looked curiously at the newcomers, others ignored them.

Brennan switched off the engine and they clambered out, stretching their cramped limbs after the long drive. For a few moments, they stood indecisively alongside the Land-Rover, unsure of the next move. Then a woman in a white laboratory coat came out of a large red-brick building nearby, which bore a faded notice proclaiming it to be the Medical School. She waved, then walked briskly across the parking space towards them.

'You must be the party from Wales. They told us on the radio that you'd arrived.'

She was middle-aged, short and dumpy, with dead-white hair. Her face was lined from the horrors they had all suffered, but she was pleasant and businesslike. Brennan introduced himself and his two companions and they all shook hands with her. Stupidly, his mind took time off to try to remember when he had last performed this simple, civilised act.

'Come on up to the Headquarters Room. They're expecting you.'

They followed her into the building and down a corridor to a hall on the ground floor. It seemed to be a food factory, where a dozen men and women were processing vegetables, drying them for storage or potting them up in glass jars. They had no time to look closely as they were hurried through, but what did excite them was that the room hummed with the noise of electric motors, driving slicers and mincers – and in the ceiling, fluorescent tubes glowed brightly to lighten the darkness of an overcast day. To see electricity being used so liberally was a great novelty, used as they were to the meagre output of small petrol generators.

Beyond a pair of swing doors, a wide staircase led to the next floor. Brennan noticed that the atmosphere was warm and Casey must have had the same idea, for he put out a hand to touch a radiator as they passed.

'It's bloody red hot!' he whispered in amazement, but before they had a chance to discuss this latest marvel, they had reached the administrative centre. Doc Mervyn was overcome with nostalgia, for he told them later that he had come up to Addenbrooke's several times in the old days, to lecture and attend clinical meetings – and this floor was one of the places he used to visit. Brennan appreciated what must have been going through the old doctor's mind, as he compared the esoteric medical debates of 1998, with the anxious discussions that were to take place there that day.

They entered another large room with 'Pharmacology Classroom' still displayed on a plaque above the door. It had recently been divided into two halves by an unpainted chipboard partition. Through a glass window in this screen, he could see an Operations Room, with a small telephone exchange manned by a woman. Behind her, a large table was covered with radio equipment, tended by two men wearing headsets.

'That's our nerve centre,' said the short woman, following their gaze. 'We have to keep a pretty close watch on our eastern sector – there are scouts out there with radios, as far away as the Norfolk coast.'

In the other half of the divided hall, several men and women were seated at a long trestle table, one using a wordprocessor, the others wielding screwdrivers and soldering irons as they serviced various pieces of electronic hardware. None of them looked up, they remained intent on their work with an intensity that Brennan found rather unnerving.

As they watched, another door opened behind them and they turned to see a short, stocky woman enter. She had grey hair cut in a masculine crop above a square face which was relieved by sharp blue eyes. Dressed in a faded blue denim jacket and jeans, to Brennan she gave off an indefinable aura of self-confidence and latent power. The laws of natural selection had had a new lease of life since the disaster, forcing the strongest personalities to the top. For better or worse, Brennan himself was a prime example of this predominance of the fittest.

'I'm Mavis Strickland, comrades. I suppose you could call me the Commissar of this little lot!' Her voice was eager and decisive as she held out her hand to the newcomers. The woman introduced the contingent from Wales, having asked all their names on the way up the stairs.

'As you might guess, we tend to run this place on rather socialist lines.' Looking at Strickland's blue Maoist style outfit and the ant-like industry they had seen so far, Brennan was hardly surprised by this opening statement.

'Don't we all these days?' he replied gruffly. 'There's no other way.'

The plain woman frowned slightly. 'The alternatives are anarchy – or tyranny, the rebirth of facism. From what I've heard, there's a lot of both sorts in this poor island, especially up north.'

'And some down in the far west, I can tell you!' broke in Casey. 'That bugger Mellars for one.' This was his pet theme, his dislike of the former Bristol barrister who had set himself up as the 'Fuhrer of Somerset', a sardonic nickname coined by his antagonists.

Brennan shrugged his large shoulders at all this. He wasn't there to argue ideologies – not in a Britain whose total population was probably less than fifty thousand.

The woman who had brought them in waved a hand at the other door and they went through into a room which contained a large bare table surrounded by chairs.

'This is our Council Chamber, where all the hard decisions are taken' said Mavis Strickland, her light tone barely concealing her pride at being so well-organised. They all sat down and three other people hurried in to join them around the table. They were followed by an elderly man carrying a large tray laden with bowls, bread and a jug of steaming soup. At a side table, the short woman was pouring mugs of tea from a large vacuum flask.

'You must be cold and hungry after that long drive,' said Strickland. 'Have this for now and we'll give you a decent meal before you set off home.'

The woman passed around the mugs and smiled as she watched them sipping it appreciatively. 'We found a whole warehouse full of Orange Pekoe. It should last at least twenty years, unless it goes mouldy on us.'

The Cambridge commissar turned to introduce the rest of her politburo to the visitors.

'These are John Lovatt, Mary Spencer and Edgar Lambert. You've already met the tea-lady, Joyce Fuller. We're five of the seven members of the Cambridge Soviet, which does its best to run this outfit.'

Inwardly, Brennan groaned at this description of their organisation. The reappearance of political labels and dogmas – especially ones that had faded many years ago with the disintegration of the USSR – made him despair of ever seeing a new type of society arise from the ashes of the old.

Strickland seemed to read his thoughts.

'We have to start off on the right foot, Brennan. Disaster has levelled us all down to equality. I was Reader in Political Science at Trinity and my comrade John Lovat there, drove a van for the railways. Now we are both equally unemployable in those roles, so we are equal in every other way too. And that applies to all of our people here.'

Mervyn James, once a rabid Tory, broke in impatiently. 'We'd like to get back tonight. Can we get on with the business?'

The leader nodded. 'Sure, sure. Tell us in detail what your proposals are.'

Brennan opened the shabby briefcase that had once been the property of the Ministry of Defence. The embossed Royal Coat of Arms could still be made out faintly on the creased leather of the flap. He took out some papers and smoothed them out on the table alongside his soup bowl. There was no real need for papers, the situation was too simple, but he had some figures written down about the population and settlement areas of the groups that were known to him.

'You already know that we represent the Welsh Marches group, for want of a better name. It covers south and west Wales, and some of the Welsh border country, down to Gloucester.'

Strickland nodded. 'So your man Beverley told us last week. What exactly are you in the organisation?'

Brennan turned up his hands in a Gallic gesture.

'Never really thought about it. I suppose you could call me the "General Manager". Like you, everybody's equal, though we don't use your Marxist vocabulary. If enough of the, let's call them "shareholders", don't like the way I manage, then they can tell me so and I'll quit.'

Edgar Lambert, a lean, haggard-faced man with a look of an undertaker, stared at Brennan from under bushy eyebrows.

'I thought I'd heard that you originally had some official status?'

Brennan ran a thumb down an imaginary crease in his documents.

'Well, I was a colonel in the Army Staff College when the troubles began. I was posted to the headquarters of Western Command near Brecon with a brief to keep that part of the country going after the government and the Royals fled to Bermuda. They even promoted me to Brigadier in the last days, but when the whole thing went pear-shaped, I was left a general without an army.'

He sighed and drank the rest of his tea. 'So I suppose in some ways, I'm still trying to carry out my original orders – more than five years later – by trying to organise people over in the West. But now that all my superiors have vanished or are dead, their orders don't matter one way or the other.'

Mary Spencer, the other woman, restlessly rolled a pencil back and forth between her fingers. She was dark and bespectacled, middle-age and intense. Brennan made a bet with himself that she was another politically-minded university don.

'Were you elected or did you just assume command of your group?' she inquired in a rather plummy voice.

Brennan tried to conceal his irritation.

'Neither, it just sort of happened! I was looking after a handful of survivors near Brecon at the beginning and when small groups progressively joined together, people seemed to want me to carry on being the organiser. At least, no one told me to bugger off!'

'So what sort of numbers have you got down there?' asked Lovatt, the railway van driver. He seemed a pleasant, open sort of man, thick-set and gingery.

'It's really a loose federation of about five smaller groups, stretching from Pembroke across to Gloucester, and up to Worcester. Altogether about four thousand people, but spread very thinly over a hell of a big area.'

Lovatt stroked his beard thoughtfully. 'That must be about ten per cent of the whole population, if we can rely on rumours.'

Casey spoke up again. 'We've made exploratory trips from the South Coast right up to the Lake District and we reckon there must be about thirty thousand left in that area. Probably another twenty thousand in the rest of the country. The big cities bore the brunt of the destruction and there's virtually no one left in any of those.'

'We can vouch for that in London,' grunted Lambert. 'Several years ago, we sent scouting parties down there. It's a desert fifty miles across, all the centre and most of the suburbs burnt out from a fire-storm, the rest empty.'

'We don't know what the situation is in Scotland,' added Mervyn. 'Too far for us to get up over Hadrian's Wall.'

'Not many left in Ireland, by what we can gather,' added Brennan. 'We're getting increasingly desperate raids from there across the Irish Sea. They are becoming a menace – they refuse to cooperate with us at all, they just swoop in to steal whatever they can.'

Strickland and her colleagues digested this for a moment, while the guests tucked into the soup and bread. Eventually, the Commissar broke the silence.

'You've obviously done a lot more travelling than us. We've tended to stay at home and get things organised within a much tighter enclave. That's how we've got so far advanced with our industrial projects. But now it's all being threatened by the increasing problems along the east coast.'

'That's partly why we came,' said Brennan. 'We had heard rumours about the boat people, then we had your message. Beverley brought back confirmation after his trip here last week.'

He paused and looked hard at the faces opposite. 'You're too small to survive if things get rougher. You surely realise that?'

Strickland assumed a rather mulish expression, but Brennan could see that her pride in her small island of civilisation was being eroded by a constant fear of annihilation. The former Brigadier shuffled the papers in front of him. 'I'll leave these with you. They're details, such as we have, of our sector and the other groups who've agreed to cooperate with us. They cover all the ground west of a line from about Bournemouth up through Wiltshire to the West Midlands, then along the Pennines to Lancashire – apart from some of the West Country, where this fascist guy holds sway.'

Brennan pushed the documents over to Strickland. 'It's the eastern side of the country that we're anxious about – and you're a key part of that, as you're bearing the brunt of the pressure from the continent.'

Strickland looked down at her stubby hands resting on the table. 'What sort of cooperation are you thinking of?'

'Anything – everything! We're not after any takeover, if that's what's worrying you. But we want to share our skills, pool our resources, especially technical know-how. We must have better communications, almost all our electrical stuff has decayed. That's where you could help a lot.'

John Lovatt looked sternly across at Brennan. 'So what's in it for us, to put it bluntly?' he demanded.

The dark woman nodded her agreement. 'We've certainly got the electronic know-how all right. So what have you got to offer in exchange?'

Brennan pointed a finger in the direction of the radio room. 'You're all set up to watch the danger coming from the coast – but what can you do about it? Very little, from what I've heard. You've not got the manpower nor the hardware to fight them off, especially if they start coming in force.'

Strickland looked as if she was going to make indignant denial, but Lovatt forestalled her. 'You're right, unfortunately – so what can you do about it?'

'We have the material, the men and the experience to help fend off your unwelcome visitors. Regrettably, we've had quite a bit of practice against the Irish lately.'

'Troops for transistors, eh?' Edgar Lambert wasn't sneering, but he sounded disillusioned.

'You won't get much electronics done if your men are killed and your women taken into slavery,' grated Mervyn.

'There's another thing,' continued Brennan. 'There are a few kids coming along at last, so we've got to get some education going soon. Once our generation dies off, the young ones will have even fewer people to work with – and none of our residual knowledge unless we pass it on. We've just got to prepare them before we kick the bucket – and the larger the pool of expertise, the better the teaching.'

He deliberately emphasised the education aspects, correctly guessing that their academic background would make them rise to the bait.

Doc Mervyn weighed in again with his characteristic lack of finesse.

'And if Brennan here is too hesitant to say outright, I'll tell you that we want to resist any outside interference, especially from Germans. He's a professional soldier and we have the means to protect what's left of our heritage. As he says, we've had to do it already, with the Irish coming at us time and again.'

Strickland looked worried and Brennan mentally cursed the old doctor for his lack of sensitivity. The Cambridge don obviously had an internal conflict between her political idealism and the practicalities of survival.

'We want no revival of nationalism,' murmured Strickland piously. 'If I wasn't an atheist, I might be tempted to think that all this was divine vengeance, a retribution for man's endless aggression.' She waved a hand to embrace the world. Mervyn was even blunter when he retorted.

'Damn fine Marxist you'd be, lying in a gutter with a German bullet in your head. It's "united we stand, divided we fall", madam! If you want to call me a neo-fascist, fine – but I prefer to stay a live fascist than a dead Commie!'

Brennan, inwardly despairing, lifted a placatory hand.

'All right, doc, we don't need to labour the point. All we want to know is whether you will come in with us. Just agree to swap information, resources and communications. Maybe some exchange of personnel – perhaps mixing the blood will increase the fertility. God knows we need it – our whole group's only got thirty kids under five years of age.'

Joyce Fuller clicked her tongue sympathetically. 'I think we're doing better than that, given our much smaller population.'

Brennan plunged on before Mervyn could put his big foot in it again. 'Both of us need some interchange of teachers to fill gaps in our knowledge. You're great on the science, but we're getting pretty good on transport. We might even get a railway line working before long.'

Strickland drummed her fingers on the edge of the table. 'And what about leadership?'

Brennan turned up his hands in a gesture of indifference. 'No problem. Just carry on as we are. No loss of sovereignty, just some give and take on a mutual basis.'

'Just like the Co-op in the old days,' added Mervyn, with a touch of sarcasm.

The stocky leader of the socialist republic of Cambridge looked along the faces of her comrades. They said nothing, but she seemed to take their lack of objection as consent.

'We've talked this over already, after your man came with his overtures the other week. Given certain assurances, we see no reason not to cooperate with you, as long as we can back out if we don't like the way things are going.' She looked again at her colleagues, rather uneasily this time. 'In fact, we urgently need some advice on the mounting problem of these boat people. They're pressing us quite hard now and don't seem the slightest bit interested in negotiating any settlement. In fact, they killed the last two people we sent to talk to them.'

Brennan nodded his understanding. 'Your problem today, but it may be ours tomorrow.' Putting more papers and maps on the table, he spread them out in a wide arc and jabbed his finger down on one.

'Now if we can get down to particulars: these show what equipment we've got available in each of our groups – and what we badly lack. Can we go through them one by one, to see how we can help each other?'

CHAPTER TWO

THE early spring dusk fell as they left Cambridge for home. Strickland had pressed them to stay until morning, but Brennan was uneasy at being away from base, even for a night and decided to get back.

As Casey drove cautiously with the headlights cutting a swathe through the empty roads, Brennan began to wonder, in spite of his claim to Strickland, how long they would be able to keep their transport going. The bright lights of the Land-Rover, including a small searchlight mounted on the roof, reminded him that one of their biggest worries were the vehicle batteries. Diesel and petrol were still to be had in plenty, from village filling-station tanks, small-town depots and even abandoned road tankers – though admittedly, much of the petrol was becoming useless after more than five years' storage, unlike diesel which seemed to last indefinitely. But it was the lead-acid batteries that were the problem, most of which had by now seen the best of their useful life over the period since the disaster struck. They now spent a lot of time searching for new batteries that had never been filled with electrolyte, so that the plates were still virgin. He hoped that the Cambridge people might be able to help, though he doubted that even they had the capacity to build new accumulators. Unless something was done, they would be reduced to using horses and bicycles within a couple more years, as even getting a stretch of railway working was not going to solve much.

To pass the time during the long drive, necessarily even slower in the dark because of the many obstructions in the road, the three men talked about these well-worn problems for the umpteenth time.

'It's not only the batteries, it's the tyres,' complained Casey. 'Even some of the new ones from the depots are starting to perish. Not even the comrades we just left can make tyres.'

The conversation wandered from one shortage to another, repeating the familiar old themes, until they tired of it and fell silent again, their eyes scanning the darkened road for wandering cows and other obstructions.

All these problems they had discussed were a part of the constant worry that Brennan had in trying to organise the surviving community. So many of the men and women, though able to carry out simple, repetitive tasks, seemed to have lost all initiative and resourcefulness. Living from day to day, almost meal to meal, they existed in perpetual bereavement, submerged in the memories of the horrors that had engulfed them and their families. In the early days, there had been many suicides, but apathy seemed to have brought even those to an end. Quite a few were psychiatric wrecks, unable to do anything but sit in a stupor, needing constant attention from others.

Brennan sighed and almost wished that he could become one of the passive majority – it would be a damned sight easier to sit on his backside, he thought, than to voluntarily knock himself out, trying to keep things going. But that was his nature, he recognised ruefully – he knew he could never stand back and watch others stumble over things he could do much better himself.

The Land-Rover droned on through the wasteland of southern England. Alongside him, Mervyn was sound asleep, probably dreaming of a world in which there were still theatres, golf and plenty of children. On the other side of him, Casey drove in silence, also wrapped in his own thoughts, leaving Brennan to continue the endless ramble through his memories and his worries for the future. He thought of Gwen waiting for him to get home, if home was a word he could use for the abandoned college that housed them all in Caerleon.

Gwen. It was strange, he mused, that many men only used their surnames these days, yet virtually all the women were known by their softer first names – though he had some reservations about calling the formidable Ms Strickland 'Mavis'. No one called him anything else but

'Brennan', even Gwen herself. He had to make an effort to remember her surname, which was Sutcliffe.

His own Christian name meant nothing to him these days, especially since he had lost his wife and children. But Gwen – she was now as much his wife as Margaret had ever been, even though no clergyman had murmured the old rituals over them. There was probably not even a Registrar left alive in their half of Britain, to enter any legal details into the records.

Brennan thought again of Margaret, though the recollections were becoming fainter with the passage of each year. Brennan had buried her and the two boys himself, in a hole he dug in the garden of their new married-quarters at the Crickhowell garrison near Brecon. He shuddered again at the memory of those two cataclysmic months – memories that flooded his mind several times a day, and would do so until he died. Two months, in which nine-hundred-and-ninety-nine people in every thousand had died, and an even greater proportion of children, who had been virtually exterminated. Gwen did her best for him, when even now the horrors came in the night. She was stronger, she had had no husband or children to lose – not even a near relative. Though Brennan found some peace with her, she could never replace what was lost – Gwen was something new, not a surrogate for what had once been. She knew it and accepted it, her virtue was that she held no resentment, taking Brennan for what he was – a strong leader.

At forty-one, he was a decade older than Gwen. A strikingly beautiful woman, she had been in her element in the media life of London. Originally an actress, she had become a television presenter, then a producer for one of the larger independent companies. Welsh by birth, she had been spending a holiday with friends who kept a private hotel near Monmouth, when the bottom had started to fall out of civilisation. She knew that if she had been in London, she almost certainly would not have survived. But Gwen was a born winner – Brennan felt that she was probably the most adaptable woman he had ever met. He suspected that if she had the facilities and an audience, she would have been back making television documentaries within a week of the disaster's end.

His musings came to an abrupt end when Casey suddenly stopped dead in the middle of the M4, to change places with him for his turn at driving. From there he had to concentrate on the darkened obstacle race of the motorway for another two hours, until he gave the wheel back again to Casey near the Bath interchange, as Mervyn's eyesight was not good enough for night driving.

On this last lap, Brennan went back to thinking about Gwen and his other problem, their senior nurse Liz Peterson. Not to put too fine a point on it, Liz was in love with him and though he gave her little encouragement, he couldn't deny that he was attracted to the dark-haired girl. He had done nothing about it, but recognised a potential time bomb in the situation. Brennan was not sure if Gwen actually loved him, but he was king and he knew that she was determined to be queen, at least until something better came along. Gwen was wonderful, beautiful, sensual, marvellous in bed and damned effective out of it – but he always had that awareness that should a greater king come along, then it might be 'kiss and goodbye', unlike Liz, who was the steadfast, loyal type who would stick by him 'for richer, for poorer!'

He felt guilty even thinking about the problem and forced his mind on to something else. There was no shortage of matters to worry over, especially concerning the place where they all lived, which Brennan feared might soon have to be abandoned. Just outside Newport, which had once been the third city of Wales, was the small town of Caerleon. It had become virtually a suburb of the now derelict city, though nineteen hundred years earlier, it had been a great fortress and garrison town, the Roman 'City of the Legions', which had given it its name.

Behind Caerleon, at the foot of a hill running down to the River Usk, was a building that looked down on the ruins of two different millenia. A large, red-brick edifice of 1930s vintage, it had been a training college until the devastation came. Although Caerleon, along with most of Newport, had perished in flames, the college had managed to remain unscathed, mainly because it was set apart from the town and had been virtually empty of students during vacation time.

Now it housed over five hundred people, almost the whole surviving population of south-east Wales. The dozens of former classrooms and dormitories provided both the communal living-space and the private accomodation for the pathetically few family remnants. There was a sickbay and even a schoolroom and kindergarten for the score of jealously-guarded youngsters, the most valuable commodity in present-day Britain.

Brennan, as the leader – or 'manager', as he preferred to call himself – had no more privileges than anyone else at Caerleon. He could easily have claimed them, but he chose otherwise – not from any egalitarian motives, but from sensing that he would function better that way. Gwen often urged him to carry more authority and to distance himself from the rest, but he stubbornly resisted her wish to become more obviously the 'First Lady'. Until society recovered sufficiently from its present paralysis – if it ever could – he felt that there was no point in adopting any outward trappings of authority.

In Cambridge, he had recognised that even Strickland, a self-professed Marxist, ruled the enclave much more rigidly than their alleged communism required. As a senior Army officer, Brennan had become well used to the privileges of rank and the social prestige that had gone with it. He had enjoyed the status and would do so again, if the circumstances returned. But until then, he was content to keep a low profile and get his satisfaction from the knowledge that his real power lay in his ability to lead others into getting things done.

Once again, his reverie was disturbed by Casey swerving to avoid some wandering animal, but his mind soon returned to Gwen. He doubted if she felt the same satisfaction in 'doing good works'. Though she could successfully affect the common touch when needed, she had the dormant urges of an empress. Brennan knew that even after five years, she still sorely missed the whirl of London life. Gwen had been riding high in the media world, she had been at the peak of her attractiveness, success and sexuality when the collapse came. Although he knew that her profound common sense told her that all this had gone for many decades, if not for ever, he felt that she was yearning for something or someone to fill the gap. Being the boss's woman was as good as she could get for the moment – though Brennan also hoped that she was in love with him, which would be quite a bonus, while it lasted.

He smiled wryly in the darkness. Poor Gwen – where else could she run to now? There was no bigger king, no better hole in which to shelter, other than the one she had with him. She was empress to an emperor in a scuffed leather jacket, bumping along in a rusty diesel state-carriage, on the way back to the Royal Palace at Caerleon College. His mood softened, as he realised that he was being hardly fair to her. She was a great girl, hard-working, cheerful, popular and talented – especially beneath the blankets. But if a more powerful emperor came along – well, what then?

Casey cut in on his thoughts, as the vehicle made another sudden swerve.

'We've got to send a gang down to clear this flaming roundabout, Brennan,' he growled. 'One day we're going to capsize here and kill the damned lot of us!'

The Rover was bumping over the central reservation again and slowly making its way up the wrong side of Junction 25, one of the main exits to Newport. The slip road that rose from the motorway on the correct side was blocked by fallen masonry from burnt-out houses on the corner of the overpass. Casey used the headlights and searchlight to pick his way through rubble on the opposite ramp, eventually reaching the intersection with the Caerleon road. The surface cleared again and they gathered speed on the last couple of miles of the home stretch.

'It must be bloody late,' grumbled Mervyn, groaning himself awake and peering through the side window into the damp darkness.

'Straight to our pits, lads!' ordered Brennan. 'Leave the chat until the morning – though everyone will be as curious as cats to know how we got on in Cambridge.'

He didn't feel like a public debate at one o'clock in the morning, not after an eight-hour drive on derelict roads. As they reached the final stretch, he reflected on how different the reality of a wrecked Britain was from the ideas of some of the science-fiction writers who had revelled in such stories a few years ago. Their idea of post-apocalyptic devastation was of nuclear-fused cities surrounded by sylvan countryside, where all the survivors needed to do was to walk into the village shops and help themselves from the packed shelves of goodies. The other popular scenario had been of a sudden plague that gently wiped out most of the population, leaving the lucky few to wander around intact cities, ambling into Harrods and Fortnum's, carting off the caviar in a Rolls-Royce taken from a Piccadilly showroom.

Brennan sighed as he thought about the reality. No one had foreseen that the greatest destroyer of all would be fire – almost without exception, the cities had perished from flames. Not the flash fire of hydrogen bombs, but the much more mundane ignition from lit matches and cigarettes dropped from nerveless fingers, from gas and electric fires knocked over by convulsing feet, from televisions and electrical equipment overheating after being left on by their dead or dying owners. From Westminster to Warrington, flames had consumed most urban areas in the first few weeks of the disaster.

As for well-stocked shops, the curse had not been quick enough for that. During the two months when the plague was at its height, factories had come to a halt, transport had seized up, ships and aircraft full of imports had failed to arrive and all the complex machinery of commerce had rapidly declined into chaos. Panic buying, then looting by those who were infected last, had left most of the shops empty – and at the end, most were burned down as the towns and cities blazed.

For the few survivors, finding supplies had been bad at the beginning and in many ways, was just as bad now. Of what was left in the still-intact shops, the perishables had quickly perished and the tinned and bottled food had been used within a few months. Only when the new communities had become better organised and transport restored, could much wider areas be combed for surviving shops and warehouses.

His endless nagging worries were jerked back to the present as Casey bumped the long-suffering Land-Rover off the road and squelched across a field to bypass some blocked streets and reach the driveway of the college, set on a gentle rise above the little town. The first lights they had seen for over two hundred miles glinted in the night.

'They must have got the Yanmar going again,' grunted Casey, as he coasted into the parking area at the back of the three-storied building. 'It can't last much longer, unless we can find a new set of brushes for it.'

The diesel generator, salvaged from a police station in Chepstow, had been running almost continuously for three years and was on its last legs. It would have been a great advertisement for its Japanese manufacturers, but Brennan doubted if anyone was still alive on those distant islands.

Some of the lights gleaming through the windows above were low-powered electric bulbs, the rest were paraffin lamps and candles – another cause of the fires that had devastated Britain after the National Grid had failed. Casey switched off the engine and they sat motionless for a moment, savouring the silence.

'Let's hope the bleeding thing will start again in the morning,' muttered Mervyn. His words brought back a flood of worrying details into Brennan's mind, from failing car batteries to political alliances, but for tonight, he intended pushing them aside. As he wearily stretched his long legs through the opened door, he thought longingly of a bed, with Gwen inside it, warm and clinging.

Then he suddenly had a 'déjà-vu' experience – he was getting out of another Land-Rover, in another time, another place. A smartly dressed staff-sergeant was holding the door for him as he saluted. Was it Cyprus or Hong Kong or Aldershot? The feeling passed as quickly as it had come and sometime Brigadier A.K. Brennan, late Major in the Royal Gloucesters, tramped wearily toward the back door of the college. A self-loading rifle was slung over the shoulder of his crumpled coat and a battered briefcase holding papers of national importance swung from his other hand.

CHAPTER THREE

THE assembly hall of the college was probably one of the most normal-looking places left in Britain. Tubular chairs stood in tidy rows, lit by a weak springtime sun that filtered through long windows that were dusty, but intact. The stage, where once prize-giving and amateur dramatics took place, was set with a table and a few chairs. All the adults in the community were there, save for a few who were sick or upstairs in careful attendance on the few precious children. The scene looked like a local political meeting before a by-election – but the Welsh Assembly was long burned out and Westminster was inhabited only by scavenging dogs.

The only effective government in Wales and the southern Marches sat on the stage and looked down on the electorate – almost all of it for fifty miles around, for they had all converged on Caerleon for company and protection. A few rugged farmers still stuck it out in isolated places, but the countryside was largely deserted. Fear and loneliness had driven most people together, for there were virtually no families left intact. In most households, all had died and it was rare for more than one to survive from a family group. The land was peopled by widows and widowers, the number of surviving couples being counted on the fingers.

Brennan looked down on the rows of faces and once again saw the stunned and uncomprehending expressions on so many, even after five years. Many would never fully appreciate what had happened, but would go to their deaths in this state of numbed shock. Though they might go through the daily round well enough, maybe talk of mundane things, eat, sleep and even make love, there was an element of automatism in the behaviour of many. Perhaps one in ten had come to some sort of acceptance with what had happened – mostly the younger, more resilient folk. Only a very small core, people like Mervyn, Casey, Gwen and himself were the true survivors, some of them actually relishing the situation. Deep down, even Brennan recognised that this challenge, for all its horror and heartbreak, filled some need in his own personality.

The meeting had been going on for half an hour and Mervyn James was on his feet, just finishing a factual description of their previous day's journey. The audience was listening intently, as any news of contact with the outside world was a prized rarity these days.

'. . . so they seem to have about the same proportion of survivors over there as we do in these parts, though they claim to have a few more kids than us. Probably the whole country – maybe the whole world – has lost about the same percentage of their population.'

The old doctor paused to look around the few hundred faces below him, some haggard, some blank, a few almost permanently tearful.

'The Cambridge lot confirm that about one in every thousand of us survived,' he repeated slowly. 'Though London and the cities had it much worse, perhaps because of the crowding together and all the troubles that followed – fires, other diseases, no medical services, food or decent water.'

The physician fell silent and Brennan could almost hear the memories of the audience raking over the familiar images of desolation in their minds.

Mervyn looked across, a questioning look on his face. 'Over to you, Brennan? I've told them what we saw, so perhaps you can talk about their reaction to our proposition.'

He sat down wearily behind the table, slumping between Casey Wallace and Lance Prichard, a good-looking young artist from Swindon, blond of hair and whose rather languid appearance hid a constitution like a tiger. The others on the platform were Beverley Truman, a former Home Office civil servant, and Roger Mellars, the leader of the West Country community, about whom Brennan had very mixed feelings. Mellars had turned up unexpectedly the previous day, having driven up from his base in Glastonbury.

Taking his cue from the doctor, Brennan stood up and leaned his fists on the table. The ranks of faces lifted expectantly to this big man, his heavily handsome face lined with the hardships of the past few years, but relieved by his calm, deep-set eyes.

'Not a great deal more to say, really. The doctor has told you about everything we saw, and it was quite impressive. Technically, the Cambridge lot are streets ahead of any of the other groups, including us. They have a great deal to offer, some things we badly need, like electrical gear. They're also very well organised – perhaps too well organised for some of our old Tories!'

He grinned briefly as he glanced across at Mervyn, who merely grunted.

'So there's nothing but advantage in us joining with them in some form of cooperation. They're willing to join our federation, for what that's worth, as long as they don't have to do anything that they don't fancy.'

He stopped and looked expectantly around the large hall, where the thin sunlight streamed through the faded yellow curtains on the long windows. It fell on a thick-set, middle-aged man in the front row, who stuck up his hand and called out a question. He was a former mechanic and had once been a regional trade-union secretary and still hankered after the levers of power.

'If they're so well set up, why should they bother with us?'

Brennan acknowledged him with a friendly nod. Alfred Ashe always asked the first question in any meeting, but for all his frequent bluster, he was a good-hearted man, another of the magic five per cent.

'It's simple, Alf. They're technically strong, but they're small in number and very isolated out there in East Anglia. They're basically university men and women, with a lot of idealism but not good at defending themselves. The boat people are breathing down their neck and it's only a matter of time before they get overrun.'

Mervyn, who frequently bickered with Alfred Ashe over now-extinct political views, couldn't resist cutting in.

'Not to beat about the bush, our comrades in Cambridge are basically college pinkos who are good at organising workshops and radio sets, but haven't a clue about guarding their own patch. They need us to help keep the Jerries at bay!'

Brennan nodded agreement. 'Regrettably, we've gained fighting experience against the Irish since last year – and we've got the equipment since we collected all that Army stuff recently. But the main thing is numbers – they're too small over there to hold out for long, so it's a trade-off between their technology and our fire-power.'

'Protection in exchange for car batteries, is that it, Brennan?'

This came from alongside him and Brennan looked down to see a faint sneer on Roger Mellars's sleek face. He still looked like the sucessful lawyer he once was and just to be different, always wore a business suit and a Marlborough tie, a somewhat incongruous uniform in the present circumstances. His long face, topped by slicked-back dark hair, wore an almost permanent expression of bored condescension.

'Yes, Roger, if that's how you see it. They'll not be making many batteries if the Germans and Friesians do to Cambridge what they did to the survivors of Ipswich and Colchester – murdered them all!'

There was murmured approval around the table, but the people in the hall stayed silent, except for an elderly man who lurched to his feet unsteadily from his chair at the end of the second row. Above a crumpled and greasy black suit, a clerical dog-collar lay frayed around his throat. One corner of his mouth dropped in the aftermath of a slight stroke, but his voice, though slightly slurred, had a desperate strength. He had been a lecturer in a theological college, though he had retired some years before the disaster struck.

'The world is in ruins and already you're talking about pacts and armies and guns! My God, my God, is it any wonder that we're punished like this!'

He raised his emaciated arms towards the ceiling in a dramatic gesture, and continued to harangue the platform. 'The iniquities of the world brought this upon us – a society rife with sin, the churches empty, marriage ridiculed, half the children bastards, sodomy paraded as a virtue! Now our leaders wish to wage war against the pathetic remnants of our fellow men!'

He fell back into his chair and began weeping uncontrollably. A faded woman alongside patted his shoulder in an awkward attempt at consolation. Brennan looked down with compassion on the old priest.

'I know, Canon Gilbey, I know how you feel, but what would you have us do? We can't turn the other cheek these days. Twenty-six people died last year when the raiders from Wexford attacked us at Carmarthen – and as I said just now, Colchester was virtually wiped out last August. I know things are probably worse in Ireland and parts of the Continent, but those people refuse to live alongside us – they pillage and rob unless they're driven off. Can we let the little bit of civilisation we've so painfully saved here go the same way?'

There was silence in the hall, but again it was broken by the scrape of a chair alongside him. Roger Mellars stood up and Brennan sank back on to his seat with a sour look on his face.

'I think Brigadier Brennan is wrong,' he began, deliberately setting out to annoy the local leader by using his obsolete military title. 'I've made the offer before – and it's the main reason for my coming here again this time. Give up this huge and useless area you have in Wales and the Midlands – it's indefensible. Move down to the West and join us there. With five thousand people from your so-called Federation, we could really get things moving. We could set up a barrier zone across Somerset and Dorset – from the Bristol Channel to the south coast – and concentrate all our efforts in the counties west of that line. Then we could thumb our noses at any attempts at invasion from the east, or the Irish, as we'd have plenty of people and all our resources concentrated in one compact area.' His face became flushed and his advocate's eloquence from his old profession swelled into his voice.

'With your present population spread so thinly from Chester to Salisbury, how can you ever hope to build and defend a meaningful society – and now you're talking about diluting it right out to Cambridge?' he declaimed. 'How many children have you got in that vast area – little more than a hundred! In thirty years there'll be almost no one left, unless we all consolidate into the tightest concentration possible. We must do it now, while we are still strong enough to build and organise! So come down to the West Country to settle – all of you!'

He thumped the table with his fist and sat down with a flourish. Brennan grudgingly admitted to himself that the younger man certainly had the gift of the gab – no wonder he had been such a successful barrister a few years earlier.

There was a wave of murmuring and a few muttered 'hear-hears' from the rows of chairs in the hall. For once, something seemed to have penetrated their apathy. It was obvious that Mellars's invitation had attractions for at least some of the audience, but Mervyn was not going to let him get away with it unchallenged. He came from a hardy farming family in Carmarthen and was not one to suffer rogues gladly. Without getting to his feet, he barked across at the lawyer so that the whole hall could hear.

'Come down to Somerset with you as El Supremo, I suppose! You don't want settlers, you want more serfs. I've heard about your precious fascist regime down there – so no thanks, chum!'

Roger Mellars looked amused at the old doctor's outburst.

'You call it fascist, we call it efficient. Those who have skills naturally direct the work of those who have nothing useful to contribute except their muscles. It's survival we need, not lip-service to some outdated, ineffective democracy. What difference is there between my system and that of the comrades in the Cambridge Reds? Or for that matter, you people here, where Brennan, for all his posing as a 'manager', is really the chief of the tribe?'

The murmuring and muttering swelled in the large hall, some for and some against the persuasive speaker.

'We can get rid of him any time we want by the democratic process, that's the difference!' called out Alfred Ashe from the front row. He had an ingrained faith in the power of the elected committee and the ballot box.

Mellars smiled sardonically. 'You really think that would happen? You couldn't get rid of the best man you've got, so where's the sense in fooling yourselves? You've got no real choice – in situations like this, the cream always comes to the top, and only a meritocracy can survive. Without Brennan here, who led you out of the wilderness in the first place, your outfit would be a shambles inside a month!'

Although this was about the first compliment that Brennan had received in five years, he had no wish for it to have come from Mellars. He disliked him on several counts: he couldn't stand his blatant conceit, he didn't like his dictatorial regime in the West Country – and last, but by no means least, he resented the way that the man undressed Gwen with his eyes every time he looked at her.

The argument went on for some time, with speakers from both floor and platform putting the case for and against a move to the western counties. Brennan pointed out that he had no authority to speak for the other groups in their loose federation, the ones near Gloucester, Worcester, Chester and the like. It became obvious that the majority in the hall were in favour of staying with Brennan, but he ended the session with the reminder that Caerleon was a free community, not a prison camp.

'Anyone who wants to go with Mellars is perfectly free to do so. All they have to do is find some way of getting there – and they're equally welcome to come back if they don't like it. However, I'm not sure if that offer works both ways . . . eh, Mellars?'

That parting shot left the lawyer silent for the moment and Brennan took the opportunity to call the meeting to an abrupt close, as it was almost time for the midday meal. The cooks who had been in the hall hurried back to their steaming cauldrons. In the three years that the college had been their home, the useless gas and electrical equipment in the kitchens had been replaced by solid fuel cookers dragged from other buildings. There was an almost limitless supply of coke and coal for them at the steelworks and fuel depots that lay within a twenty-mile foraging distance. While the meal was being made ready, many of the commune got themselves drinks of either home-made beer or wine from a makeshift bar, then sat at the rows of tables in the dining hall.

The members of the 'management' sat at one table with Mellars and his lieutenant, Wayne Addis, a surly strong-arm man with a blonde cropped head, who rarely opened his mouth. Brennan tried to curb his dislike of Roger Mellars, as the man was his guest and these hard times had revived the traditions of hospitality to all visitors who came in peace.

'Great to have such good beer,' said the former lawyer appreciatively, as he set down his empty glass. 'We've got down to the last of the bottled stuff that survived in the pubs and shops. Strictly rationed now.'

Gwen had come to sit alongside Brennan, her shoulder-length blonde hair swirling across the top of a plain black dress that emphasised her willowy figure. He noticed that today she was wearing more make-up than usual. Food may have been in short supply, but the surviving shops had enough cosmetics to last into the next century. Now she sat between him and Mellars, refilling both their glasses from a large jug of ale.

'You should make your own like us, Roger,' she said, in the dulcet voice that once was so familiar on television. 'We've a couple of keen amateur brewers here – though I suppose they've turned professional now, as it's all they can do to cope with a few hundred thirsty throats every day.' She smiled gaily at Roger Mellars and lifted a glass of red plum wine in salute. 'I prefer the Chateau Caerleon to the beer, but here's to your health, sir!'

Brennan raised his glass with the rest of them, but his lips were tight with jealousy. Something told him that unless they were careful, trouble might come of Gwen flirting with Mellars. He looked at her covertly as she talked animatedly with the leader from Glastonbury. As the drink circulated, everyone's conversation opened up and even the more withdrawn, bemused survivors managed a few words with their neighbours. Sunday was the time when the community relaxed a little and it was only then that lunch-time drinking took place, though the bar was open every evening.

As he sipped his cloudy beer, Brennan watched his lover and listened to her chattering away to Mellars and those sitting near him. Gwen Sutcliffe always dominated any company by the sheer force of her personality. Apart from her stunning good looks, she had a vivacity which never failed to lift the spirits of anyone she was with. He recognised that she had that rare quality of making everyone she met feel as if she really cared about them – about what they did and what they felt. The shy ones she would draw out and the brash ones she would parry with a roguish impudence which put them in their place without injuring their pride. Gwen was a born Public Relations woman and Brennan thought again what a personal tragedy it must have been when the crash deprived her of the outlets for her natural talents. As the power stations whined to a halt and the news-presses and studios became silent, at one stroke Gwen had lost the means to communicate with the millions of her audience – now she was reduced to a few hundred souls, reached over the makeshift PA system that 'broadcast' within the college buildings.

He listened to her with mixed feelings, as she turned on the charm, her long fingers gesturing eloquently at Mellars.

'Roger, let's face it! You don't have enough people down west to make a proper go of it. Why don't you give up trying to attract our folk down there and march yours up here to join us?'

Mellars smiled into her beautiful face, his eyes bright with desire, both for his cause and for Gwen herself. Both of them knew that their conversation was irrelevant, they were just using words as a vehicle for intercourse. Just verbal at the moment, but a glowering Brennan sensed that Mellars was already imaging Gwen in bed with him. The Somerset leader continued to mouth the worn old subject of survival as his eyes devoured the blonde, until Brennan could bear it no longer. He broke it up by leaning across and pushing himself into the conversation.

'We're going to have to fight these boat people sooner or later. Are you going to help us or not?' It was more a demand than a question. 'Because if you don't, sooner or later, you'll have to face them on your own.'

Roger Mellars tore his eyes reluctantly from the woman. 'I thought you, as the big Army man, would be able to sort them out in half a day!' he drawled sarcastically. 'Surely you don't need my fascist Panzers, as you probably call them?'

Brennan scowled at him. The military jibes were becoming tiresome.

'It's not going to be funny, Mellars. From what I heard in Cambridge, the Germans are going to be no walkover. They're desperate and there's a hell of a lot of them, more arriving every week. They've apparently moved down the Dutch coast as well and are coming across from there now, together with some Danes and local Dutch.' He paused to drink from his glass. 'And many are staying here, not just making raids for food and equipment. East Anglia and even the Kent coast have permanent German camps now. We're going to need all the men we can spare to give them a short sharp shock, as they used to say.'

'It's a devil of a long way for my lads. Some would have to come from beyond Exeter to get to East Anglia,' murmured Mellars, his eyes straying back to Gwen.

'We'll worry about that when the time comes,' snapped the bigger man. 'The point is, are you with us in this – or not?'

Mellars stared into his beer glass. 'I don't like it, not one little bit. We can't afford to lose people, especially the younger, fitter ones who have to do the fighting. But I suppose, if it comes to a showdown, we'll have to bail you out!'

'You're not doing us a favour, Mellars – it's your survival as much as ours. If those raiders settle and decide to push west, we'll all be in big trouble.'

The lawyer emptied his glass before replying. 'If only you'd see sense, Brennan and bring all your people down to us, all this expeditionary force stuff would be unnecessary. We could secure every road right across the neck of the West Country. Then we could get on with the rebuilding behind the defence line, without frittering away our time and resources by dashing all over bloody Britain to swat continentals as if we were trying to get rid of bedbugs.'

Brennan's retort was interrupted by the sound of a makeshift gong, summoning them to the serving counters. They joined the rest of the crowd at several orderly queues that were quickly served with a large, fairly appetising meal. Vegetables were restricted in variety because it was still early in the season, but they had ample potatoes and root crops to accompany fresh chicken and pork.

Back at the table, Mellars wanted to know where the food came from. 'Are your farms nearby?'

Casey was the one with least in his mouth at that moment. 'They're all within five miles now, since the Irish caught us on the hop last year. Before that, we had farmers who stuck to their land up to twenty or thirty miles away, but now they're too scared to stay so isolated.'

'We're spread all over the three counties,' replied Mellars smugly. 'Lack of labour is our problem, not fear of attack.'

Mervyn grunted, his grey whiskers sticking out like a gorse bush. 'You've been lucky so far, the Irish haven't yet started crossing the open end of the Bristol Channel to reach you. But they will, they'll start hitting your exposed settlements and soon you'll have to pull down to the south coast, out of reach.'

'Even that may not be enough,' put in Beverley. 'The Cambridge people had heard that there had been raids by the boat people as far west as the Isle of Wight.'

The conversation gave way to the serious business of eating, until the second course was called, suet pudding with cream. Casey sighed. 'I could murder a rice pudding. Haven't had one for years . . . it was always my favourite in the old days.'

Mervyn shook his head slowly. 'Talking of rice, it's hard to think that several thousand million people are presumably dead in Asia. Think of China, Japan, India! What's happened out there, I wonder?'

Gwen was the best qualified to know of the last anyone in Europe had heard of the East, through the final scraps of satellite contacts coming in to the fading media channels.

'This all started out there, of course,' she said sadly. 'They were hit earlier than us, by about a month. The last radio links failed after eight weeks, but we knew that the general situation was the same as here. The only difference was the density of population, with the far greater speed of cross-infection. God, imagine somewhere like Shanghai or Calcutta, with almost everyone lying dead!'

There was silence for a moment as they struggled with their private memories – mostly of Swansea or Cardiff, rather than Calcutta. Roger Mellars broke the silence, as their unfocussed eyes looked down at their empty plates. For once, he forgot to ogle Gwen or needle Brennan.

'Doc, you must know more than any of us about the medical side of the catastrophe. We've only one GP left with us, and he really hasn't much of a clue as to what actually happened. Was it really anything to do with HIV or that mad cow BSE, like some of the rumours said?'

Mervyn, the one-time consultant physician, seized the rare chance to give a medical lecture. 'Certainly nothing to do with either of them. It was a new strain of meningoencephalitis, which has been around since man himself.'

'What's that in plain English?' asked Casey.

'A virus infection of the brain. There are several types, many of them carried by mosquitoes. There was a big epidemic just after the First World War, following the influenza epidemic that killed millions.'

'Was this the same thing, then?' demanded Mellars.

'No, viruses mutate all the time. This was a variant of some sort. In 1999 there was an outbreak in Malaysia of a very virulent strain, which killed most of those infected. It died out quickly, though there was a rumour that the Yanks were even considering 'nuking' the town where it broke out. Then when New York was hit, they were spraying the whole city from helicopters to kill the mosquitoes. It was the West Nile strain of virus.'

'But those epidemics were due to mosquito transmission,' objected Gwen. 'That couldn't have happened this time, surely?'

Roger Mellars got in a quick appreciative smile at her, but for once, his curiosity got the better of his lust and he turned back to listen to Mervyn.

'So what happened?' he asked.

'Somewhere in south-east Asia – probably China, as that has the largest pool of individuals to allow virus mutations – this new strain suddenly appeared in a fantastically virulent form. The laboratories only had time to give it a name – MJB-Seven. They had no chance to work on it or try to develop a vaccine, as the scientists themselves were soon dead. Not only did it kill every sufferer within seventy-two hours, but its contagious properties became incredible. Instead of being spread by mosquito bite, the virus rapidly appeared in all bodily secretions, so any contact – coughing, sneezing, excreting, even talking – contaminated everyone around. Almost immediately, it got into the food and water, so everyone got infected.'

Brennan had heard all this before, but Gwen still seemed fascinated by the most horrible story in the history of mankind.

'You mean that even we survivors had the virus in us? I thought that some escaped being infected. So how did we escape – none of us were even ill!'

Mervyn shrugged helplessly.

'God alone knows – if there is a God after all this! It's a fact that everyone became infected, unless there are some people still isolated in some hidden South American valley. But for some reason, about one in a thousand didn't develop the disease at all. There was a suspicion, though there was never time to follow it up, that some of those who had an abortive infection with polio earlier in life, somehow had a natural cross-immunity to MJB-Seven.'

'But I never had anything like polio when I was a kid,' objected Casey.

'No, I said it may have been an abortive episode, because virtually everyone in advanced countries had received polio vaccine as a baby. Mind, I don't know how that idea squares with the vast numbers in developing countries who never had polio vaccination – though they may all be dead there, for all we know. If there are survivors, maybe they just had a naturally abortive attack of polio – or infection from some milder variant that gave them the same cross-immunity.'

'Like cowpox against smallpox?' suggested Gwen, getting another admiring look from Roger Mellars.

'Why MJB-Seven?' asked Casey.

'Stands for "Mutated Japanese-B Type Seven",' replied the doctor soberly. 'A little thing about one ten-thousandth of a millimetre in size, that has brought mankind almost to the point of extinction.'

'So how did it kill so quickly?' demanded Mellars.

'Brain inflammation, a very rapid type. You remember the symptoms – how can we ever forget them! Headache, sickness, drowsiness and death from respiratory paralysis.'

'But many virtually dropped dead without warning – that's why we had all the crashes and the fires!' objected Casey.

'That's because this virus also had the nasty property of being haemorrhagic. It interfered with blood coagulation and many of the early cases, when there was still time to have autopsies, revealed that they had had sudden massive brain haemorrhages, which killed or disabled people instantly with a kind of stroke.'

Mellars looked accusingly at the old doctor. 'Your medical fraternity didn't do much good, did they? Couldn't they have found some antidote or vaccine or something?'

Mervyn sighed, but Brennan was not sure whether it was for the failure of the medical profession or at Mellars's stupid question. 'I said just now, there wasn't a chance, especially as most of the doctors and laboratory workers caught the infection straight away from their patients and their samples. Remember it took thirty years to develop a vaccine against HIV and AIDS. The first sign of MJB-Seven was in Bangkok and within forty-eight hours, there were cases in Tokyo, Sydney and Dehli, thanks to air travel.'

There was another pregnant silence. None of them needed reminding what had happened next – that within another few days, air passengers spread the infection to every other continent, though better isolation facilities delayed the massive spread in the West for a few weeks, compared to Asia.

'Has it definitely gone for good now?' asked Mellars almost fearfully, after the doctor's revelation of the genesis of the disaster.

Mervyn James shrugged again. 'Who can tell? We don't know what's going on even a few hundred miles from here. But I haven't heard of a single new case since that terrible couple of months over five years ago.'

'So everyone susceptible to it just died, leaving us behind?' observed Gwen.

'It looks like it – and by definition, we survivors are immune, unless it mutates again and comes back in a different form. Though I think that's unlikely now, with such a tiny surviving world population.'

'And it didn't affect any animals?' asked Casey, a devoted dog-lover.

'Only some primates, apparently, like the higher apes. At least, the ones in zoos died, we've no idea what happened in the wild.'

Gwen was temporarily subdued. 'What about the kids now? Are they going to be safe from it?'

'Again, we can't tell. They were the worst affected in the population, far less than one in a thousand children survived, perhaps because fewer had those antibodies to protect them. The new babies born since the disaster will at least have passive immunity from their mothers to start with. All we can do is hope that MJB-Seven has gone away for good.'

He suddenly looked as grey in the face as his hair and beard. 'No medical science, no laboratories, no research – nothing any more!'

Brennan broke in harshly. 'So all we can hope for, is that the disease has burnt itself out after killing everyone at risk. So just keep your fingers permanently crossed!'

CHAPTER FOUR

THAT evening, Brennan walked arm-in-arm with Gwen down near the River Usk. Dusk was falling and it was cold. Mellars had left in his truck for Somerset and the college had subsided into a sleepy mood after the evening meal.

Brennan slipped his arm around Gwen's shoulders and she snuggled up against him, warm in her donkey jacket, with a long woollen scarf wound around her neck. He had a duffel coat and a peaked cap like those continental students once wore. For a few moments at least, they felt contented and detached, as if the crumbling world was someone else's problem for the rest of the day.

They ambled slowly along the river bank, where the brown water swept round in a wide curve down towards Newport and the sea, a couple of miles away. A long field ran down to the water's edge from the Roman remains. The amphitheatre and the foundations of the barrack blocks of the Second Augustan Legion were disdainfully unchanging, indifferent to the problems of two millennia later. Behind them, the rusted railway line and the weed-covered remains of some burned-out bungalows lay between them and the college, a quarter of a mile distant.

'No colour this time of day, my love,' observed the woman, her latent artistic talents surveying the scene with a painter's eye. 'All greys and black and a bit of brown.'

Brennan gave her a squeeze. 'It's greening up again now – the spring's here as usual, oblivious of our troubles.'

'What will it bring, though? More problems?'

'The spring's supposed to stimulate a young man's fancy! And the older man's, hopefully. The sap will be rising in all of us, never fear.'

He felt cheerful again; maybe it was seeing the back of Roger Mellars a couple of hours ago. She reached her face up to kiss him and he felt his own sap rising, momentarily, then they walked on downstream. There was a companionable silence for a few moments.

'It's been quite a couple of days, Gwen. The trip to Cambridge and then having Jolly Roger up here.'

She looked up at him and smiled her secret smile. 'You're as jealous as hell, aren't you, old Brennan?'

He bridled at this, with false indignation. 'Jealous of him? That jumped-up lawyer's nark! Why the hell should I be jealous?' Brennan lied energetically and they both knew it.

'I think he's quite a dish, actually.' Gwen was being archly provocative and her man took the bait. He took his arm from her shoulders and pointed it at the horizon, where the river vanished into the mist. 'Somerset's down that way, woman. When are you leaving?'

'Don't be so silly! Just because I fancy someone, it doesn't mean that I want to rush off with them. I fancy you a whole lot more, Brennan!'

He stopped walking and turned her towards him, almost roughly pulling her against his broad chest. Brennan was considerably taller and being so close, she had to crane her head right back to look up at him. 'I prefer you in bed, Tarzan, it doesn't hurt my neck so much as this,' she complained.

'Shut up and kiss me again. I was too tired last night, after that bloody long drive.'

'At least that's a change from having a headache,' she teased, as she strained up to reach his lips. They clung together in the mist, two lone figures in bulky clothes. After a while, she laid her head against his chest and he held a hand on her hair, stroking it gently, almost absently as he stared down the river, where the thickening shadows were beginning to hide the banks.

'This place has seen some changes, Gwen,' he said eventually. She raised her head and they began walking again, slowly through the dampening grass.

'What sort of changes, lover?'

'The river – it must have been thick with galleys in Roman times. They were here for well over three hundred years – almost as long as from us back to the Plague and the Great Fire of London. There were terrible catastrophes, too.' Gwen played up to his reflective mood. 'The Romans saw their civilisation collapse around them, just like us. It's a kind of déjà vu, I think. It's happened here again, just as it did to them, only worse this time.'

Brennan nodded in the gathering dusk. 'I try to imagine it sometimes – the ships rowing up this stream from the sea. They brought all their provisions in that way – maybe we ought to develop sea transport a bit more, if we can find someone who knows a bit about boats.'

Gwen slipped her hand into his again and squeezed it. 'You're an old romantic, my love. You've too much imagination for a professional soldier.'

'A former professional soldier, please. You're like your new toyboy. He kept making cracks today about my army rank.'

'You're still one, Brennan, from your feet right up to the top of your head. Perhaps more than when you had a rank and a uniform. A real commander now, not just a chair-bound staff officer.'

Brennan grunted. 'Ironic that my last official orders were to organise the administration of Wales and the West. I'll bet the G.O.C. Western Command didn't have all this in mind, when he gave me that job!'

'What happened to the top brass in the army? Did they get away?'

He hunched his shoulders in a gesture of disinterest. 'Last seen heading towards the sunset in a fleet of Transport Command Hercules from RAF Lyneham – together with what was left of the Cabinet and senior Civil Servants. Hoping to get to Bermuda, they said – though as the disease was just as rife in North America, I can't see what they hoped to gain.'

'Knowing those crafty swine, they probably went somewhere quite different, like Greenland! Perhaps they're still there, keeping their heads down.'

Gwen was scathing about the total failure and rapid desertion of the government, though it was difficult to see what else they could have done, while their world crashed around them.

Brennan grunted his agreement. 'Wherever they went, we sure never heard a word from them again, nor the Royal Family, who went a fortnight earlier. Not in five years, so I doubt we'll ever know what happened to them.'

They walked on, a comfortable silence settling on them again. Behind them, the dim lights of the community began flickering in the distant college windows, but ahead and to the sides, the greyness began to thicken.

'Better turn back soon, love. We don't want to fall down the bank in the dark. The tide's coming in fast, too.' Twice a day, the huge tidal surge of the Bristol Channel changed this part of the lower Usk from a muddy ditch into a brimming lake. But Gwen tugged at his hand.

'Just down to the bend, Bren. I don't want to go back yet. I'll leave those damned tapes until the morning.'

Gwen's main job in the commune was running the primitive news and entertainment service, which consisted of a series of loudspeakers dotted around the building, wired to a tape-deck and hi-fi amplifier. Through this, she relayed a rather repetitive diet of music, leavened with some disc-jockey chat and internal announcements, which passed as news bulletins.

This sparked a chain of thought in Brennan's mind as they strolled.

'Remember those funny plastic boxes with a glass window in the front, Gwen?' he said innocently.

'What boxes?'

'I forget what they called 'em . . . oh, yes, television sets, that was it.'

She gave him a swift kick on the ankle. 'Swine! That's not at all funny. When the telly went, my whole career went down the pan with it.'

'Sorry, love,' he said contritely. 'I didn't mean the sets as much as the viewers. How many billion man-hours a day did humanity spend staring at the box? And within a few weeks – poof! The whole business only lasted about fifty years, yet at the time it was hard to imagine a world without it.'

The woman nodded in the gloom. '*Sic transit gloria* and all that! I wonder if we might be able to hook up a small closed-circuit system at the college. There's plenty of video equipment knocking around in undamaged houses and shops – and any number of tapes. It's not too difficult to put it together . . . but the power supply is so unreliable.' She brightened up at a thought. 'Maybe if these Cambridge electronic wizards are going to help us, we can really get something going.' Even the thought of being behind – or in front of – a television camera brought a new sparkle into her voice.

'Not much of an audience, though,' mused Brennan. 'A lot of trouble to reach a few hundred people, all within shouting distance of each other.'

Gwen pouted a little at having cold water being poured on to her dreams. 'That would be one of the attractions of Roger's scheme to amalgamate down in the West Country. We'd have far more people in a smaller area, and things like radio and even television would be more worthwhile then. If we had more security, folks could spread out again into farms and villages – they could have communications like radio, from your Cambridge pals.'

Brenann's jaw tightened, but he wasn't sure himself whether his attitude was objective or was coloured by his dislike and jealousy of Mellars.

'The price is too high where Roger is concerned, Gwen. His reputation is too tarnished by the way he treats his people down there. But I've often thought that we ought to collect everyone we can find in the whole of Britain and maybe move to somewhere totally defensible.'

'Like the West Country!' she said with stubborn persistence.

'No, it's too big, too open to the east and has an enormous, indefensible coastline. I was thinking of somewhere like the the Isle of Man, where we could set up a really concentrated community with a normal population density. Then we could restore almost all the things we used to have in the old days.' He kicked moodily at a clump of grass. 'Maybe we can one day, but it won't happen until the Irish cool down – and until we can get a consensus on how to organise things. Otherwise we'll have a hopeless mishmash of communism, fascism, feudalism and God knows what! We're just not ready for it yet.'

Gwen was about to begin arguing again, when suddenly Brennan grabbed her arm in alarm, rather than intimacy.

'What the hell's that? Look there, downriver!'

He stood stock still, his eyes straining in the fading twilight. For a moment, he thought he was having some kind of time warp hallucination, as he fancied he saw three Roman galleys swinging round the distant bend in the river, some five hundred yards distant.

Gwen's keener hearing immediately dispelled his imagined visions.

'I can hear engines, Bren! They're motor boats.'

He stared for a brief few seconds longer, just to make sure, then turned and dragged at Gwen's hand.

'Run, for God's sake! It's the bloody Irish again.'

They pounded back along the river path, into the deepening dusk. It was now almost half a mile back to the college, but both of them were in good condition and they ran fast and easily. When they had covered half the distance, reaching the road beyond the old amphitheatre, Brennan slowed down momentarily. 'They've come up from the sea with the tide, damn them,' he panted. 'If only we'd had radio, I could have kept a lookout permanently at the mouth of the river.'

'What are we going to do?'

Brennan unzipped his heavy jacket, feeling for the big automatic pistol he kept holstered on his belt. 'We'll call out the guard.'

Gwen grabbed his elbow in alarm. 'You're not going to do anything stupid, are you?'

Brennan grinned, in spite of the tense situation. 'I'm not in the heroics business, my sweet. I'm just going to sound the alarm.'

Gwen backed off apprehensively and put her hands to her ears, as he held the big Browning up in the air and pulled the trigger three times. The shots sounded shatteringly loud in the still evening air.

'Come on, keep running!' They pounded along a tarmac path, over the rusted railway line and up another field with ruined houses at one side. The college was now silhouetted above them, at the foot of Lodge Hill. There had been no response to his alarm signal from the direction of the river, but as they neared the hedge around the college, they saw brighter lights come on and torches flickering outside. A few more yards and they heard shouts and boots crunching on the gravel of the car park, then figures came racing down towards them in the near-darkness.

'Brennan? Is that you?' It was Casey who was shouting.

'Yes, with Gwen. Get back and sound the alarm!'

Doc Mervyn blundered up behind Casey. 'What's going on, for Christ's sake? Was that you shooting?'

'It's the Irish again, damn them! At least three big motor cruisers are coming up river. Get to stations, all of you!'

They all raced back to the car park, through a gap in the laurel hedge, where Brennan stopped to get his breath back as the others ran inside. He thanked God they had practised this before. They had had to fight Irish raiders in Pembrokeshire and Carmarthenshire twice in the past two years. Since then, he had the foresight to scour the remaining army establishments and police stations for equipment and to keep up arms training for all able-bodied men and women. They had repeatedly held field exercises with a couple of hundred of the fittest people, who formed the backbone of their defence corps.

By the time he reached one of the rear doors with Gwen, whistles were blowing and a handbell, salvaged from the local school, was clanging maniacally. Inside, feet were pounding along corridors and although it seemed chaotic, everyone actually knew what they were supposed to do in such an emergency. A pattern soon emerged from the hubbub, as the 'troops' made their way down to the main hall, whilst the non-combatants moved to relative safety both upstairs and down into the basement. These were being shepherded by Liz Peterson, a former staff nurse and Fay Morgan, a middle-aged woman who had once been in the Queen Alexandra's Royal Army Nursing Corps.

'I'll go and see that the kids and the old folk are doing what they should,' said Gwen briskly. She reached up and gave Brennan a swift kiss on the lips.

'Look after yourself, old man,' she murmured, then ran to the swing doors to the main corridor.

Brennan hurried to the large storeroom near the kitchens, which served as their armoury. Already Lance Prichard was handing out weapons and ammunition to a queue of younger men and women who had lined up at the door. These in turn ferried them to the defenders in the hall. The guns included many 'Caliburns', the newest self-loading rifles issued to the armed forces just before the disaster, replacing the

SA 80 model. Nine months ago, Brennan had organised a foraging party which had cleaned out the armouries of his old military establishments at Brecon and Crickhowell, as well as raiding the big depots around Hereford and Tewkesbury to obtain more weapons, spares and ammunition.

'What's the drill, Brennan?' asked Lance. 'D'you want heavier stuff as well?'

'Grenades, two rocket launchers and two heavy machine guns. Tell everyone to assemble in the car park in three minutes. I'll get the Ferret started.' He turned to Casey, who was collecting his beloved twelve-bore shotgun.

'Get upstairs to the top floor and fire a couple of flares towards the river. They must already know we've seen them because of my pistol shots, so there's nothing to lose by seeing what's going on.'

His army training switched into gear automatically. It would have been untrue to say that he was enjoying this, but there was undoubtedly something about military command that got his adrenaline flowing. He had a pair of henchmen who were also ex-Service: one was Bill Fleming, an elderly but very fit former warrant-officer with infantry experience in the Falklands and Ulster. Phil Robson was younger, but was an ex-marine commando who had been in the Gulf War and in Bosnia and Kosovo. They were marshalling their troops into two over-size 'companies' when Brennan reached the car park.

'Robson, get straight out on to the fields and advance a line of men all across the river side of the college so that they can't slip through towards us. The buggers may already have landed – they were little more than a quarter of a mile away when I saw them.'

The ex-marine, a big man with a face like granite, went off at a trot, taking forty men and women with him, vanishing through the straggly hedge into the fields beyond. There was a prolonged whining of a self-starter, as their one and only armoured vehicle, an old Ferret reconaissance car, burst into life. Brennan thanked his lucky stars that both the battery and the degraded gasoline were still good enough to get it started.

Before he could do any more, there was a bang from over his head and a few seconds later, a brilliant white light illuminated the countryside. Before it died, Casey fired another and again the surroundings of the college were turned into a soot-and-whitewash picture.

There was a yell from one of the upper windows. 'They're moored against the bank. Four of them, big buggers! Two fishing boats and a pair of Grand Banks cruisers!' The flare went out and the darkness was even blacker by contrast.

Brennan yelled at the old warrant-officer. 'Fleming, get your lot spread out around the perimeter of the car park. No shooting until targets are identified, in case Robson has to fall back here.'

Beverley, the suave ex-Whitehall man, was driving the scout car and it now rolled up to let Brennan swing up into the turret. This had a heavy machine gun as the only armament, together with a searchlight mounted on the turret rim. As Brennan cleared the gun for action, Casey came rushing out of the kitchen door.

'Doc's set up a casualty station in the cellar – Liz is with him and the two other nurses and that medical student,' he reported. 'All the civilians are bedded down on the back of the first floor, the kids and old folk are in the cellar.'

Brennan nodded, satisfied that in spite of the dark and the surprise, everything had been battened down and the troops readied within ten minutes. Casey clambered up into the car and crouched behind the driver.

'All set, Bev. Take it away, down towards the river!' He had to bend and shout down into the interior of the Ferret, as the intercom had never worked on this vehicle, which had been salvaged from the ruins of an army transport depot near Tewkesbury. He suspected that it had been destined for a military museum. They also rescued an armoured Land-Rover returned from Northern Ireland, but this had no fixed armament like the Ferret.

As they rumbled away, he realised that not a shot had been heard yet, apart from his own pistol signals and only circumstances suggested that an attack was imminent. But those boats could be nothing else than another Irish incursion, desperate people seeking food, supplies and even slaves to bolster their small communities across the Irish sea. For a moment, Brennan wondered if they could be Germans, who were known to have made landings as far west as the Solent. But it was inconceivable that such small craft would have come all the way around Land's End . They had to be Irish, making the short passage across from Wexford to Pembrokeshire and then along the coast into the Severn Estuary. Once again, he cursed the fact that they had no early-warning system – a sentiment that he thought must have been shared by his ancestors twelve hundred years before, when the Vikings swarmed across the Irish Sea to rape and pillage the Celtic settlements hidden up every creek and river valley.

The four massive tyres of the Ferret climbed up a low bank and through the hedge into the adjacent field, then back on to the side road and over the railway line. Brennan's eyes were now adapted to the gloom, faintly lit by an invisible half-moon shining on to the low cloud cover. He could just see the gentle slope of the meadows running down past the Roman ruins towards the river and the low hills on the other side, but as yet there was no movement anywhere.

'See anything, Brennan?' called Casey from down below.

'Damn all so far. Let's have a bit of light on the subject. Bev, stop here a moment.'

The car jerked to a halt and he switched on the searchlight. A bright pencil of blue-white light stabbed through the dusk, the beam sharply defined by the thin ground mist rising from the damp fields. Almost immediately, a burst of automatic fire opened up from ahead and Brennan instinctively ducked as a stream of tracer sailed overhead.

'Christ Almighty, turn that bloody lamp off!' wailed Casey, a fraction of a second before Brennan's finger hit the switch.

'Bev, full right, quick!' The armoured car lurched away, bumping over tussocks of coarse grass. Even in the brief moment that the searchlight had been on, Brennan had glimpsed a line of men advancing across the next field, the one nearest the river.

'Give me that Very pistol and some flares.'

Casey handed them up from inside the Ferret and seconds later, man-made daylight again burst over the meadows, a vivid white arc in the sky revealing the intruders, but leaving the defender in shadow. Instantly, there was a fusillade of shots from Robson's men, who were spaced out in a line roughly parallel to the oncoming raiders. There were a few yells of pain from the lower field but the long range and transient light made any hits a matter of luck. Brennan joined in with a burst from the turret gun, but stopped as soon as the flare burnt out, to save precious ammunition.

'This is bloody useless! They could walk right past us in the dark without us seeing half of them!' he snapped.

'I reckon we'd be better off pulled tight back to our perimeter,' snarled Casey, his voice tight with anxiety. He was another old soldier, having served in Northern Ireland twenty-five years earlier. Brennan called down to Beverley to drive rapidly along the lower field boundary to their right, in front of Robson's squad. He shouted at them as he passed to fall back to the college, then had the Ferret turned down towards the river.

'Where the hell are we going now?' demanded Casey in alarm, poking his head up above the turret rim. He had to shout over the noise of the engine as they bucked and bounced over the hummocks in the rough ground.

'Let's see what we're up against,' snapped Brennan. 'Keep your head down!'

They burst through the hedge into the field where they had seen the line of attackers and almost immediately were met by yells and a ragged volley of shots, both single and bursts of automatic fire. Some of these clanged off the plating and Brennan ducked down to be almost nose to nose with Casey.

The raiders were obviously shooting at the noise made by the Ferret, as it showed no lights and the gloom was almost total now in the thicker mist along the river.

'If we had some light, we could pick off the whole ruddy lot!' ranted Casey.

There was a sudden lurch and a scream from below. 'Run one of the sods over, anyway,' yelled Beverley from the driving seat. The shots died away, the last one coming from behind them.

'We're through their line, so get down to the river, see how many they've left on their boats.' A moment later, they swerved on to the muddy path along the bank and Brennan cautiously raised himself above the turret. The glint of the water silhouetted a couple of shadowy craft moored tight against the river's edge.

There was no light on the nearest boat, which seemed to be a large cabin cruiser, but as they roared up, a series of bright yellow flashes studded the night and again bullets clattered against the side of the Ferret. Casey had taken over the machine gun and as they passed alongside the boat, he raked it from stem to stern with a continuous burst of fire.

'Next one coming up!' hollered Beverley as they drew level with the second craft, a squat vessel which Brennan recognised as a small commercial fishing boat. He could dimly see a tall wheelhouse like a sentry-box and from it, someone was firing at them with a machine pistol.

'Get nearer, Bev!' he yelled. The Ferret swerved away in a tight circle, rocking on its suspension to come back for a second pass, this time with two wheels off the path, almost on the muddy bank. In unison, Casey and Brennan lobbed grenades on to the drifter's deck, almost at the base of the wheelhouse. There were two almost simultaneous flashes and 'crumps' and the firing ceased abruptly. By the brief light of the detonations, Brennan had seen several forty-gallon metal drums lashed together on the after-deck of the first cruiser. As the armoured car circled away again, he prodded Casey's shoulder and shouted in his ear. The other man swung the machine gun around and when Brennan switched on the searchlight for a brief sighting, Casey fired a long burst at the drums. There was a flash as sparks and hot metal ignited the reserve fuel supply and in seconds, a gush of flaming diesel and gasoline swept the deck with a flood of fire.

There was a groan from alongside Brennan and he looked around to see Casey clutching his left shoulder. As they ducked down, he grabbed a torch clipped to the inside of the turret coaming. A quick look showed blood coming from between Casey's fingers.

'Home, Bev, as fast as you can. Casey's bought one!'

'Just a furrow across the skin – looks worse than it is,' muttered the man with the big nose. He did not seem to be badly injured and Brennan sighed with relief. Pulling a shell-dressing from a metal box inside the Ferret, he slid it inside Casey's anorak and urged him to keep pressure on it until they got back. Then he peered over the rim again and hooked a new belt into the ammunition feed of the gun. Beverley was driving obliquely back up the field towards the college, but now the whole scene was lit up by the red glow from the flames leaping up twenty feet from the doomed motor cruiser. By its light, he could see men running across the upper field in a ragged line, some already disappearing towards the railway line and the college.

'Let's give them a few up their backsides, Bev,' shouted Brennan, swinging the turret round to rake down the line of bandits as they came level. With his finger hard on the trigger, he saw several fall under the withering fire. As the driver turned to run parallel behind the scattering line, Brennan loosed off intermittent short bursts at the attackers, until they dispersed so that there were no more targets, especially as the light from the burning boat dimmed as they left it further behind.

The car now bumped its way across the old railway and with gears whining, began crossing the last open ground to the college. Casey had dropped down into the spare seat below to nurse his arm, and Brennan had the turret to himself. He risked another quick pan with the searchlight and saw a number of dark figures loping across the field. Beverley managed to run one down but Brennan was afraid to fire ahead, in case he overshot and hit some of Johnson's men who should be waiting around the college perimeter.

Brennan was just about to swing the gun around to fire backwards, when there was a deafening blast and the front offside of the vehicle leapt into the air. It fell back with a sickening crunch and came to an abrupt stop, the engine still running. Beverley scrambled up from the driving seat, helping Casey out as he came. 'Get out, fast! They've blown our front wheel off with something.'

Brennan helped the injured man to clamber over the edge and with Bev holding him around the waist, the three dropped to the ground. Brennan fell to the grass in a crouch and dragged the others down with him, fearful that the Irish would open fire on them – but help was close at hand.

'Here comes the cavalry!' yelled Beverley, as men rushed down from the hedge around the college, firing their weapons in both directions at what was left of the line of raiders. In the flickering red light of the distant fire, it was like a Hieronymus Bosch painting of hell, as the enemy were driven away for long enough for Robson's men to gather up the trio and hustle them the remaining few yards to their perimeter.

'What's been happening up here?' shouted Brennan above the now sporadic gunfire.

They reached the ragged hedge and doubled across the car park, bending low until they reached the back door. The marine waited until they were inside the porch before answering.

'They've spread out a lot – no real targets in the dark. I think they must be almost all the way around the building by now, but there can't be that many of them.'

Brennan wiped a mixture of sweat, smoke and Casey's blood from his face. 'Better pull everyone back into the car park. We'll be shooting at each other unless we know where we all are,' he commanded. 'I've got to get a weapon for myself, now that the damned tank is busted. They must have some sort of shoulder rocket launcher to have knocked that out – probably from some old IRA cache!'

While Robson blew his whistle and shouted orders, Brennan took Casey inside and handed him over to one of the older men who was acting as a medical orderly. 'Take him to the doc and get his shoulder fixed up.'

He next went to the armoury and got a Caliburn, slinging a bag of spare magazines over his shoulder. By the time he got back to the rear door, the outside defenders were filing in.

'Anyone hurt?'

'Three gunshot wounds, one fairly serious. They've all gone downstairs to the sickbay,' answered Lance Prichard. 'Not sure if anyone's missing, it was all a bit confused out there in the dark.' Even in the heat of battle, he managed to sound languid.

There seemed to be a lull outside, as Brennan could hear no shooting.

'I want a man with a gun at every first-floor window, all the way around the building,' he snapped. 'Then I want two rocket-launcher teams on the top floor facing the river . . . now!'

People rushed off to carry out his orders, mostly men, but with a few young women among them. Brennan ran up the wide stairs to the first floor, the best vantage point to see what was happening around the walls. Robson was behind him and they stood each side of a large window on the landing, cautiously peering out.

'Phil, there were four boats, large cabin-cruiser or small drifter size. How many men d'you reckon they could carry?'

'Doubt if they could get more than twenty on each, Brennan. That makes about eighty all told, though there could be less.'

'We knocked off at least half a dozen with the Ferret and wrecked one of the boats. We should outnumber them at least three to one, but I don't want to lose any of our people, so we'll play it carefully, right?'

He edged forward and looked out of the window. The light from the burning boat was on the other side of the building, so the back car park was in total darkness.

'Porter is sitting in the main doorway with a heavy machine gun,' said Fleming, who had followed them upstairs. 'I've got gun teams on all the other doors and men at every window, so we can't be rushed.'

Brennan nodded in the gloom. 'We want all the lights out, except in the basement casualty station. And I want to light up the outside with flares when needed.' He slammed his fist into his palm in frustration. 'God dammit, if we only had some communications, even just a bloody internal phone system!'

Outside there was a sudden commotion and a flare arched up from a window and slowly sank towards the hill. In its brief, greenish light, they saw three figures coming from the perimeter hedge in a crouching run. As if joined by strings, both Brennan and Robson crashed the muzzles of their weapons through small panes of glass in the latticed window and started firing. Two of the interlopers fell to the ground and the third turned tail, just as the flare died.

'Keep your eyes peeled for more. I'm going upstairs!' Brennan ran up the two next flights, making for the top floor. It was almost pitch black, but they were all used to mooching around the building in poor light. Moments later, he was in a bedroom facing the river, one that normally housed one of the few mothers with a small child. These were now sheltering in the basement and the room was almost filled with three men and a woman, clustered around a rocket launcher on a tripod. He hurried to the window and looked out.

'Right, we want to sink those bloody boats, while there's still some light from that fire!'

The sash window was already pushed up as far as it would go and they looked out over the meadows to the flames licking up from the charred hull of the Grand Banks cruiser. The dim shapes of the two boats ahead of her and the fishing boat astern were just visible.

'Think you can do it?' he asked the team. 'You were pretty good at the practice sessions.' The girl, a stocky, amiable soul who looked as if she had spent much of her previous life on a farm, grinned back at him.

'They're almost at the limit of our range, but I'll do my best, boss,' she replied, settling the back end of the launcher tube on her shoulder. She put her eye to the sight, as one of the men slid a long finned rocket into the back of the tube. Brennan hastily moved away and waited while she carefully aligned the launcher. There was a roar, a whoosh of flame and the room filled with acrid fumes. Coughing, they all rushed to the window and yelled with delight as an explosion disrupted the foredeck of the fishing boat that Brennan had fired upon from his armoured car.

'Bloody marvellous! You got it first crack,' he yelled, giving her a smacking kiss on the cheek.

'Beginner's luck,' she said modestly – and probably truthfully, already putting her eye back to the sight for another shot. The added flames from the fishing boat now clearly showed up the remaining two craft and as Brennan turned to leave, another rocket sped out of the window. Without waiting to see the result, which was hardly likely to match the first success, he hurried along the corridor to where the other rocket team had just got their first missile away. They had plenty of ammunition for these launchers, as they had raided the Royal Ordnance Depot outside Hereford and carried away everything they could lay their hands on from the one bunker that they managed to blow their way into.

'Come on lads, don't let a girl beat you! Sue has just blown one out of the water.'

The gun-layer, a sandy-haired Scot, grinned at him. 'I'll have the others in a wee while, never fear. Then the Paddies will have to swim home.'

Brennan left them to it and clattered back down the stairs to the front door to see that the gun team was in good shape. 'Some of them are running back down the field already,' yelled Fleming excitedly. 'They must have seen their return ticket going up in flames. Shall we go after them?'

'Hold it a few minutes. We don't want to walk into an ambush.'

He ran back to the rear door, but just as he reached it, he heard a noise that gripped his stomach in sudden fear. It was the characteristic 'crump' of a mortar. He had given no orders for any of their own to be used, so it must belong to the raiders. A second later, there was an explosion and a series of crashes from the upper floor, with a shower of masonry falling into the rear car park. He heard distant yelling from upstairs and as he reached the back door, he heard the mortar go off again. This time, it fell short, landing beyond the pine end of the college. There was tremendous shattering of glass as almost all the windows blew out on that side.

'We've got to stop this!' he shouted, calling to Robson and Lance to come to him, as he sheltered in the outer porch. 'Bev, streak upstairs and see what damage has been done. And tell those rocket teams to try to nail that mortar. Frighten the sods to death, if they can't hit them!'

Another mortar shell hit the roof, tiles cascading down to the ground. Thankfully the gunner was inexpert and was firing high, over-compensating for the previous shortfall, but it was only a matter of time before he got the range, especially if the roof timbers began burning to give him a clear target. A mortar, if allowed to straddle the college with even half a dozen good shots, could wreak havoc and do irreparable damage, especially if the building caught alight. The whole community could be wiped out – that mortar had to be stopped.

'Come on, Robson, follow me with your squad.' He yelled over his shoulder at his lieutenants as he went off in a crouching run. 'Fleming, take your men through the front door and around the other side. Get up to the hedge and fire some flares over the top field – that's where that flaming thing is sitting. We've got to get it – and quick!'

He reached the shelter of a high brick wall opposite. This ran down to the left, where it joined the hedge that rimmed the car park. Boots clattered behind him but thankfully they were not fired on. In the lee of the wall, he quickly checked his rifle and shoved his shoulder bag of spare slips around on to his back. 'Right, come on – let's get this bugger!'

Keeping low, he raced for the hedge and barged his way through with a brawny shoulder, falling to the grass the other side. A dozen men burst through after him and they wriggled across the cold, damp ground.

A few yards further and Brennan stopped to raise his head cautiously. The air smelled strongly of smoke and the flickering orange light came not only from the burning boats, but from flames now erupting from the college roof, which was burning briskly at the nearest corner. Then a white flare burst high overhead, though the illumination was slightly dimmed by the haze of smoke.

At first sight, the upper part of the field seemed empty, but before the flare died away, he saw a few dark shapes moving in the middle distance. A sudden gout of flame accompanied the 'crump' of another mortar shell taking off. He poked the muzzle of his Caliburn forward and let off a long burst at the shadowy group fifty yards away. Another flare burst in the sky and on each side of him, all of Johnson's squad began hammering away at the mortar site.

'Closer! Get closer!' he screamed, scrambling to his feet and loping off in a crouch, his rifle at the ready. Suddenly, someone came from his left at twice his speed, fully erect and running like hell. Even in the poor light, the slim build and flash of pale hair gave him away as Lance Prichard. Yelling like a dervish, Lance veered to the left to get out of the line of fire of their own men. There were answering shouts from the raiders in front and a ragged fusillade of flashes revealed their return fire.

'Cover him! Fire to his right!' howled Brennan, fearful that the rash young hero might be hit by shots from enemy or friend. He straightened up and raced after Lance, firing with his weapon held stiffly out in front of him, pounding down the slight slope towards the Irish position. One more shell took off and crashed into the upper wall of the building, before the reckless young man reached the mortar team. As he ran, Brennan saw him spraying them with continuous fire at close range. He stopped firing himself for fear of hitting Lance, but as he closed the distance between them, he saw that all opposition shooting had stopped. As he arrived at the now silent mortar, Robson and his men were closing in on each side. There were several bodies lying on the ground, none of them still moving.

'Are you OK, Lance?' Robson gripped the blond man by the arm.

'If we still had Victoria Crosses, I'd get you a couple, you damn fool!' panted Brennan. He was about to slap Lance on the back, when the younger man crumpled and collapsed slowly to the ground. Robson stared down in horror.

'Jesus, boss, I think he's dead!'

CHAPTER FIVE

LANCE had fully recovered by the time he drove the three-ton truck down to Cardiff Castle. The bullet that had furrowed his scalp had come within a few millimetres of killing him, but after Mervyn had stitched it up and he had come round from the concussion, Lance rapidly returned to normal and was fully fit for the evacuation of Caerleon six weeks later.

The truck was full of the last of the beds from the college. With two of the younger men jammed alongside him in the cab, Lance picked his way down from the M4 interchange into the city. Many roads had been blocked with the debris of collapsed burnt-out buildings and wrecked vehicles, but working parties had cleared a single lane down to the civic centre. The beautiful public buildings of white Portland stone were still standing, but most were windowless, with blackened streaks on the walls, the interiors being roofless shells. Only the main university building seemed to have escaped, still rising serenely from the forest of unpruned trees and shrubs of Cathays Park, which was carpeted by rank weeds.

Beyond the park, the shopping streets had been ravaged by a fire-storm that had burned for a week, with hardly an intact building in the whole city, apart from the ancient tower of St John's church and the huge Millennium Stadium. To add insult to injury, the River Taff had flooded repeatedly, the worst being two years ago, during one of the freak storms which were becoming more frequent as the climate continued to change. With the huge sluice-gates out of action at the Bay Barrage, the water had covered much of the city centre, leaving a tide mark of mud four feet up every wall, washing burned beams and rubble down every street.

The only other structure in the Welsh capital that was virtually undamaged was the huge castle, its defiant square mass sitting in the very heart of the city. The great walls, some Roman, some Norman and the rest a Victorian re-build, were untouched by the destruction of recent years. Even the ornate public rooms built along the western wall were intact, as the dinners and receptions normally held in them were cancelled as soon as the plague began, so that the fire risks had been negligible in the empty chambers.

After the Irish attack, Brennan had called another general meeting, at which there was almost unanimous agreement that the Caerleon College was now both uninhabitable and indefensible. The raiders had been driven off, the remnants escaping in the two surviving boats, taking their wounded with them, but leaving twelve dead lying around the college. They had wreaked considerable damage to the building with their final mortar attack. The roof had been shattered in two places and the timbers of the attics set alight. Two of the gables and the walls beneath had collapsed and much of the window glass had been blown out. Though they had managed to patch up the place to keep out the worst of the weather, the building was beyond repair. Brennan's other fear was a return visit by a stronger force, eager for revenge, as the college was poorly defensible and too vulnerable to attack. The idea of moving to Cardiff had occurred to him before, but they had been so firmly settled in Caerleon that it took the trauma of the Irish assault to tip the scales and get them to move the dozen miles further west.

Now the transfer was almost complete and the last truck was arriving, to be followed later in the day by the coaches with the remainder of the people. The Army Bedford, salvaged from the regimental depot at Brecon, whined its four-wheel drive down Kingsway between the blackened remains of the Hilton Hotel and the high walls of the castle. Swinging round the south-east bastion, past the rusted traffic lights, Lance slowed down ready to turn into the main gate opposite the rubble-choked High Street. The portcullis had been restored to working order and a gang of men were just finishing the new drawbridge, in place of the dummy that had acted as a ramp for many years. The moat had been grassed over long ago, but now steel cables had been passed through the old chain holes above the gateway and attached to the outer ends of the new drawbridge. Inside the Castle Green, they were hooked to the drawbar of a farm tractor, which could rapidly pull the massive wooden structure vertically up against the entrance.

Two guards stood under the raised portcullis, each carrying Caliburns, and waved the truck through on its third journey that day from Caerleon. Lance stopped alongside them, annoyed at their slackness in not challenging him.

'How d'you know we weren't Irish?' he snapped. 'They may have hijacked the truck on the motorway and be doing a Trojan Horse act with thirty fellows in the back, armed to the teeth!'

One of the guards, a black-haired youth from Cardigan, grinned and made a rude gesture with his fingers.

'Because we had a radio check ten minutes ago from the Gabalfa sentry post, saying that Lance had just passed through!'

Lance grunted – he had forgotten that since their contacts with Cambridge, they had aquired half a dozen VHF transceivers, complete with rechargeable batteries, which had revolutionised their communications.

The truck rumbled through the archway and entered the grassy seven-acre ward inside the battlemented walls. Lance saw Brennan way over to the left, talking animatedly with Gwen Sutcliffe. His eyes narrowed slightly, taking in her willowy figure and stunning legs. Lance had long fancied her himself, but she was the 'governor's woman', worse luck.

Or was she these days, he wondered? He wasn't alone in suspecting that the path of true love might be beginning to go a little crooked – but even if it was, he doubted that there was anything in it for him, or any others in this community.

He parked the truck near them, alongside one of the entrance doors to the west range. Here the high walls merged into the ornate buildings of the residential quarters, partly medieval, partly a gilded folly created at the command of the Third Marquis of Bute, alleged to be the richest man in the world in the last quarter of the nineteenth century. As he climbed out and began helping the others to carry in mattresses,

Brennan and Gwen walked away towards the steep mound in one quadrant of the compound that carried the ruined Norman keep, which was now Brennan's headquarters. Beyond it, the further half of the great grassy square looked like a caravan site, with five rows of touring and residential vans parked closely together.

'If you felt that strongly, I still say that you should have gone down west with the rest of them,' snapped Brennan. They had had this conversation a dozen times in the last fortnight.

'Don't be so damned stubborn, Brennan!' she flashed in return. 'I don't want to go anywhere. I just say that after the fiasco in Caerleon, we should have joined forces with Roger. There's safety in numbers – but now we're even fewer, since those fifty took off for Somerset.'

Brennan felt the exasperation rising within him like a spring tide.

'Yes, fifty went – and four hundred and fifty stayed with us! Ones who can't stomach his "Little Hitler" methods. Roger and I are like oil and water, Gwen – we'll never mix. I only hope we can at least stay allies against the boat people, but as for combining, it's just not on.'

She wheeled around to face him, her high-cheekboned face taught with annoyance. 'You're just bloody jealous! I hope you're not going to endanger the whole community, just because of a personal hang-up over me!'

Brennan became openly angry, partly because there was some truth in what she said. 'Look, Gwen, either settle down here and stop bitching about it – or pack up and go down to your fascist friend!'

He turned on his heel and strode off towards the steps to the high ruin of the octagonal keep, inside which some sheds had been erected as temporary accommodation. He hating falling out with her, yet he was full of self-justification for what he knew had been the right decision to move to Cardiff.

The woman watched him go, mixed emotions running circles in her mind. They had taken a bad knock at Caerleon, when the Irish had half-destroyed their home. She wondered if Brennan was going to survive, now that some of his followers had drifted off to Roger Mellars. Gwen loved a winner and fond as she was of Brennan, it was success – and the prospect of continued success – that attracted her to a man. But she had enough insight to know that adrenaline and calm decisions didn't go together, so she breathed out heavily and walked away steadily towards one of the trailer caravans, where her new audio studio was being fixed up by their only electrician.

Lance watched this little scene with interest as he humped his beds to the doorway, where another team took them in. He failed to hear the last part of their dispute when they walked away, but the body language was crystal clear as Gwen marched towards the caravan and Brennan stumped off towards the keep. He was never one to miss an opportunity and as soon as the truck was empty, Lance walked across to the caravan.

'How's it coming along, Gwen?' he asked. The blonde was standing over Eddie, the middle-aged electrician, as he fiddled with a screwdriver at the base of a microphone. She turned her head and smiled at Lance, though he saw the tension in her face.

'Almost ready for the big opening,' she said smoothly.

Lance climbed up into the small caravan, a fourteen-foot tourer towed in from a driveway in the suburbs. Eddie had run in a power line from the new diesel generator hidden away in the crypt against the Roman wall, where its rattle would not be heard. It was far more powerful than the worn-out petrol model they had in Caerleon – this one had been an emergency back-up generator for a local hospital and now provided all the kilowatts they needed.

Ernie had ground lines running from the van to the various residential quarters to feed a battery of loudspeakers. There was no shortage of audio hardware out at the HTV studios at Culverhouse Cross, which unlike the BBC in Llandaff, had largely escaped fire damage. The caravan was now equipped with CD and DVD players and Eddie had even looted a turntable to play old 33 and 45 records for those who wanted nostalgic music.

Lance stood very close to her as they stood watching Eddie's final prods with his screwdriver. Gwen was well aware that she was the object of admiration and not a little lust from a sizeable proportion of the community's menfolk, but she had always managed the situation admirably, keeping them at arm's length without causing any embarrassing confrontation. She was flattered in an amused way and several of the men, including Lance, could have been on her list of 'possibles' if she had not had more important fish to fry. He had several times edged his way towards an open declaration of his interest in her, but Gwen kept the relationship on a light level – a cheerfully mild flirtation.

Lance hung about, pretending an interest in the final stages of the broadcasting rehearsal, waiting for a better opportunity. It soon came, as Eddie rose from the chair in front of the microphone and made for the door.

'Just keep on talking, Gwen. I'll go round the speakers and see if the levels are right.' He vanished across the green, leaving them alone in the caravan. Gwen slid into the revolving chair in front of the console and Lance moved to stand behind her, his hands on her shoulders.

'Couldn't help noticing you having a few words with the boss,' he said softly. He could not have chosen a worse time to attempt a chat-up routine, as she immediately put a finger to her lips and tapped the microphone.

'Shush, Lance – we're on air!' she said mischievously. He reached across her shoulder and clicked the switch on the base of the microphone to 'off'.

'Come on, Gwen! We've all noticed that you are having some problems with the old man recently.'

'That's none of your damn business, Lance,' she said quietly. 'So just turn that mike on again, please.'

'You know how fond I am of you, Gwen. If you need anything, I'm always here,' he said, rather unctuously.

'Thanks, Lance – but no thanks,' she replied, with more steel in her voice this time. Reaching out, she clicked the microphone on again and kept her hand over the base to shield the switch.

'Testing, testing, testing – how's that sound, Eddie?' She bent towards the microphone, sliding her shoulder from under his hands.

Lance realised that this was not the time or the place for him to make any headway with her and with a shrug of resignation, he patted her back and moved to the door.

'Remember, Gwen, I'll always be around if you want me.' He stepped down to the ground and as he walked away, Gwen momentarily switched off the microphone to murmur to herself.

'Not this time, Lance – but don't stop trying, there's a good boy!'

Brennan was in a sour humour for a time, but there was so much to do that he worked it off by the evening. He had to check that the move from Caerleon was complete and later in the afternoon, made a quick final trip there with Beverley in one of the Land-Rovers. They walked through the deserted rooms, covering every floor, then came back down to the car park for a last look at the outside. The roof was in a sorry state and many of the shattered windows were roughly boarded up.

'It served us well for a couple of years, Bev,' he observed, rather sad that the old building would now be left to disintegrate at the mercy of wind and weather. 'Better than that Tesco warehouse near the Severn Bridge.'

Beverley Truman's aristocratic features grimaced at the memory of the first year the survivors had spent in that place, huddled in sleeping bags and blankets on the floor of a building like an aircraft hangar, with no privacy or vestige of comfort. This was when Brennan had drifted into becoming the leader – he had brought a handful of survivors down from Brecon in a couple of army trucks and gradually collected more and more isolated people from farms and hamlets to congregate in the warehouse. Here they survived on scavenged tinned food from stores within a ten mile radius and vegetables foraged from farms, gardens and allotments. For transport they depended on a couple of vehicles salvaged from Brennan's army depot. Over the next two years, he had scoured most of south and west Wales for all remaining survivors, until the eventual numbers had made the Tesco depot so inadequate that they had to move to the college in Caerleon.

'There were only half as many of us then, but it was still a God-awful place to live,' drawled Beverley, as they stood gazing up at the battered college. He was thirty-six, a tall dark-haired man with a long nose and rather weak chin concealed by a small goatee beard. In Brennan's estimation, Bev was one of the best-adjusted members of the group. Born in Henley, he had gone to Harrow and then studied history and politics at Oxford. The Civil Service was his obvious destination and he had been a public relations guru at the Home Office when the plague began. Hurriedly taking leave of London, he had fled with his wife to the Cotswolds, but like so many others, found that distance was no protection. His wife had died and due to his own inexplicable immunity, within weeks he had become the only living person in the ominously-named village of Lower Slaughter.

A supreme egoist and something of a snob, he was not the most popular man in the community, but Brennan got on well with him, as he was efficient, highly intelligent and very knowledgeable. He could always be relied upon to do what he was asked and in any emergency, he was a rock of dependability. As a bonus, he was a wizard with any form of motor vehicle, his former passion being sports cars. Without his expertise, their transport would have given up the ghost long ago. Like their solitary doctor, they had only one professional motor mechanic in the community, but John Parsons was so chronically depressed that it was hard to get him to even lift a spanner.

With a last nostalgic look around, the two men climbed into the Land-Rover and set off for Cardiff and their new home. They drove through a pleasant May evening, the daylight hours lengthening after the long winter and early spring. The motorway was gradually being encroached upon by the countryside, the hedges and verges creeping inexorably across the hard shoulder, with islands of grass and weeds pushing up everywhere through the cracked tarmac and the joints in the concrete sections of the carriageway. Japanese knotweed was rampant, especially in the wetter places and nettles, brambles and bracken were enjoying an exuberant comeback after centuries of suppression. It was now all so familiar to the two men, that the signs of nature reclaiming its heritage was as unremarkable as their frequent dodging of crashed and blackened vehicles, though this evening Beverley was moved to comment on the increase in animal life.

'Must be the good weather, Brennan. Looks like a bloody nature park out there.' He waved a hand at the scrubby fields stretching across towards Cefn Mably, just outside Cardiff. A herd of horses was stampeding merrily in a thunder of hooves, watched moodily by a dozen cows. Along the thickened hedge was a score of bedraggled sheep, staring suspiciously at a pair of dogs slinking past them. A pair of buzzards circled over a thicket of young beech trees that were pushing up in the middle of what had been a cornfield and Brennan knew that when dusk fell, the foxes and badgers would be out in force.

'Another few years and we'll find it hard to use the roads because of this growth,' observed Beverley, as the Land-Rover crushed a small bush that had pushed up through the asphalt. 'Let's hope Ruddy Luddy makes some progress with his railway project before then!'

Ruddy Luddy was their nickname for Bruce Ludlow, a wild, untidy extrovert with a shock of red hair and a full beard to match. Unusually amongst the generally sombre members of the community, he was always cheerful and noisy. A former railway engineer whose job had also been his main passion in life, Ruddy had been a member of several railway preservation societies and was now claiming that soon he could get a small steam locomotive running again. For the past few months, he had been spending all his spare time at a former steelworks near Newport, where he had found an old oil-fired shunting engine parked in a corner, presumably earmarked years ago for some industrial museum. Now Ruddy was trying to persuade Brennan to give him a team to clear debris from outside the shed to allow the loco to be moved on to the main line. He had even sweetened the plea with the promise of a working JCB to help clear the obstruction, if they could find a good battery to start it with.

'We'd better have a community meeting after supper tonight,' said Brennan. 'We can bring up this business of the railway then – and anyway, we need to mark our first night in the castle with some sort of formality. So let's hope the beer and wine travelled well from Caerleon!'

The banqueting hall was too small to feed all the community at one sitting and overflow trestles were set up in other parts of the rambling accommodation. William Burgess, the Victorian architect and designer who dreamed up this mock Gothic extravaganza, had built endless communicating rooms and corridors in the block that formed the south-western corner of the castle, surmounted by the huge clock tower, its gilded hands now forever stuck at twenty past eleven, after the city power supply had finally failed more than five years ago. The rest of the new inhabitants ate in some of the adjacent rooms, which were decorated like a child's fairy-tale book, with murals of medieval scenes, mythical animals and dark wood carved into a multitude of curlicues. The high ceiling carried ornate beams and fanciful corbels and though now covered in dust and grime from the burnt city, the roofs above were sound and weatherproof. Brennan wondered what the place would be like in the depths of a hard winter, as the central heating system was probably irreparable. However, being originally a nineteenth-century reconstruction, most rooms had cavernous fireplaces and there was no shortage of wood and coal.

When everyone had eaten a good meal prepared in the kitchens below, the children and their carers, together with a few of the oldest survivors, went off to the beds now ranged in dormitory chambers, whilst the rest crowded into the banqueting hall, after the trestles had been stacked against the walls. All the chairs were in use and the younger members leaned against the walls or sat in the window embrasures. The home-brewed wine and beer was circulated and the community settled down to what was essentially a tribal gathering.

Brennan stood in front of the assembly, his back to the huge fireplace that reached up into the darkness of the beamed roof, the bare bulbs strung along cables from their new generator giving an adequate, but not generous illumination. On benches each side of him sat his 'management committee': Doc Mervyn, Beverley, Casey, Lance, Ruddy and a few more activists. Brennan looked around the sea of faces, who though tired after days of upheaval and resettlement, were looking expectantly at their chosen leader.

'I'll keep this short, folks,' he began. 'We've had our second move since we came together and surely this one must be the safest yet. It was re-built by the Romans seventeen hundred years ago as a defence against Irish raiders – so what's new!'

There was feeble laughter from some parts of the hall, but most looked deadpan, their strained faces waiting for some reassurance about the future.

'It did the job all those centuries ago and I don't think we need fear the fellows from across the water again. We've now got lookout posts along the coast at Nash Point lighthouse and on Penarth Head, both with radios, so we'll have plenty of warning if they come again.'

Two pairs of young volunteers were doing weekly stints at these places, one about fifteen miles west of Cardiff, the other on the headland which overlooked the entrance to Cardiff Bay. Up in the lofty clock tower, aerials poked out high above the city streets, keeping a twenty-four hour radio watch, both with their own outposts and with Cambridge, who had supplied all the equipment.

Brennan spoke for a few minutes, quietly reassuring the fainter spirits and then going on to some practical details of how living arrangements would be organised in their new home. Finally, with a meaningful glance at Gwen, who sat at one end of the front row, he touched on the sensitive issue of the defection to Somerset.

'We've lost a few of our friends for the time being, but it's a free country – at least it is here! And maybe when they find that life in Glastonbury is not all it was cracked up to be, they'll come back.'

'If they can get out!' called a cynical voice from the back.

Brennan shrugged. He didn't want to get into an argument and cause more anguish amongst friends of those who had gone over to Mellars. The autocratic barrister was reputed to run the western counties along the lines of a police state, with a bunch of hard-line cronies who regimented every aspect of their community's life, irrespective of the wishes of individuals. Mental and physical coercion were used instead of consensus and there were rumours of confinement and beatings for those who were reluctant to toe the party line. No one from South Wales had ever been invited to visit the other side of the channel, so all they had to go on was rumour. But tonight, Brennan kept off these aspects and hoped that those who had gone over to Glastonbury would find the adverse reports of Mellars's regime to be exaggerated.

As usual in these community sessions, his short address ended in general discussion and he was glad when questions began to flow.

'What do we do now we're here, Brennan?' called a burly man who had once been a smallholder near Ross-on-Wye. For the last three years, he had been farming just outside Caerleon, but the move had taken him away from the land he worked.

'John, you know the score, we've been through it with you. I don't see why you can't keep using the plot near Caerleon, but keep it for arable farming. You need only go out there for ploughing, sowing and reaping. The cattle we're bringing here.' He swept his arm to point north.

'There's hundreds of acres just over the castle wall, in the Park and Blackweir beyond. Great pasture and plenty of fertile flat ground alongside the river for cultivation.'

'What about flooding?' asked another voice. 'That ground could be under five feet of water again.'

'That was because the barrage was jammed shut,' cut in Ruddy. 'We've looked at it and we're going to blast the gates permanently open, as soon as Brennan can pinch more explosives from his army depots.'

The manager nodded and continued to extol the farming prospects.

'Within six miles of here, there's plenty of good farmland, all around the edge of the city. Agriculture is going to be our main priority, as it's all we'll have to live on once we've liberated everything still edible in the warehouses. But we can still keep on some of the established farms in Gwent – with our early warning system down the coast, there's no fear of a surprise attack in future.'

A long discussion began about exactly where and when the agriculturists among them could get started and the general feeling was one of optimism. Then a middle-aged woman stood up, her face lined with sorrow, deep grooves each side of her downturned mouth betraying her depression and unhappiness.

'Never mind the farming, what are the rest of us going to do?' she demanded. 'We talk about Somerset, but this place looks like a prison as well – high walls and a single gate with armed guards!'

Brennan suppressed a sigh. Though he was profoundly sorry for Maude Butler's unhappiness, she never failed to come up with complaints and accusations that did nothing to help the general morale. She had lost every member of her family within a week – husband, parents, children, siblings, cousins – but so had most of the others in the community.

'Maude, the walls are to keep people out, not to keep us in,' he said as gently as he could. 'You know all too well what happened in Caerleon. We came here to prevent that ever happening again. The gate is open to all of us, you can walk out any time you want.'

'But what are we to do in the long run?' persisted another voice, a younger woman who sounded more petulant than anxious.

It was Mervyn who leaned forward on his chair to answer this question. 'Now that we've seen what Cambridge has achieved, we can be encouraged to start becoming better organised. There's so much to be done, it's frightening.' He jumped to his feet and waved a hand as if encompassing their whole world. 'Look, we've got one doctor here, that's me!' He tapped his chest dramatically. 'I'm sixty-six, I could have a coronary or a stroke tomorrow – then where would medical knowledge be? And almost the same goes for our electrician, our plumber, our mechanic.'

'What are you trying to say, doc?' called another voice. 'That we start a medical college?'

Mervyn slammed a fist into his palm. 'Yes, exactly! And an engineering college and a plumbing college! We've got a few kids coming along and more to follow, but unless we leave them a legacy of our knowledge, they'll be in a hell of a worse state than we are now. Little better than savages, unless they have an inheritance of some sort of technology.'

He sat down abruptly and Brennan took over again.

'We've discussed this in the committee and feel that now we're settled in a big city, we need to trawl it for every useful item we can find. As Doc Mervyn says, we need the biggest source of reference material we can gather together, so that existing knowledge isn't lost. The big libraries are all destroyed, even in the university and medical school, but we need to scour the suburbs for books, tapes, CDs and videos before they deteriorate even more. There must be doctors' houses with medical books that have survived the fires – we need everything we can salvage to build up a database from which we can start teaching each other.' He warmed to his theme and became almost passionate. 'There's work for everybody – some as salvage parties, others storing and indexing. We need to save every book that we can find, on every conceivable subject, for it's the last store of knowledge our kids will ever have. Everyone with even partial ability in some subject, must begin teaching others.'

The idea suddenly sparked enthusiasm amongst the community – the prospect of doing something other than merely surviving from day to day appealed and soon there was a lively discussion going on.

'We can use our new broadcasting system,' declared Gwen. 'Between the gossip and the music, we can have short talks by our experts, so while you are peeling potatoes or minding the kids, you can listen to Doc telling you how to set a broken arm or Eddie explaining how a dynamo works!'

The talk of salvaging books moved on to reclaiming as much useful material as possible. Though they had been raiding shops, homes, depots and factories around Caerleon and Newport for several years, this was on a random basis, looking for things they needed at that moment. Now Lance proposed a systematic search of all unburned buildings to recover anything useful before rust, damp and rats destroyed it.

'There are several empty warehouses just off Western Avenue and down near Rover Way where we could store tons of stuff. We want more tools, tinned food, furniture, clothing, blankets – you name it, we're going to need it, sooner or later.'

The committee agreed to start drawing up plans and rotas for salvage and reclamation parties. Everyone knew that searching houses was going to be a grisly job even after the passage of five years, with all the hundreds of thousands of deaths that had occurred, but familiarity had partly inured them – and by now the vast majority of victims would be skeletalised and less offensive.

'What about transport, if we're hoping to carry loot home by the ton?' asked Beverley.

Brennan looked at Ruddy Luddy, who had gravitated by default into the role of traffic manager, both rail and road.

'We've half a dozen trucks still running, but we'll bring in some more. No shortage of vehicles, it's batteries that are the problem.'

'Have to tow-start them, unless we can come across a depot with some new batteries that never had acid put in them,' suggested Lance.

'And salvage some of those starter-boosters, now that we've got a fair bit of electric power,' added Beverley.

'The time will come when we'll be back to horse traction,' observed Ruddy, with a tinge of satisfaction. 'Together with my steam locomotive, we'd be set for ever then, and sod the internal combustion engine!'

Tired from the day's efforts, the meeting gradually broke up and the inhabitants of the castle drifted off to their beds. Though most of them were sleeping in communal rooms, with anything from four to a dozen beds in each, quite a few who had acquired partners had a room to themselves, even if the room was on wheels in the castle quadrangle. Two weeks earlier, one of the foraging parties had come across twenty touring caravans parked undamaged in a sales yard. This had sparked the idea of raiding holiday caravan parks along the nearby coast, which provided an unlimited number of vans. Many were towed back to the castle and now stood in rows inside the huge grassy space within the curtain walls, providing some comfort and privacy to over two hundred people.

Brennan and Gwen were lodged in one of them, a sixteen-foot Clubman tourer. It had a large settee which opened into a double bed, but tonight they lay silently one on each edge. Under the heavy duvet, they were both naked, as usual, but there seemed no prospect of any intimacy, not even the comforting wrapping of arms around each other. The spectre of Roger Mellars was present, almost as palpable as if he had been lying between them.

Brennan stared up at the ceiling of the caravan, dimly seen in the distant glint of the one bulb burning over the inside of the castle gateway. Tired though he was, sleep eluded him as myriad thoughts and problems chased through his mind, all against the background of Gwen and her ambivalence about wanting to join the Glastonbury group. She lay quietly a few feet away from him: he knew she was not sleeping either. Stubbornness and pride made Brennan force his thoughts to trucks, locomotives, supplies of medicines – anything other than that supple body lying within arm's reach. How were they going to assemble and retain all the knowledge of their generation for the use of the future? Was Ruddy going to get his railway working? What was going to happen in East Anglia, with these increasingly anxious reports coming from Cambridge? When were they going to have to fight the boat people? Should he make another tour of the Midlands soon? Could they rely on support from that area if the Germans made a concerted attack?

Then, almost like a snake sliding under the duvet, a hand searched until it found his. He felt his fingers squeezed and a moment later, a warm breast pressed against his bare shoulder and a head rested against his. With a groan of release, all thoughts of trucks and guns vanished and he rolled over to pull the woman close to him, their legs and arms entwining and their lips meeting in a delicious reconciliation that almost made the dispute worthwhile.

CHAPTER SIX

THE news on their radio link the next day was not encouraging. Mavis Strickland's technicians in Cambridge had given them a reconditioned Japanese shortwave sideband transmitter which had once belonged to a radio 'ham' in the suburbs, together with a 1990 state-of-the-art communications receiver. They had a wide range of frequencies available and with the tall mast on the roof of Addenbrooke's Hospital and a long whip aerial on the castle clock-tower, they could communicate quite well. Cardiff's precious equipment was in the command hut in the Norman keep, fed from the clock-tower by coaxial cables salvaged from the television studios.

That morning, Brennan was in the hut poring over duty rosters when Wayne, the young man on radio-watch, rapped on the trestle to get the boss's attention.

'Cambridge are on the air, they want to speak to you.'

Brennan slid his chair along and took the headphones. He heard Strickland clearly from almost two hundred miles away, there being no competition from other radio traffic or man-made electrical static.

'Our scouts have seen an increase in the arrivals along the coast over the past few days,' she reported. 'With this calm weather at sea, a dozen fishing boats and even a few sailing yachts have arrived around the Harwich area.'

'Are there many people with them?' asked Brennan.

'Hundreds more, joining those already there. And more further down the coast, near Clacton. Altogether, there must be a thousand or more camped in the ruins or living in old tents and shacks.' Strickland went on with more details of places and numbers, the worry in her voice plainly evident.

'Any idea if they're armed?' asked Brennan.

'Our guys can't get that near. They have to lurk in clumps of trees and ditches a mile or more away, for fear of being seen. We don't want to lose any more men.'

Brennan was able to determine that so far, none of this increasing immigration had tried to push very far inland. He signed off with an exhortation for the Cambridge people to keep constantly monitoring the situation and to keep in daily touch with Cardiff.

Later that morning, the 'Executive Committee' met in the 'council chamber' – the other hut inside the Norman keep This was a large lean-to fitted against one of the walls, with a corrugated metal roof that made a hell of a noise when it rained.

Brennan had decided on using the keep for the command post, because in the awful event of a massive attack, it was the most defendable refuge on top of its steep mound – exactly as Robert Fitzhamon had decided over nine hundred years before, when he had built his fortress within the ruins of the Roman enclave. The half dozen 'Ministers' of that shabby Cabinet were joined by a handful of others, mainly those with specialist skills like the two former soldiers, the electrician and mechanic, as well as a couple of the nurses, including Liz Peterson – and their only medical student, Tan Chen Swee, a Singaporean who had been studying at the University of Wales College of Medicine. Apart from one Indian lady, he was the only Asian survivor, as they seemed to have been even more hard-hit than Caucasians, perhaps for some genetic reason.

The conference shed was bare apart from two half-circle Formica tables rescued from a hospital dining room. These were placed edge to edge with a ring of folding classroom chairs around them. Brennan began the proceedings in this spartan version of Parliament, by telling them of the message from Cambridge that morning.

'We're going to have to fight them sooner or later – and it sounds as if it's going to be sooner,' said Casey, in his usual pessimistic way.

'And we must do it in a way that minimises our own casualties,' observed Beverley in his over-cultured voice. 'Especially if we begin by fighting on behalf of Strickland's lot.'

Brennan nodded his agreement.

'That means having the best weaponry and equipment we can muster. Which ties in with what we were talking about yesterday – and our planning here this morning.' He went on to outline the need for a comprehensive sweep of the whole South Wales area for everything of use, from encyclopedias to machine guns.

'What about this educational idea?' asked Gwen, who was there as their media expert-cum-disc jockey.

'We've got to get on with it straight away!' snapped Mervyn. 'Remember, I might have my coronary this very night, so our medical school must start right now.'

'Where are we going to hold all these classes?' asked Gwen. 'All the rooms in the castle are full of beds.'

Casey suggested hauling in a few more big static caravans, which could be assigned to different specialities and this sensible idea was soon agreed upon, as there was plenty of parking space inside the huge compound.

'Right, tomorrow we begin trawling the county for everything useful,' said Brennan. 'One party had better concentrate on getting some more trucks and vans – that's you, Ruddy. And identifying all the accessible diesel supplies.'

The dishevelled redhead grinned. 'I know of a whole train of tanker wagons full of diesel in a siding near the Severn Tunnel. Once I've got my loco going, I can pull 'em out one at a time and bring them down here.'

'If we start bringing tons of stuff back to these warehouses, we'll reach a point where we won't have a clue what we've got or where it is,' objected Lance. His swept-back blond hair concealed the scar from the Irish bullet, but the others remembered his courage, which was strangely at odds with his laid-back affectations.

'Then let's start a database,' countered Beverley Truman. 'Plenty of PC's knocking about and now that we have a reliable power supply, there's no reason why we shouldn't get computerised.'

'Can you handle that?' demanded Brennan.

'I can set it up, no problem. There are a few women here who used to have secretarial jobs, so they can soon learn to input the data.'

'We should get a few of the older kids in on that,' said Gwen firmly. 'They're the ones who need to be brought up with all the skills we can possibly teach them.'

'OK, let's set up one van as an IT centre,' determined Brennan. 'That's all down to you, Bev. Your time in Whitehall won't all be wasted, after all.'

Beverly grinned. 'Right, computers it will be – though we won't get much joy out of the Internet or emails.'

There was a pause while all of them suddenly remembered how the World Wide Web was going to revolutionise all aspects of life – until it vanished within a few days.

With a mental jerk, Brennan brought them back to earth and the rest of the meeting went ahead, planning their big foray into the surrounding countryside. Different teams were allotted to specific targets and the available transport was distributed between them, though Bruce Ludlow was to urgently seek out some extra vans, trucks and trailers, beginning that afternoon.

They broke up after an hour and went with their lists fluttering to organise their teams. Brennan was gathering up his papers when Liz Peterson came back into the empty shed and came to stand close alongside him.

'I suppose Doc Mervyn will be running the medical school? Who else will we need in that team. Obviously Tan, he's almost a doctor – but what about us three nurses?'

Brennan had the feeling that she already knew the answers and was just making an excuse to get him alone. If it wasn't for Gwen, he would be quite happy with that, for Liz was an attractive thirty-year old former Staff Nurse, dark and petite, good-looking without being too exotic.

'Of course, Liz! You're just as important as doctors. We need anyone with medical experience, from an ambulance driver to a first-aider.'

She put a hand lightly on his arm. 'We're still very thin on the ground, Brennan. Mervyn is a physician, but he knows as much about operative surgery as our electrician. God knows what we'd do if someone needed an emergency operation, even an appendectomy.' Her face became genuinely worried. 'And if we do get into a war situation over in East Anglia, who's going to deal with serious casualties?'

Brennan turned slightly so that he gently disengaged her hand from his sleeve. 'These are the things that your medical group are going to have to sort out, Liz. Thanks for reminding me, I'll talk to Doc about it. There's a chap in the Worcester group who was a surgical registrar – we'll have to get him down to give courses to your lot.'

'We've got no obstetrician – not even a trained midwife here, though Gloucester has one,' she said.

'All goes to confirm what we said: we must share expertise as fast as we can. We could do with a dentist, too, but I don't know of one anywhere. Maybe Cambridge has one?'

Picking up his battered briefcase, he began moving towards the door of the hut. Reluctantly, Liz Peterson followed him, her brown spaniel eyes fixed on the broad back of the big man that she adored so much.

By the evening, Ruddy Luddy was back with a series of useful vehicles. His team had gone out with three Land-Rovers, one of them a breakdown truck and they returned from a trawl around Cardiff with two Ford Transit vans, a one-ton DAF truck, a MAN low-loader and a Bedford furniture van. The team had taken out several of their precious heavy-duty batteries to get the new vehicles started, though one of the vans had to be hoisted up and towed home, as both front tyres were flat. They had taken out a portable compressor to top up sagging tyres, which most vehicles needed after five years of disuse, but this Transit's front wheels had been slashed, for some unaccountable reason.

They now had a dozen useful carrying vehicles lined up in the castle yard, the tanks all topped up with fuel ready for the next day's foraging. The diesel came from a BP road tanker that they had found full of the fuel in a depot at the docks and which was now parked outside in Castle Street.

After the evening meal, the fifty men and women who had volunteered for the first day's searching, stayed in the dining hall after the trestles had been cleared of the dishes. Brennan and Beverley read out the rosters for each team and gave the leaders clipboards with orders to record what they had found and where it was to be stored. Earlier that day, Lance had taken a party to break open the two warehouses that they had identified, ready for the reception of their loot. One had been empty, apart from the skeletons of several refugees, but to Lance's surprise, the other had been half-full of assorted new clothing, presumably having been a distribution centre for South Wales retailers.

'We've enough anoraks, jeans, socks and T-shirts to last us all for a decade!' he declared. 'To say nothing of designer dresses, brassieres and nylons!'

When the business for the morning had all been settled, many went off to bed for an early night, though a few stayed to watch some entertainment. Now that they had adequate electric power, a few large-screen television sets had been recovered from intact houses and DVD players were able to screen nightly films and features. These were again rescued from private collections, as virtually all the stores were either burnt out or had no stock after the looting that had occurred in the first few frenzied weeks of the epidemic, when gangs of still-healthy youths robbed anything they could lay their hands on.

Brennan occasionally watched a film, as it was something of a novelty after the primitive facilities in Caerleon, where they had little power to spare. But the sight of the normal world of a few years ago filled him with sadness – even the brash American comedies or soaps filled with synthetic domestic drama. The trivia of everyday life and the streets filled with traffic and bustling humanity seemed a cruel reminder that Armageddon had been just around the corner.

Tonight, he just took Gwen by the arm and led her off to bed in their two-wheeled home.

The medical expedition took one of the larger Transit vans to seek their particular type of treasure. Tan Chen Swee was the driver, with Fay Morgan and Mervyn James alongside him. In the back were two helpers, Thomas who had been a hospital porter in Merthyr and Richards, a former professional snooker player. They were both quiet and withdrawn, but willing enough when told what to do.

'Pity we don't have a chemist or a dispenser amongst our five hundred people,' bemoaned Fay, as they drove slowly up towards the motorway. She was the second of the two nurses, Liz Peterson having stayed behind to look after the sickbay, which had one man with an acute asthma attack and two with what seemed to be influenza.

'I've a hazy recollection of some pharmacology, though most of it's related to heart disease,' said Mervyn, 'But no doubt Tan here is red-hot, he must have taken his exams in it.'

The Singaporean grinned. 'That was over five years ago, Doc. A lot has happened since then.' More stoical than many, he had no idea what had happened to his family and friends in his home city-state. At least most of the others had seen their loved ones dead and terrible though it had been, at least they were able to draw a line under the horror. Yet Tan knew absolutely nothing of what had happened five thousand miles away – and probably never would.

He drove them steadily through the ruinous suburbs, even managing another smile when Fay facetiously warned him that they were approaching a speed camera at the side of the road. They passed the huge University Hospital on their right, but made no effort to divert towards it – a previous visit had confirmed that it was a roofless, blackened shell with nothing of any value remaining. Even the extensive library, which would have been so useful to them, was a heap of ashes, populated only by pigeons.

The chemist's shops in the capital had all been trawled long before and the few items of value taken from them. Now they were casting their net wider, into territory that had not been combed before.

'Where's the first stop?' asked Fay, who in a rather stark way, was still attractive in her fiftieth year. Tall and slim, she had long black hair that contrasted with her pale, classical features; several of the children referred to her as 'the witch' behind her back. After fifteen years nursing service in the army, she had taken up physiotherapy in civilian life and at the time of the disaster, was working in a private sports clinic in Oxford. Never having married, she had fled from the early deaths to her home town of Cardiff to stay with relatives, but the plague had followed her and much to her dismay, she had been the sole survivor of the whole suburban estate where her aunt had lived.

Mervyn James thought her a nice woman, unaware that Fay had considerably stronger feelings about him. Though he was sixty-six and always looked as untidy as if he had just staggered out of bed, he was a fit, dynamic senior citizen and she never missed an opportunity to be where he was – hence today's trip, as she had bargained with Liz Peterson to be the accompanying nurse.

'We'll try Bridgend first, see if there are any surviving shops, then have a look at the hospital,' said the doctor. When they reached it, the centre of the medium-sized town, about eighteen miles west of Cardiff, was totally choked with decaying traffic and fallen masonry scattered across the narrow streets of the centre. Tan got as far as he could, then switched off the engine.

'It's our feet from here on,' he said cheerfully, as they all piled out, carrying empty holdalls and suitcases in the expectation of some successful pillaging. They picked their way along the deserted shopping street, where about half of the buildings were roofless from five years of extreme weather distorted by global warming. The pavements and road were thick with shattered rafters, broken slates, tiles and window glass, some of the latter from the looting of the early days. When they reached the main street, one whole side had been burnt out and fallen masonry had collapsed on to the road and parked vehicles.

The only sound was the cold wind moaning through the ruins, apart from the barking and howling of some distant dogs. After the surprise at the Membury Service Station, Mervyn was cautious and had an automatic pistol in the pocket of his anorak in case of trouble, but it seemed as if no living soul was within miles.

They looked in every shop as they passed, but most had been estate agents, building societies or clothes shops. One mini-market tempted them to step through the smashed plate glass windows to have a quick look around, but there was nothing on the shelves apart from a few rusted tins of dog food and bottled herbs and mustard.

'There's a Boots over there,' said Dave, as they came out. On a facing corner was a branch of the chainstore chemists, its well-known sign on the façade faded, but a reminder of familiar days gone for ever. The glass doors were hanging drunkenly off their hinges, indicating that other looters had got there first, some time in the past five years.

As they went in, a trio of large rats scurried away amongst the mouldering debris on the floor. Smashed cosmetic bottles, shattered electric shavers and hairdryers were mixed with cameras, film , toothbrushes, hair dyes and shampoo.

They crunched over the wreckage to the back of the store where a ceiling sign still proclaimed 'Prescriptions Dispensed'. The glass-topped counter had been overturned and a ruin of cough medicines, vitamin bottles and cold cures lay trodden into the dirt and dust on the floor. To one side, a huge roof-beam from the upper storey had plunged through the ceiling, causing even worse chaos to one part of the store, which was covered in rubble and plaster.

'Very little for us here,' grunted Mervyn, surveying the wreckage.

'Some of this stuff may still be useful, even if it's five years old,' said Fay optimistically, scooping some of the intact bottles and packets from the floor into her holdall. Tan stepped behind the fallen counter and went into the dispensary behind, the others following. Water had been streaming down two of the walls from the shattered roof above the upper floor and mould and slime covered much of the shelving and benches.

'Not much here, either,' muttered Thomas, the other helper, as he surveyed the empty shelves. On the drier wall, a few books were propped on the worktop and Mervyn seized one, a large green volume the size of an old family Bible. 'This'll be useful – the ABPI Compendium of Data Sheets. Gives details of every drug on the market.'

'Five years out of date now,' objected Tan.

'So are all the drugs, so that's just right!' retorted the old doctor.

Fay Morgan opened all the lower cupboards, but they were empty.

'Someone's been here before us – though I suppose they had no stock delivered in the last weeks, anyway,' she said sadly.

Richards had picked up a sign from the floor, lying in the dirty water at the foot of another door at the back of the dispensary.

'It says "Stockroom". Must be through there.' He tried the handle, but it refused to move. 'Want to bust it open, just in case?'

Tan came across to look and rapped on the door panel. 'That's metal – it will take a lot of busting.'

After a short debate, they decided that it might be worth the effort. Going back into the main store, the four men managed to dislodge the fallen beam from the debris and carried it into the dispensary to use as a battering ram. It was an eight by four-inch timber, about twelve feet long and after five minutes violently swinging it at the lock, the door finally burst open. It was pitch dark inside, but Mervyn had a torch containing rechargeable batteries, supplied by Cambridge. Its light showed mainly empty shelves, but there was some stock left and rather than try to decide what was useful and what was probably so outdated as to be useless, they decided to sweep everything into their bags and sort it out back at base. Mervyn noticed some antibiotics which might still have some potency left in them, as well as an assortment of painkillers.

'What about those cupboards?' asked Richards, pointing to stoutly locked boxes on the walls. With a case-opener that Thomas had brought, they forced open the doors and found a small but very useful supply of scheduled drugs, including morphine, pethidine and other synthetic compounds, the sight of which delighted Mervyn.

'Right, let's try the hospital now,' he said hopefully, as they piled back into the Ford with their booty. The relatively new hospital was on the road back to the motorway and although it had escaped any fire, it was in a sorry state from the weather. Much of the roof tiling of the two-storied building had been stripped off by the repeated, ferocious gales and at least half of the windows had been broken. The wards and departments, exposed to the elements for years, were a sodden mess, with weeds and bushes growing out of window frames, bird's nests on bed frames and animal droppings soiling many of the floors.

The foraging team tramped through the deserted corridors, crunching broken glass and rubble underfoot. Most of the wards had skeletons or scattered human bones lying around and some of the beds had decayed bodies humped under the damp, mouldering blankets. Almost immune to these sights by now, the searchers looked in every ward office and broke open any intact cupboards looking for useful drugs and equipment. Their carrier bags were soon filled with syringes, needles and odd pieces of surgical equipment that might come in useful.

In the dental department, Mervyn took as many forceps and gadgets as he could find, even though he had no idea how to use them. In a deep cupboard in one ward, Fay discovered a number of brand new sheets and blankets still wrapped in plastic covers and insisted on their helpers hauling them out to the van. The hospital dispensary was a disappointment, as it had obviously been looted early in the epidemic and very little was left. They found more syringes and needles and drip sets for infusions, but there were no drugs of any significance.

It was in the operating suite that they made their best haul, as the outer doors were chained and it was obvious that no one had entered since some last survivor had locked the place on the last fateful day.

Fay Morgan had been a theatre nurse at one stage in her army career and even twenty years later she could recognise most of the surgical equipment.

'We need to take all this stuff,' she exclaimed, as she opened cupboards and once-sterile drums in the ante-room to the two theatres. Sterile packs of instruments, serried rows of artery forceps, clamps, retractors and a host of other metallic treasures stared at her from the shelves. Being stainless steel or chrome-plated, they looked as good as new and Fay shovelled them enthusiastically into their holdalls. In the anaesthetic room and the two theatres, Mervyn and Tan looked in awe at all the silent monitors and anaesthetic apparatus.

'We need some of this, lad – if we had someone who knew how to use it!' They had been fortunate so far in not being faced with a serious surgical emergency, but their luck could not last. The physician dreaded the thought that someone soon must need an urgent operation for a strangulated hernia or a serious injury. And what if one of the women developed an obvious breast cancer, he thought? Is she to be allowed to die without an attempt at a mastectomy? And what if a new baby has pyloric stenosis and would die for want of a relatively simple operation? As he looked at the mass of equipment, he vowed to get in touch with Britain's only surgeon, to begin some form of training, however elementary.

'We can't take this stuff now, it will need a special trip with several vans and more able bodies,' he said.

Tan was thoughtful. 'What's the point of taking all this specialist stuff out of a perfectly good operating theatre. Wouldn't it be better to bring the patients here when needed?'

Fay shook her head. 'No power, for one thing. Nothing would work in here. And it's too far from where all our people are. We also need some portable facilities, if we have to go away from Cardiff – especially if we have to go to help the Cambridge lot.'

Tan was full of bright ideas. 'What about a mobile hospital, in one of those big articulated trailers? I'm sure we could find another small generator for power.'

This sparked a lively discussion and Mervyn promised to put the idea to the committee as soon as possible. In the meanwhile, they carried on searching the theatre suite. The locked cupboards yielded useful drugs and anaesthetics before they left to rummage through the rest of the hospital. The laboratories provided some large bottles of alcohol and various solvents, as well as a useful selection of medical textbooks. In the consultants' offices – apart from the bones of several consultants – they found more books and by the time they left, Mervyn felt that they had the nucleus of an excellent teaching base for their embryonic medical college.

With the Transit van full to the back doors with their loot, they made their way back to Cardiff, dropping off most of the equipment at one of the warehouses, claiming a special corner for all their cardboard boxes stuffed with medical devices. Mervyn insisted on taking the books and drugs back to the castle, locking them in the big Pemberton static caravan that they had been given for their medical studies.

It was now almost dark, the era of 'Daylight Saving' long forgotten, so the tired teams gravitated to the dining hall for their evening meal and to hear what the other explorers had been up to that day. After the eating had been accomplished, jugs of their home-brew began circulating and both the foragers and those who had stayed at home sat or stood around the ornate chamber, listening to the exploits of the first day.

'There's not much usable food left out there,' said Beverley, who had led the hunt for any remaining provisions. 'We got to all of the big supermarkets in the city, but only three were standing – several had burnt to the ground and another two had been totally flooded when the river came up years ago. Two more had virtually collapsed when the roofs were blown off in the gales, everything inside was wrecked.'

'What about the warehouses?' asked someone.

'Much the same story. Several burnt out, the others had very little stock. Those last weeks must have seen continuing local demand until the population collapsed, but no deliveries – factories closed, transport disrupted – then what was left was seriously looted by the later survivors, including many of us, I suspect.' His cultured voice was strangely at odds with the terrible tale that his words evoked.

'So how much did you get today?' asked Mervyn James.

'A couple of van-loads of hopefully usable stuff. After five years, only tins are any good now, though every one will have to be checked for bad rusting or being blown.'

The doctor nodded. 'Can't risk botulism or some other bloody awful toxin. Any dried stuff useable?'

'We found half a dozen bales of pasta which looked OK, sealed in plastic. And a couple of sacks of rice, which the rats hadn't got at.'

There was a silence, as the listeners realised how little had been recovered for the sustenance of five hundred people.

'It looks as if from now on, we're going to have to rely totally on what we can grow and rear,' said Brennan, voicing the thoughts of them all.

Beverley Truman nodded. 'We may get better luck when we go out into the smaller towns and up the valleys, where the destruction may have been less. But the passage of time is the main factor against us now. Most stuff other than tins has gone off in a big way – people, animals, mould and general rot has made it useless. I wouldn't even trust the stuff in sealed glass jars, a lot of it looks a funny colour.'

'Remember the old "sell-by" dates?' laughed Gwen, with brittle gaiety. 'They were usually in days or weeks, not years. So what's in these tins, Bev? Caviar?'

'Could be, Gwen – the labels have peeled off many of them! The most useful things were looted long ago. We've got soups, tinned meat, curry, dog food, cat food . . . all sorts of stuff.'

'Well, at least we can have Kit-e-Kat sandwiches for a bit!' quipped Lance, but he failed to raise a laugh.

'As long as we can still make bread,' added Brennan. 'The only flour we'll have is what we grow ourselves, so farming continues to be the main priority.'

'Milling is the problem, we've only got one small electric machine. We need to find something bigger, so that's another search target.' The speaker was one of the farmers who had reluctantly come in a few months ago from a solitary existence near Usk and was now working a few acres just outside the city limits.

Mervyn James recounted the adventures of the medical team in Bridgend and there was an upsurge of interest in his proposition to set up a surgical facility with the equipment they had found. The idea of a mobile surgery was discussed and Ruddy Luddy was detailed to find a suitable articulated van for the job.

Ruddy was enthusiastic about his day's work back in Newport, where he was still working on his beloved steam locomotive. 'Today we got the branch line cleared out to the main track. I've had her running. There's plenty of fuel oil, so later this week we'll pull her out and fetch one of those diesel tankers down from Severn Tunnel Junction, as a trial run.'

'What about the track?' asked someone. 'Is it clear? And what about the points? Surely all the mechanism is screwed up.'

Ruddy grinned through his red whiskers. 'All sorted, chum. I've walked the track between here and Newport and done the rest on a little diesel buggy we made. It's all clear, given a couple of diversions around an abandoned train and a wreck. I've set the points with a crowbar – and we needn't bother about signals, given the amount of traffic!'

This raised a few sniggers, but Brennan saw the importance of having even a rudimentary addition to their transport, especially if it didn't rely on road vehicles with their need for petrol, diesel, tyres and batteries. It would only be a matter of time before they were driven back to horse traction and that was another issue which was filed away in his mind – the need to start collecting and breaking-in draught animals.

He was brought back to the present by the voice of Jane Purvis, a schoolteacher who ran the classes for their few children. A large, formidable woman of fifty, she stared aggressively at the world through thick-lensed glasses, but Brennan knew that she had a heart of gold and was devoted to the kids under her care. A spinster, she had lost her aged mother during the horror, but had no other close family. Brennan had observed the fairly obvious fact that some of the less traumatised survivors were those who had not been married or had children, though there were many exceptions, including himself. Jane was relating her day's work, looking primarily for books and other educational material.

'Most of the libraries have gone – Cardiff Central's burnt out, more's the pity. They had a marvellous reference department,' she said crisply. 'Some of the branches have survived, though damage to the roofs and waterlogging have ruined much of their stock. The mice, rats and woodlice have played hell with a lot of the books, too.'

'But you found something useful?' asked Liz Peterson.

'God, yes. We filled our van to the roof and we'll go back for more for many days yet. Finding somewhere to put them is the problem – there's no point in hiding them away in some distant warehouse, where no one can get at them.'

This sparked a discussion about a library, both for a repository of useful knowledge and fiction for reading pleasure. It could also be used for most of their community meetings. It was suggested that the National Museum's East Wing, which had survived fire and storm, should become their State Archive and two of the survivors who had formerly worked in libraries volunteered to categorise and generally look after the books. The discussion went on and others described their day's haul, which ranged from garden tools, useful in any small-scale farming, to camping equipment. Some of the booty sounded of little potential use to Brennan, but having suggested the hunt for material in the first place, he did not want to dampen any enthusiasm. There was plenty of storage space available in the warehouses and maybe in the distant future, everything might prove to be useful.

Next day, the search was scheduled to move further afield, to cover the populous former mining valleys and the western end of the county. The extent of their foraging was determined by the state of the roads – one smaller valley beyond Pontypridd was totally inaccessible due to the blockage of several hundred yards of road by a collapsed, incinerated factory building. Many days of work with mechanical diggers would be required to open it and the effort was not worth the likely returns.

Later in the evening, people began to drift off to bed, but a hard core remained, talking and drinking sparingly, as their brewing capacity had not returned to full volume since their move from Caerleon. Gwen sat close alongside Brennan, her shapely legs curled up on the padded bench in one of the window alcoves. Liz sat at a table opposite, saying little, but her dark eyes rarely strayed from the big man in the window.

As the talk shifted back to their educational plans, a young man pushed his way into the circle and headed for the leader, a serious expression on his face. He was one of the radio-watchers, on duty this evening.

'Boss, you'd better come over and talk to Cambridge. They sound pretty anxious to me.'

The radios, both short-wave and VHF, were constantly manned, with scheduled contacts with their two coastguard posts every hour and a listening watch with Cambridge twice a day. The latter was used only every few days, but the opportunity was always there, given the tense situation in the east. Concerned faces watched as Brennan swallowed the last of his drink and followed the lad out of the dining hall. Beverley, Mervyn and Lance hesitated for a moment, then went after him. In the communications shed, Brennan sat down before the microphone and motioned to the younger man to switch the head-set over to a speaker, so that they all could hear. The voice of the self-appointed Commissar of Cambridge came faintly, but clearly over the miles.

'Brennan, the boat-people seem to moving inland. All day, our watchers have had to pull back to keep clear of them, though they've stopped for the night now.'

'How far have they come?'

'Only a few miles, as they're mostly on foot.'

'Are they all together?' asked Brennan.

'No, they're coming from different places along the coast, but from the direction they're going, they seem to be converging on Cambridge.'

'Do they have any vehicles?'

'A few trucks and vans, as well as the odd four-wheel drive.'

Lance whispered in Brennan's ear and the latter asked another obvious question.

'How many men d'you reckon are on the move?'

'Hard to say, as they're all split up across the countryside – but several hundred, no doubt of that.'

'Any idea of what weapons they have?'

There was a silence, filled only by slight crackling from the speaker, perhaps from some distant thunderstorm. Then she came back on air.

'I was asking one of the scouts, who's just come in. He says it's hard to tell, from the distance away they have to keep, but he thinks they have only small arms. No sign of any heavier guns, unless they're in the vehicles.'

Brennan turned to have a quick word with his lieutenants, then went back to the microphone.

'At the rate they're moving, how long will they take to reach Cambridge.'

'They're very slow, just foot-slogging. Tonight they stopped to camp well before dusk, so if they do that each time, it will be the day after tomorrow before they all get anywhere near here.'

'How much resistance can you put up?'

Even across the radio waves, they could hear the suppressed panic in Strickland's voice.

'You know we're not great fighters, Brennan! We can get about a hundred men out to face them, but we've got very little armament. Mainly a few machine guns, farmers' shotguns, some rifles and revolvers.'

Brennan heard Lance groan behind him and felt like doing the same. The Cambridge Comintern might be great at reconditioning electrical equipment, but seemed hopeless at defending themselves.

'Can you help us, Cardiff? We've got two day's grace at the most.'

The former Brigadier, appointed Defender of the West by his absentee senior officers, sighed under his breath, but hardly hesitated. 'Sure, that was the deal we made. I just didn't think our alliance would be called upon so soon. But we'll get up there as soon as we can. If we leave early in the morning, we should get to you well before nightfall.' There followed a lot of operational instructions, Brennan trying to get Strickland to dispose her small force as effectively as possible.

'Strengthen the checkpoints you already have and block all the roads from the east with old vehicles or loads of rubble,' he commanded. 'Do it about five miles out of the city, to stop them driving in quickly with whatever transport they've got. And put all your armed men behind the barricades.'

Eventually, Strickland signed off, after a promise to make contact early next morning. The Cardiff contingent discussed the new situation late into the night, deciding how to manage the full-scale expeditionary force next day.

'That puts paid to our foraging for the time being,' said Beverley. 'We could have done with another cruise around the Army depots to add to our armoury, if we're going to have a battle on our hands.'

Mervyn was worried about leaving Cardiff relatively undefended, if they were going to take their best fighting men to East Anglia. 'What if the damned Irish come back when we're away?' he fretted.

'We have to take that chance. I doubt they'll come so soon, after the bloody nose we gave them at Caerleon. And they won't know we've moved to Cardiff, either. The radio lookouts will stay in place, so if any hostiles show up on the horizon, the folks here will just have to pull up the drawbridge and sit it out until we get back.'

'And how long is that likely to be?' grunted Alfred Ashe, the usually disgruntled and pacifist trade unionist.

'Not long, Alf, this will be short and sharp. Like wars in Roman or medieval times, we either win quickly – or get wiped out!'

'Thanks a bundle, Brennan!' snapped Ashe. 'Where would that leave the few who stayed at home?'

The more diplomatic Beverley Truman tried to reassure him. 'He's pulling your leg, Alf. Of course we'll sort these Jerries out – and in quick time. According to Strickland, they've only got small arms and no decent vehicles.'

'We'd better send a motorcyclist over to Jolly Roger in Somerset, to tell him what's happening,' added Brennan. 'I doubt if he'll lift a finger to help us in Cambridge, but maybe he would rally round if there was a sudden Irish raid – it would be to his own advantage to keep those sods out of the Bristol Channel.' He got up from the table and stretched his arms above his head. 'It's late, and we've got one hell of a lot to do at first light. Let's get our heads down.'

In their caravan, he held Gwen close in the low bed. They clung together, but by some unspoken mutual consent, did not make love.

'Are you going to be safe up there, Brennan?' she murmured. 'Even that last brush with the Irish was pretty hairy – Lance came very close to being killed then.'

'We have to do it, sweetheart. What could happen to Cambridge could happen to us eventually, if they're not stopped now.'

'But this isn't a handful of Paddies on a few boats. There's hundreds of these people, according to what Strickland said.'

He pulled her more tightly to him. 'We'll be fine, love. They're just a rabble at present, trudging along the roads from the coast with rifles and pistols, as far as we can tell. I very much hope we can frighten them off or even do some sort of deal before much blood is spilt.'

'It seems awful to have to kill more people, when there are so few of us left. Why are they so keen to cross over to Britain, I wonder?'

'Same goes for the Irish, Gwen. Things must be even worse over there – and on the continent. Though what could be worse than the desolation here, I can't imagine.'

She turned over and fitted her bottom into the bend of his hips, like a pair of spoons.

'Maybe someone else is pushing them west from further across Europe. Though there should be plenty of room for everyone now, so I can't see that as an explanation.'

'If we catch one, we'll ask him. Beverley speaks German fluently – and I've got a smattering from my time there in the army, years ago.'

He fell silent, recalling the time he was a mere Captain, stationed in Munster. His eldest child was born there, the boy who he later buried in a hole in the ground near Brecon. By the time he had shaken off the old recurring nightmare, Gwen was fast asleep in his arms. He was not as confident about the coming fight as he had made out and lay worrying about what would happen to her if he never came back from Cambridge. Even these morbid thoughts eventually gave way to his fatigue and well after midnight, he slid into a troubled sleep.

CHAPTER SEVEN

ALTHOUGH Brennan now regretted not having raided every military base again for more arms, ammunition and vehicles, they had acquired some extra equipment since the skirmish at Caerleon.

When their only scout car had been wrecked, they managed to repair the Ferret's front suspension from cannibalised parts, found in a Territorial Unit. Brennan also took a raiding party around the army depots that he knew so well from the old days, at Sennybridge, Brecon and Crickhowell. They found two armoured Land-Rovers that had once seen service in Ulster and a Saracen armoured personnel carrier. While Beverley, Ruddy and their mechanic worked on the vehicles to get them going, Brennan took off for a couple of hours on a solitary pilgrimage to the former Officer's Quarters. He stood quietly for a time in his former garden, alongside a pathetic mound of earth that was the grave of his whole family, and vowed to come back one day and put some kind of memorial at the spot.

The new vehicles now came in very useful for their expedition to the east. The Land-Rovers and the Ferret could join the other civilian vehicles and go under their own steam, but the Saracen, a heavy brute with frightening fuel consumption, was driven on to the low-loader truck to be carried to Cambridge.

Soon after dawn, a hundred men and twenty women assembled in the castle bailey, alongside a motley collection of transport. About twenty vehicles, almost all they possessed, were lined up – from vans through four-by-fours to small trucks. A small tanker lorry, whose lettering proclaimed it to be delivering domestic heating oil, was filled with diesel and came at the tail-end of the convoy to keep them supplied. It held almost all their remaining stock of fuel and Brennan's uneasiness about committing it to this campaign was only tempered by Luddy's claim to have found a whole train of full tankers on the railway.

A number of vehicles towed trailers in which were much of their armament, covered with blue tarpaulins. Learning from the Irish assault, Brennan had taken four mortars from the armoury in Crickhowell. They had had to blow off the armoury doors with dynamite looted from a quarry near Cardiff, but the effort was worth it, as it was an Aladdin's cave of useful weapons, ammunition and plastic explosives. One of the Transit vans was filled with food, much of it their tinned reserve, together with enough simple cooking utensils to make scratch meals during the campaign.

Amid shouted farewells, some emotional and tearful, the troops clambered aboard the vans and trucks, watched by virtually the whole of the community. The cavalcade set off, with Brennan's Land-Rover leading the column, but they got no further than the raised portcullis under the castle gateway, where he had to stamp hard on his brakes and jerk to a stop.

A wild figure dressed in a shabby black cassock was standing on the drawbridge, gesticulating and waving a crude wooden cross. Spiky white hair stood up all over his head, above a face which was flushed with anger.

'Bloody hell, it's Canon Gilbey again!' groaned Lance, sitting next to the driver. 'The poor old boy's getting worse by the day.'

The clergyman advanced on the Defender and slammed his cross against the bonnet, glaring madly at the occupants, before shambling around to the driver's window.

'You're all warmongering sinners – and you are the greatest sinner of all, Brennan!'

'Take it easy, Reverend, this has to be done, you know.'

The canon shook his cross violently, the roughly-nailed pieces of wood almost coming apart.

'Madness upon evil madness! The leaders of men have ever been consumed with anger, greed and jealousy. So much death already and you are going out to kill more poor souls! You'll rot in hell, my man.'

'I expect I will, padre,' sighed Brennan. 'But I don't want to kill anyone – far from it! With luck, we can scare these people off with just a show of force – or come to some peaceful arrangement with them.' He didn't believe a word of what he said, after Strickland's account of their atrocities, but he wanted to pacify the unstable old priest.

'You shall not pass!' screamed the dishevelled canon and staggering back to the front of the Land-Rover, he painfully laid himself down against the wheels. Thankfully, a stream of people had come out through the archway to see what was happening and several of them gently picked up the demented priest. The old lady who seemed to have appointed herself his keeper slipped an arm around him as the others led him back into the bailey.

'Come on, Augustine, there's a good fellow,' she murmured, but Canon Gilbey continued to shout imprecations over his shoulder until he was out of sight. The convoy started up again and slowly turned around the corner of the great castle, heading for the motorway interchange.

'What are we going to do with these folk who become mentally deranged, Mervyn?' asked Brennan, sad at the deteriorating state of the old priest.

The physician grunted sardonically. 'Half of us are already deranged in some degree! Depression, paranoia and the rest of it. We've already got a score of people who have been totally incapacitated from the beginning. Thank heavens that others are prepared to look after them.'

It was true that in the early days, there had been many suicides, as lonely men and women, deprived of their dead spouses and families, saw no point in going on with their lives. These thoughts, and the endless replaying of personal tragedies, kept most of the travellers quiet for much of the journey. Brennan expected to take until evening to get to Cambridge, even though they started soon after dawn. Apart from the diversions and difficulties due to obstructions, they drove quite slowly, not wanting to stress the old vehicles more than necessary, as well as economising on their precious fuel.

Two motorcycles had gone ahead of them, one ridden by the intrepid Beverley. He had suggested that scouts would be useful to check the state of the road ahead, as one never knew if some bridge had recently collapsed or trees had blown down across the carriageway. Another one had gone off to Glastonbury with a letter from Brennan to Roger Mellars, telling him of the Cambridge emergency and inviting him to follow them up there to add his strength to the battle.

The morning passed uneventfully, and they stopped in the middle of the M4 somewhere near Reading to eat their bread and meat and drink some of the cider and beer they had brought.

'No chance of being breathalysed today, folks,' said Casey, the only ex-policeman among them. He had been a uniformed sergeant in the Gwent Constabulary when the disaster struck and had seen every one of his fellow officers lost, as well as all his own family.

'We'll stick to this booze or to tea as much as possible' ordered Mervyn in his best doctor's voice. 'We haven't got our filter system here that we have at home – and I wouldn't trust the stream or river water in this part of the country, even after five years.'

Brennan thought of the remains of over fifty million corpses leaking into the groundwater and was thankful that he was drinking from a bottle of their home-brew, made from spring water from a Monmouthshire mountainside.

They set off again, through a thin drizzle blown by a gusting westerly wind, but just before the Slough turn-off, their luck ran out. One of the Transit vans began to emit clouds of steam and had to pull over. The convoy stopped and a quick look under the bonnet showed that the top radiator hose had burst, the old rubber having perished. They had no spare and no time to start searching for a replacement from any abandoned vehicle on the roadway.

'Hitch its trailer to one of the Land-Rovers,' ordered Brennan. 'We'll have to distribute its load and passengers amongst the others.' He pitched in with the rest and within minutes, weapons, ammunition and stores were packed into the other vans. The crews squeezed themselves in elsewhere and they were soon off again, with everyone keeping their fingers crossed that another vehicle would not succumb to old age. On the M11 to Cambridge, the fuel truck blew a front tyre, but thankfully it carried a spare wheel and willing hands had it changed in record time.

The weather had deteriorated badly and it was now blowing a gale, whipping driving rain across the flat East Anglian countryside. They were running later than Brennan had anticipated and dusk was coming down by the time they passed the ruins of Stansted Airport. Beverley roared back on his Yamaha to refill his tank from jerrycans of petrol carried on the fuel truck and reported that there was no signs of any activity for at least the next ten miles ahead.

'I don't think we'll make Cambridge tonight, in this weather,' he said, water streaming from his leathers. 'Better to get there early in daylight in the morning.'

The leaders huddled in the lee of a van and agreed that it would be best to camp overnight.

'Duxford airfield is only a few miles further on,' suggested Bev. 'There's one hangar still standing, we could all get in there for the night and stay dry.'

Forty minutes later, they arrived outside one of the maintenance hangars of the old RAF base, which had become the Imperial War Museum's aviation shrine and home to several historic aircraft societies.

'I had a look at the place in daylight when I came back some time ago,' said the machinery-loving Beverley. 'The large hangar which had that early Concorde and a Sunderland has burned out, as well as most of the rest of the place. But one building looked fairly intact, apart from a few bits of roof blown off.'

They found the large aircraft-entrance doors rusted up, but several of the smaller doors were not only open, but knocked off their hinges. There had obviously been some early looting, but there was little of use to anyone. There were many aircraft scattered around the hangar, some seventy or more years old. A few were in pieces, being renovated when the curse arrived. However, apart from one or two enthusiasts who walked around in the gloom staring at these now-useless machines, the travellers had little interest in anything other than getting dry and warm. In a space under the intact part of the roof, they soon set up their camping equipment for cooking, heating and light. Within an hour they had containers of Cardiff stew ready to eat and with mugs of hot tea to wash down bread and cheese, they felt almost comfortable as they rolled into their sleeping bags on the floor and settled down to sleep.

Brennan, old soldier that he was, set a guard on the line of vehicles outside and took the first couple of hours' watch himself. He found a wooden chair and sat just inside one of the outer doors, where he could stay out of the blustery wind. The rain had stopped and breaks in the racing clouds allowed light from an almost full moon to illuminate the vans and trucks. Soon, footsteps behind him heralded Lance Prichard, who claimed he couldn't sleep and wanted some company for a while.

'The "eve before the battle" and all that stuff, Boss,' he said airily, but Brennan could sense the underlying tension in his voice.

'We'll be all right, Lance – as long as you don't repeat your heroics at Caerleon and get your head completely blown off this time.'

'No way, I'm keeping it well down tomorrow. What d'you think will happen up here?'

Brennan shrugged his big shoulders inside his leather jacket. 'Have to wait and see. If it's just a rabble with a few pop-guns, maybe we can scare them off with a few mortars dropped in front of their noses. Depends on how many of the buggers there are.'

Lance peered out of the glass door at the litter being hurled along the roadway by the wind. 'Hell of a night – maybe they'll be so miserable after their march from the coast that they'll turn round and go home?'

'Where's home for them, I wonder?' mused Brennan. 'Poor sods risk crossing the North Sea in piddling little boats, just to get to another wrecked country.'

'Must be even worse on the continent, then. We need to find out why, if we can. Though according to Strickland, these Jerries prefer shooting to talking.'

They fell silent for a while, listening to the howl of the wind and clatter of loose sheets on the damaged roof of the hangar. Since the climatic changes of the last decade, violent gales were commonplace, though the winters were getting even milder and the summers even wetter.

'Pity to see all those great old planes in there.' Lance jerked a thumb over his shoulder. 'No one to fly them, no one even to come and look at them, except us.'

'Didn't you once say that you had a pilot's licence?'

The slim young man nodded. 'My old man treated me to a flying course as a twenty-first birthday present. Afterwards, I managed enough flying to keep my licence. Maybe I could have afforded a little plane one day, if. . . .'

So many times Brennan had heard these 'ifs' and 'maybes' – and uttered them himself.

'A small plane would be damned useful for getting around to see what's happening in the country. But I suppose it's impossible?'

Lance glumly agreed. 'I'm sure that somewhere there's quite a few planes in flying condition . . . but no aviation fuel. The Germans once made a diesel-engined aircraft – pity they didn't persevere.'

'What about jet-power? They use kerosene . . . that lasts, doesn't it?'

Lance grinned. 'There's easier ways of committing suicide, Boss! I can just about manage to fly a little Beechcraft or a Cessna.' He squatted on his heels in the dim moonlight, looking up at the impassive figure of their leader. 'In a way, Brennan, things haven't changed so much for you as for the rest of us.'

'What d'you mean? My world's gone, the same as for the rest of us!'

The younger man gestured in embarrassment. 'God, I don't mean your personal tragedies, like we've all had – family and that. But you were a senior Army officer, used to organising people and commanding things to happen. That's basically what you've still been doing these past five years – now you're even leading armed troops into battle, so what's new!'

Brennan grunted a grudging agreement. 'I suppose you're right, in that sense. What about you?'

Lance grinned in the darkness. 'I've had a real career change, chum! I went to art college in Reading and then became a graphic designer. My last job was designing sets for the theatre and films . . . a far cry from charging round the countryside with a machine gun!'

'Which do you prefer, lad?' Brennan was not much more than a decade older than Lance, but felt like his father.

'Got to make the best of it, haven't we?' His voice became sadder, as he recalled that he was engaged at the time of the plague. 'I lost my girl. She died in my arms, Brennan. I'd gone back to Swindon when it started, to be with her. By the time I got back home to Reading, my parents had gone too.'

They had all replayed their private hells to each other many times, as if in the retelling, a little of the horror might be rubbed away. The two men sat silently for a few minutes, then Lance got to his feet.

'I'll have a bit of a kip, then I'll come and relieve you for a few hours. Don't forget to put the cat out!'

He went back into the hangar and threaded his way through the sleeping bags to reach his own. He lay under the wing of an old Heinkel, wondering if any of the men he might have to kill tomorrow were descendants of the plane's designer.

Strickland and her lieutenant John Lovatt leaned over the table in the 'council chamber' at Addenbrooke's Hospital, several Ordnance Survey maps spread out in front of them. She raised her head to speak to Brennan.

'An hour ago, our scouts reported by radio that the nearest of the hostiles had reached Newmarket Heath. A big group of them camped out on the racecourse overnight. The main stand is burned out, but maybe they got some shelter in the ruins, with weather like last night.'

Brennan leaned across to look down at the map. 'That's about ten or twelve miles away from the city?'

'Yes, with the A1304 running straight towards us. They could be here within a few hours. And their other main party is coming up from the south – they're near Haverhill on the A1307, which aims them straight at Cambridge.'

'Any more of them or are they all in those two battalions?' Brennan unconsciously used a military term.

'We've only got six observers out, but two of them report smaller groups walking the minor roads between the other main forces. There may be more that we don't know about – we can't cover every road in the area.'

'What are they doing, just marching?' asked Mervyn.

Lovatt shook his head sadly. 'One of our men was near enough to see them looting a farm near Bury St Edmunds. There are still a few loners out there who refused to come in to Cambridge, even though we warned them several times.'

Something in his voice told Brennan that this was not the whole story. 'What else did he see?'

'The swine took all they could from the farmhouse, killed the few pigs and poultry and took them to their trucks. When the farmer and two other men and a couple of women tried to stop them, they just shot them, fired the house and drove away!'

'The bastards. At least it eases our conscience about dealing with them later today,' grunted Mervyn.

'I hope you can keep them out of the city. I hate to think what they'll do if they get in.' Looking pale and intensely worried, the Cambridge leader glanced around at the faces of the visitors, seeking reassurance. Six of the Cardiff men were there, with a few of the members of the local Comintern facing them across the big table.

'No sign of any of them on the motorway when we came up a couple of hours ago,' commented Beverley Truman. 'But if some are near Haverhill, they're only a few miles from us.'

'What preparations have you made so far?' asked Mervyn.

'All the kids, old folks and many of the women have been brought inside the hospital compound. The rest of our able-bodied men and younger women are out on the two main roads into the city from the east.'

'Did you put up roadblocks, as we suggested?'

'Yes, we loaded trailers and trucks with rubble. We can tow them aside if you need to get your own vehicles through.'

They discussed the situation urgently for a few more minutes, eating sandwiches and drinking tea as they talked and looked at the maps. The rest of the Cardiff force were being fed downstairs in the dining hall. It was now about nine o'clock in the morning and the weather had eased off, so that although there was a brisk wind, there was only the occasional shower. When they finished eating, Strickland led the way downstairs. As they passed the radio room, Brennan jerked a thumb towards the women operators.

'We need to keep in touch both with your spies out there and between the various groups, both your men and ours. Will your communications be up to that?'

Edgar Lambert, the lean, haggard Cambridge man nodded. 'I'm looking after that. There should be no problem on the VHF side, the range is quite short now. We've rustled up ten transceivers between us, and the women in there can patch through any of them to talk to anyone else.'

Out in the compound, Brennan assembled the men and women he had brought from Wales and following rehearsals back at home, they split into four groups, dividing the various items of armament equally between them. These were unloaded from their vans and the heavier weapons like the mortars and heavy machine guns loaded into the pair of ex-army Bedford trucks and the two armoured Land-Rovers. Two other Land-Rovers carried spare ammunition and some basic food and water to last the day.

Staff Sergeant Bill Fleming and former marine Phil Robson took charge of two of the companies and Lance and Beverley the other pair. The old Saracen was rolled off the low-loader truck, after having been persuaded to start with a good battery provided by Strickland's boffins. The repaired Ferret was being used by Beverely as his lead vehicle and soon they were ready to go.

'Who are you leaving behind here?' asked Brennan, as he prepared to swing up into the Saracen with Casey and eight armed men.

'Including the older women and kids and those unfit, about two hundred men and women,' answered Lovatt. 'We've no weapons for them, apart from those in the perimeter posts – and even if we had, few of them would know one end of a gun from the other, including myself.'

Brennan managed to restrain his comments at the military apathy of these people, who had known for many months of the growing threat along the coast.

'We'll have to see about that when we've sorted these buggers out today,' he shouted above the roar of the Saracen, as Casey revved up the engine in a cloud of blue smoke.

He climbed inside and slammed the back door shut. The ugly vehicle resembled a flat steel coffin on six massive wheels. A snout-like bonnet had a radiator shield of thick horizontal bars, above which was the flap of the driver's window. It was a troop-carrier, rather than an armoured car and ten persons could sit along the side-benches in bone-rattling discomfort.

Brennan scrambled to the front to sit alongside Casey and they moved off to head the other heavier vehicles, which carried forty of his troops. Behind them came the vans, giving the rest of his army a lift to the barricades a few miles down the road.

'We'll send them back when they've dropped their passengers,' he yelled in Casey's ear. 'No point in exposing delivery vans to stray bullets.'

Each of the groups had a Cambridge man or woman with them to act as a guide and to keep radio contact with the hospital. The one in the Saracen, a tough-looking girl in jodhpurs with a twelve-bore shotgun grasped in one hand, yelled at Brennan after they had driven for about ten minutes through suburban roads lined with damaged, derelict and overgrown houses.

'The first roadblock is about half a mile ahead!'

This was on the older A1303 road to Newmarket, which crossed over the A14 dual carriageway and was the route to the nearest body of invaders.

The roadblock was just as Strickland had described: two large trailers filled with brick rubble, blocking the road completely between the pine end of a shop and a high wall the other side. A score of men and a few women were waiting uneasily behind the trailers, carrying an assortment of rifles, shotguns and a few automatic weapons. Brennan walked forward to talk to the man whose red armband seemed to mark him out as the leader.

'Any sign of them?' he asked, staring down the narrow gap between the trailers.

'Nothing yet – but the radio-room said five minutes ago that they're on the move from Newmarket. Their four trucks are crawling along, as the rest are foot-slogging behind, so it'll be a couple of hours before they get within sight.'

The commanders of the four companies had walked over and stood around listening.

'What about the southern mob – have we heard anything of them?' asked Lance.

As the local man shook his head, the girl with the shotgun had her VHF set to her ear and was talking rapidly to the control room.

'They're on the move as well. Marching between Haverhill and Linton, the main route to the city, but further away than the lot on this road.'

Brennan looked at Beverley Truman. 'We'll try to sort this lot out first, but to be on the safe side, you'd better take the Ferret and one of the Ulster Land-Rovers and go down south with one company in some of the vans. Don't go too far, but set up an ambush in case they reach you. Keep in touch by radio and if things get nasty, we'll send the cavalry!'

Beverley gave a brisk salute, which for some reason didn't seem at all inappropriate even in those bizarre circumstances. As he ran back to his vehicles, Brennan watched him go with some misgivings. For all he knew, he was sending Bev to his death against a far larger force – he only had Mavis Strickland's assumption that the Germans were poorly armed. With a sigh, he turned to the man with the red armband.

'Right, let's get on with the show. Can you let us through?'

The locals had a farm tractor waiting nearby and it dragged one of the heavy trailers aside to let their vehicles pass. With the Saracen whining ahead, they drove down the main road, which now left the built-up area and was passing between overgrown fields and hedges that were rapidly becoming scrub and woodland. After a few miles, Brennan peered out of the open front vents, searching the flat countryside for a suitable place for an ambush.

'Hills are as rare as cockerel's eggs in this bloody place!' he grumbled, but eventually they came to the top of a long rise. Here the dead straight road stretched away gently downwards for over a mile, ending in a sharp bend. Near them, on either side, patches of dense woodland provided good cover and on the right, a large house was set in the trees almost on the edge of the road. Casey stopped the six-wheeler and Brennan got out to talk to his three company commanders.

'We'll wait for them here. Lance, take your lot across the road, we'll keep the other two companies this side. Hide the heavier vehicles well back in the trees and send the vans back to the roadblock until we radio them to come and pick us up,' he ordered optimistically.

Everyone piled out and unloaded their weapons and ammunition. Casey took the Saracen behind the shelter of the house, then saw that beyond it was a weed-filled rectangle surrounded on three sides by low buildings.

'Must have been a riding stables or a stud farm,' he shouted. 'Plenty of room for the trucks in here, out of sight of the road.'

Within minutes, under the firm direction of the four former professional soldiers, eighty men and women were dispersed along a few hundred yards of road, just inside the scrub and trees on either side. Two mortars were set up, as well as four heavy machine guns and two of the rocket launchers. Two dozen men were spread out at the lower end of the wood at right angles to the road, in case the enemy tried to outflank them.

Brennan stood in the middle of the road and stared down the empty mile. He lifted a loud hailer that Strickland had provided and his amplified voice resounded between the trees.

'Now comes the hardest part,' he shouted. 'Waiting for the bastards to arrive!'

He walked down the road beyond the trees for a few hundred yards and then came back again, making sure that nothing of his force was visible. Back at the stud farm, he turned to Anna, the Cambridge girl, who looked quite at home here in her riding pants.

'Any news from base?'

She lifted the VHF and spoke a few sentences, then listened for a moment.

'One of the scouts has gone off the air – either his set's failed or he's been killed or captured. The other one's skulking in the fields and says that the leading trucks must be almost within sight of where we are now.'

'What about our other group, that went south?'

Anna spoke rapidly again into her transmitter. 'They've stopped near Sawston, a couple of miles short of the other hostiles. No problems so far.'

Brennan walked back into the road and used the loud hailer again. 'This is your captain speaking! We should be able to see the first of them in the distance within a few minutes. So we're going quiet now –

not a sound until we scare the hell out of them.'

He switched off and went back to the Saracen, where Casey was waiting, a Caliburn automatic rifle slung across his shoulder. He wore a belt strung with grenades and his ugly, heavy face had an expression of quiet contentment.

'A bit like the old days in Bosnia, boss,' he said. 'I didn't carry grenades in Belfast!'

Brennan recognised the need to ease the pre-combat tension with old jokes and reminiscences and went along with the older man's mood.

'I missed Bosnia, but caught Kosovo. I was in the Gulf, too, but all I saw was smoke and bloody sand.'

'It would be nice to have had a few of the old SAS lads here with us,' said Casey, pensively. 'Though Phil Robson's no fairy, coming from the Marine Commando. And Bill Fleming is old enough to have been in the Falklands, by God!'

All this was ancient history to them, but they felt the need to talk, to reassure themselves that they were professionals, albeit leading a bunch of amateurs.

Brennan walked restlessly to the corner of the house and peered down the road, but it was still empty as far as the eye could see. When he came back, Casey Wallace had a question for him.

'When they do show, what are we going to do? Zap them first or try to talk them into going home?'

This was the very question that Brennan had been agonising about for the past few hours. He had fobbed off the curses of Canon Gilbey with the promise that he would negotiate before shooting, but now that the balloon was about to go up, it was not that simple a choice.

'If we lose the element of surprise, Casey, we're going to have to slog through a fire-fight – and by the sound of it, there's a lot more of them than there are of us.'

'The bastards have already killed plenty of Brits already, by all accounts,' agreed Casey. 'I can't see them throwing in the towel just because you threaten them on your new loud hailer. We'll end up with a lot of us dead if we don't hit them first.'

His lieutenant's common sense tipped the scales for Brennan. The Reverend Augustine Gilbey or not, he had no intention of going back to Cardiff with several van-loads of corpses – if any of them ever got the chance to go back.

'Right, we'll give them all we've got to start with! I'll make sure Bev does the same with his company.'

After another covert look down the empty road, he got Anna to call up control and was patched through to Beverley.

'Nothing in sight yet, boss,' came the cultured accent of the former Home Office official. 'We're nicely dug into two buildings each side of the road.'

Brennan told him of their decision to strike first, fast and furiously, and with a fervent expression of good luck, broke the connection, just as Casey called out that something had appeared at the far end of the road. Confident that his voice could never reach for a mile, he called out to Robson and Fleming that they were to whack the enemy with all they'd got, as soon as Brennan's side opened the batting.

'We need to get their vehicles with the first salvo, OK?'

Getting waves of assent from the trees, all went silent again and Brennan slipped with Casey through the wind-rustled trees almost down to the front line on their side of the road. He lay in the tangled weeds, full of new spring sproutings, and scanned the road through his field glasses. There was no sun to reflect off the lenses and give him away, so he studied the distant bend in the road for a long moment.

'Two trucks so far, going very slowly,' he reported to Casey, who had crawled up beside him. 'Ordinary flat-bed delivery lorries, two or three tonners, by the look of them.'

'What's on them, can you see?'

'Hard to tell, they're head on to us. Wait a minute, there's men on the second one, standing up, shoulder to shoulder.'

There was a few moments' pause, then he spoke again. 'Another bigger van coming round the corner, looks like a small furniture van or a big horsebox.' He handed the glasses to Casey who took a long look.

'The first truck has got something sticking out over the roof of the cab. Looks like a heavy machine gun.'

Brennan took the binoculars back and agreed with Casey's diagnosis.

'We need to take that bugger out straight away, or it could do us a lot of damage. Slip back and tell one of the rocket teams to target it, but don't fire until I say so.'

Casey slid away and Brennan continued to watch. The vehicles had stopped and a few moments later it was clear that they were waiting for the foot-sloggers to catch up, as round the bend in the road, between more trees, came a ragged column of men. They were ambling, not marching and were in a disorderly straggle across the road, about three or four abreast. They caught up with the trucks, which began moving again at walking pace and as they came nearer, the column of men still shambled around the curve in the road. Brennan estimated that at least three hundred men had appeared before the column ended, incongruously having a horse and cart as its rearguard.

'We'll wait until the leading trucks are almost up to our front line,' he muttered, as Casey returned. 'Otherwise, if we fire too soon, the main column will be too far away to get the best result at this angle.'

Casey wriggled back again to the rocket launcher on their side of the road and lay waiting for a sign from Brennan.

The 'hostiles' came on steadily, the trucks whining in second gear as they came up the slope at walking pace. The defenders could see three faces behind each of the windscreens of the two trucks and the big van. The latter had a jagged hole cut in the front panel above the cab where the muzzle of a machine gun was poking out. Brennan had rehearsed their plan of campaign before they settled into their ambush positions, so that there would be no duplication of attack on one vehicle at the expense of missing out on the others. The numbers of hostile trucks was not known beforehand, but his men and women knew who were to concentrate on alternate vehicles.

The lead truck drew almost level, a Leyland Daf three-tonner with a heavy machine gun mounted high up behind the cab. The sight of it eased what was left of Brennan's conscience, as there was now no doubt about the intention of this column, who were patently intent on wiping out Cambridge.

He signalled the start of hostilities in a spectacular way, by traversing the windscreen of the Leyland with a burst from his Caliburn SLR. As the glass disintegrated, the truck swerved across the road as the driver was hit. A second later, a short-range impact from a rocket launcher exploded the cab and the crew of the gun above.

Almost simultaneously, all hell was let loose as the other rocket teams blew the second truck and then the panel van to smithereens. The leading foot-soldiers were caught up in a hail of flying debris, which worsened when the van suddenly blew up in a ball of flame, as it presumably carried spare fuel and ammunition.

The long column of walkers were paralysed for a moment by this utter catastrophe apparently arriving from nowhere, but then they dived for the edges of the road. Brennan had chosen his spot well, for his own front line was exactly at the edge of the wood, beyond which was no cover, only open fields of weeds and brambles. All his troops opened up with their small arms, a mixture of Caliburns, SA 80s, old FNs, even a few Stens from an army museum. Those nearest the road lobbed grenades down the verges and the two tripod-mounted machine guns wreaked havoc amongst the Germans further down the column.

It was a complete rout and during the first few moments, not a shot was fired back by the shattered column. Then the survivors in the first ranks began running back down the road, cannoning into those who had been out of the field of fire, until the whole 'battalion' was in full flight. The horse and cart, which had been a long way back at the tail of the column, wheeled around and galloped away into the distance, boxes and packs falling from it as its driver belaboured the beast into top speed. The small arms fire of the ambushers ceased as the fugitives fled out of effective range, but the mortar teams sent two shells crashing into the roadway behind them as a final incentive to make themselves scarce.

Halfway back to the bend in the road, someone must have tried to halt the retreat, as a number of men flung themselves on to the roadway and the verges and began firing rifles and a few automatic weapons at the still unseen defenders hidden in the trees. Brennan heard a few bullets whining overhead and chips of bark flew from a couple of tree-trunks nearby, but the gesture was futile at that range.

'Drop another couple of mortars on them,' he yelled. 'That'll stop their antics!'

A few more moderately well-aimed shots blew fountains of earth and some tarmac out of the road and as Brennan had predicted, the defiance ended abruptly as the braver marksmen began a crouching run to follow their fellows down the road.

'Follow up in the Saracen and the Rover!' shouted Brennan. 'The rest of you stay in position.'

Casey started up the Saracen and Brennan and his eight-strong team piled aboard. They roared down the road, followed by the armoured Land-Rover, weaving past the wrecked trucks and the burning panel-van. Many bodies lay inert on the road, but he left it to Robson and his men to see if any were still alive.

As they drove down the straight, the enemy had just reached the bend in the road, a rabble with no apparent leadership. Brennan suspected that their 'officers' had been in the leading vehicles.

When the Saracen roared up behind the tail-end of the fleeing men, they dived for cover to the sides of the road, where the trees began again.

'They're just melting away,' yelled Casey over the noise of the engine. 'We can't flush the sods out now, they're scattering amongst the trees.'

They saw the horse and cart hammering away in front of them, but Brennan tapped the driver on the shoulder and made a motion to turn back. As they passed a few men dodging between the trees, he let fly a few bursts through the front vent and the men in the back fired through the side ports at any target that presented, but it was more a gesture than a serious effort.

'That'll do, Casey, take us back. They'll be spread across half the county soon, we can't chase them all.'

They revved back up the slope to the site of the ambush and stopped in the road. Robson was coming cautiously down the road from the trees, his weapon at the ready in case any of the fallen enemy was lying doggo and took a pot-shot at him. Behind him, on either verge, Lance and Fleming were leading their companies with equal caution, looking at the casualties to see if any were alive. Those involved in the explosion of the trucks were undoubtedly dead and most of the others who had been hit by automatic fire or grenades and mortars were also beyond help. By the time the search parties reached the limit of destruction, they had found four still alive, but Doc Mervyn, coming behind with his large medical bag, pronounced two of them beyond aid, especially in the absence of any surgical or transfusion facilities. Both were unconscious, one with a leg almost detached and a severe head wound, the other with a gaping abdominal injury. He gave them both a massive injection of morphine to prevent them from suffering any pain should they recover consciousness before they died.

'What about these two?' demanded Lance, pointing to the other pair, who were groaning amongst the nettles at the side of the road.

Mervyn hurried to the nearest, who was trying to sit up. It was a man of between thirty and forty, very fair-haired and dressed in a long field-grey overcoat that looked as if it was German Army surplus.

'He's had a bang on the side of the head, but seems otherwise all right,' shouted the doctor, as he helped the victim to sit upright. 'Anyone speak German?'

To Mervyn's surprise, the man answered in excellent English, though his voice was rather slurred.

'I'm Dutch, actually. Are you going to shoot me?'

'Only with morphia, if necessary. Are you hurt anywhere else?'

With another groan, the man put a hand to his aching head. 'I do not think so. I was thrown to the road by an explosion. Are you a doctor?'

'Yes – our commander will speak to you while I look at the other survivor.'

Mervyn left the Dutchman slumped on the road, a huge bruise on the side of his head growing more prominent by the minute, while he went across to the other man. This was an older fellow incongruously wearing a dark business suit, which was torn and stained, one side being badly scorched. His face and neck were peppered by small lacerations and bruises from debris blown from the road by a grenade. One side of his face was reddened and superficially burned, as was the back of his right hand. None of the injuries was deep and thankfully his eyes were spared. This time, Mervyn had no luck with his English and the man stared up at him fearfully from where he was lying in the road, muttering something in German. The doctor gave him some morphine, then took some swabs from his bag and moistened them from a bottle of antiseptic. He gently cleaned up the face of the German, picking out embedded bits of gravel and road dirt, to the accompaniment of groans and hisses of pain. Meanwhile, Brennan had come across the Dutchman and crouched alongside him.

'Don't worry, we're not going to hurt you.' He waved a hand at the carnage on the road. 'Sorry about all this, but it was you or us. I don't think your lot were carrying those machine guns just for ornament.'

The man grinned weakly. 'You were right. These bastards were going to do to Cambridge what they did to Ipswich and Colchester. I am not with them voluntarily. My name is Jan Beelan, by the way.'

His English was almost too perfect, as was often the way with folk from the Netherlands, thought Brennan.

'Well, Mister Beelan, we'll take you back with us. I presume you don't want to walk back to the coast to join your friends?'

'My God, no! Please keep me with you, I can hardly believe I've escaped.' He suddenly groaned again and put a hand to his head.

'We'll have a long talk when you feel better. Lance, can you get a couple of chaps to help him into the Saracen. What about this other fellow?'

He walked over to where Mervyn was closing up his medical bag. 'How is he, doc? Will he live?'

'Yes, as long as those burns and skin wounds don't go septic. He doesn't seem to understand any English.'

The man, dark-haired and very thin, lay on his side on the road surface, his knees pulled up into an almost foetal position. He was shivering uncontrollably, either from fear or shock, but his eyes were open and aware. Brennan tried some of his rudimentary German, unused since he was stationed there many years earlier. The man muttered something through chattering teeth, but it was incomprehensible.

'Better put him in the Saracen as well, Lance. You'll have to carry him, by the look of it.'

A few of the other troops had come nearer and were looking somewhat aghast at the sight of what they had done to these victims. As the two survivors were loaded, Phil Robson came across and indicated the scene of mayhem with a sweep of his hand, where some thirty bodies lay on the ground.

'What are we going to do about them, sir?' he asked, the title coming automatically in this reversion to his military days, though in normal circumstances no one ever called Brennan 'sir'.

'We can't leave them here for good, but it would take us ages to dig graves and I'm worried about Beverley's situation over on the south front.'

'Why not leave them to the Cambridge people,' suggested Lance.

'They've got a JCB digger that they could bring out. We could give them an armed guard if they want it, though I think the hostiles have gone off to lick their wounds for the time being.'

His suggestion was accepted thankfully and everyone began moving back up to the stable-yard to get organised for departure. Anna of the jodhpurs got on to her radio again and reported the rout to Cambridge Control, with a request to get a digger out for the burial task. Then she was patched through to Beverley on the Bury St Edmunds road and to Brennan's great relief, he answered straight away. He spoke to Bev for a minute or two, then signed off, turning to the others who waited expectantly for his news.

'He did even better than us, by the sound of it! Bev ambushed a much smaller force than ours, with just two trucks and a van. He dropped a mortar shell just in front of the van and blew the radiator off, then the whole mob turned and ran, leaving their vehicles in the road.'

'Any casualties on either side?' asked Mervyn.

'Not a scratch on our folks. Two of theirs killed, they've buried them and didn't pursue the rest. The hostiles left a machine gun and some ammunition behind. Sounded a proper fiasco!'

The doctor nodded, then reported that both the mortally-injured men to whom he had given morphine injections, had already died.

Back at the stable-yard, they radioed for their transport to come and pick them up and while they waited, they took stock of the situation. They had only one casualty: one of the girls in Robson's company had a large wood splinter in her upper arm from a stray shot that hit a nearby tree. Mervyn cleaned and dressed it and the girl seemed more pleased than distressed at being the only one with an honourable war wound.

'What's going to happen next, I wonder,' queried Lance. 'That seemed too easy to be true. Are they going to come back for more?'

Brennan leaned against the massive bulk of the armoured car, his

Caliburn held at the trail like a farmer out for foxes.

'They won't try anything for a while, I'm sure. But we mustn't be complacent. This took them by surprise, they were expecting only to be up against the softies from Cambridge.' He looked guiltily around for Anna, but she was some yards away.

'Now they know that it's not going to be a walkover, they'll be far better prepared next time. There are plenty of old military depots in East Anglia, especially around Colchester. I'll bet they've already got the message and will get themselves tooled up much better for next time.'

'We can't stay in Cambridge for ever, nannying Strickland and her crowd,' objected Mervyn.

Brennan agreed, his strong features grim as he weighed up the long-term prospects.

'I don't think Cambridge can survive, if they come back at it hard. It'll take the Germans weeks or months to get organised and better armed, but eventually they'll be back.'

He pushed himself off the Saracen and buttoned up his worn leather jacket. 'We'll have to go back and talk it over with Ms Strickland – and see what out new friend from Holland has to tell us.'

CHAPTER EIGHT

JAN Beelan turned out to be a 38-year-old electrical engineer from Rotterdam, where he had once been the technical manager of a large auto-electric repair company. Brennan felt that he would be a very useful addition to their scanty pool of experts, when he pleaded to join their Cardiff community, rather than stay in East Anglia.

When the returning expeditionary force reached Addenbrooke's, they received a heroes' welcome from the locals, but Brennan was more delighted to be reunited with Beverley's squadron, who were all safe and sound. Strickland and her colleagues laid on a celebratory meal that evening in the dining hall and the leaders of both groups sat at one long table. Jan Beelan was included, as it seemed so obvious that he was delighted to be released from the coercion of his former companions. The other captive was in the sickbay upstairs, having his injured face attended to.

'They forced me to join them on their damned boats, so that I could help them get some motor transport going over here,' said Jan bitterly.

As they ate an excellent meal of soup, roast pork and a selection of vegetables from Strickland's capacious freezers, a picture of what was happening in nearby Europe began to emerge.

'I just don't understand why you lot are so keen to invade Britain,' demanded Mervyn, in his usual blunt fashion.

'Don't blame me, doctor, I had no choice,' replied Jan. 'But if you think conditions here are rough, you should see the other side of the North Sea.' He waved his fork at the warm, well-lit dining room, with plenty of food on the tables.

'It's not like this everywhere,' warned Lance. 'Our friends in Cambridge must have the best conditions in the country. You won't find it quite so cosy back in South Wales.'

'So what's the motive for this sea-borne invasion?' asked Mavis Strickland, getting back to the point.

'One is the sea itself,' explained Jan. 'Since this freak weather of the past few years and a steadily rising sea level, much of the Netherlands is flooded again. All the great dykes have been breached, there's no pumping any more and at least half the country is under water. The IJsselmeer, what you used to call the Zuider Zee, has reformed and extended itself greatly. Some of north-west Germany is also flooded, so I've heard.'

'Parts of the Essex and Suffolk coast have had the same problem – miles of it are permanently under water now,' agreed Edgar Lambert.

'But on its own, that wouldn't account for this mass exodus,' objected Beverley.

Jan Beelan began to shake his head, until he found it was too painful. He now had a great discoloured swelling across one side of his head.

'Sure, we are so few in numbers that what's left of the land is enough to live on. But most of the towns and cities have been flooded –including Amsterdam and Rotterdam – so we had far less than you to plunder for food and supplies. The main factor is that other people have moved in from further east, pushing us into the sea. There have been endless fights and even exterminations.'

'Why are they coming west, then, if your patch is so unattractive anyway?' asked Mervyn.

'It's only hearsay, but it seems that there have been several nuclear disasters out there somewhere in the east. Many of the surviving Germans have fled and even some Czechs, Hungarians and Poles. And they are being displaced by Russians and Ukrainians that panicked them into fleeing west.'

There was a silence. This was about the last thing anyone wanted to hear.

'You don't mean nuclear weapons?' demanded Mervyn.

Jan shrugged. 'The only news is rumour, but I don't think so. I would suspect, being an electrical engineer myself, that some abandoned nuclear power plants have gone on fire or their reactors melted down, with no one left to take care of them.'

'Like Chernobyl, you mean?' asked Lance Prichard.

'Could be, but there's no hard news, only tenth-hand rumour passed around. But it's sent many hundreds of surviving Germans and even some Danes down to the North Sea coast, which is far as they can get, without crossing to England. And they were followed by Austrians, Hungarians, Romanians, even a few Russians. They all pushed into the Netherlands and Belgium.'

Brennan put down his knife and looked at Mervyn. 'Chernobyl affected us here, all the way from the Ukraine. I still remember it – they couldn't sell sheep from North Wales for years, because of the radioactivity in the grass. Is there a risk for us?'

The old doctor shrugged. 'Potentially, yes. But there's nothing we can do about it. We can't even tell if it's happening, as we've got no detection instruments. But as far as I can tell medically, no one has suffered from leukaemia, though without proper diagnostic facilities and hospital laboratories, we can't even be sure of that!'

'What about the British nuclear plants?' asked Lance. 'Would we even know if one or two of those boiled over, if they were way up north?'

'I suspect yours had better fail-safe systems than some of those badly-designed and poorly-maintained plants in the East,' said Beelan. 'Some of the easterners claimed that there had been deaths from radiation. It certainly was one of the reasons for this trek westwards. There have been huge floods in Germany too, in the Rhine and Danube valleys, that pushed even more people out.'

'How much of the population is left, generally speaking?' queried Strickland.

'Before the Netherlands was invaded about two or three years ago, it seemed that about a tenth of one percent survived. One in a thousand, in other words.'

Mervyn nodded. 'That's roughly what we calculate here. So there must be half a million survivors across Europe. Did you have much organisation in Holland, some kind of administration?'

'It was slow forming, as we were so few in number, but after a year or two, there were two main groups, one the north-east and the other in the south. But when all these invaders pushed in, it went to hell again. More like a prison camp or a slave colony.'

They kept talking through the rest of the meal, then adjourned to a former students' lecture theatre, where they were served home-made fruit wine and continued to question the Dutchman. It was such a novelty to get news of somewhere beyond this island of Britain, that people were reluctant to give Beelan a rest.

'As I said, two or three years ago, these people started to come in from the east, mostly Germans but some others as well. We were just settling down then and when the number of these intruders became too much, we resisted. That's when things turned nasty and they forced themselves into our communities. Some on both sides were killed, the organisation crumbled and it became sheer anarchy, with dozens of small groups fending for themselves and fighting any other who tried to take what they had.'

'So how come there was enough organisation to mount this cross-channel migration?' asked Beverley.

'About a year ago, another few truckloads of Germans crossed the border. I think they came from Rostock or somewhere in what used to be the old east Germany. They had guns and were very belligerent. At least they stopped much of the squabbling between the smaller groups in North Holland – mainly by shooting them! They soon set up a sort of dictatorship, under what you might call a warlord, a guy named Gustaf Fischer, who it seems had been an officer in the German Army. They all called him 'Major', anyway.'

Mervyn leered at Brennan. 'You're not alone then, Brigadier. You've got competition amongst the Jerries, even though you outrank him!'

The former soldier scowled. 'That's the last thing I need, to compete with the *Wehrmacht*! But it makes things more serious, if there's a professional soldier against us. He won't be caught again like he was today.'

'Maybe he was killed in that first truck we hit today,' suggested Lance, but the Dutchman shook his head. 'No, he stayed back in Colchester. He sent some of his thugs to head up those columns.'

'So how did you get mixed up in this?' asked Brennan.

'Fischer's gang were soon reinforced by many more Germans and some Poles and Czechs. They imposed their rule on the rest of us and soon the Dutch there were well outnumbered. I must admit they were better organised at foraging for food and getting more vehicles on the road, but there was no vestige of democracy. You did what Fischer and his lot ordered, otherwise you starved or were even beaten or shot.' He touched his head tenderly. 'It was well worth this blow on my skull to get away from them. I had no one left behind – my wife died in the first weeks and we had no children.'

'They made you come across to England?' asked Lance.

'I was made to work on their transport in Holland and when they decided to move over here, I was forced to go with them. Today I was given a shotgun and made to walk in their column, but I was told my main job was to fix any of the trucks if they broke down.' He smiled wryly. 'But even I couldn't have mended the damage you did to them!'

Brennan scratched his nose thoughtfully. 'I'm still not clear why these Germans decided to cross the sea to come here? How did they know it wasn't even worse in Britain?'

Jan Beelen sipped some blackberry wine appreciatively. 'I heard that some Germans fishing off our coast got blown out to sea in some of this terrible weather we now get so often. They found shelter in some little harbour in Essex and went exploring. The place struck them as being in better shape, with some fields of corn and farm animals. When they got back, Fischer sent a couple of boats to reconnoitre and decided things were better this side.'

Mervyn grunted. 'That's when the trouble started, I suppose. They massacred a lot of people in several of the coastal towns.'

Jan sighed heavily. 'They boasted about that, when more boats came back to collect settlers. The plan was – still is, I suppose – to shift almost everyone over here. They've been collecting boats and repairing them all along the coast. I know, because I've had to fix some of the electrics for the starters and ignition – it's a hell of a job, as we have hardly any batteries now and very little gasoline, only diesel.'

'Join the club, we have the same trouble,' commented Lance. 'Who's this other chap we saved today, the German?' he added.

'I have never seen him before, I'm sorry. But I can find out tomorrow, my German is fluent now, unfortunately!'

Brennan looked at his wristwatch, a reliable old wind-up type that needed no batteries. 'It's getting late and we've had a busy day. There's a lot to talk about tomorrow, then we need to make sure that mess out on the Newmarket road has been cleared up. I think we ought to spend the following day in making a few sorties in the Saracen and Ferret to make sure that those bastards really have gone back to the coast. Then we'll be on our way home the morning after that.'

The leader of the Cambridge Soviet nodded bleakly. 'We certainly need your advice about defence in the short term – and unfortunately, I think I know what you're going to recommend for the long term!'

Brennan had plenty to occupy his mind as their convoy wended its way steadily westwards two days later. One concern was that they had failed to make radio contact with Cardiff the previous day. Their routine signal at noon had gone unanswered and in spite of reassurances from the others that probably the Cardiff transmitter was faulty, he could not dismiss images of another Irish attack from his mind. Fears of a pillaged community and an abducted or ravished Gwen kept creeping into his mind, even though he knew that with their warning posts on the coast and the impregnable walls of the castle, this was almost impossible. They had left well over a hundred active men and women behind, to protect the older folks and children. There was a sufficient supply of small arms for defence until they returned, so he kept telling himself that some tired electronics was by far the most likely reason.

He was also concerned about the situation in Cambridge, for they had left a very nervous community back in the old university city. Strickland's community was bolstered somewhat by Brennan leaving them additional weapons and the armoured Land-Rover, but he was doubtful if they had the numbers or determination to fend off anything more than a skirmishing attack by Fischer's brigands. He had told Strickland to put stronger roadblocks on every road into Cambridge, even on the west side, in case they were covertly outflanked. All the remaining farmers in outlying areas were to be persuaded back into the city and more radio-carrying observers were to be sent out eastwards as an early-warning system.

'I think we're only buying a bit of time,' he grunted to Casey, who was driving their own vehicle back along the M4 near Reading. 'The place is so vulnerable, stuck out in the flatlands with no natural defences.'

'We've got to worry about ourselves in the long run – there's a hell of a sight more Germans, Czechs, Austrians and the likes, than there are of us. If they get the idea that Britain is some kind of paradise for them, eventually we'll be fighting them all the way back to Pembrokeshire!'

Conversation stopped while Casey threaded his way between two rusted trucks and a burnt-out coach which almost blocked the three lanes of the motorway on the westbound side. He was unable to get to the clear lanes on the opposite side, as the crash barriers were still intact along this stretch. There was a stiff wind blowing, which seemed to be increasing in force with every minute and the ragged trees which lined the road were swaying dangerously, branches and twigs falling on to the already littered road surface. Behind them came the rest of the vehicles, including the two coaches and the low-loader with the Saracen. They had some extra vans which Strickland had given them, loaded with electrical equipment and tools, in anticipation of their future move to Cardiff.

After a while, there was a voice from the back, where Liz Peterson and Fay Morgan were seated sideways over the wheel arches, their feet on ammunition boxes. Thankfully, their role as casualty nurses had not been needed.

'What about these two chaps you captured?' asked Liz. 'Do you think they can be trusted?'

'I'm sure the Dutchman can, he was overjoyed at being liberated.' Mervyn sounded in no doubt at all about it.

'Does that go for the German, though?' asked the older woman. 'If he's a doctor, then we're going to have to work with him, when he recovers. I don't want to feel uneasy about him.'

'We'll make damn sure he's OK first,' reassured Brennan. 'I can't see that he's going to turn out to be a saboteur or anything. He should be glad to have ended up in a decent place.'

The German had been quite unwell the previous day, as his burned face and hand had become swollen and Mervyn had been afraid that his numerous cuts might turn septic. He had filled him with antibiotic, which though long out of date, still seemed to work quite well and this morning he had seemed much better. He was travelling in one of the vans with the 'troops', having Jan Beelan to keep him company. Jan had questioned him at length the previous day and in spite of his groggy state, the man had been quite forthcoming and seemed more than willing to change sides and stay with the South Wales group. Intriguingly, he turned out to be a paediatric surgeon from a university hospital in Aachen, almost on the German-Dutch border. Though when in his shocked condition after being almost blown up, he seemed to have no English, a day later he could speak stumblingly, but well enough to hold a conversation. Both Brennan and especially Mervyn hoped that the damage to his hand was only temporary, as a surgeon would be an invaluable asset to their meagre medical team.

The slow journey went on, the weather worsening until a full gale was blowing. Near the Bath interchange, they had to stop to pull aside an electricity pylon that had been blown across the carriageway. Thankfully, it was not a particularly large one, which would have totally defeated them, but even the forty-foot tangle of rusted metal took the combined efforts of two trucks and a Land-Rover to drag it aside sufficiently to let them pass.

The Severn Bridge was swaying ominously when they reached it and Brennan stopped the cavalcade to allow only one vehicle at a time to cross, both to limit the weight and the possible loss of life if it should finally plunge into the estuary below. Thankfully it held and an hour and half later, they were driving past Cardiff's civic centre to the massive and almost impregnable castle that was now their home.

A nasty surprise awaited them as they drove across the drawbridge.

CHAPTER NINE

'WHAT the hell d'you mean, she's gone?' snarled Brennan.

Alfred Ashe, who had been left in charge while Brennan was away, stood his ground and glared back.

'Don't yell at me, Brennan! It's a free country, you said so yourself. If they wanted to go, I couldn't stop them. I argued with them, but that Mellars is a very persuasive fellow!'

'And a bloody liar into the bargain!' yelled the leader. 'For God's sake, Arthur, why didn't you warn me by radio what was going on?'

'Because he took the damned thing, that's why,' retorted Ashe, his pugnacious face red with anger. 'He said it would be more use down in Somerset, now that it was unlikely that you would be coming back.'

Brennan swung round on his heel to face his henchmen, standing equally appalled behind him on the gravel in front of the West Range of the castle buildings. The convoy was drawn up on the grass inside the walls and most of the troops were crowding forward to see what the fuss was about. The women and older people who had stayed behind when the combatants had left, were coming out of the castle buildings and their caravans to press around the central figures. Brennan, his face dark with anger, held up his hands for quiet.

'Those of you who stayed home already know this only too well – but for the benefit of those of us who have just returned, I have to tell you that Roger Mellars came here as soon as our backs were turned and made off with fifty of our people and some of our equipment . . . including Gwen Sutcliffe!'

There was a buzz of protest and shouts of 'shame' and 'the bastard!'

Those returned from Cambridge who had left partners and lovers behind, hurried across to the residents to see if they had also been deserted like their leader. Mervyn, his beard fairly bristling with indignation, stepped forward until his nose was almost touching that of Alfred Ashe.

'Alf, what the bloody hell has been going on? We haven't been away five days and we get back to a major catastrophe!'

With Casey, Lance, Beverley and Mervyn almost squeezing him against the wall, Ashe repeated the news that he had just given to Brennan. The gist of it was that the day after they left for Cambridge, Roger Mellars arrived with several trucks and two old passenger coaches. As he was hardly an enemy, he was admitted into the castle, where he promptly claimed to have heard from a motorcycle courier that he had sent to the Cambridge area, that Brennan's force had been routed. Mellars asserted that the city had fallen to the boat-people and he made an impassioned speech to the community to escape while the going was good and come down to Glastonbury, where they would be safe behind his promised wall of steel across the West Country peninsula.

There was a heated confrontation between him and Alfred Ashe, backed up by some of the younger men and women who were loyal to Brennan – but the majority of the activists had gone off to fight and most of the remainder were the older, more vulnerable people. What seemed to tip the balance was Gwen Sutcliffe's decision to throw in her lot with Roger – which Ashe thought was strongly influenced by Mellars's assertion that Brennan was either dead or a captive.

He had adroitly commandeered the short-wave radio, cutting off any opportunity to confirm with Cambridge what was happening. It seemed that Gwen had tried to get through to Strickland's control room, but the operators said that there was no response. In hindsight, it seemed that Mellars had threatened the radio men to provide that convenient excuse.

In the end, a few score of the community had gone away in the buses and trucks, taking some of the armaments and electrical equipment. They had even towed away a few of the better caravans, including the communications van which Gwen used for her domestic broadcasts.

'And that's it, Brennan,' ended Alfred bluntly. 'He had about thirty of his roughnecks with him, under that thug Wayne Addis. Some of our lads tried to oppose him, but they were locked in one of the castle chambers until they left – and the rest of us were more or less threatened with a roughing-up if we persisted in defying them. They loaded up and drove away – there was nothing we could do about it. If we were to believe him, you were either dead or not coming back here.'

Lance saw the look on Brennan's face and knew he was preoccupied with Gwen's defection. For once, his low-level jealousy of his boss concerning the beautiful Gwen was submerged both in sympathy for Brennan and by concern that she had done the dirty on them both by going off voluntarily with that shit from Somerset.

Even in the face of such unexpected adversity, Brennan's ingrained sense of order and leadership prevailed and grim-faced, he set about organising the emptying of their trucks and the dispersal of the tired warriors after their long journey. Delegating the many tasks to his 'senior officers', he strode around checking on everything, but his mind was working at top speed devising a plan for bringing down retribution on the treacherous barrister from the West Country.

Within a couple of hours of their return, they were being fed stew, bread, cold meat and boiled potatoes in the dining halls of the castle. As soon as they had finished, Brennan beckoned to all his lieutenants and they marched off with mugs of hot tea to the command hut in the keep, for a council of war.

'Now then, where do we go from here?' demanded Brennan bluntly, though he already had a general idea of what he was going to do, which included hanging, drawing and quartering Roger Mellars.

'It's better than the bloody Irish, which was what we feared when the radio went down,' said Mervyn placatingly. 'At least we know where our folks and the material have gone – and no one's been hurt or killed.'

'And we can go down to sort the bastard out and get them back!' snapped Lance viciously. He had visions, which he kept to himself, of Gwen in bed with the slimy lawyer of Glastonbury.

'How much stuff is missing, Ruddy?' asked Brennan.

The hairy engineer, who had not gone with them to Cambridge, was unusually subdued, the fiasco having temporarily dampened his cheerful nature. 'I wasn't here when they came, I've been camping over in Newport to get this engine working,' he admitted. 'Not that I could have stopped them, anyway. But I checked this morning and about twenty automatic rifles, some shotguns, a dozen pistols and an old Bren gun have gone from the armoury. He took the communications radios and some assorted electronic spares, but nothing vital.'

'We had nearly all our good armament with us, thank God,' said Beverley. 'So he didn't get any heavy stuff, like rocket launchers or heavy machine guns. And we've got quite a reserve stock of weapons in the warehouse in Western Avenue.'

'What about vehicles?'

'Nothing important – a couple of vans, one Land-Rover and a few of the caravans. We can replace all those in a day's scrounging up the valleys,' replied Luddy.

'We've brought a spare short-wave set and some more VHFs back from Cambridge,' added Lance.

Brennan held up a large hand. 'Right, those are important details, but we need to decide on the big picture. What are we going to do about Mellars?'

Lance ostentatiously looked at his wristwatch. 'Leave tonight – go down there and zap the treacherous bugger!'

Mervyn, keeping to his usual role of elderly sage, held up a restraining hand. 'Hang on, let's not do anything hasty. This needs careful thought. We're not up against murderous pirates like in East Anglia, so we can't go blasting our own people to get revenge. Calm down and wait.'

Lance and Brennan caught each other's glance and quickly looked away. Almost telepathically, they knew that the other was thinking of Gwen and Roger Mellars – and Lance did not want Brennan to know that he was thinking that.

These nuances were lost on Bruce Ludlow, who was oblivious of any sexual tensions in the community, being more in love with pistons and connecting-rods. 'Are we ready for another confrontation, so soon after Cambridge?' he asked. 'Surely we need to check on fuel supplies, the state of the vehicles and the weaponry.'

Mervyn swiftly backed him up. 'Certainly we can't go dashing off in the morning, like we did for Strickland. Mellars isn't going anywhere, after all.'

Brennan reluctantly grunted his agreement. 'Right, we need at least a day or two to get organised. I think we might need some extra transport. We ought to get hold of some more coaches – there's no point in bumping our troops around in trucks when they could sit in a decent seat.'

Beverley had got up from the table and taken a thin volume from a plank bracketed to the wall, which served as a book-shelf.

'We need to get some Ordnance maps of Somerset if we can find any, but for now this road atlas will have to do.' He riffled through the pages and laid it open on the table, where the others craned their necks to look at a double-page spread which included Somerset. 'Has anyone been down there in the last year or two?' he asked. There was general shaking of heads.

'Only the chap we sent to ask him to help us at Cambridge,' said Ashe. 'And that dull bugger was one of those who went back with him this week, so we can't ask him what he saw.'

'The problem is that we have no idea what his set-up is like down there,' growled Brennan. 'Has he fortified the place, are there road-blocks, what defences has he got, if any? We know nothing, so it'll be a blind operation without some previous intelligence.'

Brennan was covering all the disadvantages, before asking for suggestions as to how to get them solved.

'What about another motorcycle recce first?' suggested Beverley. 'I'm quite happy to slip over there and have a snoop. I can be there and back in less than a day.'

'Worth thinking of, though it might give our intentions away if you're spotted.'

Mervyn snorted derisively. 'He knows damned well we'll come for him. All that stuff about knowing we were wiped out in Cambridge was a pack of lies – he can't have had any idea of how we got on.'

'I can't see how Gwen and the others fell for that,' complained Lance. 'How could they believe that Roger knew what was going on almost two hundred miles away?'

'Perhaps she didn't need much persuading,' said Brennan bitterly.

There was an embarrassed silence as the others digested his unexpected suggestion. The less sensitive Ruddy jumped in with some wishful thinking.

'Pity we can't get a light plane in the air. If only we had some usable fuel, I'm sure Lance could get one of those Pipers from the Aero Club off the ground. He could be over Glastonbury in a few minutes.'

'Well, we haven't, so let's not fantasise,' growled Mervyn.

Ruddy was not totally crushed. 'The petrol we've got still works OK in motorcycles and the few non-diesel vehicles we've got. After I've got the locomotive sorted, I may go down to the airport and have a look.'

As they wearily left for a well earned sleep, Brennan walked across to the parked caravans with Mervyn. 'After we've sorted Mellars, we'll have to get on with preparations for Strickland's immigration here – then start thinking about the big battle with the Germans. Sooner or later, they'll have to be crushed in a big way. Once they take Cambridge, they'll start spreading further west, with their beady eyes on the Midlands and then us.'

The old doctor sighed. 'We don't need this, Brennan! We should be ploughing more fields, raising more cattle and getting on with educating all the younger ones. Why the hell do we have be diverted by war all the time? I'm beginning to think old Canon Gilbey is right – the human race is doomed to fight itself into oblivion.'

Brennan put an arm around the physician's shoulders. 'I know, old friend. But we just have to keep plugging on, dealing with every crisis as it comes. Maybe we'll get through it eventually – it's either that or give up the ghost right now.'

Mervyn grunted and plodded off towards his own van, leaving Brennan to climb into his Avondale and his now lonely bed. As he opened the door, he felt someone materialise behind him. His nerves already stretched, he swung round defensively but relaxed when, in the dim light from the distant gate lamps, he saw that it was Liz Peterson.

'Brennan, I just wanted to say I'm sorry about Gwen,' she murmured, coming close and putting a hand on his arm.

'Thanks, Liz. But it's not only her, it's all the others that concern me. They were conned by that swine.'

'I think she was, too. Someone said that she was crying when Roger Mellars told us that your expedition had been badly hammered by the boat-people. I think he probably suggested to her that you were dead.'

She made no move to leave as he stood with his hand on the door-handle and Brennan knew she was waiting for an invitation to come inside with him. For a moment, he was tempted, but then he decided it was too soon to burn his bridges with Gwen.

'We'll see what the next few days bring, Liz,' he said gently, moving his arm so that her hand fell away. 'Thanks all the same. I'll see you in the morning, there's a hell of a lot to be done.'

She stood for a moment looking up at him, then quickly kissed him on the lips and hurried away into the gloom.

CHAPTER TEN

BRENNAN woke at six next morning and went for breakfast with a steely resolve not to dwell on Gwen's defection, but to fill every moment of the day with mind-numbing activity. There was certainly plenty to do, and all those remaining in the castle were similarly single-minded about teaching Roger Mellars the price he must pay for his deception and piracy.

Beverley, dressed in a long black raincoat and carrying a machine pistol across his back, was the first to leave on his Norton to reconnoitre the Somerset enclave. He took one of the VHF handsets, in the hope that its range would extend across the Bristol Channel, which was in line of sight with their lookouts on the Glamorgan coast. Given the comparative ease with which a motorcycle could weave around obstacles in the road, he reckoned on being near Glastonbury within two or three hours. A full tank of petrol would easily get him there and back, so hopefully he would be home later in the day.

Brennan saw him off with some misgivings, as he had done a few days before in Cambridge when he had led the sortie down the Haverhill road. The suave former Civil Servant always seemed to volunteer for the most dangerous jobs but, like Lance, he did it with such an air of unconcern that most people failed to recognise the risk he was taking.

Back inside the castle arena, Brennan walked over to the mound and climbed the steep steps to the keep. Here he found Alfred Ashe and Jan Beelan huddled over the radio equipment that they had brought back from Cambridge. The Dutchman was sitting in front of the transmitter, a complicated-looking Japanese Yaesu, connecting up the aerial input. Alongside it was a large communications receiver, an ICOM R9000. Brennan was wondering where Strickland's men had found such sophisticated gear, when Alf spoke to him.

'Jan's got it working alright, he seems to know his way around these things.'

The Dutchman swung around on his stool to face Brennan and looked up with a wry smile. 'Until I got married and couldn't afford it, I was a radio 'ham', as you call it. Do you want to talk to Cambridge at eight o'clock?'

'Sure, but can Mellars listen in to what we're saying to them?'

'I am afraid so, now that he's got your other equipment – if anyone there knows how to use it.'

'What about the VHF transmissions, are we monitoring them as well?'

Beelan pointed to one of the smaller sets on the table. 'Both the coast stations and your colleague Beverley are on the same frequency, so we'll get anything they send us.'

Brennan left them to it, impressed by the Dutchman's quick grasp of the problems and his obvious expertise with electronics. It was fortunate that the only two survivors of the rout turned out to be an electrical engineer and a surgeon, when they could equally well have been a fish-fryer and a nightclub croupier.

Down in the castle grounds, all the vehicles were being filled up with fuel from the tanker, which Bruce Ludlow was waiting to take down to a fuel depot in the docks to refill it with diesel and to look out for some more usable petrol.

'That joke about the aircraft last night gave me an idea' he said, beaming irrepressibly. 'The only petrol that remains OK after a few years is that in full, sealed containers. Maybe one or more of the aviation tanks at the airport is full – that would see us through for a long time, just using motorcycles and a few small petrol generators.'

'And help your aircraft idea, I suppose,' grunted Brennan. 'Why don't you try for a Boeing 747, there's sure to be one in the British Airways body shop down there.'

'I'll keep that in mind, boss! But first, I want to get my railway working. Then you could take a couple of Chieftain tanks up east if you wanted!'

Luddy said this as a joke, but Brennan filed the idea away in his mind for future consideration. His next stop was the infirmary, a large room on the first floor of the Marquis of Bute's opulent Victorian residence, built into the West Wall of the castle. Here he found Tan Chen Swee and Liz Peterson in a little anteroom they used as an office-cum-treatment room, adjacent to the small ward where Fay Morgan was chatting to one of the three occupants. Tan and Liz were drinking tea and offered him a mug while he asked after the patients.

'The girl with the war-wound has been up, to have her dressing changed,' said Tan. 'No problem there, the tree splinter came out cleanly in one piece.'

'What about our German chap?'

Liz looked at him over the rim of her cup, her big brown eyes making him think uneasily of last night's kiss. 'He's fine, the swelling on his face is going down nicely.'

'And his hand is going to be OK,' added Tan. 'Thank God for that, him being a surgeon.' His Singapore English was sing-song, but as perfect as the Dutchman's.

'Any idea of his sympathies? Is he for us or against us?'

Tan's smooth face creased into a smile. 'He's very grateful. I think he expected to have been shot when you found him on the road. When I said that we wanted him to get well quickly so that he can teach us some surgery, he almost burst into tears with gratitude.'

Brennan swallowed his tea and made for the door, all too conscious of Liz's eyes continually seeking his. She had always made it clear that she was attracted to him, but since Gwen had disappeared, her inclinations were becoming all too obvious. He found her very attractive, in a way that was totally different to Gwen's 'in your face' glamour. The nurse was petite, dark and quiet, but she had a way of looking from under half-lowered eyelids that promised hidden talents. Her hair was a black helmet with a straight fringe across her forehead, like Cleopatra. Brennan knew little about her background, except that she was almost thirty, had never been married and had been a Staff Nurse in the Royal Gwent Hospital in Newport.

Trying to put her from his mind for the time being, he went back to the main gate and crossed to a doorway in the high curtain wall that stretched all around the castle in a huge square. Inside, there was a long passage in the thickness of the wall, supported by concrete buttresses put there when the castle was renovated in the nineteenth century. The outer wall of the passage was Roman masonry, over sixteen feet high, still as good as the time when it was built seventeen hundred years before – as a protection against Irish raiders!

The spacious passage was used as their armoury, with a metal grille and a heavy door closing it off from the castle arena. Lance was inside, with Phil Robson and Bill Fleming, checking all the arms that had been returned the previous evening.

'I'll get a squad of chaps cleaning and oiling this morning,' said Fleming, slipping easily back into his soldier mode.

'I sincerely hope we don't have to hammer Mellars like we did the Germans,' said Brennan. 'But we certainly have to give him a show of strength when we go down there. You can't negotiate from a position of weakness.'

'When are we likely to move on him, chief?' asked Phil Robson.

'Depends on what we learn today, both from Bev when he gets back – and from any radio contact, if we ever get one.' He fingered the tube of a rocket launcher appreciatively. 'These did the trick in Caerleon and Cambridge – we must try to find some more as soon as we can. When we've sorted Jolly Roger, we must do a trawl of all the military bases we can find and collect everything that might be of use. We've plenty of storage space now.'

Lance went over to where a brace of mortars stood on their tripods. 'And these are worth their weight in gold – though gold's bloody useless these days!'

Bill Fleming looked worried as he surveyed their armaments. 'I hear the guy who's running the Germans is a former *Bundeswehr* major. He won't take kindly to what we did to his force this week. I'm afraid that he'll take a leaf out of our book and go searching for even heavier weaponry for a return match.'

Brennan picked up a Caliburn and pulled the slide back to check the action. 'Exactly what I said earlier, Bill! There must have been a hell of a lot of stuff left over in Eastern Command, even more than we had this side of the country. And we can't stop them getting their hands on it.'

Lance joined the chorus of pessimism. 'And they've got the same chances of getting military vehicles as us, if they put their minds to it. The Jerries are by nature pretty efficient. I don't think they'll be using a horse and cart next time.'

'The one thing they haven't got is radio' said Robson. 'Unless they overrun Cambridge and collar some VHF sets and batteries.'

'We must make sure they don't. I'll be urging Strickland to get out of there as soon as she can and bring all of their technology with them. In fact, I'd like to start shifting some of it now – that's partly why I asked her for more radio sets to bring back with us.'

The soldierly mind of former Warrant-Officer Fleming was mulling over what had been said. 'I'm sure the Jerries will nick whatever stuff's in Eastern Command, so let's hope they don't push over south of London to Aldershot and Hampshire. That area must be even thicker with military material . . . they could even pick up tanks there!' He was only half-serious, but Brennan's mind leapt ahead at the suggestion.

'You're right again, Bill. I think we should go over there ourselves very soon and take what we need, then destroy anything useful that's left. In the long run, I doubt we'll be able to stop them overrunning the Home Counties, so let's not leave them anything nasty to hammer us with.'

Cursing Roger Mellars for interrupting what might well turn out to be a campaign for their very survival, Brennan stalked away to the next focus of activity, which was Ruddy Luddy briefing a search party on what they needed in the way of fresh vehicles. While he went off to loot diesel, two teams of men and women were going up the Taff valley to find more vans and small trucks in working order. They took some precious spare batteries with them to get suitable vehicles started, together with jacks and tools to cannibalise other wrecks for wheels.

By the time he had been around everyone, giving some consoling words to those who had lost friends to Glastonbury and encouragement to others who were working hard to get everything ready for their imminent foray to Somerset, it was time for him to go back to the keep.

He found Alfred Ashe and Jan Beelan still hunched over the Yaesu.

'Beverley called in just now to say that he was on the M5 just past Brent Knoll,' announced Alf. 'He's going on one of the minor roads towards Glastonbury, in case there are roadblocks on the main roads.'

'He can't get too close on a motorbike, they could hear him coming miles away on that flat land,' mused Brennan. 'But knowing Beverley, he'll have some plan up his sleeve.'

'It's almost eight o'clock,' said Alf. 'Time for Cambridge.'

As they waited, Brennan wondered what the real time was. After five years, with no broadcast time-checks and the batteries of electronic watches and clocks exhausted, timekeeping was somewhat arbitrary. They weren't even sure of the date, to within a few days.When they went to Cambridge, for convenience they synchronised their wind-up watches with Strickland's time, which was alleged to be approximately correct by some means which he had not enquired about.

Now as the red figures on the radio's digital clock flicked to 0800, a voice called them up from the other side of the country. When they had acknowledged, the operator said that Strickland wanted to speak to them. Conscious that Roger Mellars or one of his minions might be listening, he was cautious about what he said.

'We have a major problem over here, but you needn't concern yourself over it. How are things your end?'

As they were using duplex working on separate frequencies for receiver and transmitter, there was none of the 'Over' routine needed as with the VHF sets and Mavis Strickland responded as if they were on the telephone.

'Nothing new, thank heaven! Our watchers have pushed almost to the coast and have seen the hostiles withdrawing right back to their camps there.'

Brennan's reply was pessimistic. 'I suspect it's the calm before the storm – they'll be smarting from their defeat and keen for revenge. We think here that they'll be foraging for better arms and transport after seeing how we behaved, so try to get your spies to see what they're up to.'

Strickland's worried voice betrayed her anxiety about the future. 'We had a meeting of the whole community last night.' Brennan was glad to hear the commissar use this phrase, rather than 'Comintern' or 'Soviet', as it suggested a change of attitude in the face of danger. 'There was a clear vote to ratify the agreement to join you in Cardiff, especially from the women and the few families we have. They're fearful for the safety of the kids here.'

'The sooner the better, you can send them as soon as you like. What about bussing down the women and children straight away – and as much of the technical stuff as you can spare. It would be a disaster if the Germans got their hands on radios and batteries.'

'Right, but we're short of long-distance transport. Can you provide any?'

Brennan was in a quandary at this. If Mellars was listening, he didn't want to let on that they needed their transport to mount an imminent invasion of the West Country. He decided to fudge the issue.

'We've got problems in that area ourselves, after coming up to you. It'll be at least a few days before we can get any decent vehicles on the road again.'

They spoke for a few moments more about the dismantling of equipment in Cambridge and the need to keep a close eye on the enemy's movements, especially if they moved on Colchester and other places with military depots. As they prepared to sign off, Brennan tried to get a covert warning to Strickland.

'We'll talk again tomorrow, but we need to keep off the air as much as possible. The bloody Irish have been sighted off the coast again,' he lied. Brennan wanted to end this before anything revealing was said. 'I'll explain when we see you, I'm signing off now. Keep an eye on those Jerries.'

He put the microphone down in front of Jan Beelan, who more formally ended the connection with the Cambridge operator.

'Bloody difficult to avoid saying anything, when you know that the creep from Glastonbury may be listening,' he growled. He made for the door, giving one last instruction as he went.

'I'm going out with a few of the lads around the farms to see if we can pick up a couple more four-wheel drives. I'll take one of the VHFs, so let me know if anything significant comes through.'

He clattered down the steps from the keep, feeling at twenty past eight in the morning as if he had already done a full day's work.

The Vale of Glamorgan, a fertile coastal plain that stretched some twenty miles west of Cardiff, was a jungle. Once a lush farming area, dotted with fashionable commuter homes for the city's upper middle class, it was now an overgrown wilderness of tangled weeds and spreading scrubland. The narrow roads that meandered between the pleasant villages were choked with encroaching vegetation and the ubiquitous Japanese knotweed was sprouting everywhere after its winter hibernation. The countryside was a paradise for foxes, badgers, packs of wild dogs and prowling feral cats, who all seemed to have arrived at a balance of coexistence where each lived off the others and the profusion of smaller animals that infested the wild fields and woodland.

Though some of the smaller lanes were already totally impassable, Brennan's old ex-army vehicle pushed its way through the medium-sized roads, in spite of the horsetails and other tough weeds that were forcing their way up through the cracked tarmac. This time he was driving himself, at the wheel of a 1970s 101 Forward Control Land-Rover – a big, ugly, angular beast designed as an artillery tractor. With its 3.5 litre engine, it guzzled their precious petrol, but for vehicle recovery, it was ideal. Still in camouflage green and black, they had recovered it from some enthusiast's garage in Bridgend and now Brennan was sitting high above the front wheels, listening to the throaty rumble of the V8 as he urged the old warrior towards a large farm at top of this lane. He knew from an Ordnance map that they were near a village called Flemingston, about twelve miles from Cardiff. Only a mile or so away was the huge RAF airfield of Saint Athan – which reminded him again of Ruddy's ludicrous idea of getting an aircraft into the sky.

It was early afternoon and so far they had found one Nissan Patrol and a Toyota Land-Cruiser. They had towed these to the main A48 trunk road, which was relatively clear of obstructions, to be recovered by their breakdown truck and taken back to the castle. Brennan had called up on his VHF for this to be done, hoping incidentally that if Mellars could hear him as well, it would reinforce the belief that they were short of usable vehicles. From the Vale, Somerset was clearly visible across the Bristol Channel, a mere fifteen miles between the coasts. Cardiff reported on a different pre-arranged frequency that Beverley had called in to say cautiously that he was on his way home and would report when he arrived, rather than over the air.

Now they were approaching this new farm, poised just above a shallow valley.

'Let's hope there's something useful here, then we can go home,' said Casey, sitting beside him. He had his favoured shotgun strapped to the Dexion radio rack behind their heads, though here on home territory, he had little expectation of trouble. In the back of the Land-Rover, having a rough time due to the primitive suspension, were two younger men, complete with their tools and air compressor.

The Forward Control ground its way up the narrow lane, crushing the weeds under its massive sand-tyres. No other vehicle could have passed this way in years and when they rumbled past a rusted gate into a large farmyard, the quarter-acre of nettles and docks gave the same message of desertion. On two sides, there were large 'Atcost' barns of cement block and wooden palings, under corrugated roofs. Between them the track passed into another yard, where the roof and chimneys of a substantial farm-house could be glimpsed. One end of the barn in front was an open implement shed, half-obscured by vegetation, but the high cab of a large red tractor could be seen at one end.

'That any use to us?' asked Casey.

'Maybe in the future, but we can always come back for it, now we know this place is intact.' Even in the countryside, many of the farms had burnt down due to candles and oil-lamps, overturned by collapsing victims after the electricity had failed. Brennan gunned the truck across the wilderness of the farmyard to get nearer the big shed, where a baler and a flail-cutter were rusting alongside a large reversible plough and various other agricultural implements.

'If things were only more peaceful, we could get places like this back into production,' said Brennan longingly. If only they could settle this nonsense with Roger Mellars and keep the Germans at a long arm's reach, so much could be done to haul themselves back to some semblance of civilisation, especially if the extra people and technology from Cambridge could be added to their community.

Selwyn, one of the lads with them, pointed over Casey's shoulder at a pair of high wooden doors next to the Massey Ferguson tractor.

'What d'you think that is? Could be a garage.'

Brennan stopped outside the doors and switched off the burbling engine. He climbed cautiously down from the high cab, his foot feeling for the ring on the front wheel. By the time he got around the front of the 101, Casey was already rattling the padlock on the doors.

'Locked, so there must be something worthwhile in there.'

Selwyn had jumped down from the back and advanced with a brick that he picked from the ground. With a few heavy blows, the hasp tore out of the softened wood and Selwyn and Casey heaved against one of the doors, which was jammed against debris and weeds outside. With a crack, one of the rusted hinges went and the door lolled half-open.

'Look at this, just the job!' called Selwyn, the first to get his head inside. The others looked and saw an immaculate Range Rover 2.5 DSE, a top of the range diesel four-wheel drive.

'Looks like new, just a bit of dust on the cellulose!' enthused Edgar, the other young man.

They pushed both doors wide open and saw that indeed, the red Range Rover was one of the best-preserved vehicles they'd seen.

'Must have been in this box ever since the . . . the troubles.'

Even now, many people had difficulty in putting a name to the catastrophe which had brought their normal lives crashing to the ground. Brennan looked at the sound wooden planking which formed the walls and roof of the garage.

'No wonder they built a decent nest for it – one of these would have cost well over forty grand new.' He had looked at the Y-registration plate, which told him that it had been bought right at the start of this terrible century.

'The tyres are a bit soft, but they're otherwise OK,' said Casey. 'So, let's get the compressor in here – and a spare battery. She may even start, to save us towing her home.'

Edgar was the 'hot-wiring'expert and with Selwyn, they put a new battery in place.

'The fuel gauge shows almost empty, but there should be enough to see if she'll start,' announced Selwyn.

While Casey and Brennan dropped the Forward Control's tailboard and manhandled the petrol-engined compressor into the garage, the two lads cranked the Range Rover's engine over on the new battery. Nothing happened for a time, then there was a splutter and then a roar. The diesel came to life for the first time in five years, to the accompaniment of cheers from the two young men. As it dropped back to a tick-over and Selwyn squeezed the clutch and brake pedal to test the feel of the hydraulics, there was a lesser clatter as Brennan pulled the lanyard of the compressor engine and began inflating the tyres, which were down to half their normal pressure.

He was on the last one, when there was a dramatic interruption.

CHAPTER ELEVEN

THERE was a shattering explosion from just outside, ear-splitting even above the noise of the compressor and the Range Rover's engine. As the four men inside gaped in surprise, there was a brief pattering overhead, as lead shot rained down on the corrugated roof. The two younger men ran behind the vehicle whilst Brennan and Casey flattened themselves against the walls behind the half-opened doors.

'Jesus, I left my gun in the cab,' hissed Casey. Before his companion could reply, there was a quavering cry from outside.

'Come out, you bastards! What are doing in there?'

Cautiously, with his hands held up, Brennan advanced to the doors and peered out. A wild-looking apparition stood in the yard, holding a double-barrelled shotgun. He had fired once into the air, but now the muzzle was pointing rather shakily at Brennan's stomach.

'Take it easy, sir! We thought the place was deserted, like everywhere else.'

The man with the gun stared at him, with a look of incomprehension on what could be seen of his face, which was covered with a straggling iron-grey beard that looked as if it had been trimmed with a garden shears. He had a shock of hair pulled to the back of his neck and tied with a length of orange binder twine, another length of which secured a dirty fawn raincoat around his waist. A pair of mud-caked wellington boots completed the ensemble.

Brennan had been in many tight spots in his life, but now he wondered, almost dispassionately, if that life would end so abruptly and unexpectedly in a farmyard from a shotgun blast.

But what did happen was almost as unexpected. The man, after a few seconds' silent scrutiny of the intruder, suddenly dropped his gun and fell to his knees in the weeds. With his forehead almost touching the muddy soil, he began weeping uncontrollably.

Amazed and embarrassed, Brennan hurried to him and crouched alongside, putting a consoling arm around his thin shoulders, which were racked with sobs. Casey came cautiously out of the garage and prudently picked up the fallen shotgun and removed the one intact cartridge, before coming to bend over the pair. The weeping soon ended in a series of sniffs and the man raised his head to wipe his nose and eyes with a very dirty hand – his face was not much cleaner. He looked up at Brennan with red-rimmed eyes.

'I haven't been called 'sir' for over five years – in fact I haven't been called anything!' He struggled to get up, with Brennan and Casey helping him to his feet. 'You're the first people I've seen for more than five winters. I thought I was the only one left in the world.'

'There's quite a few left, several hundred of us in Cardiff,' replied Casey. The man stared at him as if Cardiff was a place on Mars.

'This is your farm?' asked Brennan. The man gave a last sniff and spat upon the ground.

'It is indeed – and I haven't set foot outside it for what must be four winters.'

Brennan wondered why he calculated in winters, rather than years or even summers, but assumed it was a cardinal point in a farmer's calendar.

'I'm sorry we were messing with your Range Rover, but we thought it was abandoned. It's a long story, I'm afraid.'

The man stared at the four strangers almost fearfully and for a moment, they thought he was going to break down again.

'It's been a shock, hearing voices again and seeing something on two legs. All I've had to talk to was the likes of him.' He jerked a finger at the corner of the barn, where a young border collie was peering fearfully through the nettles at the first humans he had ever seen, other than his master.

'We'd better have a talk, I think. My name's Brennan, by the way.' He introduced the others and the farmer, who seemed to be in his fifties, said that he was Godfrey Traherne. It seemed something of an effort for him to recall his name, after five years' disuse.

'Come around to the house. This takes some getting used to.'

Casey was on the point of suggesting that a strong cup of tea would do his nerves good, until he realised that Traherne had probably not tasted it for at least four years. Selwyn switched off the two engines and the two lads followed them around the barn into a smaller yard in front of a large farmhouse. Part of the roof had been stripped off in a gale and some of the window glass had been blown in. As they crossed a patch of churned mud to a side door, Brennan saw that beyond a gate on the other side of the yard, was a field with rows of vegetables and some roughly ploughed land, as yet unplanted. Traherne caught his glance and expained. 'That's what keeps me alive – spuds, cabbage and the like. And a few fowls, ducks and a couple of pigs, which I have to keep breeding on.'

'How do you manage to plough, Mr Traherne,' asked Selwyn, who came from a farming family in Powys.

'Couple of Shire horses, that I saved early on from a neighbour, who used to show them. I ran out of diesel for the tractor in the first few months.'

He led the way into the farm kitchen, which was in an indescribable state of squalor, with dirty cobwebs, unwashed dishes and dust-covered surfaces signalling utter apathy and neglect. The only items seemingly in use were one chair at a large table and a Raeburn solid-fuel cooker, on which were a couple of blackened saucepans.

Godfrey Traherne pulled out a few more chairs from the table and absently brushed off years of dust with his hand.

'Sit down, I can't give you anything to drink other than water. Not even milk these days. There's plenty of cows running wild, but it's almost impossible to catch one that's in milk.'

Brennan whispered to Edgar to run out to their Land-Rover and fetch a bottle and a few moments later, Traherne almost had another emotional crisis when he was presented with his first beer in half a decade. When they were sitting around the table, the farmer waved a hand apologetically around the room.

'I know it's a hell of a mess, but I've not had the heart to do anything about it. I thought I was just going to survive alone until I died. I thought more than once of using the twelve-bore on myself, to hurry it up.'

There was a silence as each man thought his private thoughts.

'I just use one of the beds and eat in here. The rest of the time, I'm grubbing enough food from half an acre and seeing to the remaining animals.'

Gradually, as his tongue loosened up after such long disuse, his story came out. He had been a fairly successful farmer in the difficult years for agriculture, working about a hundred and fifty acres of good land. Godfrey had a wife and three children, the eldest son helping him, together with a hired farmhand. When the pestilence had arrived, first his wife and daughter had died, then later both his sons.

'I nearly went mad then . . . I had the muzzle of my gun actually in my mouth at one stage. It was his mother that saved me – for good or ill, I don't know.' He pointed to the collie who lay quietly by the cooker.

'I was so fond of the bitch, that I couldn't bear to think of her left alone. Daft, isn't it?'

Traherne went on to relate how he had buried his family, taking them on the tractor to Flemingston churchyard, where he dug their graves himself – a story which brought back poignant memories to Brennan, who had done the same in his garden near Brecon. Left alone, Traherne had almost gone mad, but kept himself alive by eking out what was left of his tinned food and by growing vegetables.

'What about your neighbours?' asked Casey.

'In the first few weeks, when people were dying like flies, we tried to help each other, but it became chaotic. The water and electricity failed, the phones, radio and television went – we tried to stick together in the village and managed to find a bit of food from the local shops in Llantwit Major and Cowbridge, but as more and more died, everything went to hell. The shopkeepers were dead, there was nothing much left in the shops anyway. Then there was looting and violence. So I decided to stay home and sit tight, until some help came from outside.'

His listeners nodded sadly, the story was so familiar to them. They had all expected some magical rescue party, the cavalry galloping over the hill with tinned food and medicines. But no one ever came!

'Then my eldest boy died – I took him away on the tractor too and came home and waited for the plague to finish me off as well. I lay on my bed and prayed for death, but nothing happened!' He shook his head as if shaking off an angry wasp. 'I don't need to tell you this, you must have suffered the same way. But why were we spared?'

Brennan explained the doctor's suspicion that some cross-immunity with poliomyelitis might be answer, but Traherne shrugged it off.

'I never had a day's illness in my life, let alone polio. I think it's God's will, somehow, though why he took my poor Glenda, who was ten times a better person than me, I'll never understand.'

Brennan hoped that he was not going to launch into a tirade about God's wrath, like Canon Gilbey back in Cardiff, but the farmer subsided and carried on with his story.

'After Owen died, I just gave up. For weeks, I didn't go out, almost died because I didn't want to eat. Eventually, I roused myself, took the Range Rover and went round all my neighbours and even further afield. Not a soul was still alive. A few of the houses had burnt down and I think some must have left home, for their cars were missing.' He passed a hand over his eyes again, which had become moist once more. 'I came home and stayed here for many more weeks. That was when those terrible storms began, I thought I was going to lose the whole roof. When I did go out again, it was on foot, as I wanted to keep what diesel I had left for ploughing. I walked to Llantwit and even to Cowbridge, but there wasn't a soul about anywhere. Half the place had burnt down and there was awful storm damage as well.'

Brennan explained that by then, their embryo community had made a trawl of the towns and gathered up any survivors to take to their refuge in the Tesco warehouse near the Severn Bridge.

'There was no way we could get around all the thousands of farms and isolated houses, so there may well be other people still living alone like you.'

'We've found quite a few over the years,' explained Casey. 'Some wanted to stay put and keep farming, but then this Irish problem began and it wasn't safe to leave people out there on their own.'

Now it was Brennan's turn to explain what had been happening in the wider world of southern Britain, from the time of the pestilence up to the recent campaign against the Germans. Traherne was an intelligent man and the civilising effect of meeting human beings again – and a bottle of home-brew – rapidly restored his mental and emotional equilibrium. Brennan did not touch on the current problem of Mellars, as he felt this was irrelevant to Godfrey's situation, but probed what the farmer might wish to do next.

'This has been one hell of a shock, I need some time to get my mind around it. But I don't want to come into Cardiff, that's for sure. I've got this land under cultivation and some animals that I'm responsible for.' He looked around the utter desolation of his kitchen. 'Maybe I'll do something about this, now that I know that I'm not the last person left on earth!'

'We can leave you some diesel, we've got a couple of spare five-gallon cans in the truck. That would get your tractor going, if you use the battery we put in the Range Rover,' said Casey.

'I'll send someone down with the tanker when we get a chance, to fill up the diesel storage tank I saw in the yard,' promised Brennan. 'Then you can come up to Cardiff in your posh Range Rover and see our set-up. We've got other farmers who go out to their land each day. We had to do that after the bloody Irish started picking off people who were out on their own, but we've got that sorted now.'

As they left, Traherne offered them the Range Rover, but Brennan decided that the farmer needed it more than the community. They left on amicable terms, Godfrey Traherne having received a new lease of life and promising to get much more of his farm back into production, supplying Cardiff with produce in return for diesel – and some more bottled beer!

On the way back, they discussed this remarkable afternoon, putting aside any fears of yet another battle to come in Somerset.

'Do you think there are more like him scattered around the countryside?' asked Selwyn.

'Bound to be, statistically,' mused Casey. 'After all this damned trouble with Mellars and the Jerries has been settled, we had better make a thorough tour of the country areas to see if there are any more stragglers.'

'Or get Luddy's aeroplane to drop leaflets!' suggested Edgar, facetiously.

On the way back, they made a detour into the nearby airfield at Saint Athan, which had been one of the RAF's major maintenance establishments. There were no aircraft on the aprons and a few quick forays into the hangars showed that no serviceable planes were left.

'I think they used everything that would fly to ferry out the Royals, the government and senior civil servants,' commented Brennan, rather sourly. 'I know the surviving top brass from the Armed Forces flew out of RAF Lynham towards the end and I suspect they took everything they could from here as well.'

'But they didn't take those!' said Selwyn exultantly, as they rounded a hangar and came into a parking area where a dozen vehicles stood intact in their grey RAF paint. 'Land-Rovers, a mobile crane, a JCB and four three-tonners.'

'Nothing we can do about them today, we've got no diesel and we gave our last good battery to Robinson Crusoe!' muttered Casey.

'Not to worry, we know they're here and no one else but us is going to steal them,' replied Brennan philosophically. 'This is another place to send Ruddy Luddy – he'll have an orgasm at the sight of that mobile crane and another JCB. Maybe he can find some full tanks of aviation fuel, too.'

He turned the Forward Control for home and an hour later, they rumbled over the drawbridge into the castle.

CHAPTER TWELVE

To Brennan's great relief when they returned, Beverley was back safely from his expedition. As they sat over the evening meal in the crowded dining hall, he reported what he had seen, in typically relaxed tones as if he had been out bird-watching.

'Not a lot, actually. I couldn't get too near Glastonbury because they've closed off a lot of the roads.'

'You mean with checkpoints?' asked Mervyn, his whiskered chin wagging as he chewed on some less-than-tender mutton in the stew.

'No, most of them are roadblocks, pure and simple. A great heap of rubble dumped right across the road, impassable to anything but a tank.' He sipped appreciatively from a glass of the new batch of mead. 'There are only a few manned guard-posts, on the major roads in to the town from Wells, Street and Shepton Mallet. There are barbed wire fences across the fields ringing the town, with the Tor sticking up in the centre.' This was the famous conical hill that rose four hundred feet behind the town. It had a medieval church tower on the top, which could be seen for many miles across the flat fenland of the Somerset Levels.

'How did you manage to get even that near, Bev,' asked Casey, pulling his big nose out of a tankard. 'That bike of yours makes quite a racket.'

The smooth-faced emissary smiled. 'Pedal-power, that's how. I hid the motor behind a wall about five miles out, somewhere around Westhay, where I'd seen a bicycle outside a shop. The tyres were flat, but it had a pump and they stayed up long enough for what I wanted.'

'That was still risking it, a moving object in broad daylight,' objected Mervyn.

Beverley shook his head. 'There were other people about. I saw some working in the fields – those that weren't flooded – and some on the roads, though I kept well away from them. They haven't pulled right back into the town, like us, because they've not suffered these attacks from the bloody Irish, I suppose.'

Brennan was puzzled by Mellars's tactics. 'I don't understand why he's got roadblocks so close to Glastonbury, if he claims he runs most of the south-west. What about this "Wall of Steel" that he boasts about, a defence from the Bristol Channel to the English Channel?'

'A load of nonsense, as far as I could see,' answered Beverley. 'There was no challenge anywhere on the motorway as far as I went – and none until Glastonbury was well within sight. I think he has a small enclave there and that's all.'

'He always was full of crap,' growled Casey. 'He's trying to enlarge his little empire by conning other folk into joining him – or by kidnapping them, which was what he really did here.'

Brennan was silent, thinking of Gwen and privately tormenting himself by wondering to what extent she had gone off of her own free will.

'So what are we going to do about it, Brigadier?' snapped Mervyn. He used Brennan's former rank only when he wanted to snap the big man out of one his frequent reveries.

'You'll have to make a frontal move on the town,' said Beverley. 'I couldn't see any way of sneaking in round the back. And this time, we're the attackers, so there's no chance of an ambush situation like Newmarket.'

'What about going in at night?' suggested Lance.

'Look, this isn't going to be a blitzkrieg,' growled Brennan. 'The more I think about it, the less I want to start a shooting match.'

'But the bugger can't be allowed to get away with it,' said Mervyn.

'Like Richard the Lionheart at the Siege of Acre, we're going to blockade his town until he sees some sense.'

'Richard ended up massacring everyone, which included beheading all his prisoners!' commented Bev drily.

'That's not on the agenda!' replied Brennan. 'But confrontation with an overwhelming force seems the safest way. We'll take everything we've got down there and sit outside his checkpoints until he lets us in.'

After the meal was finished, Brennan called a general meeting of all the community and once again, the cleared dining hall was filled, though the loss of half a hundred to Somerset gave them a little more space. Their 'general manager' stood in one of the window bays, his six feet two inches giving him a commanding height over the people seated on chairs and benches.

'These are difficult days, folks. We have so much to do and these repeated crises are interrupting our work,' he began. 'But they must be settled – and as quickly as possible.'

Though most had heard various versions of what had taken place in Cambridge from those who were there, he gave an unvarnished account of the ambushes and the likely threat that was to come, once the invaders had time to regroup and get better equipped.

'The Cambridge community have accepted that they cannot stay where they are, as the place is indefensible and they are badly equipped, both materially and psychologically, to resist a determined attack.'

There was a buzz of interest at this, as it was not common knowledge that Strickland had agreed to decamp.

'They have about three hundred people and we can't accommodate that number inside this place. Anyway, I don't know yet whether they want to integrate completely with us or set up a separate community.'

A voice from his left broke in, Alfred Ashe wanting his usual say in things. 'Surely we can find a big building somewhere in or near the city for them? Now that we are bound to get a few hours' warning of any more Irish attacks, they could quickly be brought inside here if there was an emergency.'

Brennan agreed and promised to discuss it with Strickland at tomorrow's radio contact. 'They'll need some sort of factory facilities for their technology, so maybe we can find something in one of the surviving industrial estates for them. It'll be a marvellous boost for us – we're providing food, shelter and defence for them, in return for their expertise in all sorts of useful things – and think what a contribution they can make to our educational projects!'

'They've got more kids than us, too' added Mervyn. 'That can only be good for both sides, to have a bigger pool of young people – in a few years, a bigger genetic pool too!'

There was more chattering and whispering at this and Brennan held up his hand for quiet.

'That's the good news – but as you know only too well, there's bad news, too. We have to have a confrontation with Roger Mellars and settle this dispute once and for all. With the extra folk coming from Cambridge, he must be made to see that his nonsense about pulling everyone back into the West Country is totally unacceptable – especially as he's been lying about it all along.'

Brennan then explained about Roger Mellars's deception and the fact that his claim to a secure Utopia in the West Country was all falsehood. The fact that he had refused to contribute any help to the campaign against the East Anglia hostiles was further evidence of his lack of good faith. When he had finished setting out the problem, Brennan stood back and motioned for Beverley Truman to take the floor.

'As you know, I've been down there today on a motorbike,' began Beverley. 'All Mellars has got there is the town of Glastonbury and some undefended farming country around it. His talk about sealing off the West Country from sea to sea is sheer bullshit! I suspect there are other small independent groups down in Devon and Cornwall, which are quite separate from his. He's been conning us all along.' Brenann moved forward again. 'Bev obviously couldn't get in to see what conditions are like in Glastonbury, but we have to go down there and sort him out. As far as I'm concerned, not a shot need be fired. If the damned man had any sense now, in the face of this German threat, he would join with us, instead of trying to fragment us.'

There were rumbles of agreement and a few calls of 'Zap the bastard!' from some of the more youthful members.

'So the day after tomorrow, we'll take our full force down there and have a showdown. With luck, we'll bring back our people – or certainly as many of them as wish to come home.'

As he said the words, he wondered whether Gwen would be amongst them. He caught Liz Peterson's dark eyes staring at him from a nearby chair and his thoughts jumped forward unbidden to the possibilities that arose if Gwen elected to stay with Roger Mellars.

As promised, Thursday morning once again saw the departure of their 'army'. The previous day had been spent in energetic preparations, in which almost the whole community was involved. This time, they added two more coaches to their convoy, to accommodate the extra men and women in less discomfort than rattling about in trucks. When the cavalcade streamed out through the castle gate on what, in spite of Brennan's best intentions, might turn out to be a gun-fight, it seemed particularly incongruous that one large luxury coach had 'Bebb's Continental Tours' emblazoned on its panels, and the other sported 'Ferris's Holidays' below a row of European flags. The other vehicles were those which had been to Cambridge, the trucks carrying mainly equipment and food supplies to support the extra troops, who now numbered more than two hundred.

The trusty Alvis Saracen was on its low-loader, followed by the Ferret scout car. As they left, most of the residents who stayed behind came out to wave them off, many in tears and the rest in a sombre mood, wondering what the outcome of this latest escapade would be.

In the lead was Casey, driving one of the Land-Rovers with Brennan alongside him and Mervyn and Beverley in the back with a pile of weapons between them. This time, Mervyn had made sure that Canon Gilbey was safely in bed, mildly sedated with one of the drugs they had collected in Bridgend. The convoy negotiated the now-familiar obstacles on the motorway as far as the approach to the old Severn Bridge, where they stopped to allow the rest of the vehicles to catch them up. As was so often the case in this altered climate, it was raining heavily on to the bedraggled countryside, with rumbles of thunder over to the south-west. Casey looked dubiously at the sagging bridge deck, thankful that for once, there was little wind to further stress the failing suspension.

'Phil Robson is going to dispatch them over one at a time, like we did before,' Brennan said, reading Casey's thoughts. 'It can't be long now before the whole damned thing falls into the sea!'

'One more winter storm like we've been getting these past few years will finish it off,' agreed Mervyn. 'As if the world hasn't had enough of disasters, even the bloody weather's turning against us!'

They waited until the twenty-three other vehicles had crawled past them and passed gingerly over the bridge, then followed up as a rear-guard behind the Saracen. Once across, Casey gunned the Land-Rover back to the front of the column.

'Are we going to stop well back from Mellars' hideout or go straight up to his first roadblock?' asked Casey.

Brennan twisted around to consult Beverley Truman.

'You've been down here, Bev? What do you think?'

'We need some sort of base camp to leave the transport – and if we're stuck here in a siege for some days, then we'll need a place to eat and sleep. I suggest we pitch camp somewhere just outside Street – there's a village called Walton on the road in from the motorway.'

Street was a relatively modern annexe to Glastonbury, situated a couple of miles to the south, where the huge Clarke's shoe factory and Retail Village had been the main features of the town.

'Clarke's is all burnt down, as far as I could see from the distance, but Mellars has got a roadblock outside it, so Street must be included in his enclave,' explained Beverley.

By now they had reached the Almondsbury interchange, where the M4 and M5 motorways crossed by a complicated system of flyovers.

'It's a nightmare on the south side,' warned Beverley. 'Not so bad on a motorbike, but you'll have your work cut out to get through this next quarter-mile.'

In fact, it turned out to be impossible, as a multiple collision and fire involving at least a dozen vehicles had blocked the southern end. Casey waved down the convoy to a halt while he tried to weave a passage through on to the southbound M5. After threading the Land-Rover through a welter of rusting, burned and overturned cars, vans and trucks, he was finally brought to a halt. There was a total blockage of even the multiple lanes where the road to Filton turned off. A petrol tanker appeared to have crashed and caught fire, leaving a huge area of incinerated road surface and other vehicles almost welded into blackened destruction. On each side of it were further crashed and abandoned cars and lorries, making further progress impossible.

'I didn't realise it was this bad when I came across!' said Beverley. 'I just took the bike down the embankment and scooted well clear of this mess.'

'Now what do we do?' asked Casey. He had stopped alongside a police Vauxhall with flat tyres and a smashed windscreen. The driver's door was wide open and a scatter of human bones lay on the seat, partly hidden by the remains of a rotting uniform.

Brennan cursed under his breath. 'It would take us hours to drag enough of this stuff aside with one of the big trucks.'

Mervyn, who lived for years in the Bristol area, had the obvious answer. 'We'll all have to back up and reverse, then go back down the M4 towards the new bridge, but turn off on the M49 spur to Avonmouth.'

The hardest part was turning the convoy, especially the coaches, but after much swearing and blaspheming in the pouring rain, they set off back down the hill towards the river until they found a gap in the central crash barrier to get across to the westbound side. From then on the going was easier, though once they had regained the M5, crossing the high-arched viaduct over the Avon was again a difficult exercise in dodging wrecks.

Once through the gap in the Mendip Hills, the dead flat area of the Somerset Levels stretched before them. Soon, between breaks in the streaming rain, they could glimpse the strange conical hill of Glastonbury Tor in the far distance, across countryside that looked more like a lake than former farmland.

'It's reverting back to what it was like before the Romans,' remarked the historically-minded Mervyn. 'Now that the sluices aren't being controlled and there's no pumping, this flooding is likely to be permanent. All this land is barely above sea-level.'

'Glastonbury used to be called the "Isle of Avalon", as I recall,' added the classically-educated Beverley. 'Didn't the water used to come right up to the foot of the Tor?'

Mervyn nodded. 'It was "Ynys Witrin" in Welsh – the "Island of Glass". Some years ago, the archaeologists discovered one of these prehistoric lake dwellings nearby. Things are just going back to what they were centuries ago.'

Brennan was more interested in the present. 'Many of the roads are going to be under water – Mellars may have got himself a ten-mile wide moat around his fortress!'

'The A39 from Bridgwater runs along the Polden Hills towards Glastonbury,' said Beverley, who had reconnoitred the area. 'They only form a low ridge, but they keep the road well above the floods.'

He turned out to be right and when they turned off the motorway at Junction 23, their only problems were wreck-dodging, rather than ploughing through water. Even the rain eased off by the time they got to Walton, a ribbon settlement about three miles south of Glastonbury.

So far they had not seen any signs of life, the houses on either side of the road being the usual desolate picture of abandonment, damage and decay.

'Is this the place you reckon we should stop, Bev?' asked Brennan, looking unenthusiastically out of the side window at the drenched village. A mixture of houses of different ages and sizes, a church, a few shops and garages and a large shed with a faded sign saying 'Farm Cider For Sale' lay uninvitingly under a grey sky.

'We need somewhere to pull all these vehicles off the road,' said Casey.

'Why, are you afraid of blocking the traffic?' grunted Mervyn, with a flash of his old sarcastic manner. 'Why not pull them all into a circle, like the old Western wagon-trains?'

There were fields behind the houses lining the narrow road, but Brennan didn't want to risk getting bogged down in mud. 'There's a pub down there, let's see if their car park is big enough for us.'

They moved along a few hundred yards and saw a public house on the right, with a large car park behind a ranch-style fence, which was almost invisible under a profusion of brambles and bind-weed. There were half a dozen cars on the further side, one burned out, but there was enough room for most of their own vehicles. Soon the convoy was settled and the Saracen rolled off its wagon onto the road. The potential besiegers assembled alongside the pub, which had lost one side of its red-tiled roof, but seemed otherwise intact. Some of the men went exploring inside, to find that it had been stripped of anything useful – their hope for some surviving bottles of whisky or a full pressure keg of five-year old ale were soon dashed.

'At least it's a roof over our heads,' said Brennan, as he looked into the two large bars and a hall-like annexe which must have been used for dances and other functions. 'It's one o'clock, we'd better have something to eat and drink.'

As everyone foraged in their packs and pockets for their rations, Brennan held a briefing with his 'staff officers'.

'We're almost within shouting distance of Street and within sight of Glastonbury itself. We must assume that someone there has already heard us arrive. Twenty-five engines make a hell of a row.'

'We'd better deploy some sentries and scouts straight away, sir.' Once again, Phil Robson had reverted to his old military mode of speech. At Brennan's nod, he hurried away and Lance asked what the next step was.

'We'll go in through this Street roadblock, whether they like it or not. Take the bull by the horns and see what happens. But let's eat first.' He dipped into his once-official bag and pulled out a plastic box with slices of bread, boiled beef and home-made cheese, which was the staple ration for almost everyone.

'We're OK for drink for a few days, quartermaster?' he asked Bill Fleming, who after several decades, had again taken on his old duties of looking after supplies.

'We've got a few dozen crates of beer for tonight, and plenty of clean water in steel kegs in one of the trucks.'

Ever since installing themselves in Caerleon, they had filtered all their water through a system salvaged from a large hotel. With mains pressure having been zero for more than five years, they had taken water from a stream, using a small petrol-driven pump, trying not to think how many corpses may be leaking into it within its catchment area. In Cardiff, Mervyn had vetoed using the river that flowed alongside the castle, flowing as it did through the former populous mining valleys containing half a million dead bodies. Every day, they sent a large tanker-trailer up to a holding reservoir at Llanishen on the outskirts of the city and carefully filtered it. All that was used for drinking or cooking was boiled first, though Mervyn and Ruddy were working on a scheme to chlorinate it, using equipment stripped from a swimming pool. So far, the doctor's caution had paid off, as there had been no serious gut infections amongst the community.

When they had eaten, Brennan assembled everyone on the road outside and detailed about a hundred and fifty men and women to climb aboard the covered trucks and bigger vans. Robson and Fleming rode on the first and last, the Ferret armoured car and the Saracen leading the column. The remainder of the force were left at the inn with the coaches and other transport, setting up a perimeter guard equipped with small arms and one of the mortars. Mervyn, Fay and Liz Peterson stayed with them with their medical kit, again fervently hoping that their services wouldn't be needed.

Before Brennan climbed into the Ferret with Casey as driver and Beverley as gunner, he conferred with the two returned scouts, who had gone cautiously through the fields and houses towards the roadblock at Street.

'They've got a great heap of rubble across the road near Clarke's Village,' one reported. 'There's a farm gate across the narrow gap with a couple of chaps standing behind, but I didn't see any sign of a blockhouse or a machine gun, like there was near Cambridge.'

'There's a double barbed wire fence stretching across the fields from it,' said the other young man. 'Looks more as if it's meant to keep people in, rather than out!'

'That may be nearer the truth, son,' said the commander. 'Right, let's do it then, boys!'

He clambered aboard the old armoured car, and with the Saracen close behind with Lance driving, the expedition drove off. The rain had stopped, but thunder still growled far away as they covered the short distance to the edge of Roger Mellars' enclave.

They breasted a rise where there were old traffic lights at a junction and looked down the slope, seeing the large expanse of Clarke's factory compound on their right. It was now a wilderness of trees and scrub, surrounding the derelict remains of many buildings. Ahead, the road descended through a wide weed-choked expanse of what used to be grassy verge, to the barrier that the scout had described.

'Give it some welly, Casey!' yelled Brennan down the hatch. 'Show the bastards we mean business!'

CHAPTER THIRTEEN

THE Ferret zoomed down the slope towards the gate, over which three startled faces became clearer as they approached. For effect, Beverley traversed the turret, so that the 7.62 machine gun swung away, then came back, its perforated barrel-guard depressing as it centred on the guards.

They stopped ten yards from the gate and Brennan yelled at the men, 'Open this gate, we're coming through!'

After a hasty consultation, the oldest man, a black-bearded bruiser in a donkey-jacket and peaked cap, yelled back defiantly.

'We've been told not to let anyone in! Clear off!'

The three had self-loading rifles slung on their shoulder and Brennan was ready to duck down in the turret at any sign of hostility.

'Either you open the gate or we knock it down!'

Casey revved the Daimler engine to emphasise the point, but the sentries behind the gate unslung their rifles and the two on either side of Blackbeard ducked behind the butresses of rubble. As the brave but foolhardy centre man worked the bolt on his weapon, Brennan shouted at him again.

'Look, we can do this the easy way or the hard way! If you open the gate and stand back, no one will get hurt.'

For reply, the man levelled his rifle at Brennan. 'I told you, no one comes in without the Chief's permission,' he yelled back.

'The bugger's off his head, trying to hold up an armoured vehicle with an old FN,' shouted up Casey above the noise of the now idling engine. He closed down the grille in front of his driver's port, in case the guard took a pot-shot at him.

'Push his gate down, Casey, then turn so that Bev can cover these guys while the rest of the vehicles come through.' With no intercom, Brennan had to shout his orders down the turret. With a roar, the Ferret lurched forwards and the steel plating of the wedge-shaped nose knocked the gate clean off its hinges before running over its buckled bars. Casey made a tight circle in the road behind and stopped as Bev waggled the machine gun barrel threateningly at the three guards, who now dropped their weapons and flattened themselves against the inside of the shoulder-high barrier of old bricks and earth.

The Saracen thundered through behind them, followed by the procession of trucks, whose occupants had their own guns at the ready over the tailboards.

'Damned useless defences,' snapped Brennan. 'Lucky for Mellars it's only us and not the Germans.'

'I doubt that he was expecting us so soon – and not at this back entrance. He might have thought we would come down from Wells,' suggested Beverley. The last truck passed, the discomfited guards gaping at the strength of the invading force.

'They can't even tell the town that we've arrived, as they've got no radio or phones,' observed Brennan, as they started up again and rapidly overtook the column to take the lead once more.

They passed a sheepskin factory closed long before the plague began, then came alongside the rise of Wearyall Hill, beyond which was the dramatic cone of the Tor, the grey stone tower of the ruined church of St Michael on the peak. They swung past a roundabout and found themselves on the outskirts of the small town of Glastonbury. The main road in had been cleared and the rubble and debris of burned and damaged houses had been stacked along the edges, already vanishing under grass, weeds and the opportunist buddleia.

'Some of these houses are being lived in,' said Beverley, pointing at smoke coming from some chimneys and boarded-up windows where the glass had been lost. As they went further into the town, turning a corner into a narrow street, people began appearing, mostly peering fearfully from doorways and shattered window frames, though some were on the pavement. Compared with the Cardiff community, the clothing of these Glastonbury inhabitants looked threadbare and ill-fitting. The people they saw had a furtive, hangdog appearance, which reinforced Brennan's concerns about the regime under which they were forced to live. A little further on, two men in blue boiler suits and peaked caps were standing near a battered truck which was at the side of the road. Half a dozen men were shovelling rubble into it, presumably for the construction of more barriers. As the Ferret approached, they dropped their tools and ran behind the lorry to gaze apprehensively at the military cavalcade that was passing.

'Where the hell is Mellars's opposition?' demanded Brennan. 'Is this some kind of trap?'

'He can't do much without heavier weapons than he seems to have,' replied Beverley. 'He got nothing substantial from his raid on us.'

Around the next corner, the question was partly answered. A massive barricade of debris twelve feet high, had been piled from side to side of the street, butted against commercial buildings at each end. Another elongated heap had been placed in front of the narrow gap in the centre, so that the only way in was by filtering around either end of this barrier, effectively preventing a ram-raid attack on the entrance. In the buildings on each side, sandbags had been stacked in all the window openings, leaving small gaps for defenders to fire through.

A few more poorly-dressed men, some still clutching shovels, scuttled behind the barrier as they approached, vanishing through a heavy metal grille that was being pulled across the inner entrance.

Casey came to halt fifty yards short of the obstruction and waited for orders.

'This is a bit more like a defence,' said Brennan, almost approvingly.

'We could blast it apart with our mortars, if it came to it,' observed Beverley. 'And those window embrasures wouldn't last two minutes under heavy machine gun fire or the odd rocket!'

'Don't get too bloodthirsty yet, Bev. We're supposed to talk our way out of this one, remember? I'll have old Canon Gilbey damning my soul again if we as much as scratch anyone!'

The Saracen drew up alongside them and Lance called across from his driver's hatch. 'What happens now, boss?'

'Negotiations, old son. If we can find anyone to negotiate with.'

He bent down in the turret to ask for Strickland's loudhailer, which was handed up to him.

'While I try to get some sense out of someone, get Robson and Fleming to organise some patrols to go off each side from here and reconnoitre their perimeter. Get them to see if the centre of the town is all walled off like this.' As Lance acknowledged the order with a wave, Brennan had an afterthought.

'I don't think there are any trigger-happy folk outside this inner sanctum, but tell them to be careful and for God's sake not to shoot unless they're fired on.'

Lance reversed the troop-carrier back along the line of Land-Rovers and trucks, while Brennan scanned the roadblock for any signs of life. He saw some movement in two of the windows in the shop buildings at either side, but no one appeared at the main entrance.

'I presume Jolly Roger and his men have sealed up the other roads in the same way,' he said to Beverley. 'Glastonbury seems to have reverted to a medieval walled town!'

He pressed the switch on the loud hailer and raised it to his mouth.

'In case you hadn't guessed, we're from Cardiff! We don't want any trouble, unless you force it on us. I want to speak to Roger Mellars, so can you get him here straight away, please.' The amplified voice reverberated between the buildings on either side, but there was no response. Brennan tried again.

'Come on, you're not all deaf. Somebody – anybody – please come out here and talk to me. I need to meet your leader.'

He caught Beverley smirking at him from lower down in the turret.

'What's so funny?'

'You sound like a Martian just landed on earth! "Take me to your leader" and all that!'

In spite of the potentially fraught situation, Brennan grinned, but business was business and he raised the loud hailer again.

'Come on, let's be having somebody! I need to talk to Roger Mellars.'

After a few moments, they heard the gate grating on the road surface as it was slid aside. A burly man appeared, also dressed in a blue cover-all like a welder's suit, wearing a cap suspiciously like a police officer's. He had a rifle in one hand as he stalked around the end of the barrier and approached the armoured car. Brennan saw that on his belt, there was a holstered revolver.

'Put that rifle down on the ground!' shouted Brennan. As Beverley swivelled and depressed the turret gun to track the man across the roadway, Brennan kept up the pressure.

'And don't let your hand wander near that pistol, if you want to keep your head on your shoulders!'

The heavily-built man, who had a drooping black moustache, glowered up at Brennan, but with obvious ill-grace, placed the rifle on the tarmac before coming closer to the green and black vehicle.

'What do you want? This is private property!'

'Ha-bloody-ha!' retorted Brennan. 'Were you one of the thieves who came over to us a few days ago?

The man's scowl deepened. He had a red, lined face and coarse, pitted skin. 'I know nothing about that. Why don't you clear off and leave us alone?'

'Chance would be a fine thing, chum! But you give us back everything you stole, including our people, and we'll gladly leave you to stew in this miserable dump!' He waved a hand expansively at the derelict town clustered at the foot of the isolated hill. 'Now cut the crap and go and tell your boss that Brennan is waiting outside to talk to him. If he doesn't come out, we're coming in – and don't think that pile of earth is going to stop us!'

The man looked anxiously from side to side as fifty armed men and women broke away from the line of trucks and loped off into the side lanes on either side of the main street. Brennan had scavenged a few score camouflage-pattern fatigue outfits on one of their raids on the Breconshire army establishments and he had previously arranged with Robson and Fleming that these were to be worn by the first wave of troops to be deployed. Those left in the trucks wore a motley collection of anoraks, bomber jackets and jeans, but he correctly thought that a first impression of uniformed troops might have a good psychological effect.

As the local fellow saw these slip away around the perimeter of the inner zone, he looked uneasily at the Ferret, the Saracen and the brace of armoured Land-Rovers. It was obvious that these visitors meant business.

'OK, I'll send a message and see what he says. He knows you're here, anyway, from the bloody noise you've made!'

'Can't you get him on the phone or radio?' asked Brennan provocatively, knowing that they had neither, as they had stolen only one VHF set from Cardiff and the big short-wave equipment was useless except for talking to another similar set.

'We don't have any phones,' snarled the pseudo-policeman. 'I'll have to send a runner up to the Tor.'

'Why the Tor?'

'Because that's where our headquarters is, at least on the lower slopes. Most of the centre of the town is burned or ruined.'

Brennan was glad of this information, every little helped if it came to a showdown.

'OK, I'll give him half an hour from now.' He looked ostentatiously at his wristwatch. 'Then we're coming in to find him.'

He dismissed the man with a flick of his wrist, then dropped down into the turret. It was all part of his plan to keep ascendancy over the defenders. Through the gun port, he watched the man trudge away, pick up his rifle and vanish behind the barricade, the gate squealing as it was pulled shut again.

'Let's see if that squeezes Jolly Roger out of his burrow,' he said to Beverley. 'I'd better make sure that everything is alright back at the ranch.'

He used the hand-held VHF set to speak to Mervyn back at the pub, using a different pre-arranged frequency from that used in Cardiff, in case Roger's men were monitoring it with their single purloined receiver. The doctor reported that all was quiet, but they were standing by in case Brennan needed any reinforcements. After about twenty minutes, in which there was no action other than a few glimpses of men behind the upper windows of the central gate, Robson came back with a report from his patrols. His tall figure in mottled green and black came striding across the street, a floppy jungle hat with turned-down brim jammed on his head.

'All the side streets have been filled up with rubble, but on the two other main streets into the town, there are gates like this one.' He hefted his Caliburn on to his shoulder. 'They've been there a long time, plenty of weeds growing over them, so they haven't been put up recently just for our benefit.'

'Where are our lads and lasses now?' asked Brennan.

'Hunkered down near the other gates, but far back enough not to be tempting targets. Shall I leave them there?'

'May as well. Send a truck over to each platoon, with some water and grub, in case they have to stake those places out for some time.'

As Robson went off, Brennan had the impression that he was enjoying this return to what for him had been normality when he was a professional soldier, something to take his mind off the death of his wife and daughters. That made two of us, he thought wryly.

The quiet descended again and they whiled away the rest of the time in discussion.

'This Glastonbury set-up is not really what we expected from the line he spun us before,' said Brennan. 'Listening to Mellars, you'd think he was running the whole of the West Country, not just one little town.'

'I think he uses this as the central base and literally farms out a lot of country all around,' replied Beverley. 'When I came on the bike, I saw houses occupied up to ten or fifteen miles out, mostly farms. If the Irish came – or god forbid, the Jerries – he'd be in big trouble without any outer defences.'

'How does he control those folk out there, I wonder? I presume they are the ones who bring the food into the main community here.'

Beverley jerked a thumb back down the road. 'Those guys in the boiler suits and police hats look uncommonly like enforcers! Those rumours we heard about a police state seem likely to be true. Work or get worked over, seems to be the motto here!'

'It's amazing how a few people can hold the majority down.'

'Not when those few have the guns and the majority don't,' answered Beverley. 'Remember Saddam and the Iraqis – or a dozen other dictators. Come to that, the Norman Conquest and even the Roman occupation was by a tiny minority. To start a revolt, it takes guts and a willingness to die.'

Brennan agreed. 'I suppose that's why Roger won't join us in tackling the Irish or the Germans. It would mean giving his people arms – and that might be suicide for him and his cronies.'

Casey climbed up from his cramped driving seat to stretch his legs.

'Why didn't we rumble this guy before?' he asked. 'All that crap about building a Hadrian's Wall across the West Country to protect his empire, when all he's got is this!' He waved a hand over the turret rim.

'He always discouraged us from coming down here . . . though in fact, he only came up to us twice. I'm not even sure how he got to know about our groups.'

'Through Gloucester, I think,' said Casey.'We haven't heard much of them lately, come to think of it. Nor Worcester.'

'When we get a few more radios from Strickland, we can give them one each and keep in touch more closely,' promised Brennan. 'I'm hoping they can pull in more farmers and strays from the Marches. They need their numbers bumping up, Gloucester's got less than two hundred people.'

Further chat was cut short by the grating of the gate across the ground.

'Someone's coming out,' snapped Casey, sliding down to his seat again. Brennan looked across the road and saw the moustached man, this time without his rifle, leading another figure across from the barricade.

'Who the blazes is this?' drawled Beverley, squinting through his periscope. 'Looks like a sky-pilot, with that dog-collar.'

As the pair approached, the man with the police cap dropped back and allowed the other person, rather portly and middle-aged, to come up to the side of the Ferret.

'I understand that you are Brigadier Brennan?' he asked, in a rather high-pitched, plummy voice. A round bland face was capped by a wiry thatch of grey hair. He wore a blue anorak over black trousers and shirt, with a clerical collar around his neck. Brennan hoped that he was not another half-crazed canon like Gilbey – more clergymen seemed to have survived than doctors.

'That rank has been redundant for many years – but yes, I'm Brennan.'

'And I am Richard Whyting, the vicar of St John's. I'm not sure that my rank is redundant yet, so I'm carrying on with my duties, much as I imagine you are doing.'

With a muttered 'Keep me covered, Bev,' Brennan hoisted himself out of the turret hatch and clambered down to the ground over the large spare wheel attached to the nearside. He took the hand that the parson stuck out and shook it, again wondering at the odd feel of this unaccustomed civility.

'Good afternoon, vicar. I was expecting Roger Mellars.'

The clergyman cleared his throat as if about to deliver a sermon.

'He asked me to come in his stead, to make some exploratory enquiries.'

'There are no enquiries to be made, sir. He committed theft and abduction in Cardiff when my back was turned. I want whatever he took returned at once. The matter is not negotiable!'

The priest's benign expression faded. 'That is rather harsh, Brig . . . er, Brennan. I understand that the people involved came of their own free will.'

'Then they can leave again of their own free will, if they wish!' retorted Brennan. 'But the radios and weapons Mellars stole, didn't jump into his trucks of their own free will, nor the Land-Rover.'

Richard Whyte was a full head shorter than the ex-soldier and craned his neck upwards as he replied.

'Roger doesn't see it quite that way, I'm afraid.'

'I don't give a damn how he sees it. I want all that stuff back and I want to talk to all my people. Either by arrangement or by force!'

The vicar shifted uneasily from foot to foot.

'I have been asked to mediate in this dispute, being a man of the cloth,' he brayed. To Beverley and Casey, listening intently from within the car, he sounded so much like a stage caricature of a clergyman, that they wondered if he was an impostor.

'There's nothing to mediate about, Reverend,' said Brennan patiently. 'The leader, or whatever he calls himself, of this enclave is a thief and a liar. When he discovered that the majority of our able-bodied community had gone off to help defend another group against foreign invaders, not only did he decline to offer any help, but he took the opportunity to come and raid us, by deception if not actual force.'

Whyte puffed out his cheeks and looked indignant. 'Those are harsh words, sir. I'm sure you've misinterpreted the situation.'

'Then either get Roger down here to explain the misunderstanding – or we'll come in and confront him. Down the barrels of a large number of guns, if needs be.'

The pink face paled at the ultimatum. 'I'm sure there'll be no need for that, Brennan. I'll do my best to bring you face to face.'

'Please do that, vicar, and quickly. I'll give Roger another half hour, then we start destroying this checkpoint. Is that understood?'

He stood back to indicate that the interview was over and after some hesitation, the clergyman nodded a farewell and hurried back towards the gate, followed by the surly man with the moustache.

Brennan climbed back into the Ferret and checked his watch again.

'If he doesn't show up, then we're going in at the thirty-minute mark,' he said grimly. 'I'm not going to be fobbed off by some damned sky-pilot mouthing platitudes.'

Twenty minutes later the familiar squeal of the gate sounded again and three men in boiler suits and caps came across the road, the moustached man in the lead.

'You're to come with us to meet the chief,' he announced. 'Only two of you, without any weapons.'

Brennan gazed down at him from the turret, an amused smile on his face. 'You must be joking, chum! We come in with these three vehicles and their crews.' He indicated the Ferret, the Saracen and one of the armoured Land-Rovers, which had another large machine gun on top. He thumbed at the other drivers and with a series of roars, all three engines started up – thankfully first time, as the batteries had had a good charge on the trip from Cardiff.

The three local guards hopped back from the vibrating Ferret, mouthing protests, but Brennan shouted down to Casey and waved a beckoning arm at the other vehicles.

Slowly, they passed behind the first barrier and swerved through the inner barricade until the snout of the armoured car was almost touching the heavy metal gate, which had only been drawn aside enough to let the three men through. As these came galloping up, Brennan yelled at them over the roar of the engines.

'Pull it back or I'll knock it down!'

With a thunderous scowl, the one with the moustache motioned to three men who were hidden behind the barricade and they dragged the heavy grille back on its rudimentary castors. 'They must have pinched that from the railway station!' yelled Beverley from below.

On the other side of the barrier, Magdalene Street stretched ahead, straight into the centre of the town with the ancient abbey ruins on the right. The roads had been cleared of rubble and though many of the shops and buildings were burned or derelict, a number were being lived in, with people at their doors and smoke drifting from the chimneys. Brennan was surprised to see several horses and carts further up the street. There were almost no motor vehicles anywhere and he assumed that Mellars was very short of fuel and batteries, compared to themselves.

'Where now, I wonder?' said Brennan, half to himself. Casey halted the car while the other two vehicles came up behind him. The three men in boiler suits stalked angrily to the side of the Ferret.

'You shouldn't have done that!' one yelled.

'Just shut up and show us where we'll find Roger Mellars!' retorted Brennan, in no mood to bandy words with stroppy underlings.

The guards were in a dilemma – their orders having been totally ignored, they were afraid to confront the invaders with any threat of force, given the impressive weaponry on top of two of the armoured vehicles – and the sight of multiple gun-barrels poking out of the ports of the Saracen, which was obviously filled with troops.

'All right, follow me, but slowly,' grated the first man grudgingly.

There was a Triumph motorcycle on its stand nearby and kicking it into life, he went ahead, then turned right and went up the narrow High Street. At the top, he led them on to a side road which passed between houses and into a narrow lane which started to rise as they approached the green hills that were the backdrop to Glastonbury. They wound around for half a mile, between overgrown trees and hedges, with houses concealed behind them. Some were abandoned, but others were occupied, as furtive faces peered out at them every few yards.

At the base of the Tor, which now rose steeply above them, they drove into a wide courtyard faced by a large double-fronted Victorian mansion. Behind it, several rows of barrack-like wooden buildings were terraced into the hillside, suggestive of an army camp or temporary school accommodation.

The house was in excellent condition, with obvious recent repairs to the roof, intact window glass and well-tended grass verges to the wide gravelled area in front.

'Roger does himself well, by the looks of it,' yelled Beverley from below.

'At the expense of his minions, I suspect,' replied Brennan cynically.

Ignoring the hand signs of the motorcyclist, the three armoured vehicles swung across the gravel and stopped in an arc before steps leading up to a large porch, their guns directed threateningly at the white front door. As Brennan stood up in the turret, that door flew open and a tall man with blonde cropped hair emerged, an automatic pistol in his hand. Brennan recognised him as Wayne Addis, Roger's chief thug, who had accompanied him to Caerleon just before the Irish raid.

'I'd put that back in your pocket, Wayne, if I were you!' he bellowed, as the engines throttled back to a tick-over. With a look of angry amazement on his narrow face, Addis stared at the three military vehicles menacing the house, then ducked back inside and slammed the door.

'Great welcome!' commented the urbane Beverley. 'Think they'll invite us in for tea? It's about the right time.'

'Switch her off, Casey. Come up and stand by the gun, in case there's any funny business. Bev's coming in with me.'

He hauled himself out of the turret again and slid to the ground. Walking to the Saracen, he motioned for Lance to come out as well.

All the while, the fellow on the motorcycle glowered at them suspiciously, then hoisted his bike on to its stand and ran around the back of the house. Brennan, wearing battledress like the other two, with a red beret on this head, started up the steps to the front door.

'I don't think Roger will dare shoot us on sight' he said hopefully. 'He knows what would happen if he did.'

As they reached the top, the door opened and Wayne Addis appeared again, this time minus his pistol. 'You'd better come in, now that you're here,' he said tonelessly.

Brennan pushed past him into a large hall with rugs on the tiled floor.

'Where is he?' he asked bluntly.

Without replying, Addis went to a door on the left and opened it, standing aside to let them through into a large room with a curtained bay window. It was carpeted and had several matching settees and armchairs around a coffee table in front of a large Adam fireplace. There was antique furniture against the walls but Brennan had eyes only for the figure seated on one of the settees. Gwen, in a smart dress he had never seen before, stared up rather fearfully at this large man in combat uniform who had burst in clutching a rifle and seemed to fill the whole room.

'Hello, Gwen – enjoying your holiday?' he asked cynically.

CHAPTER FOURTEEN

'THIS is rather a surprise, Brennan!' said a voice behind him. Swinging around, he was aware for the first time of Roger Mellars sitting in an armchair opposite. He got up and advanced with his hand outstretched, which Brennan pointedly ignored, putting his hand instead into an inside pocket and pulling out a folded sheet of paper.

'Here's a list of the material you stole from us. I want it all back – now! And I want to talk to the people you conned into leaving Cardiff.' He turned back to Gwen. 'And that includes you, madam!'

The barrister's façade of an urbane gentleman began to falter.

'Now look here, Brennan—' he began, but the bigger man cut him short.

'Cut the crap, Roger! You've been caught with your fingers in the till. If you'd come to Cardiff openly and made your pitch with the people, fair enough – though from what I've seen here, they'd have been mad to listen to you.'

Mellars bristled at this. 'They came of their own free will, dammit!'

'Bullshit! You conned them with stories of your West Country paradise, stretching from shore to shore. All you've got is a derelict little town, a mob of gangsters to enforce your dictats – and a handful of unhappy, cowed citizens skulking behind an earth wall, while you play El Supremo in the only decent house in the place!'

Roger's handsome face flushed with indignation, but before he could answer, Brennan swung back to the lovely but apprehensive woman on the settee.

'Is this what you really want, Gwen? Are you happy with swapping a decent community for this Stone Age hideout ruled by a third-rate robber baron? If you are, good luck to you, you'll need it! If not, then come home with us!'

With the vicar twittering anxiously in the background and Wayne Addis glowering from near the door, Roger Mellars changed his tack. He became the reasonable, persuasive advocate that had once made him such a success in the Crown Courts of the Western Circuit.

'Look, old chap, there's been an unfortunate misunderstanding here.'

'Not on my part, there hasn't!' growled Brennan.

'We heard that you'd had a trouncing in Cambridge and might even be dead. Going to Cardiff was an act of mercy – we knew most of your active people had gone away with you, so we offered sanctuary to those who were left, if they wanted to come. For all we knew, the Jerries might have been belting down to Cardiff to finish the job!'

'You're a bloody liar, Mellars,' said Brennan calmly. 'For a start, there was no way you could know what had happened in Cambridge. You had no radio until you stole ours.'

'We sent motorcycle scouts up there, we do it regularly.'

'I don't believe you. The Cambridge people have never heard of you. And where did your alleged spies get such a ridiculous story, when we trounced the opposition within half an hour?'

Mellars wriggled expertly, after years of practice as a lawyer. 'I presume they spoke to some idiot outside Cambridge, who gave them false information, either from ignorance or malice. Anyway, I'm sorry if our chaps got it wrong.'

'Oh, come off it, Roger! All your brave motorcyclists saw was us going off up the motorway – so you took the opportunity to come over and rob us. Did you really think you could get away with it?'

'It wasn't like that at all!' snarled Mellars, losing his temper. 'In any event, these days everyone has to take chances when they are offered. Anyway, who are you to talk? I hear on your radio that you're taking over Cambridge and dragging them down to live under your regime.'

Brennan took a step forward and prodded Mellars in the chest with a large finger. Wayne Addis stiffened and his hand moved towards his belt, but Lance, who had been keeping a sharp eye on him, jerked up the muzzle of his machine pistol as a discouragement.

'Mellars, you're a fool as well as a liar! You know damn well that we're under constant threat from both Ireland and the Continent. Cambridge has survived so far, but it's indefensible in the long term – just as you are, if you hang on in this piddling little enclave with just a pile of earth for protection.'

Both the men were becoming steamed up and the rotund priest hurried around the settee, his hands held up placatingly.

'Gentlemen, gentlemen! I'm sure we can come to some amicable arrangement without resorting to harsh words or violence!' He pushed himself between the two men who were squaring up to each other like a pair of cockerels, while Gwen looked on white-faced, but with an inner frisson of excitement, knowing that part of their antagonism was over her.

Brennan suddenly stepped back and his shoulders relaxed as he deliberately released the angry tension that had built up inside him.

'You're right, vicar, there's no need to get steamed up' he said evenly. 'I want three things and I'm going to get them! The stolen goods returned, the opportunity to speak to the people you brought from Cardiff – and a private talk with Gwen Sutcliffe here.'

He jerked his head around to face Mellars again. 'And in spite of everything that's happened – and my undisguised dislike of you personally, Roger – I'm offering you the same as Cambridge. You're welcome to move all your people to Cardiff, as this shambles of a place just isn't safe. It's a toss-up who hits you first, the Irish or the Germans.'

Mellars shook his head sullenly, but the Reverend Whyte took him by the arm and steered him across the room, murmuring in his ear.

Brennan took the opportunity to move to the settee, where he stood towering over Gwen, who looked up half-defiantly, but with anxiety showing on her beautiful face.

'Come on, we've got to talk!' he said, almost roughly. Bending, he took her hand and pulled her up and led her across to the door.

'Out of the way, Wayne! I presume there's another room here somewhere?'

Sullenly, the bodyguard moved aside and Brennan pulled Gwen

across the hall to another half-open door, which led into an empty dining room, with a dozen chairs around a long polished table. He kicked the door shut behind him and pushed the woman on to one of the chairs.

'Now let's have a bit of sense from you! Did that slimy bastard force you to leave the castle or did you want to come here with him?'

Gwen looked up at him, then her face crumpled and she burst into tears. She groped for his hand, but he backed away.

'It was a bit of both!' she sobbed. 'He was so sure that you were in awful trouble in Cambridge – maybe even killed.'

Though he expected it, this was not what Brennan wanted to hear.

'I know you've fancied him ever since you first saw him. So have you slept with him?'

She didn't answer, but dropped her face into her hands as the sobs racked her. Brennan chewed his lip in his own anguish.

'Doesn't matter, we've got far worse problems that that,' he said gruffly. 'Look, you must come back, you can't stay in this dump, even if Roger has got himself a nice house. It's not safe any more.'

She gave a few sniffs and raised her head, her eyes reddened and moist.

'I'm so sorry, Brennan. Really sorry. I thought that maybe I'd never see you again.'

'Well, you didn't wait long to see if I'd turn up. But answer my question, are you coming home?'

She nodded through her sniffs, wiping her eyes with her fingers.

'Right, that's settled. Jolly Roger can come as well, if he wants to. You can set up house together in Cardiff.'

That provoked another burst of weeping, but Brennan was already moving to the door. 'Get your things together, if you have any. We'll be leaving as soon as I've settled a few matters with the Lying Lawyer!'

Back in the other room, Brennan found Mellars and the vicar murmuring in earnest discussion, with Lance and Beverley still keeping a wary eye on Wayne, who hovered just inside the door.

'Is Gwen alright?' asked Lance anxiously, as soon as Brennan reappeared.

'She's decided to come back with us, if that's what you mean,' he answered gruffly. Beverley gave Lance a warning glance, willing him not to pursue the subject at the moment. Brennan walked across to where Roger and Richard Whyting were arguing and brusquely interrupted them.

'Right, let's have some sense. I want to see my people straight away, while you produce the stuff you pinched from us. That includes the Land-Rover and the radio, right?'

The vicar gave one of his bland ecclesiastical smiles, once reserved for seeing off his parishioners at the church porch after Matins.

'Indeed, yes. We've lodged them in St John's itself, the church is one of the few large buildings with an intact roof.'

'Right, you can take me down there in a couple of minutes, padre. Meanwhile, Mellars, I want a few words with you.'

He grabbed Roger by the arm and drew him away towards the bay window.

'I'm willing to forget this silly escapade of yours if you act sensibly in future.'

'Don't patronise me, soldier,' snapped Mellars huffily. 'Say what you have to say and then clear off!'

Though Brennan felt like punching him on his aristocratic nose, he controlled himself. 'Gwen wants to come back to Cardiff. I gather you've had your wicked way with her, so if you're serious about her, then I've told her you can come back with us. And that goes for your whole outfit, as you'll not survive here much longer.'

The former barrister sneered at the bigger man. 'Don't talk such nonsense, Brennan! Do you think I'm going to shack up in a bloody caravan in Cardiff and play poor relation to you? No way, you just take your miserable crowd back – and that includes Little Miss Muffet. She's not all that great between the sheets, anyway – quite a disappointment, in fact!'

A figure suddenly materialised alongside the pair and before Brennan could prevent him, Lance had felled Mellars with a ferocious fist blow to the mouth. Roger staggered back and fell into an armchair, mouth welling blood from a split lip.

'Keep your foul comments to yourself, you evil bastard!' hissed

Lance, furious with rage at the lewd comment about the woman he coveted himself.

Wayne Addis started forward, groping at his belt for his pistol, but Beverley stepped forward and pointed his own weapon two-handed at the bodyguard. Brennan held up his hands to the room, as the vicar ducked down behind a settee. 'Alright, alright! Just cool it, everyone.' He bent and grabbed Roger by the shoulders and hauled him upright again.

'Back off, Lance! And you keep your nasty remarks to yourself, Mellars. I'll ask you again, will you consider abandoning this place and bringing your crowd over to Cardiff, as the Cambridge community is doing? We can find you somewhere outside the castle to live – the fort is a safe haven if we get attacked.'

'Go to hell, Brennan! Just take you stuff and your people and clear off. That's if they'll want to go?'

'The choice is theirs, I'll not force them. But I can make a good guess as to their answer. And maybe some of your folk would prefer to get out of this dismal prison camp.'

Mellars flushed with mixed rage and panic. 'Don't you even think of taking any of ours! We're thin enough on the ground now, that's why I was keen to have some more volunteers.'

Brennan shrugged. 'The option is always open. Now, vicar, where's this church of yours? Lance, you wait for Gwen and bring her back to the gate in the Land-Rover. Keep the Ferret and the men here – if there's any funny business from these people, you can shoot the place up!'

Ignoring Mellars, who was wiping a trickle of blood from his chin with the back of his hand, Brennan beckoned to Beverley and the priest.

'Come on, padre – you can have a lift in the Saracen to this church of yours. Then we'll collect our property and be off.'

The journey home was both uncomfortable and embarrassing. Brennan forsook the Ferret for one of the armoured Land-Rovers, driving it himself, with Mervyn alongside and Fay Morgan in the back with Gwen. Riding in that vehicle was rather like being inside a water cistern on wheels, noisy and claustrophobic from the heavy plating covering the whole surface. In one way, Brennan was glad of the drumming roar, as it made communication almost impossible, especially between the driver and the passengers at the back. Relations between Gwen and himself were fraught, to say the least. He could just about hold a conversation with Mervyn, who was close alongside and they went over the events of the day as they drove at the head of the column, back towards the motorway.

'Back to the status quo, more or less,' shouted the old doctor. 'We've got everything back and Roger is sticking fast to that dump.'

Brennan nodded, as he swerved to avoid a pair of horses cropping the grass that sprouted from the centre of the road. 'He'll be sorry in the long run. Hopefully, we can keep the Germans well to the east inland, but sooner or later, either the Irish are going to come at him from the coast or some more venturesome Jerries are going to push ashore in Dorset.'

'No chance of him contributing any men to the next punch-up with the boat people?'

Brennan shook his head. 'He refused, but it was pointless asking him, anyway. Now that we've seen what a piddling little operation he's got there, with so few men and damn-all in the way of weapons, he's not worth bothering with.' He raised his voice deliberately, hoping that a few words would percolate to the back seats.

As they hammered along to the junction with the M5, he went over the events of this thankfully bloodless day. He had been prepared for a proper siege of Glastonbury, but they were going home the same evening, the shadows lengthening as they turned northward on the motorway. It was only a few hours since the pompous vicar of St John's had taken him down to his church, where though the chancel had lost its roof in a storm, the nave was still intact. Here they found the fifty refugees – or captives, as Brennan preferred to call them – camping out in primitive circumstances. They had a motley collection of mattresses and sleeping bags laid out on the floor, where all the congregation's chairs had been pushed to the wall. At the back of the church, there was a proper kitchen, used in former days for light refreshments for visitors, where a couple of Aga stoves had been installed, fuelled by wood.

Most of the émigrés from Cardiff were middle-aged, as the younger men and women had gone to Cambridge at the time of Mellars' visit. There was no doubt whatsoever about their unanimous desire to get back to South Wales as soon as possible. In fact, they looked on Brennan like Moses delivering them from captivity in Egypt. Somewhat shamefaced, they made excuses, apologising for being taken in by Roger's persuasive oratory, based on the lie that Brennan's expeditionary force had met with disaster. Gleefully, they immediately gathered up their dismal chattels and marched off to the gateway in the barricade to await the trucks from Walton to pick them up. Sullenly, the blue-dungareed guards had let them out, under the watchful eyes of Lance who stood in the turret of the Ferret, Casey driving the armoured Land-Rover with Gwen Sutcliffe in the back.

Meanwhile, Brennan had taken the vicar back to Roger's mansion and made a final effort to get Mellars to abandon his enclave in favour of a safer place. With the ten armed men and women from the Saracen ranged along the gravelled area, he shouted for the man to come out and talk. With bad grace, the lawyer came to the steps outside the front door and for five minutes they bandied words without making any progress. Mellars, having regained much of his supercilious manner, dismissed Brennan's overtures with contempt. The former soldier soon gave up any attempt at conciliation and in exasperation, demanded the return of the stolen equipment. With a gesture of indifference, Mellars told Wayne Addis to attend to it and vanished into the house, slamming the front door behind him.

With bad grace, the big fair-haired thug led the way around to the huts at the back of the house. Here, several of the barrack blocks housed the police force which kept Mellars in power, but part of one long hut was their armoury.

With some of the men from the Saracen to help him, Brennan soon identified the few dozen weapons that had been taken from Cardiff. What remained belonging to Mellars was a collection of small arms, good only for scaring away a few bandits, but futile against a large force of organised attackers. Calling up one of the trucks from outside the barrier to come and fetch the rescued material, Brennan left a few men to organise its removal. Then he took the Saracen together with the

Land-Rover that had been stolen, back to the gate with the two radio-operators and drove outside into comparative freedom. They waited until the truck went in and returned with the weaponry, then the whole convoy did a single-file turn outside the gate and headed back towards the pub at Walton.

When they got there, they found that their numbers had swollen by another twenty-five souls, as some of the more daring or desperate inhabitants of Glastonbury had slipped from doorways and lanes to reach the slowly-moving trucks, where willing hands helped them aboard, ignoring the few furious shouts and curses of the police-capped custodians of Mellars' kingdom.

After a short stopover at the inn in Walton, to eat some more rations and reorganise the transport, the expedition shook the Glastonbury mud from its tyres and headed home.

CHAPTER FIFTEEN

IT took a few days for the community in Cardiff to settle down after the turmoil caused by the Glastonbury raid and the recovery expedition. Most people, even those closest to him, were wary of Brennan's mood as he went about his business with an impassive, silent air. It was worse than if he had been stamping, shouting and cursing, as this stony indifference was harder to fathom – and harder to deal with.

Mervyn James, who was the closest to a father-figure for the leader, wisely decided to let time take its course and confined his conversation to the practicalities of everyday life. There was certainly no lack of things to be getting on with, with the prospect of the migration of Strickland's people to Cardiff in the near future as well as preparations for the inevitable confrontation with the Germans before very long.

The twenty-five refugees from Somerset had to be accommodated and as a temporary measure, Bruce Ludlow took the low-loader out to a former holiday park on the Glamorgan coast and hauled in three more big residential caravans. The escapees were all men – women were few in Glastonbury and children almost absent – so they had no problem in settling them in the vans.

'When the Cambridge crowd comes, they can go with them to wherever we fix them up,' said Luddy cheerfully. Brennan talked to all the new arrivals in turn and found no reason to be concerned at having Mellars's former men in their midst. Most of them had been working in the fields outside Glastonbury and were quite happy to carry on helping with the agricultural activities that were being started in the huge Bute Park behind the castle. Another useful addition was a man who had been a veterinary assistant – and another a retail pharmacist in Wells. But the prize, as far as Luddy was concerned, was a middle-aged man who had been in charge of a tractor repair workshop in Shepton Mallet.

The radio was re-installed in the command centre to double up with the new equipment and the daily contacts with Cambridge went on as before. Thankfully, Strickland's spies reported no attempts on the part of the boat-people to move further inland, but it was obvious that they were working away to improve their transport.

After walking on eggshells as far as Brennan's relations with Gwen were concerned, his closer associates were relieved on the third day to see the two talking together outside her broadcasting caravan, parked just inside the main gate. She had resumed her disc-jockey and news-caster functions as if nothing had happened, though her patter was definitely more subdued than in the past.

Mervyn and Lance were walking from the keep towards the mess-hall for breakfast when they saw the pair standing rather stiffly together at the door of the van.

'I'd love to hear what they're saying to each other,' said Lance wistfully. 'I think the Boss has taken this harder than he's letting on.'

'I'm bloody sure he is!' retorted the old doctor. 'It's a bit hard when, as soon as you turn your back, your girlfriend buzzes off with some Flash Harry and is in bed with him before you can say knife!'

'D'you think they'll patch it up?' asked Lance, his feelings torn between sympathy for Brennan and his own ambitions where the blonde was concerned.

'Doesn't look like it, does it?' said Mervyn, as Brennan turned on his heel and marched away, while Gwen stepped up into her caravan and slammed the door with unnecessary vigour.

However, an hour later, when they met for a 'management conference' in the command hut, Brennan showed no outward sign of anger or bitterness. In fact, the observant Mervyn thought he looked and sounded less uptight, as if he had arrived at some decision and was prepared to live with it.

'There's a hell of a lot to be done, fellers!' he began briskly. 'I want to get as much fire-power collected as we possibly can and then scotch any attempts on the part of the Germans to grab any.'

'That means Hampshire and Wiltshire, I presume,' mused Beverley. 'We can't do anything about East Anglia, the Army bases there are right on their doorstep.'

The chief nodded. 'We have to take what we can from the south and then wreck anything useful that's left to stop them getting it.' He paused to point at an old Mobil road map of Britain pinned up on the wall.

'When he was still with the Jerries, our Dutch friend Jan Beelan heard rumours of some landings along the south coast, perhaps even as far west as Portsmouth. I'm afraid they'll strike inland from there into areas where there's plenty of Army stuff remaining.'

Mervyn craned round to look at the map. 'Do we know if anyone is still living down that way?'

'Jack in Gloucester told me some time ago that there's a few small settlements around Chichester and Southampton, living off the land,' replied Beverley. 'They're only a few score in number and wouldn't last five minutes if the boats came in there.'

Brennan scribbled something on a sheet of paper laying before him. 'Right, a priority is getting over to the Salisbury Plain and Aldershot areas to comb it for good transport and weapons. Ruddy, how's your railway project coming on?'

The amiable engineer was enthusiastic. 'We're almost ready to roll, boss. Give me a few days to suss out the line as far as Swindon and if it's clear, I think we can pull half a dozen trucks that far.'

'Take as many strong men as you need to get it done soon. It would be great if we could carry heavy loads that far without having to dodge up and down the roads.'

'Sure, though it'll have to be via Gloucester. The Severn Tunnel has been full of water for years!'

Lance was fond of teasing Ruddy Luddy. 'Railways? I thought you were into aircraft now?'

The ginger-haired man beamed. 'Funny you should say that! When we fetched those caravans yesterday, I made a quick visit to Cardiff Airport and checked on the fuel storage tanks. Most were empty, but they'd had jet fuel in them, anyway. Stuff like kerosene, no good for anything except stoves.'

'So what's the big news?' asked Lance.

'One tank was full – with aviation gasoline! A few thousand gallons of Avgas!'

Brennan actually smiled. 'Is it any good after five years?'

'It was full to the brim when I climbed up and dipped it. The rod was still in place and the manhole bolted down to keep it airtight.'

Mervyn looked suspiciously at the tubby engineer. 'Great for our motorcycles and small generators, as well as cars, if it's still OK. But you're not even thinking about finding a plane to put it in?'

Ruddy shrugged. 'No harm in experimenting. There should be a whole fleet of little aircraft over at the Flying Club on the other side of the runway. We could fuel one up and Lance could at least see if it would taxi up and down.'

'Thanks a million! It's not as easy as that, trying to start an aero-engine after five years,' grunted Lance.

Brennan held up a large hand. 'Alright, let's leave it for now. The railway is a bigger priority.'

But Bruce couldn't resist getting in the last word. 'Sure, boss – but wouldn't it be nice being able to fly over the countryside and see when those German buggers are coming?'

Privately, Brennan thought it would be a great idea, but for now there was more pressing business. The Cambridge contingent were ready to start dismantling their electronic workshops and other technical facilities. They were going to be transported piecemeal back to Cardiff and with the threat of another attack from the coast at some unknown time, the sooner they started, the better. The rest of the meeting was devoted to the logistics of shuttling trucks back and forth and worried about diesel supplies, Brennan wanted a rail-tanker brought down from Severn Tunnel Junction, if Ruddy could get his locomotive up and running.

When they broke up for a meal at midday, Lance wandered off with assumed nonchalance and made his way to the radio caravan. Slipping inside, he found Gwen just signing off her morning session and putting on a long-playing tape loop of nineties popular music to last through the lunch break.

This was the first time he had spoken to her alone since she returned, as she had kept very much to herself these past couple of days.

'Just wanted to say how glad I was that you came back with us, Gwen,' he opened, rather lamely.

She looked back at him wanly. Without her usual make-up, apart from a hint of lipstick, she looked very pale and with her hair dragged back through a ring at the nape of her neck, she was not her habitual glamorous self. Still, he thought, she was probably the best-looking woman left in Britain and risking a rebuff, he slipped an arm around her shoulders. This time she did not shrug it off, but laid her cheek against his shoulder.

'I made right fool of myself, didn't I, sonny boy?' she murmured.

He grinned as he rested his own face against the top of her head.

'Well, you don't seem to be exactly flavour of the month in certain quarters, old girl. How are things in that direction?'

'What do you expect, Lance? I've blotted my copybook in a big way . . . and can you blame him?'

'I gather you're not – er, well you know?' said Lance diffidently, fishing carefully for some indication of his chances.

Gwen lifted her face and for a second, a smile reminded him of her old self.

'No, Lance, we're nor "er" at all! I'm back sleeping in our old caravan, but the big man has found a bed somewhere else.'

'Maybe I'll call on you for a cup of cocoa one evening?' he said, emboldened by her answer.

'Cocoa? You'd be lucky, my lad. The damp saw that off years ago.'

'OK, I'll settle for tea and sympathy.'

Gwen smiled at him. 'I'm the one that needs the sympathy, Lance. I'm the scarlet woman of Cardiff Castle now. In years to come, I expect they'll say my ghost haunts the battlements!'

He bent and gave her swift kiss on the lips. 'If there's any haunting to be done, it'll be me, sweetheart – creeping around your caravan at midnight.'

She gave him a push, but the coquettish manner in which she did it, sent him off to look for his meal with a smile on his handsome face.

Spurred on by Brennan's exhortations, Bruce Ludlow took a working party that same afternoon to his precious locomotive, sitting in a huge prefabricated building that had been part of a steelworks near Newport. Like most of the Welsh steel industry, it had been driven out of business by foreign competition some time before the plague hit the world, but most of the rolling mills and other machinery were still there, rusting away all the faster since half the huge roof had been ripped off by gales. Thankfully, the old oil-fired locomotive, earmarked by the company receivers for sale to a preservation society, had been tucked away in a corner where the adjacent walls and roof were intact, so it had escaped most of the rain. It had spent many years shifting long trucks piled with steel billets and rolled rods from the mills to assembly yards some distance away, where the main line sent a spur through the perimeter fence into the works. Another smaller building had caught fire and collapsed across the track a few hundred yards from the main mill and most of Ruddy's efforts had been in clearing the debris with a rescued JCB, so that the engine could be brought out to the shunting yard and from there to the main line. This afternoon, Bruce and four of his fellow railway enthusiasts arrived in an old Transit van filled with tools, to contemplate their next move.

'We know the loco will go, we've tried her up and down often enough,' observed Maldwyn. Though he had once been a financial adviser in Merthyr, he had also been a devotee of the Great Western Railway and a frequent visitor to the GWR Society in Didcot. In fact, it was his secret ambition now to see if any of the larger engines had survived at Didcot and might possibly be resuscitated.

'It's the main line that's going to be the problem,' said Ruddy, stating the obvious. 'We've checked it as far as Gloucester, but we need to survey the rest of the way, if we're hoping to get as far as Swindon.'

In previous months, they had constructed a small open railcar, little more than a diesel engine scavenged from a lorry, mounted on a four-wheeled platform. With this they had explored the main line as far as Gloucester, having to alter points with a crowbar and often remove obstacles from the line, the most common culprits being fallen trees. In Lydney Station, the line was blocked by an abandoned two-car motor-train, still with the remains of its dead driver at the controls and a few more mouldering corpses in the coaches. They had no way of starting it, but thankfully, they were able to bypass it on a parallel loop line. Their fear was that somewhere else, another defunct train would be standing on a stretch of single line, with no way of getting around it. Thankfully, there was no major obstruction as far as Gloucester and no collapsed bridges, which was Ruddy's other nightmare.

'So what are we going to do about it?' demanded Maldwyn.

'Why not fetch one of those oiltankers, as a test run,' said Bruce. 'Brennan's going to need a helluva lot of diesel, if there're ferrying all that stuff from Cambridge. It's easier than taking the road tanker back and forth to the Severn Tunnel to keep filling it up.'

As excited as small boys, the four men fired up their precious locomotive, which had a full bunker of fuel-oil from their previous exploits. The engine was bigger than the usual works shunter, as six or seven long platform trucks filled with new steel bars and rods needed plenty of muscle to move them. The loco was known as an 0-6-0 from its three coupled wheels each side. It carried its water in a pair of large saddle tanks and worked equally happily in either direction.

Within an hour they had steam up and with the four of them crowded on the footplate, they moved out of the works on to the main line, which used to carry a huge volume of passenger traffic from Carmarthen to Paddington – and in the more distant past, from the Irish ferries at Fishguard.

'We're off, lads – give us a celebratory blast, Maldwyn!' exulted Ruddy. The Great Western fan gave a few blasts on the whistle as they cautiously rattled over the points on to the main line. The sound was more like a flatulent cow, as though the rest of the machinery worked well, five years desolation had done something evil to the acoustics.

The eight-mile journey went all too quickly for the delighted crew and soon they entered the sidings, a wilderness of rusted tracks, buried in rank grass and tall weeds. The junction was where the main line split, one branch entering the long tunnel under the Severn estuary, the other running along the north bank of the river to Gloucester. In the heyday of the rail system, it was a busy marshalling yard and numerous parallel tracks still lurked amongst the smothering vegetation.

'We've got to get her across there.' Bruce Ludlow pointed at a line of ten tanker wagons standing against the buffers on one siding. By dint of much levering of points by Maldwyn and his helpers, Ruddy manoeuvred the locomotive on to the right track. Getting extremely filthy from thick red rust mixed with black oil, they uncoupled the end tanker from its fellows and hitched it to the front of 'Ivor the Engine', as they had decided to christen their new toy.

Releasing the long brake-handle on the wagon needed much swearing, sweating and blows from a sledgehammer, as years of corrosion had seized it, but eventually Ruddy opened his regulator and to the cheers of the others, the tanker moved slowly away from its fellows, with strident squeals from its long-neglected axle-boxes.

Cautiously, they hauled the precious cargo back along the line and went past the steelworks and carried on towards Cardiff. Ruddy had checked this part of the line on their buggy and knew that they couldn't get right into Cardiff Central, as a building right against the line had been involved in the fire-storm that had destroyed much of the city. One wall of the five-storeyed office-block had crumpled right across the track and to clear the mountain of debris would have needed weeks of work with bulldozers, as well as having to re-lay a new section of the damaged lines.

'We'll heave-to at the container depot,' decided Bruce as he slowed to a crawl when they approached a retail park a couple of miles outside the city centre. The main line passed close behind the park, where the long-legged gantries of a container yard still stood like yellow storks.

Luddy took his train on to a short loop and stopped in a spot where their road-tanker could come alongside. Maldwyn unhitched and Ivor was puffed out the other way, back on to the main line. They had a discussion about whether to leave the engine in Cardiff, but as their van was in Newport, they made that the excuse for another ride back up the line. As they were about to leave, Fred, one of the other men, spotted a guard's van standing at the end of one of the container spurs.

'Why not take that with us? If we're going on longer journeys, we could kip out in it, to save taking a tent.'

Again with behaviour that was more like a schoolboys' outing, they seized their new toy and with Maldwyn and Fred on the rear platform of the van, they set off for Newport to put Ivor to bed.

*

After the evening meal, another Cabinet meeting was held in the keep. There was a lot to discuss, as Cambridge had been on the radio earlier and reported that they were sending six lorries filled with technical equipment down the next day. They only had about ten decent-sized trucks and were not too well off for diesel, so Brennan, having heard of Ruddy's success in bringing more fuel by rail, decided to send them a new supply by means of Cardiff's road-tanker.

'We could do with another of those, there must be a few knocking around somewhere,' he suggested. Alfred Ashe actually volunteered to take a party to commandeer one the next day, an unusual gesture from one who was generally reluctant to offer his services for anything physical.

'Has Strickland any more news of the Jerries?' asked Beverley.

'Nothing new, many of them seem to have pulled back further south into Essex, where it's harder for her spies to keep track of them. It's too far for VHF contact, though she's putting some guys halfway to relay messages.'

'Essex is where Colchester is,' said Lance. 'I wonder if they're after the military stuff, like we suggested?'

'Almost certainly, after the trouncing we gave them,' grunted Brennan. 'This guy Fischer isn't daft, especially if he's ex-*Bundeswehr*. He'll be collecting all the firepower he can lay his hands on. Their weak point is communications, thank God.'

'Makes it all the more urgent for us to get down to Aldershot!'

As he spoke, Mervyn ran his fingers over his beard, which he had trimmed neatly since their escapade in Somerset. He had also had a haircut and Brennan wondered if it was because the old dog had finally succumbed to Fay Morgan, who made no secret of her partiality for the doctor.

'I thought of going within the next week,' he answered. 'We can tank up Strickland's trucks when they arrive and turn them around the next day to get another load of whatever she wants to send down. Then we can spend the next few days finishing our trawl of the valleys, hopefully getting some more good towing vehicles and a couple of low-loaders. After that, we take a convoy up to Hampshire and Salisbury to see what we can find.'

Bruce Ludlow as usual, was brimming with bright ideas. 'Look, if you bring whatever you liberate back to Swindon, by then maybe I can get Ivor the Engine up that far. Give me a couple of days to explore the track beyond Gloucester. I can take half a dozen chaps, a truckload of tools and the JCB on a flat wagon to deal with any nasty obstructions. We've even got a guard's van to camp out in now!'

'How are you going to bring vehicles back, Luddy?' asked Lance.

'Easy! I saw a line of empty car-transporter wagons at the Severn Tunnel! And there's plenty of flat-bed wagons for guns and anything else you fancy. You just get 'em alongside the line at Swindon. Providing there's no bridges down, I'll bring them home for you!'

His enthusiasm was infective and after some more discussion about the details, it was agreed that Bruce would go off in the morning to survey the rest of the track.

'Now what about this immigration from Cambridge?' demanded Mervyn, who saw himself as Director of Social Services as well as Chief Medical Officer. 'We're already overstretched for accommodation in the castle, with these extra folk from Glastonbury. They could sleep in more caravans, if we fetched them, but the kitchens and the ablutions can't cope properly with many more.'

'There'll be a total of about three hundred, when they all come – including about twenty small children,' announced Liz, on whom fell much of the organising for the babies' welfare.

'That'll almost double our population!' exclaimed Fay Morgan. 'No way can we have all those in the castle.'

This sparked off another round of suggestions and argument, but finally a consensus of opinion decided that the part of the university that had escaped fire should be given over to Cambridge.

'They should feel at home there, with so many academics amongst them!' grunted Alfred Ashe. It was true that the main building of the university, only a few hundred yards from the castle, was an imposing classical building of white Portland stone, containing innumerable rooms off its long corridors.

'They've even got the old Student's Union across the road for a dining room and kitchens,' added Lance. 'They were the only two bits of the college to survive the fires.'

'What about all their electronics stuff and machine tools that they're shipping down here?' asked Mervyn.

'A lot of it can be put in the science blocks in the same building,' suggested Ruddy Luddy. 'We'll have to find them another decent diesel generator, but we know where to look now that we've done a recce of the hospitals.'

'And any heavier machinery can go in the warehouse next to our store on Western Avenue,' said Brennan. 'That's only a couple of miles away, we've got plenty of transport now.'

'While it lasts,' corrected Alfred, reverting to his more usual gloomy self. 'I still say we should be collecting and breeding horses, ready for when your fancy vehicles all pack up. You don't need a battery to start a carthorse!'

Bruce nodded sagely. 'Point taken, Alf. But I think we've got a year or so left in the trucks yet. That's the beauty of my locomotive, it'll work for as long as the fuel oil lasts – and by then, we'll have got a coal-fired loco going.'

Brennan nipped further flights of fancy in the bud with a demand for hard planning of timetables and duty rosters for the next few days. When this was thrashed out, they adjourned, most going across to the dining hall for a pint of home-brew or a glass of fruit wine. Long before midnight, almost everyone had turned in, but Lance waited quietly in a corner, nursing a beer until he saw Brennan leave. The younger man stayed a few more minutes, then padded out into the castle bailey and made his way across to the eastern side where all the caravans were lined up in rows. Some still showed dim lights behind their drawn curtains, as there were plenty of replacements available for their small gas cylinders. Lance tapped softly on the door of one of these and in a moment it opened, to reveal Gwen Sutcliffe in white silk pyjamas, rescued from an undamaged boutique in Monmouth.

'Lance, I guessed it had to be you!' she whispered in mock annoyance. 'You never give up, do you?'

'Never! Can I come in?'

She stood aside and pulled him in, shutting the door with exaggerated care. 'What'll the neighbours think?' she hissed dramatically.

Lance tried to slip an arm around her shoulders, but she pushed him away and pointed to one of the long couches that had not yet been pulled out to form a bed.

'Sit there and behave yourself, boy!' she commanded.

When he reluctantly moved away from her and did as she ordered, Gwen sat on the seat opposite, just out of range of his hands.

'Are you doing the rounds of all the unattached young women?' she demanded.

'Only the most beautiful ones – and they're in pretty short supply.'

His smile lit up his face and she felt a lurch of desire, against her better judgement. Though he was fair instead of dark, he reminded her of the lean and handsome young men that used to smile out of French movie magazines.

'No point in asking what you want, Lance,' she said with disconcerting directness. 'Your hormones are making the van quiver!'

Lance grinned again. 'I thought you might want a little TLC, Gwen. You've had a rough time lately, what with the big man swatting Jolly Roger off you, then giving you the elbow himself.'

She reached out and gave his ear a painful tweak. 'Less of that, young man! How d'you know it wasn't me that gave him the elbow?' she exclaimed indignantly.

'The gossip in this place is usually pretty accurate,' he replied smoothly.

'Well, for once it's wrong! If you must know, the decision to cool things was mutual,' snapped Gwen fiercely.

Lance lifted his hands defensively. 'OK, OK! I just thought I'd check that you were all right.'

'At midnight, with me half-undressed? Pull the other one, Lance!'

Again he gave her an impish smile. 'I'd gladly do that, sweet, if you'd let me get a bit nearer.' He quickly moved across to her couch and pulled her to him, but she turned her face away and he found his lips buried in her hair. She resisted, then sagged against him and began to cry softly. This was the most effective weapon she could have used, as although Lance was not actually bent on ravishment, he had hoped for a rapid surrender. Now with a weeping woman in his arms, his ardour was suddenly turned into gentle sympathy. Stroking her golden hair, he kissed the top of her head.

'Come on, love, it'll all come right somehow.'

Gwen shook her head and burrowed against his shirt-front. 'I was taken in by that bastard Mellars and fell for the line he was shooting,' she murmured. 'I can't believe I was that stupid!' She raised her head and stared up at Lance. 'God, how things have changed! When I was in with the London set years ago, I ate people like him for breakfast.'

'What about people like me, love?'

Her volatile mood changed rapidly and she smiled up at him. 'You're fine, Lance. I always was a sucker for a good-looking guy! That's how I lost my virtue so easily to bloody Roger the Lodger.' She sniffed the last of her tears away. 'And it's why I fell for Brennan, too. Big, masterful, dominant – all the things that turn me on.'

Lance was silent, not knowing how to respond to that one. Though he greatly admired the Boss and was totally loyal to him in anything other than women, he didn't want to queer his own pitch with Gwen by extolling Brennan's obvious virtues. Lost for words, he reverted to behaviour that had served him well since his student days. Sliding both arms around her slender body, he kissed her full on the mouth and groaned, 'Oh God, Gwen, you're so bloody beautiful! I'm crazy about you!'

She stiffened, then relaxed and took his face in both her hands, to seek his lips with her open mouth.

'Here we go again!' she murmured, half to herself. 'But why the hell not, if the other one doesn't want me any more?'

Though Lance had assumed that Brennan had taken himself off to bed, he had in fact gone up to the keep to check on the radio watch. There was no real need for this, but he was restless and knew he wouldn't sleep for an hour or two. A permanent radio vigil was kept in case Cambridge or one of the coastal lookouts sent an emergency signal and a rota was organised to have an operator listening throughout the twenty-four hours. Tonight, he was mildly surprised to find Jan Beelan sitting in solitary state in the radio room, listening to the slight hum from the live equipment.

'I felt it was right for me to do my share,' explained Jan in his impeccable English. 'I am so grateful for being rescued from those bastards and being given such a good welcome here.'

Brennan pulled up another chair and chatted to the Dutchman for a while, both to keep him company and to hear more about conditions on the mainland of Europe. Starved of any news from outside their part of Britain for five years, any description of life elsewhere was a welcome novelty.

'What happened to your government?' asked Brennan. 'Ours just emigrated early in the troubles – I'm not even sure where it went, though it was supposed to be North America.'

Jan shrugged. 'No one knows the truth. Our Royal Family was much less in the public eye than yours, but I think they died along with most of the population. Some of the ministers and senior army and police officers did their best to hold things together, but of course most of them died within a few weeks.'

'What was the last you heard of other countries? The radio links went on sporadically for a while here, but eventually went quiet.'

Jan Beelan shook his head sadly. 'You probably know more than me about that. Our newspapers and television stopped after about three weeks, when the power supply failed. There was an emergency radio service for about another week, as most survivors had battery-powered transistor radios – or radios in their cars. According to that, every country in the world was affected, as determined by their last radio transmissions, most of them asking for help.'

The two men fell silent, reliving the awful few weeks, five years ago.

'Did you lose a family, Jan?' asked Brennan, gently.

'A good wife and two children,' he replied soberly. 'I wish to God it had been me instead, but I suppose they would have a bad time trying to survive without me.'

'The same with me, a wife and two kids,' answered Brennan. 'As to the God you mention, I used to have a general sort of belief in him, but after this, I've become a devout atheist!'

The Dutchman nodded fervently. 'I know what you mean – if there is some supreme being, is he just perverse in causing so much suffering – or is he playing some sort of game with his creation, like a child pulling his toys to pieces? Either way, I want nothing to do with a God like that!'

They talked for a time, each finding in the other a similar philosophy and outlook on life. At one in the morning, Wayne appeared to start a new four-hour shift. As the two older men got up to leave, Brennan pointed at the equipment on the table, its pilot lights glowing green and red.

'You've never had so much as a whisper on that from anywhere else?' he asked.

The younger operator shook his head and Jan Beelen agreed.

'Since I've been standing watches, I've tried a number of times, searching the whole frequency band – but there's been absolutely nothing. The rest of the world is silent.'

They left the keep and clambered down the steep stone steps to the bailey, where the Dutchman said goodnight and went off to a bed somewhere in the West Range. There was a half-moon flitting in and out of drifting clouds and Brennan, still feeling too wide awake to sleep, sat on a low wall to contemplate the cosmos. The wall was the stump of a high rampart the Normans had built to reduce the size of the Roman fort to a more manageable area. As he rested his bottom on the stones, he wondered what man had cemented them together, all those centuries ago. He felt himself entering a descending spiral of morbid introspection and shook himself out of it by looking up at the sky, now all the clearer from the absence of street and city lights. Away from the moon, between clouds, he could see a myriad of stars and from dim memories of Army orienteering courses, he could still name some prominent navigational markers. They stared back at him, totally uncaring about Earth's predicament. Then he realised that the light that entered his eye from most of them, had left them long before the plague, when his wife and children were alive and happy.

The thought soured him and he dropped his gaze to ground level, just in time to hear a caravan door close softly a hundred yards away. There was now no light behind the window, but from its position, he knew it was the van he had shared until recently with Gwen Sutcliffe. His eyes, now well adapted by his star-gazing to the dim light from the lamp over the castle gate, saw a figure walking away, keeping to the grass to avoid crunching the gravel. As it passed between him and the distant bare bulb, he had no difficulty in recognising the silhouette as that of Lance Prichard.

Brennan sat where he was, trying to analyse his feelings. Strangely, he felt no urge to run after the younger man and fell him to the ground in a fit of jealous rage. Instead, he felt as if a disembodied hand was slowly drawing a line across the page of his life on which was recorded his time with Gwen Sutcliffe. He felt almost bemused because he had no anger or hatred for Lance, which he felt he should have, given that it was now so patently obvious that Gwen had wasted no time in changing partners once again.

Brennan sat quietly, listening to his own steady breathing and wondering why he was not beside himself with righteous anger. Earlier on that day, he had had a low-key, but none the less bitter conversation with Gwen, who seemed to feel that he was patronising her with his offer to forget what had happened in Glastonbury. He still yearned after the woman, but was it pure lust or did he love her as well? And was that ambiguous love now extinguished once and for all? He didn't know, but he felt suddenly older and more resigned. Lance was nearer Gwen's age, and she was always a sucker for a handsome face and a roguish smile – but was she going to make this a permanent affair or was it a quick flirt? He liked the man a lot and hoped that he wouldn't get hurt over this.

Wearily, he got up from the cold medieval stones and made his way back into the warren of rooms in the Victorian fantasy that was the West Range. As he found his bed in a room with three snoring men, he resolved that what he had seen tonight would remain locked in his head. He would say nothing to anyone, especially Lance. As sleep eventually came uneasily to him, it was not Gwen's face that hovered in his mind, but a long-dead wife who he missed more than ever before.

CHAPTER SIXTEEN

THE next few days were ones of strenuous activity for the Cardiff community. Teams went out to continue their scouring of fresh areas for material, concentrating on the once densely-populated ribbon settlements up the many valleys that stretched for thirty miles north of Cardiff. On the first day, Brennan deliberately sought out Lance Prichard and arranged to go with him and four others down into the Vale of Glamorgan. Here in addition to general scrounging, they wanted to check on Godfrey Traherne, taking him some more diesel for his tractor and Range Rover, as their promise to send the tanker down had been frustrated by the Glastonbury expedition.

Brennan felt that being with Lance might in some way avoid the danger of a schism that otherwise might develop between them. His odd feelings of the previous night had persisted, in that he felt not the slightest jealousy of the younger man. After all, he reasoned, Lance had made no move on Gwen until it was clear to everyone that Brennan had moved out. She had made it clear, both by her rapid alignment with Roger Mellars and by her spirited rejection of Brennan's offer of reconciliation, that she was her own woman and free to take up with whoever she fancied. Though part of his mind whispered that he was lying through his own teeth, Brennan decided that he was well rid of her and that Lance was welcome to try his luck.

Now they sat side by side in the front of a Ford Transit van and behaved as normally as on any other day. Brennan wondered covertly if Lance had any concealed guilt about cuckolding 'the Boss', as he called him, but there was no sign of tension in his easy conversation.

When they reached Traherne's farm, they were surprised by the transformation of the place. With the few gallons of fuel that they had left him on their first visit, the farmer had used his tractor to flail all the weeds in the lane and yard and had cut a couple of acres of hay in the nearest field. He had run out of diesel at that stage, but used an old horse-rake to collect the hay and make a rough rick in the yard, covered by a tarpaulin. His whole attitude was transformed from the defeated, apathetic figure they had met previously.

'You really kicked me back into life, Brennan!' he exclaimed, taking them into a house which was hardly recognisable as the squalid hovel that they had seen before. It was tidy and relatively clean, as was Godfrey himself, who had washed, shaved and abandoned his scruffy overall for a decent shirt, trousers and a flat cap. He was delighted with the new drums of fuel and repeated his intention to get the farm really working again, so that he could supply Cardiff with produce.

'It'll take some time, but I'll comb the deserted farms around here for anything I can grow or breed by next year,' he promised. 'I found a few fowls next door with new chicks, so I'll start raising them for eggs. I'll round up some of the stray cattle and bring them in – and some of the sheep, but it'll take time to get organised.'

Brennan promised to canvass in Cardiff for volunteers who would like to take up farming and they left Traherne in good spirits, especially as they brought him a dozen flagons of home-brew.

As they drove down the newly-cleared lane to the narrow country road to the deserted village, Lance unfolded the tattered map of the area and studied it closely.

'You know, we're not far from the airport. I was just wondering if there was anything in what Ruddy said about this aircraft idea. Daft as it sounds, why not take a look, as we're so near?'

Brennan was also intrigued by the idea, but played hard to get. 'You're off your head, like Bruce himself,' he grunted, but when they reached Cardiff International, he turned into the approach road and drove the van up to the front of the terminal building. It was a scene of utter desolation, with many of the large plate-glass panels of the Departure Hall smashed and a great swathe of blackened masonry above, where fire had spilled out of some of the windows of the offices above. Luggage trolleys lay overturned on the pavement and abandoned vehicles were dotted around the building. Lance pointed to the large public car park a few hundred yards away.

'Look at that – damn near full! Where've they all gone?'

Hundreds of cars lay rusting, waiting for owners who would never return. Brennan could see a few four-wheel drives amongst them and earmarked these for recovery at some time.

'I suppose when the plague started, many people who could afford it thought they'd escape overseas. Maybe some of them did, for all we know – though I doubt it.'

'The Flying Club is over on the other side,' said Mostyn, one of the other helpers, who had lived in the nearby town of Barry. He pointed across the main runway to a group of buildings, one of which was a small hangar.

Brennan looked around at the chaos in the terminal. 'Nothing for us here, boys. We may as well drive over there, it's a long walk.'

They took the van through the smashed checkpoint between the terminal building and the control tower and drove over the grass-grown parking apron and then across the main runway. On the other side, they saw that several small private aircraft had been wrecked by the bad weather, one crumpled on its collapsed wing, another actually blown bodily against a brick wall and a third upside down on the concrete.

'Doesn't look very hopeful,' said Mostyn.

'Let's try the hangar before we give up,' replied the ever-hopeful Lance. Part of the roof of the big corrugated iron shed had been stripped off and lay scattered around the apron. The big sliding doors were closed with a chain and padlock, but by now, the crew were expert at breaking and entering. With a crowbar from the van, they snapped the chain and levered back the rusted doors enough to slip inside.

Three small planes were inside, two of which were irreparably damaged by parts of the roof falling on them. The other seemed intact, a bright yellow biplane of ancient appearance.

'Bloody hell, that must be almost as old as Mervyn!' exclaimed Lance, enthusiastically.

'What is it, a Wright Flyer?' asked one of the other lads incredulously. Lance was walking around the small plane, his hands touching the dusty lower wing almost affectionately.

'It's a Tiger Moth, a DH 82! De Havilland built thousands of them in the thirties and forties.'

Brennan looked dubiously at the fragile-looking aircraft. He had flown in a few small Army planes, but nothing as archaic as this.

'It's a museum piece, Lance. Surely no possible use to us?'

The fair-haired man came back from a circuit round the plane, a big grin on his face.

'I flew one of these just once – it belonged to the instructor who taught me to fly on Cessnas. Dead easy to handle, it was one of the main trainers before the last World War.'

Brennan looked from Lance to the plane and back again. 'Are you serious about this? You reckon you could fly this Yellow Peril?'

Lance sobered up a little from his sudden euphoria. 'If the damn thing will work, yes! If we get decent gas for it and check out the engine. Ruddy and especially Beverley could do that – Bev's a wizard with the internal combustion engine.'

'Cars, yes! But this is an aircraft engine' objected Mostyn.

Lance shook his head. 'These Moths have what's essentially a car engine, only upside down, with the crankshaft at the top. The Gipsy Major is just a four-cylinder motor, giving about 145 horsepower, if I remember rightly.'

'Is that a lot?' asked Brennan, who was no expert on machinery.

'Put it this way – Bev's motorbike can go a damn sight faster than this, which does about eighty on a good day with a following wind!'

Brennan walked up to the plane and peered into one of the two open cockpits. 'Looks pretty crude to me. But you think it's worth pursuing the idea. Would you trust yourself up in this thing?'

Lance shrugged. 'As I say, depends on whether we can start it and how it sounds when it's going. At least they're magneto-fired, so there should be no problem with ignition. The prop has to be swung to start them, no batteries needed.'

They stood talking for a while and Lance couldn't resist clambering into the rear cockpit and fiddling with the controls. The rudder, elevators and ailerons all seemed to waggle satisfactorily and for a moment

Brennan was afraid that Lance was going to start making 'Brrrrm-brrrrm' noises like a small boy!

Eventually, they tore him away from his new toy and levered the hangar doors shut. 'The hardest part may be getting these fully open,' quipped Maldwyn, pointing to the five year's accumulation of rust, leaves and dirt that clogged the runners of the big doors.

'Let's see if Bev can get the bloody engine started, before we worry about getting it out,' growled Brennan, as they walked back to the van – but secretly, he was as excited as Lance at the possibility, however slender, of having an eye in the sky.

When Brennan returned to Cardiff, he found that the convoy from Cambridge had arrived and was parked all along Castle Street. It was too late to start unloading them at the university or the Western Avenue warehouses, so the drivers and their escorts were taken off for a meal while beds were found for them in spare caravans.

Brennan found two faces he recognised, as John Lovatt and Edgar Lambert – Strickland's lieutenants, were in charge of the convoy.

They sat with the Cardiff management committee to talk while they ate, Brennan being anxious to hear of the situation in East Anglia.

'It's too damn quiet, after that battle you had,' said Lovatt. 'But I'm afraid it might be the quiet before the storm.'

'The boat people have pulled right back into the coastal towns in Suffolk and Essex,' added Lambert. 'Our observers can't get near enough to see what's happening in built-up areas, like they could in open country.'

Lovatt, the former railway worker, put down his knife and fork on an empty plate and gave a satisfied sigh.

'Good grub, this! I think I'm going to like living here.' After a long swallow of the local ale, he added to what his companion had described. 'Those bastards are up to something, though. They've got more vehicles now – that horse and cart caper was bloody ludicrous! Our chaps have spotted a number of military trucks going between Colchester and Felixstowe during the last couple of weeks.'

'Any sign of armoured vehicles or guns?' asked Mervyn.

'None reported, but our guys can't get further south than Colchester.

God knows what's happening down there. If only we had a spotter plane!'

Brennan and Lance exchanged glances and grinned at each other, but said nothing to the others. For a few moments, Brennan had forgotten all about Gwen and Lance, though at other times, it took a conscious effort to push them from his mind. He had not seen his former partner this evening, for once she seemed to be keeping well out of sight.

The discussion turned to settling the Cambridge emigrants in their new habitat at the university in Cathays Park. They had brought a mass of electrical and light engineering equipment and were anxious to see it installed.

'We'll take the trucks back as soon as we've unloaded – there's a whole lot more to bring down,' said Lambert.

'We'll have to fix up your power supply as soon as we can,' offered Beverley. 'There's a nice diesel generator in Whitchurch Hospital, about five miles away. Now that we've liberated a road crane, we can swing it out and move it down to the college fairly quickly.'

The technical discussion went on for another hour and they agreed to add another ten trucks from Cardiff to the returning cavalcade, so that virtually everything could be shipped back from Cambridge on the next load, including enough sleeping bags, crockery and utensils to allow the refugees to camp out in the university until they were better organised.

'We'll collect all the buses we can find to bring your folks down as soon as you're ready,' advised Brennan. 'We don't want to be caught napping by some sudden onslaught by the Jerries.'

As the evening wore on, with endless discussion and planning, Brennan found his attention wandering, He wondered how Ruddy Luddy was faring on the railway and whether his dream of clearing the track all the way to Swindon would be fulfilled. Knowing the ebullient fellow, he suspected that if Ruddy got through to Swindon, his next target would be Didcot, Reading and maybe even London! Contemplating such ambitious plans made Brennan think of their expedition this afternoon and when the meeting finally broke up after dark, to let the weary people from Cambridge get to their beds, he cornered Lance and Beverley before they left.

'What about this crazy idea of Ruddy's to see if we can get an aircraft off the ground?' he demanded. Lance explained to Beverley their discovery of an intact Tiger Moth at the airport. 'Ruddy says that one of the storage tanks is chock full of aviation gasoline, so there should be plenty of fuel. Do you think it's feasible to get the engine running, Bev?'

As he spoke, he produced two paperback books and held them up. 'I found these in the cockpit, if they're any help.'

The other two saw that the volumes were an Operator's Handbook and a Workshop Manual for the DH 82 and the Gipsy Major engine.

Beverley's face lit up at the prospect of delving into a novel variety of internal combustion engine. 'We can certainly have a look. If the plane's been under cover, I don't see why it shouldn't still be airworthy.'

'The motor's a glorified car engine, Bev,' encouraged Lance. 'It's nineteen-thirties vintage, even if it's a forties manufacture.'

The two began an earnest discussion about inverted crankcases, scavenge pumps and magnetos, so Brennan drifted away intending to find his bed, as tomorrow promised to be another hard day. As he reached the corridor leading from the dining hall, someone came out of the shadows and spoke to him.

'Brennan, can I have a word with you, please?' It was Liz Peterson, who had obviously been waiting to waylay him. She wore a dark dress and in the gloomy passage, her face stood out as a pale oval beneath her black hair.

'Sure, Liz, what's the problem?' A few yards away, an outer door was open into the castle ward and he gestured towards it. 'Let's get some light on the subject.'

He ushered her down the few steps until they stood on a flagstoned area in the pale moonlight, as last evening's clouds had vanished.

'I wondered about the Cambridge children, as they're coming soon.'

Brennan wondered why he had the feeling that her concern was an excuse to speak to him alone.

'What about them, Liz?' he said gently. They started to walk slowly along the gravelled area, then on to the dry grass towards the lofty mound that supported the keep.

'Even with our own kids, there won't be all that many youngsters here. It seems wrong to separate theirs from ours by keeping them up in the college.'

Though this was a reasonable concern, it had not yet occurred and there could be no urgency about the matter.

'You're probably right, Liz. We'll discuss it at the next management meeting – and I can mention it to the Cambridge people before they go back tomorrow. Obviously, all the kids must go to school together, whatever else happens.'

Though this should have closed the subject, the brunette nurse continued to walk closely alongside him, steering him up the inside of the west wall, away from the occupied buildings and the caravans parked beyond the keep.

'It's a lovely night, Brennan. That moon up there doesn't give a damn for our troubles down here on earth, does it?'

This was so like his own thoughts the previous night that he smiled in the gloom at her similar sentiments. Whether she saw this as she looked up at him or merely sensed it, Liz slipped her arm through his.

'This place is like a colony of bees – every individual knows each other's business almost instantly.'

Though apparently obscure, he knew exactly what she was trying to convey. Not only was the breakup between Gwen and himself now common knowledge, but it seemed that Lance's filling of that particular vacuum was also buzzing around the castle grapevine.

'That's life, Liz,' he replied gruffly. 'Compared to all our other problems, it's of little importance.'

She squeezed his arm firmly. 'Relationships are always important. None of us can afford to be alone for ever. We all lost someone, but that shouldn't stop us starting over again.'

The next few steps took them into the shadow of the high curtain wall. The light over the main gate was a far-away glimmer and abruptly, Liz stopped walking and swung against his front. He was a full head taller and she had to look up to see his face.

'I'm so very fond of you, Brennan,' she said softly. 'You must know that, surely?'

He looked down, his mind a turmoil of images. His wife, his children, Gwen, rolled past his inner eye like slides projected on a wall and then there was a blank, which seemed to be his future. Gradually, the serene features of Liz Peterson filled the mental screen and he sighed. The prospect of a moonlit night, a very attractive woman and no possible reason to hang back, pervaded his consciousness. Slowly, his free arm went round her shoulders and his head dipped to meet her lips. It was a long kiss, but not one full of sexual passion – rather of mutual compassion and a promise of a pleasant future.

When they broke away, Brennan said gently, 'It's going to be a long day tomorrow, Liz, and it's getting late.'

She smiled and made no reply, demanding nothing more. Taking his other arm, she gently moved him back along the way they had come and when they neared the entrances to the accommodation wing, she released his arm.

'I go this way, Brennan. See you in the morning!' She slipped away like a wraith, leaving him standing, staring after her.

He sighed again. 'Now what am I getting myself into?' he murmured to himself.

CHAPTER SEVENTEEN

THE days of the week meant almost nothing now, apart from a convenient way of marking off the interval between events. Most people neither knew nor cared what the day or date was, as nothing hung on the definition. Certainly Sunday had no significance, except for a tiny handful of older people, who joined the deranged Canon Gilbey in one of the small rooms of the castle for what passed as a religious service. All the rest, with the possible exception of their two Muslims, had abandoned any belief in a God, after the catastrophe had deprived them of all their family and friends.

As there was no radio, television or printed publications, no one knew any longer exactly what the date was. Brennan had started keeping a kind of diary, recording all the main daily events of the community, but as his starting point was rather arbitrarily somewhere around the shortest day three years before, it was only accurate to within about a week or two. At least most people knew what year it was, by the number of seasons that had passed since the plague – and a former keen yachtsman had several years before worked out the moment of noon, so that their clocks and watches were roughly correct. How closely this corresponded with timekeeping in other settlements, Brennan never knew, though since their contacts with Cambridge, the latter had synchronised with 'Cardiff Time' for purposes of radio schedules.

Using this, it was Tuesday morning when the Cambridge convoy set off for home, promising to be back with the remainder of their equipment on Friday. A number of Cardiff men went with them, driving the additional trucks that Brennan had promised. A few hours after they left, a battered white van arrived, bearing a jubilant Bruce Ludlow and his team, announcing that they had indeed reached Swindon and returned to tell the tale. Ruddy sounded like Livingstone having penetrated the deepest jungles of Africa.

'We made it, Brennan! You bring your stuff to the main line near the Railway Museum there and we can bring it all back here for you in half a day!'

After the heroes had recounted their story half a dozen times – especially the episode where they pulled aside a collapsed footbridge with a chain attached to Ivor the Engine – Lance and Beverley told him about their find at the Aero Club. They almost had to restrain the man from dashing out to his Transit van that moment and racing off to the airport. 'I told you so!' he chanted. 'If Lance says he can fly the damned thing, we can get it going for him.'

After a more sober discussion, Brennan agreed that a team should go down to look at the plane that afternoon to make a 'feasibility study' as he put it. Lance, Beverley, Ruddy and Parsons, their depressed motor mechanic were the obvious choices, but Brennan suggested that Jan Beelan might also be useful, having been an auto-electrical engineer. Brennan decided not to go with them, much as he was intrigued by the possibility of a spotter plane, but he wanted to keep an eye on the new Cambridge enclave in the university, as well as make some plans for the expedition to Aldershot next week.

John Lovatt had stayed behind with three technicians from Cambridge, to see to the disposition of some of the machinery they had brought and Brennan spent a couple of hours up there, with a working gang to help push, pull and carry the equipment that he hoped in the long term, would make such an improvement to their facilities.

He also wanted to be fully employed, mentally and physically, to stop himself brooding about Gwen – and perhaps to keep out of the castle as much as possible, until he had clarified his own mind about Liz Peterson. After her absence the previous evening, Gwen had appeared as usual this morning and started up her disc-jockey and newscaster role as if nothing unusual had happened during the past week or two.

He passed her in the breakfast queue and she gave him a smile and a 'Hiya, Bren!' in a manner which seemed to have no strain or guile in it whatsoever. The sight of her beautiful face gave his stomach a lurch, against all his determination to put her out of his mind. When he went to a table with his fried eggs and toast, he found that his heart was beating faster than it should – and cursed his hormones and his weakness at being so affected.

As he finished eating and sat with a large mug of tea – Mavis Strickland had sent them two chests of Orange Pekoe – Liz Peterson slipped into a chair on the other side of the table. The mess hall was emptying now, but there were still plenty of people about, who cast knowing looks at the pair of them. Brennan cursed the incestuous atmosphere of their little community, where everyone's business seemed instantly to be everyone else's.

'You won't forget that business about the kids at the next meeting, will you?' she said. There was no coyness in her words or manner, but Brennan felt that her meaning was as clear as if she had 'I really fancy you!' tattooed across her forehead.

They talked for a few moments and again there was nothing in her words that was out of place in the smooth running of the community, but he felt her big, dark eyes fixed on his face like a pair of searchlights. Brennan was still unsure of what he wanted to do about the situation – he really liked her, he enjoyed her company, he thought her very attractive and he would be more than happy to go to bed with her, but something held him back from the inevitable commitment. He wasn't sure whether it was because of Gwen or because of Liz and he became annoyed at his own indecision. Managing to bottle up anything other than polite, amiable conversation, he waited a decent interval before he swallowed the rest of his tea and made an excuse that duty called. They parted with mutual smiles, her eyes giving him a last caress as they went their separate ways. Brennan marched off to the radio room to check for any messages, then went up to the college, through the profusion of late spring undergrowth in what used to be the formal gardens of the civic centre.

He stayed far longer than he intended, helping them to clear space in the old research and teaching laboratories and to position lathes, drills, computers, welders and a whole collection of obscure equipment in the various rooms. With John Lovatt, whom he found to be a most intelligent and sensitive man, they explored the ramifications of the building, which had housed most of the original university almost a century ago. They patrolled the long passages, peered into a hundred rooms and crossed the road to look at the large Student's Union which could provide cooking and dining space for Cambridge's three hundred.

While Brennan was acting like a latter-day estate agent, the putative new Air Force was shoving aside the rusted door of the hangar at Rhoose airport. With gleaming eyes, Beverley and Jan had the engine cowling off within minutes and together with Parsons, were poking about the Gipsy Major with grunts of appreciation and satisfaction. Ruddy was checking the integrity of the fabric-covered fuselage and wings, whilst Lance was in the cockpit, studying the handbook with a frown of concentration as he checked the controls and instruments.

An hour later, they stood on the floor of the hangar and contemplated the plane, which sat there like a great yellow butterfly.

'Needs a day's work on the engine and the control system – cleaning and lubricating,' proclaimed Beverley. 'Flush through the fuel flow from tanks to carburettor – old gasoline gets sticky.'

'And the ignition system,' added Jan, staking out his expert territory. 'Check the magneto, contact points, sparking plugs. Then we could give her a swing and see what happens.'

Bruce Ludlow, who had been investigating the side-room that lead off the hangar, pointed to its door. 'There's drums of the proper lubricating oil in there. We need to drain the old stuff and refill her, then get some of that aviation spirit from the other side of the airport. We've got a small tank trailer in Western Avenue that would do for that.'

Jan Beelan contributed some news about communications. 'The usual aircraft band VHF is installed – we would need a suitable battery, the one in there is completely dead, unless it will take a recharge. I can take it home tonight and try it.'

'What range would that give us?' asked Lance.

'A good many miles in line of sight – though I suppose this machine won't get very high,' answered Beelan.

Ruddy grinned. 'If Lance can get it off the ground at all!'

'You get the bloody engine doing four thousand revs and I'll get off the ground all right, mate!'

'How far can this thing fly on a tankful?' asked Parsons, the novelty of an aircraft engine lifting him out of his usual apathy.

'There are two tanks, holding a total of about seventy-eight litres,' answered Lance. 'That's supposed to give a range of about 250 miles.'

Beverley decided to call it a day. 'Right, we'll be back tomorrow with the fuel trailer, a load of tools and Lance's helmet and goggles!'

'Just call me "Biggles",' responded Lance, but all the others looked at him blankly, the name meaning nothing to them.

On the day before the second Cambridge convoy was due to return, Lance and Beverley invited Brennan to leave his 'boss duties' as they called them and come down to the airport for a couple of hours to witness their attempt to move the Tiger Moth. The aviation team had spent two days fiddling with the machine and when Brennan drove his Land-Rover behind their van to the old hangar across from the terminal, he saw that the doors were pushed wide open.

'We needed the Ford to shove them apart, the tracks were so rusted – but I doubt if we can ever close them again,' explained Ruddy.

The yellow aircraft had been pushed to the centre of the hangar facing the doors. Lance clambered into the rear cockpit and Brennan had a momentary stab of concern. What if the damned thing blew up in a sheet of flame, even if it never got off the ground? The fact that the pilot was sleeping with his own long-time lover, never entered his head.

There was an exchange of shouts as the other men scuttled back and forth around the plane. With chocks under the wheels, Bruce Ludlow stood ready to swing the propeller and with more shouting and a yell of 'Contact!' from Lance, he heaved mightily on one of the wooden blades. Brennan had another attack of déjà vu, in that he suddenly felt he was watching one of the old war films, which were already ancient when he had seen them on television as a youth.

Nothing happened – nor the next time or the next. With mounting disappointment, Brennan looked at the faces of the others, but curiously, they seemed not in the slightest abashed. On the next swing, there was a stuttering rattle, a cloud of blue smoke, then a hesitant rumble and finally a roar as the engine took up its revolutions. Having leapt backwards out of harm's way, Ruddy was grinning like a Cheshire cat.

'Takes a few swings when she's cold,' he yelled. Brennan realised that this was not the first time they had started the engine, but presumably he had been invited down to see if the Yellow Peril would actually move. Lance let the engine warm up and then throttled back to a steady tick-over. Beverley moved across to Brennan's side.

'This is the crunch part, according to Lance – seeing if it'll taxi properly,' he shouted.

The pilot stuck a fist over the side of the cockpit, with the thumb upraised. Ruddy and their mechanic pulled the ropes which took away the wheel chocks, then moved to hold the wing tips. The engine revved up and the propeller blurred into a red and silver circle. Slowly, with the men steadying the quivering wings, the plane moved out into the open air for the first time in over five years. A cheer went up from the watchers, as the plane taxied out on to the weed-infested concrete and headed for the lane that took it towards the runways. The main mile-long landing strip, once big enough for jumbos, went east–west, but a shorter runway crossed it at almost right angles.

As the plane speeded up above walking pace, Ruddy and the mechanic let go of the wings and stood while the others caught them up to watch the Tiger Moth bump its way westwards.

'What's he going to do, make a few passes back and forth along the runway?' asked Brennan.

Beverley shrugged. 'I don't know. It's mainly to make sure that the engine will keep running for a decent length of time.'

They watched as Lance reached the cross runway and heard the engine note increase even more. The biplane turned on to the concrete and hurried down to the other end, turned round and came back up.

'The engine sounds great!' enthused Jan Beelan. 'Not a single misfire. We put in a new set of plugs we found in the stores.'

The Moth turned again and went back down the track, but more slowly this time, and when it reached the junction with the main runway, it swivelled right.

'Hey, what's this?' demanded Bruce Ludlow, holding his wet finger up. 'There's an easterly breeze . . . surely he's not. . . .'

But he was! The roar of the engine increased as Lance opened the throttle and the little plane bounced along the runway. Its tail-wheel lifted from the ground and in what seemed only a few more yards, its bicycle-sized undercarriage left the grassy concrete as the Moth wobbled into the air and headed for the far end of the runway and the cliff edge beyond, below which the grey waters of the Bristol Channel offered a damp conclusion to any faulty take-off.

'He's up, the mad bugger!' shouted Brennan, his fears for Lance's safety surging back. The others were cheering and he had the suspicion that they knew all along that the pilot intended getting airborne if the engine seemed to be behaving itself.

This was rapidly borne out by Jan Beelan producing one of the hand-held VHF sets and speaking into it.

'Well done, Lance – everything is satisfactory?' His correct English was even more pronounced when he used the radio.

'No problems, boys, she's flying like a bird! I'll just do a circuit and then put her down. No point in tempting fate on the first attempt!'

Lance's voice was clear and Brennan realised that they must have fixed the power supply and set the correct frequencies in advance.

The Moth rose steadily until it was well clear of the eastern perimeter, then banked slowly left and climbed well above the terminal building. It carried on westwards for a couple of miles, then turned and sank down gracefully to a perfect landing at the top end of the main runway. As it taxied back towards them, Brennan, who knew little about aircraft apart from sitting in them, was amazed at the success of what had seemed little more than a dangerous prank.

'How the hell can it go so slowly and still stay in the air?' he demanded. Beverley smiled at his naïvety. 'These old biplanes are little more than a box-kite with an engine. They're only doing about thirty when they land.'

As Lance came slowly up to the apron in front of the hangar, Brennan began thinking of the possibilities that an aircraft now offered. If it could be shown that the old plane was safe enough to risk Lance's life over longer distances, they could not only have quick communications with other parts of the country, but more importantly in the shorter term, keep an eye on the aggressive boat people.

After Lance had killed the engine and they had manhandled the flimsy craft back into the hangar, congratulations were followed by serious discussion. When Brennan asked about the problems of using the Moth operationally, Lance was naturally enthusiastic.

'I can land her on virtually any flat ground that's at least a few hundred yards long. It would be a damn sight more convenient to bring her up to Cardiff and fly her off the grass in Bute Park, behind the castle.'

'With a range of only two hundred and fifty miles, you will need fuel dumps at convenient landing sites,' said the practical Jan Beelan.

'We can do that with small road tankers and trailers,' said Ruddy Luddy. 'Plenty of those knocking about the country, we can leave a few hundred gallons at various places.'

'How long will the fuel last in that tank over there?' asked Brennan, pointing across the airfield to the storage area.

'Probably go off before we use it all,' said Lance. 'A little plane like this does as many miles to a gallon as a family car – and there's a few thousand gallons in that tank.'

They went back to Cardiff in an ebullient mood, Lance promising to fly the Tiger back to the castle park within the next few days. There were plenty of other things to divert them, as next day, the second and larger load of material came down from Cambridge, together with two busloads of younger men and women, mainly those who worked with the equipment. From then on, Brennan encouraged them to become as independent as possible up in the university, though a large contingent of the Cardiff community helped them with the hard work of setting up both the workshops and the living accommodation. The new generator was carted down from Whitchurch Hospital and within a day or two, they had as much power and lighting as in the castle.

'When will the rest of you come down, John?' he asked Lovatt after the fourth day.

'We'd like to get the sleeping and eating facilities all lined up first. Then get the kids and the old folks here.'

The issue of the children coming down from Cambridge brought Brennan into contact with Liz Peterson again. Since the night they kissed in the moonlight, he had seen her daily and their relationship had been just the same as before. In the evenings, he had not deliberately avoided her, but they had always been in the company of other people and she made no move to corner him again in the dark.

Liz seemed content to play a waiting game – he was sleeping in a room with three other men and she was living in a side room off the sickbay, so there was no opportunity for them to jump into bed with each other, even if that had been on the agenda. Brennan felt too old to go romping under a bush in the park and in spite of speculative looks from a number of the others, there was no sign of any intimacy between them.

Almost the same relationship seemed to exist where Gwen was concerned. She was once more her bright self, she talked to everyone as usual and Brennan was fully included in any conversation. They never mentioned the rift that had occurred and, rather to his own surprise, he found it easy to respond to her in a completely normal way. Mervyn James, whose age and nature made him feel that he had a paternal role as far as Brennan was concerned, gruffly tackled him about his personal affairs one morning, as they climbed the steps to the command centre.

'Everything all right with you, Brennan?' he grunted. 'Plenty of the usual gossip going around, since the Glastonbury affair.'

'More important things on my mind at present, Doc.'

Mervyn shook his grey head. 'We only get one life, son. Make the most of it, whatever awful things have happened in the past.' He paused to get his breath back on the long climb. 'No doubt the grapevine has told you that I'm no longer alone in my little caravan. I'm getting older and don't see why I should stay lonely for the rest of whatever time I've got left.'

Brennan had heard that Fay Morgan had moved in with the doctor and he was happy for him, if that was what he really wanted.

'I'm marking time for the moment, Mervyn. Let's see how things pan out in the next few weeks or months.'

'Well don't leave it too long,' growled the physician. 'Make up your mind which way you want to go and do something about it. Things aren't always what they seem, you know.'

This obscure remark brought them to the entrance of the keep and left Brennan wondering what the older man was trying to tell him.

The meeting that day was largely concerned with the final move of Strickland's community and with the imminent expedition to Hampshire and Wiltshire. Both the women in Brennan's life were there, sitting as far from each other as possible. Throughout the hour-long discussions, he noticed that they never once looked at each other, though each contributed freely to the debate whenever it was appropriate. This distracted him somewhat from the business in hand, which annoyed him, but he could not help but wonder how deep Gwen's apparent discarding of his affection really went.

Later that day, he sought out Alfred Ashe, who looked after the accommodation and asked if there happened to be a spare caravan amongst the extra ones that had been brought in for the Cambridge drivers.

'Not that I want to pull rank, Alf, but I've got a lot of work to do, even at nights – and those three characters I sleep with could snore for the Olympics!'

Ashe said this was no problem, as all the extra Cambridge folk had now moved up to the college – so within hours, Brennan was established in a two-berth Abbey, three rows away from Gwen.

At half past eleven that night, there was a soft tapping on his door.

On the following Sunday, another few coachloads of people arrived from Cambridge, together with trucks carrying bedding and domestic material. Now all the older folk, children and many of the remaining women had been cleared from the old university city, leaving virtually only a holding garrison of about fifty behind the defences around Addenbrooke's Hospital. Strickland remained with them, 'like the captain of a sinking ship', as Mervyn rather scathingly put it.

Lance had made a few more proving flights with the Moth and on Monday, flew it up to Cardiff. Almost the whole community from castle and college turned out to see him make a perfect landing on a strip of newly-mown grass in Bute Park. There was great excitement amongst the crowd and Brennan thought that if nothing else, the plane was a good morale booster, as the community seemed to take the arrival of an aeroplane as another step in their return to civilisation. Privately, he had his doubts that it had much long-term significance, as it was one ancient aircraft that would last only as long as fuel and spares held out. Far more important was the development of education and farming, but he fully realised that an aircraft had far greater popular appeal than a tractor.

Bruce Ludlow had already rustled up another trailer-tank, which filled with aviation spirit, had been towed up to act as a forward fuel depot on the motorway near Swindon. Lance had pointed out that a couple of hundred yards of a clear motorway lane made an excellent airstrip and the enterprising Luddy had marked out a suitable section near the tanker, by spreading copious yellow paint over the tarmaced surface, which could be easily spotted from the air.

The radio links with Cambridge continued to record the absence of any obvious activity on the part of the continental settlers along the coast, which Brennan thought ominous, given the inevitable reaction which must come to the rout which they had suffered. Strickland pointed out that since the shrinkage of the Cambridge enclave, they now had fewer 'spies' out with less radio equipment, the bulk of which had been sent to Cardiff. Brennan discussed this at the Monday management committee meeting and asked Lance if he was prepared to make an early reconnaissance from the air.

'We'll need some fuel taken by road up to a point much nearer them – say on the M11,' replied the intrepid aviator. 'Even refuelling near Swindon won't leave much margin of safety, if I'm going to swan around East Anglia for more than a few minutes.'

'Let's hope the Jerries don't pick up some SAM missiles from their searching in Colchester,' said Mervyn, half-seriously.

'You keep well up out of danger, lad!' warned Brennan. 'Even a rifle could do that yellow kite a lot of damage, let alone a heavy automatic weapon or a rocket launcher.'

'A damned bow and arrow could knock that thing out of the sky!' growled Mervyn, who like Brennan was concerned for the safety of the impetuous Lance. They still remembered his reckless attack on the Irish at Caerleon, which almost got him killed.

In preparation for the epic flight, Lovatt's electronics wizards fitted a short-wave transceiver into the plane, in addition to the hand-held VHF set. They powered it from a small motorcycle accumulator, which would last a couple of days between charges – with the admonishment not to try any aerobatics, as the acid would run out if he tried to loop-the-loop! They contacted Cambridge and arranged for them to monitor the same frequencies when Lance went up to East Anglia in about a week's time, as he wanted to make a number of longer flights with motorway landings, before committing himself to enemy territory.

Life in the castle went on around all these new events. The school was expanded to take the additional children from Cambridge, the specialist classes were getting under way, with people learning a variety of skills, from brewing to MIG welding and from computer literacy to plumbing. The medical school started business and the German surgeon, rapidly recovering from his injuries, began haltingly to teach Tan Chen Swee and Mervyn some more surgical skills, though at the moment it was theoretical as thankfully there were no patients in need of operations. A long trailer had been found for their mobile theatre and with the two nurses and a couple of girls who wanted to learn the healing arts, the doctors were equipping it from the mass of material in Bridgend Hospital.

Brennan had finally taken Mervyn's advice and abandoned his state of celibacy. When the tap came at his caravan door that night, he had a momentary doubt as to who might be outside – blonde or brunette?

It was Liz Peterson and this time there was no prevarication or hesitation on the part of either of them. She stayed the night and then came every night, except when it was her turn to do night duty if there were any patients in the sickbay. They were now quite open about it, as were Lance and Gwen – it was no one's business but their own.

Brennan found Liz very different from Gwen, but he was content with that. She was quiet, gentle, affectionate and even-tempered. Gwen had far more passion, but could be argumentative, provocative and occasionally, frankly outrageous. He found himself weighing up the differences, missing the fire and challenge of the blonde, but valuing the peaceful calm of Liz's soothing nature, especially in the present period of stressful activity.

One component of this stress was the trip to Aldershot, which was upon him almost before he realised it. It took them three days to trundle their convoy around the military bases on Salisbury Plain and across Hampshire. They took their heaviest trucks, together with towing vehicles, drums of fuel, spare batteries, a car transporter and twenty men with tools and even explosives.

As former regular soldiers, Phil Robson and Bill Fleming knew many of the army establishments almost as well as Brennan. They found many places badly damaged, some burnt out, others virtually empty, as military units had been transferred elsewhere in the final panic, but there was still a wealth of material to be salvaged. Normally, these places would have been sealed up as tightly as the Bank of England, but death, desertion and previous looting had left many wide open to them. Brennan was saddened all over again as he saw the evidence of the horrific weeks, long ago.The bodily remains of soldiers scattered in barrack rooms, pathetic mounds of earth in the gardens of married quarters and even the signs of a battle inside the main gate of Tidworth on Salisbury Plain, where the remnants of the bodies of soldiers and civilians were mute evidence of an attempted raid on the camp, presumably for food.

In another regimental headquarters near Fleet, his wanderings around the camp took him into the Adjutant's office, where he found a partly-skeletalised body in a still-recognisable Major's uniform. The body was slumped over the desk, a service revolver near a mummified hand and a great cavity in the side of the skull. A curled photograph still lay on the desk, showing a smiling woman and two children. The parallel with Brennan's own history was so poignant, that even after the passage of years and the sight of countless hundreds of corpses, he could not prevent his eyes filling with tears.

But the work had to go on and after the first day's pillaging, they took their initial haul back to Swindon, relying on Bruce Ludlow's promise to shift it back by rail. Then they went on again and filled up their trucks and towed the vehicles they wanted back again to Swindon. On the third day, they headed for home with a last load culled from nearby Warminster still on their trucks.

The list of their booty was impressive, in that they had salvaged a hundred new rifles, more heavy machine guns, rocket launchers, mortars and even two anti-tank guns, with ammunition in plenty as well as military explosives, more effective than the dynamite they had looted from a quarry near Cardiff. The vehicles included a Scimitar and a Saladin armoured car, the latter with a 76 millimetre gun. A Fox scout car and a Spartan personnel carrier completed the list of armoured vehicles, together with three five-ton trucks, four Land-Rovers and a bulldozer.

'Thank God we've got Ruddy's train-full of diesel,' said Fleming. 'If we have to use this lot, we'll need to find an oil well afterwards!'

At a meeting in the keep that night, Brennan explained to the ones who stayed home, that they had destroyed or immobilised everything they could not take away – material that could have been used by the boat people if they penetrated that far.

'They can't use heavy armour, as they couldn't even start them, so we didn't bother with tanks and the like. But all the weaponry we left behind has been made useless – vital bits taken out of the firing mechanism and the like. The surplus ammunition, we blew up – and a few lovely bangs we made. A wonder you couldn't hear it from here!'

'Are you bringing all that other stuff back home?' asked Mervyn.

Brennan rubbed his beard, now iron grey at the sides. 'That was the original intention, but I'm beginning to wonder if it's necessary. If we get into a major punch up with the invaders, we want it to be as far east from here as we can manage it.'

Beverley nodded his agreement. 'I thought that all along – we'd have to take the damn stuff all the way back and perhaps lose precious time. Why not leave it in Swindon, that's fairly central.'

'Yes, Ruddy can haul a train load of the small arms and some of the smaller vehicles back, but we can store the rest where it is. That factory outlet place alongside the railway would be good cover for it.'

Bruce looked mildly disappointed that his beloved engine was not going to be put to a full test of strength, but Brennan assured him that if they needed to go to battle, he'd have plenty to haul back up the line.

'In the meantime, perhaps you could explore the track up towards the Midlands,' he said, to further mollify Bruce. 'It would be great to have easier communication with Worcester and beyond.'

They arranged to send a working party back on Ivor the Engine to sort out the military equipment at Swindon, get as much as they could under cover and to set a six-man guard on it, camping out in one of the railway buildings.

'Probably little risk of anyone pinching the big stuff, as I think Swindon is deserted,' concluded Brennan. 'But after that chap took pot-shots at us at the service station a few miles away, it's better to be safe than sorry.'

It had been a hard couple of days and the prospect of a soft bed and the gentle comfort of Liz Peterson sent him gratefully to his two-wheeled palace in the castle bailey.

After more discussions in the shed on the castle mound, the committee decided to send a small team to back up Lance when he made his first reconnaissance flight. Casey volunteered to accompany Beverley, Jan Beelan and Parsons, the morose mechanic, who between them provided most of the expertise in petrol engines. They took a Land-Rover towing another trailer of Avgas and made for Duxford, the aircraft museum where the expeditionary force had spent a night on the way to Cambridge. Leaving soon after dawn, they expected to get to the old airfield by afternoon, ready to greet Lance as he brought in the Tiger Moth. It was about two hundred miles in a direct line from Cardiff to Duxford, so would be well within the little plane's range.

The route was becoming familiar now, as were the various obstacles along the M4 and M25, until they reached the less obstructed M11.

At the museum, they camped out again in the workshop hangar and Jan and Beverley brewed tea while waiting for some sign of the yellow biplane. Before long, there was a shout from outside and when they joined Parsons and Casey at the door of the workshop, they found them staring up at the clear sky.

'Listen, can you hear it?' demanded Casey, a hand around his ear. From away to the west came a distant droning and soon they saw the Moth high above the trees beyond the perimeter fence.

They gave a bellow of triumph, heavily laced with relief. Using the small VHF, Beverley called up the pilot and Lance's voice replied almost immediately.

'Thanks for waiting, boys. Have you got the kettle on?'

'A fresh pot just made . . . any problems on the way?'

'None at all – this RAC Road Atlas is just the job. Follow the A505 and you can't go wrong!'

'Not a breath of wind down here, you can land any way you like.'

As the Civil Aviation Authority had ceased to exist, their informal radio protocol offended no one, nor did Lance's approach. With a large airfield and no wind, he just came straight in, landed and wobbled across the grass towards them, stopping almost against the wire fence that used to keep the public off the field. The engine stopped with a final puff of smoke and a backwards waggle of the six-foot propeller as Lance climbed out of the rear cockpit, goggles pushed up over a woollen balaclava helmet.

They welcomed him effusively and while Parsons and Casey pegged down the wings and tail with safety wires in case of high winds, the other pair took him off for the promised tea and sandwiches.

When the others came in, they sat around on old detached aircraft seats placed on the floor of the workshop. 'What's the country look like from the air?' asked Casey.

'Hard to tell much is wrong from up there, unless you come down very low. I did a pass over Oxford at a few hundred feet and it was a real mess. Most of the centre is burnt out, masses of fallen masonry in the streets – awful!'

Beverley, who had been an undergraduate there, was saddened at this description of the scene of his salad days. 'Any sign of people there?'

Lance shook his head. 'Couldn't see a soul from the air. No smoke from any chimney, nothing moving on the roads, not even a bike – not that much could move on those rubble-choked streets.'

'Any sign of life anywhere else on your trip?' asked Casey.

'I saw Ruddy's train chugging along between Cirencester and Swindon – I buzzed him and got a few blasts on his whistle for my trouble. Apart from that, all I saw were a couple of small fields near Hitchin that had been cultivated, but no sign of any people.'

The others were silent, mulling over the fact that in a two hundred-mile journey over the centre of England, not a soul was to be seen. It brought home to them how complete was the desolation. Was the rest of Europe – and the world – the same, they wondered?

Eventually, Casey broke the silence to suggest that they got on with servicing the plane. When the engine had cooled, Parsons checked the oil levels, the plug leads and anything else he could think of. All seemed in order and on the principle that 'if it ain't broke, don't mend it', they closed up the engine cowling, then carefully filled the tanks with the volatile aviation fuel. They wandered around the remains of the museum until it was time to cook the food they had brought. After the meal, they got into their sleeping bags and settled down on the hard floor of the hangar.

Two days later, the radio link from Cambridge brought disturbing news. Brennan was called to the keep by the duty operator to talk directly to Edgar Lambert, one of Strickland's deputies, who sounded worried and agitated.

'There's something going on along the coast,' he said. 'Two of our forward observers have seen a column of trucks moving between Colchester and Ipswich, going north. That could mean they're aiming to come towards Cambridge again.'

'Any military vehicles with them – or guns?' snapped Brennan.

'Some of the trucks were painted green or were camouflaged. They didn't see any of those armoured things you brought up here, but they had to make a run for it when the convoy came nearer. In fact, I've pulled them back nearer home – I don't want to have any more killed, like those some months ago.'

'How many of you left there now?' asked Brennan. 'Could you evacuate in a hurry if you had to?'

'About fifty of us – we've virtually cleaned the place out of anything useful now. We could evacuate in the trucks and the one coach that we kept. Do think we should pull out now?'

'Let's wait a bit and see what happens. Having your spies on the ground for as long as possible is a help, though now we've got the aircraft in your area.'

'I want to get those scouts out of there very soon,' Lambert replied firmly. 'Can't this plane of yours do a better job spotting them from the air?'

As this was the very purpose which they had intended for it, Brennan had to agree and promised to get Lance to begin overflying Suffolk and Essex. He knew that the previous day, the Moth had been flown down over London and Kent to see if there was any sign of the hostiles seeking weapons down south. Lance had reported seeing nothing on the roads, even though they could presumably have crossed the Thames – the Dartford Bridge was still intact, not having suffered like the two Severn Bridges, though all the tunnels under the river would have been either flooded or blocked by vehicles.

Brennan asked Strickland to contact Duxford on the VHF and ask Lance to start spying on the coastal region – and to contact Cardiff on the other radio when he was airborne. Within an hour, a weak but usable signal came through direct from the biplane, which was heading due east towards Ipswich. Lance reported his position and confirmed that he had heard from Cambridge about the activity on the roads and was on his way to have a look.

'For God's sake, keep well up, Lance,' advised Brennan, worried that the impetuous flier might buzz the enemy, as he had with Ruddy's train. 'We have no idea what weapons they may have picked up by now.'

'I doubt they'll have anti-aircraft missiles, boss,' came the distant voice. 'A plane must be the last thing they'll expect to see!'

'Don't take any chances, Lance – even small-arms fire could sink that thing, if you're too low.'

After promising to be careful, which Brennan only half-believed, the pilot promised to radio in at frequent intervals to let then know what he had seen. 'So in case I get pranged, at least you'll be kept up to date!' he joked, which sent a quiver of apprehension down Brennan's spine.

When the radio link was broken, he went out of the radio room into the adjacent hut, the so-called Command Centre, to look at their motley collection of Ordnance Survey maps, to find those that covered East Anglia. As he was refreshing his knowledge of the geography of Suffolk and Essex, he sensed someone behind him. Turning, he found Gwen standing in the doorway, an unusually sombre expression on her face.

'Is he all right? I heard that you had been talking to him on the radio just now?'

Brennan pulled out one of the metal-framed chairs from the table and waved her to it, sitting at another a few feet away. He looked at her lovely face, her perfect make-up and her elegant figure and wondered again how she managed to look as if she had just walked out of a studio, rather than be camping out in a bare castle in the centre of a ruined city, amongst a population mainly composed of depressives and eccentrics.

'Lance is fine, love! He seems to be enjoying himself immensely, he's already known as Biggles to those who still remember what it meant.' He felt the need to be comforting, but at the same time was embarrassed at this first acknowledgement of the rift between them, which had been so promptly filled by Lance. It was the first time since Glastonbury that Lance's name had passed his lips in her presence.

'You know what he's like, Brennan! He seems to go out of his way to put himself in danger.'

'He'll be safe enough, Gwen. That machine is as sound as a bell and the last thing the opposition expect is an aircraft overhead . . . there's nothing they can do to him, as long as he keeps well up.'

She looked far from convinced, but Brennan had no more reassurance for her and made the excuse that he must go back to the radio room.

Half an hour later, it crackled again as Lance briefly announced that he was over the coast and was heading north to overfly Ipswich at three thousand feet. By now, a few people had congegated in the bare room in the keep, news of the situation having already leaked out into the community. They all stood silently behind Wayne, the young radio operator, looking at the equipment as if half-afraid of what might next come out of it. Some of them were struck with the incongruity of a tribe like theirs, camping out in a ruined city and subsisting on salvaged food and home-grown vegetables, but being able to communicate with an aircraft on the other side of the country.

'I just hope the silly bugger doesn't do anything rash!' grated Mervyn, worriedly pulling at the end of his moustache. This set Gwen off again.

'He's not a silly bugger! He's a bloody hero!' she cried and ran from the room. With a sigh, Brennan went after her again and found her sitting at the table in the empty hut, staring at the wall with her knuckles to her mouth.

'Are you really that fond of him, Gwen?' he asked. He could have bitten his tongue as soon as he said it, but the words seemed to come out unbidden, She looked up at him, her eyes reddened and moist.

'He's a lovely guy,' she said ambiguously and something in her look stirred embers of the fire he thought was cold ashes.

Unsure of what to do or say, he squeezed her shoulder and left her to go back to the others. They stood in silence for a few more minutes, staring at the front of the radio as if Lance's words might appear on the black enamel like a teletype.

'He's turned off his transmission his end,' said Wayne. 'Saving his battery, perhaps.'

After ten minutes, the patience of one of the audience gave out and he slipped away, back to his work. Alfred Ashe was just getting restive, when there was a rushing sound from the speaker, picking up the noise of the Gipsy engine, then Lance's voice was superimposed on the background roar.

'Are you reading me?'

'Yes, Lance, go ahead.'

'There's something going on down there. A column of about thirty vehicles moving north out of Ipswich.'

'What type – can you see them well enough from that height?' Brennan leaned forward into the microphone, as the operator switched them back and forth at each 'Over'.

'Seems to be all trucks – but there's some smaller stuff, maybe Land-Rovers or the like. I'll go down for a closer look – they've all stopped, now that they've seen me.'

'For God's sake, don't get too close!' shouted Brennan, as if he could make the force of his voice carry better to East Anglia.

'No problem – they can't know where I come from. I might be from France, come to save them!'

'With a big British "G" painted under your wings?' snapped Mervyn. 'You keep well up out of harm's way, my boy!'

The link went dead and they waited in frustration for several more minutes, until the transmission returned.

'I stand corrected, chaps! There's two armoured personnel carriers and two armoured cars, something like Ferrets. And there's a tracked vehicle, with a short, fat gun sticking out of the front.They're taking a leaf out of our book.'

'Shit! Do you think they're heading for Cambridge?' rasped Brennan.

'Looks like it – nowhere else to go in that direction, with that lot.'

'Right, get out of there – now! Get back to Duxford and refuel, you may have to get out in a hurry.'

'Roger! See you back home.'

As they broke the connection, Brennan fleetingly thought that Lance's choice of 'Roger' as the conventional radio word of understanding was hardly appropriate, especially as Gwen had come back into the room – but the pilot's news immedietaly thrust such trivialities out of his mind.

'Right, Wayne, get Cambridge on the line straight away.'

As they waited, he moved back behind the others and gripped Gwen's arm. 'Lance is fine, he's just turned round and is heading back.'

She smiled at him radiantly and he wondered whether any of it was for him or all for her new lover.

'They're on the air, Brennan,' called the operator and in a moment he was speaking to Strickland. The news that a large column of presumably heavily-armed enemy was advancing on their city sent the Commissar into a flurry of anxiety, but Brennan's calm and decisive manner helped to settle her down. The situation was hardly unexpected and thanks to their forward planning, all the remaining garrison could be pulled out with an hour's notice. They discussed the final details and arranged that Strickland's convoy should join with Beverley's group at Duxford on the way down the M11 motorway and get back to Cardiff as soon as possible.

The Cambridge radio was shut down for the last time and Brennan sent a last message to Lance, telling him to let Beverley know what was happening.

'As you're flying back to Duxford, check that there are no Jerries driving across country to cut off the motorway,' was his last command before they went off the air. With the radio silent, Brennan turnd to the others in the room.

'So now we know! The boat people are now truck people and have other military hardware that may well match ours.'

'What'll they do after taking Cambridge, I wonder?' mused Mervyn.

'They'll be itching to get even with us for the hammering we gave them near Newmarket,' said Brennan gravely. 'Sooner or later we're going to have to fight this Gustaf Fischer guy to a standstill – and the further away from here the better!'

CHAPTER EIGHTEEN

A MONTH later, in the the height of hot summer weather, there was still no sign of any aggressive activity from eastern England. Jan Beelan spent a lot of time monitoring radio frequencies across the dial, in case the 'hostiles,' as the Cardiff folk now called them, had managed to acquire some communications. Thankfully, the ether continued to be empty. The problem came up again at one of the frequent council meetings, at which the Cambridge contingent was now fully represented.

'There are still transceivers to be had over there, I'm sure,' said John Lovatt. 'Like us, they could probably find them in houses that belonged to amateur radio enthusiasts. But it's the power supply that's their problem, especially with portable equipment.'

'The fact that we can't hear them talking on short-wave does not mean that they do not have VHF equipment,' cautioned Jan in his impeccable English. 'Though I agree the lack of batteries is their main problem.'

'No chance of them finding any tucked away in Cambridge?' queried Brennan, worried at the thought of Fischer having the means to communicate. This, together with a spotter aircraft, was the West's main trump card if it came to a battle.

Strickland was adamant. 'We've shipped everything useful down here and destroyed anything which might conceivably be of help to them.'

Brennan knew that as they left Cambridge, they had set fire to Addenbrooke's and all their other smaller installations. One of Lance's subsequent overflights had confirmed that they had burnt to the ground, adding to the complete desolation of the city.

In the weeks that had passed, much had been done at Cardiff, in spite of the prospect of impending war hanging over them. The Cambridge group had settled in satisfactorily and though they lived a quarter of a mile away, they integrated well. All the children, now numbering about forty, were cared for together, except the very small infants. Nursery classes and school were held in the castle, though the older children went over to the college for the more technical lessons. Adult education was booming, the enthusiasm of the Cambridge academics having had the effect that Brennan had expected. The medical school had four students, all under forty and the German surgeon had proved to be a human dynamo when it came to organising the hospital and mobile operating unit. His English had improved by leaps and bounds and Mervyn's former nightmares about a surgical emergency had largely receded.

The farming had expanded and with Ruddy's acquisition of almost unlimited diesel fuel, more tractors were reclaimed and put into service. Godfrey Traherne had kept his promise and taken on two women and a man as trainee farmers. They had rounded up stray cattle and planned to get some into milk as soon as possible. Nothing had been heard of Roger Mellars and Brennan was content to leave it that way, though some of the management committee felt that he should be told of the increased threat from the east and invited to contribute some manpower if conflict seemed imminent. Brennan grudgingly agreed, and went along with a plan to send over a messenger with the news, though privately he thought that there was little useful that Glastonbury could offer.

At this meeting, on a very hot day, the usual pattern of topics was discussed, but as always, the threat of Fischer's invaders was uppermost in their minds. A dozen people now sat around the table in the keep. Since the Cambridge contingent arrived, a general election had been held, each of the two groups providing six members chosen by their 'electorate'. Unsurprisingly, the same people as before were nominated and the twelve unanimously gave the chair to Brennan, with Strickland as the vice-chair – no way would she countenance being called 'chairwoman' or 'chairman'. That was the full extent of their bureacracy and Brennan was thankful to see that Strickland's communistic stance and jargon seemed not to have survived the journey from Cambridge.

After the domestic matters of the day had been exhausted, they turned inevitably to the main worry.

'So where are we as regards these buggers in the east?' demanded Mervyn, in his typically undiplomatic language.

'They've done virtually nothing since they went into Cambridge,' replied Brennan. 'Lance was over Suffolk and Norfolk a few days ago, so he call tell you himself.'

The intrepid flier had gained almost as many votes as Brennan in the recent poll and was everyone's hero, including Gwen's, whose caravan he continued to share.

'That's right, nothing moving apart from the odd lorry,' he responded. 'I suspect they're short of fuel and are either searching for more or conserving what they've got.'

'So what happened to that big convoy they launched at us in Cambridge?' asked Strickland.

'Most of it's still there, parked in a field off the link road to the motorway. No sign of any men around them – nor any in the remains of the city. I presume they've all been taken back to the coast.' There was a silence as they digested this.

'A funny business – what the hell are they up to?' asked Casey.

'I think Lance is probably right, they're consolidating and building up stocks of fuel and possibly more military hardware – though we've scotched any attempts at their getting material from Hampshire.'

'They'll be pissed off that their attack on Cambridge was a total waste of effort,' said Alfred Ashe. 'No captives, no loot – not even a place to live, as you set fire to it all, Ms Strickland!'

Lance looked across at Brennan. 'Boss, tell them about yesterday's flight, that's a bit worrying.'

The big man grunted. 'As you know, I've gone up with Lance a few times in the Moth and yesterday we thought we'd have a look at the south coast.'

All the other heads swivelled towards him. They hadn't heard about this before.

'We saw smoke in Portsmouth, coming from house chimneys. Most of the place is a ruin, but now some people are obviously living there, but they're not the natives.'

'How can you tell that?' asked Lovatt.

'Because there are big motor boats moving inside Portsmouth Harbour – and we even spotted one coming in from the sea. I think Jan Beelan was right, there are landings now along that coast, perhaps coming from Ostend or even the French channel ports.'

'Just as well we cleaned out the military establishments north of Portsmouth, before they could get to them,' commented Casey.

'So what's all this telling us, Brennan?' demanded Mervyn, always one to keep to the main issue.

'Not a lot, Doc! It's patently obvious that they intend to come after us sooner or later, otherwise they wouldn't have gone to the trouble of salvaging those armoured vehicles. The problem is, we don't know where they'll attack and we don't know when.'

'We've got the plane, though' said Mary Spencer, one of the Cambridge delegates. 'Surely that will be an early warning.'

Lance smiled indulgently at her. 'Yes, and we're damned lucky to have it. But we can't keep it in the air all the time and Southern England's a big place, even for an aircraft.'

Brennan agreed, looking solemn as he explained. 'We can't push our luck too far, Mary. That little plane's seventy years old, we've got no expert aero-mechanic and virtually no spares. Lance risks his life every time he goes up in it, so we have to ration its use.'

Gwen was sitting opposite him and Brennan saw her face blanch at his words. She really was fond of Lance, he thought, with an ambivalent feeling in his breast. He was living with her as openly as Brennan shared his van with Liz Peterson. The passage of time had all but removed any awkwardness between them all, though they did not go out of their way to make a foursome in the dining room or at the evening bar.

'So what do we do?' persisted Mervyn, relentlessly dragging the leader's attention back to earth.

'Can't you put a few forward observers out, like we did in East Anglia?' suggested Edgar Lambert. 'We've plenty of motorcycles and enough VHF sets to work the system.' This seemed a reasonable proposition and they kicked it around for a while.

'We'd have to pick on a few likely localties to keep watch over,' decided Brennan. 'As with the plane, southern England is too big to attempt to cover much of it. It would be too hit-or-miss.'

'You're the soldier and tactician,' grunted Casey. 'Where would you put your money on for an attack route?'

'I've thought about this a lot,' answered Brennan. 'The obvious place is down the Thames valley and the M4 corridor. The biggest force from Essex and district would come round London and down the motorway towards us, perhaps picking up another mob from the South Coast on the way.'

'So what do we do about it?' demanded Mervyn.

Brennan unfolded a couple of maps from a pile in front of him and spread them out on the big table.

'This is what we do!' he said, stabbing a finger on the map and beginning to talk.

By the time another fortnight had passed, the air of forboding that hovered over the community had largely faded, as such tense expectancy could not be sustained when nothing at all had happened.

However, the committee still held meetings every few days and Brennan kept a constant watch on the reports of the radio monitors and the motorbike spies. The forward base in Swindon was made permanent and a score of men and women lived there on weekly shifts, living in one of the intact railway buildings alongside the main line. They renovated the military equipment that had been collected on Brennan's pillaging expedition to Aldershot and kept the fleet of vehicles in good condition, ready for immediate use. In addition, the motorcycle men used it as their base, coming back there every night from their reconnaissances.

'They're going up the M4 as far as Slough and down from the Newbury intersection almost as far as Winchester,' he reported to one of the meetings. 'And occasionally, they take a look north on the A34 as far as Didcot, to make sure no one is creeping down from the Oxford direction, though I don't think that's likely.'

'How are they reporting in?' asked Strickland.

'They're back home in Swindon each night, but in case they spot something, they can make an urgent call on their VHF, as long as they're not too far away. We've got two guys in the Membury service station, which is the highest point around there, with an antenna rigged up on the roof for maximum range eastwards. They can relay it back to Swindon, where they have the other short-wave set linked to us here.'

'And they've seen nothing yet?' asked John Lovatt.

'Not a dicky bird! But the bastards are going to come sooner or later – why else would they have got themselves armoured vehicles and artillery?'

Brennan had drawn up detailed contingency plans to be put into action the moment they had advance warning. Most of the weaponry had been taken back to Swindon by Ruddy's beloved train service, to be ready on the spot. So convinced was he that the M4 corridor must be the line of attack, that he was now preparing to fortify the high ground on either side.

With Beverley, Casey and the two old soldiers, Robson and Fleming, they took a large working party up to Swindon, including a JCB and a bulldozer. They trucked out along the motorway to Junction 15, where the main road to Marlborough crossed it at right angles on a twin flyover. From here the motorway climbed steadily eastwards between chalk banks towards the Membury service station, where they had been ambushed by thieves some months earlier. On either side, the smooth chalk hills rose above the M4, with Bishopstone and Lambourn Downs to the north, before the ground fell away into the Vale of White Horse. To the south was a high, prominent ridge with an isolated tree at the eastern end and the remains of Iron Age earthworks on the other.

Going south on the Marlborough road, they turned through the village of Badbury and climbed up the side of the ridge in the tough old 101 Land-Rover.

'This is called Liddington Castle,' announced Brennan, as he stood within the grassy mounds that crowned the crest of the hill. 'It was a Celtic hill-fort right on the ancient ridgeway – historians thought it had a special significance in the Dark Ages.'

Whatever it was called, the site had a tremendous view and even to the least militarily-minded, was obviously a superb strategic position.

'We need to place our defences behind the crest, so that they can't be spotted from the east, then find a similar place on the other side of the gap.' He pointed over to the Bishopstone side.

'There's no old fort that side, is there?'asked Phil Robson.

'Unfortunately not – so we'll have to make our own. That's why I brought the JCB. It'll have to be camouflaged from the motorway – we want to catch those buggers napping again, if we can.'

Several days' work was needed inside Liddington Castle, to build defences behind without altering the profile as seen from over a mile away, up the motorway. At the back of the ancient fortifications, they used their mechanised diggers to dig trenches and make dug-outs, as well as a rough approach road up from the hamlet below. Behind these, an area was flattened off to act as a holding area for armoured vehicles, concealed from below.

'Thank God that these days, we don't have a Ministry of the Environment or the Ancient Monuments Commission, or whatever they're called!' said a perspiring Bruce Ludlow. 'They'd have had our guts for garters for bulldozing one of their precious historic sites.'

Brennan made several trips along the motorway, to make sure that nothing was visible from a distance and when satisfied, turned his attention to the northern side. Here they had a tougher job altogether, as there were no pre-existing earthworks, but with some judicious repositioning of turf, over several more days they managed to build a long, low parapet faced with grass, behind which was a similar set of defensive works to the southern side.

When the work was completed to the former brigadier's satisfaction, they had another job at Junction 15 on the way back to Swindon. Where the two long bridges crossed the motorway at the bottom of the long slope, he worked with Phil Robson and Bill Fleming to place large explosive charges under each end of both spans. They were equipped with detonators and the wires run well up into a field on the north side. Further charges were placed into holes knocked by the JCB in both east-facing approach roads, to prevent vehicles dodging the main blockage down below. All this explosive was the fruit of their foraging weeks earlier at a Royal Ordnance Corps unit on Salisbury Plain.

'I hope we won't need to blow this,' said Brennan, when everything was completed. 'It would screw up our own use of the road in the future.'

The realistic – and pessimistic – Beverley shook his head. 'Maybe in the future, we won't want to travel further east than this, if those guys have settled on the other side.'

With this sobering thought, they climbed aboard their transport and rumbled back towards the Swindon base.

Though Lance was flying sorties in the Moth every few days, it was one of the motorcyclists who picked up the first signs that something was happening in the east. Eddie Thorpe, a thirty-year-old former welder from Newport, had been a keen motorcyclist in the old days and was now quite happy to spend his time on an ex-police Norton 500, driving around the roads of southern England, with an SA 80 rifle strapped to his carrier and a VHF tucked into his leathers.

About noon on a fine August Tuesday, he had patrolled up the motorway, then turned south on the A34 which led down to Winchester and Portsmouth. A few miles south of Newbury, he stopped near Beacon Hill to have his meat sandwiches and a flask of tea. From force of old habits, he parked in a lay-by. There was a rusting Ford Focus there, but Eddie made no effort to see if the bones of the driver were still sitting inside.

He propped up the Norton and sat on a weed-festooned wall alongside the road to eat and drink. After a few minutes, his brow wrinkled, as something began to disturb the habitual silence to which he was accustomed on these expeditions. Usually only the wind, the bleating of stray sheep and the chirping of birds could be heard when his bike was switched off. Now he realised that he could hear another motorcycle engine in the distance – and it was coming nearer. It was too late to move his own machine out of sight, but dropping his half-eaten sandwich, he ran to get his automatic weapon and then scrambled up the bank behind and in a running crouch, hurried to a crest from where he could see about a quarter of a mile of the road.

Lying in the long grass, he pushed his rifle in front of him and clicked off the safety. In a moment, a motorcycle came into sight, the rider in a heavy grey coat with a flat cap on his head and goggles on his face. He suddenly saw Eddie's Norton standing in the lay-by and slowed down and stopped a hundred yards away. For once, Eddie cursed his own love of motorbikes, for he had meticulously cleaned and polished his machine. The newcomer would instantly realise that no way could this one have been abandoned five years ago.

In a dilemma, Eddie tried to decide whether to challenge the man, shoot him, or lay low. The problem immediately solved itself, as the 'hostile' suddenly revved the engine of his Yamaha, hauled the handlebars around and roared off the way he had come. Within seconds he had vanished around a bend and the noise of his machine rapidly faded in the distance, leaving Eddie to listen once more to the sheep and the birds. Shaken, he hurried back to the lay-by, gathered up his thermos and roared off to get the news back to Swindon in the shortest possible time.

Lance was airborne within an hour of the foreign scout being sighted. As soon as Eddie was well away from the lay-by, he stopped and called up the Membury listening post with the news. When they relayed it to Swindon, Lance hurriedly spoke to Brennan on the short-wave set at the depot, then drove down to the motorway landing strip and climbed aboard the Moth, which was kept ready fuelled for such emergencies. Within a few more minutes, even at the modest eighty miles an hour at which the old plane cruised, he was following the Winchester road southwards from the M4 and what he found put him straight back on the VHF to Swindon, as the battery for his short-wave radio had inexplicably gone flat.

'Get back to Brennan with this news,' he shouted above the engine noise. 'There's a column of about twenty trucks and a couple of four-by-fours coming up from the Portsmouth direction. No armoured vehicles, nor heavy guns that I can see. They're just past Winchester on the A34, going slowly northwards. Got that?' When he had the affirmative, he continued 'I'm turning east to see if anything's happening on the motorway in the London direction. I can't believe that just a handful of old trucks is going to invade us. Maybe they're meeting up with a bigger group from the east. I'll be in touch when I get back.'

When this was relayed to Cardiff, Brennan was waiting anxiously in the radio room in the ancient keep. Casey was with him and together they pored over the creased road maps covering Berkshire and parts of Wiltshire.

'Is this going to be the real thing?' asked Casey, rubbing his big nose in both excitement and anxiety.

'I think it must be, pal,' grunted Brennan. 'They wouldn't be on the road in such force, using up their scarce fuel, unless they meant business.'

'Are you going to blow the whistle right now? They could be in Swindon in less than a couple of hours, but we haven't got a hope of getting there before them.'

Brennan chewed his lip in indecision. 'Let's wait to see if Lance finds anything further up the motorway. In the meantime, I want to get Phil Robson on the line. He's still in Swindon, thank God.'

Within an hour, Membury picked up Lance's signal again and relayed it back to Cardiff. After a moment's listening, Brennan barked out a staccato list of orders for Swindon, then turned to the expectant faces of Wayne and Casey.

'The balloon's going up, boys. There's a sixty-vehicle convoy coming past Slough on the M4, including a few armoured vehicles, a big gun on tracks, the rest trucks and coaches.' He hurried past them and clattered down the steep steps to the castle bailey, heading for Gwen's broadcast caravan. Bursting in, he found her doing her disc-jockey act, but one look at his face made her pull off her headphones and stare at him, pale-faced.

'It's Lance, isn't it?' she asked.

'It's Lance all right, but he's fine! Just swanning around the sky. He's just spotted the invasion, so cut the music and put out a general alarm! I want everyone belonging to the defence force mustering in the castle as fast as their legs can carry them. Tell them to send out runners to call in all working parties. You know the drill, we've rehearsed it often enough.'

He turned to go out, but she grabbed his arm. 'Hey, what am I to tell all the folks – they'll be battering on the door in five minutes, wanting to know what's going on.'

'Tell them as much as I know myself at the moment. There's a big force of hostiles coming west towards us – and we're going to stop them, OK?'

As he went out she was already stopping the tape and her voice rang out on the speakers around the castle at full volume, calm and confident, in spite of her justified fears about her present lover's safety. Mervyn, Casey, Jan Beelan and several others were hurrying towards him as he left the van and tersely, he sent them about their business of organising a very rapid mobilisation. Already, he could hear trucks being started up and people were running to the armoury to collect their weapons.

Back in the radio room, he waited impatiently for Lance to get back to Swindon and within an hour, the pilot had landed and was on the short-wave radio from the base there. He gave Brennan a first-hand account of what he had seen, though this added little to the previous reports.

'You said you can land that plane anywhere on the motorway?' demanded Brennan.

'Sure, given a clear few hundred yards.'

'Right, I want you back in the air straight away, Lance. Take Phil Robson and his stuff back to the bridge that takes the secondary road from Newbury northwards across the motorway. It's the B4000 . . . you've got a road map with that on it, I'm sure. We've got to beat those bastards to it, so don't hang about, lad, or we're lost!'

Leaving Wayne to watch over the radio, Brennan ran down from the keep once again, wishing now that he had placed his command centre in a less exhausting position. In the castle ward, there was orderly chaos, but everything was going to plan for a rapid getaway. When he went out over the low drawbridge, rows of trucks were already lined up along Castle Street and teams of men and women were loading last-minute supplies and light armaments into them. All the heavy equipment had already been sent to Swindon and Luddy's train had done sterling service in moving both vehicles and materials to the anticipated battle zone during the preceding weeks. Leaving the rest of the organisation of a hasty departure to his lieutenants, Brennan went back yet again to the keep and waited to hear from Lance. On the success of his mission depended their own survival and probably their very lives.

Eighty miles away, Lance was happily doing his best to achieve this. Though until recently, he had not been in a cockpit for almost seven years, the Moth was easy to fly and he now felt completely at ease in the little plane. The former marine commando was in the front cockpit, with ominously heavy packages packed around him, there being more in the small luggage compartment. The extra weight caused Lance to alter the trim considerably, as he normally flew solo, but the short flight of about fourteen miles along the motorway posed no problem. He identified the road-crossing on his RAC atlas and put the plane down on a stretch of carriageway that was thankfully clear of abandoned or wrecked vehicles. He taxied almost up to the bridge, which had the usual two concrete spans across a central pier, and killed the engine. They both clambered out and hurriedly unloaded the explosives and detonating devices on to the road.

'Better swing her round now, Phil – we may have to make a quick getaway,' he suggested.

They swivelled the light plane around by pushing on her wing-tips, then hurried up the bank with the first of the charges. While Robson set them expertly in the most damaging places, Lance ferried more packages up to him, but kept an anxious eye on the road eastwards. His caution paid off, for just as the ex-soldier was wiring up the detonator cables, Lance heard the distant rattle of a motorcycle engine. Like Eddie a couple of hours earlier, the sound galvanised them into action. Grabbing their SLR rifles, which they had prudently brought from the plane, they ran one to each end of the bridge and lay down, poking the muzzles of their weapons between the railings.

In a few moments, the rider appeared in the distance, but as soon as he saw an aircraft sitting across the eastbound lanes, he came to a sudden halt. Seeing no sign of movement anywhere, he cautiously came on, legs out, his feet almost scraping the road on each side. He wore thick goggles and a machine pistol was slung across his back.

When he was fifty yards away, Phil Robson loosed off a short burst, aiming at the front wheel of the bike. With a yell of surprise, the rider fell off his buckled machine, then ran uninjured but terrified for the sanctuary of the tangled vegetation beyond the hard shoulder. Lance fired another burst to hurry him on his way and a moment later, the man had found a break in the fencing and was hammering away across the overgrown field behind.

'Let's do it and get out of here, Phil! They may be close behind him.'

Robson gathered his wires and hurried with them back down to the road. 'Better move the Yellow Peril a fair way off – this is going to be one hell of a bang,' he advised.

Lance climbed aboard, Robson swung the propeller into life and the plane taxied away for at least four hundred yards. Phil unwound his wires to their full extent and took them into a ditch behind the bank that lined the motorway. A couple of minutes later, there was an almighty explosion and the bridge spans lurched, then fell with a shattering crash and a huge cloud of dust and debris across both carriageways, completely blocking all the lanes.

Robson ran down to the Moth and climbed in, shouting, 'That'll take some moving, some of those chunks must weigh ten tons!' He had a bleeding gash on his forehead from a flying fragment, but he seemed not to notice it.

Lance opened the throttle and the Gipsy engine urged them down the road and up into the air, just short of the blackened hulk of a B&Q truck which had hit one of Eddie Stobart's leviathans.

'Home James and don't spare the horses!' yelled Lance contentedly, as he looked over his shoulder at the pall of dust hanging over their handiwork.

CHAPTER NINETEEN

'THOSE two chaps have saved our bacon,' proclaimed Casey, as he looked over Brennan's shoulder. They had a map spread on the front panel of a Saladin armoured car and Casey jabbed a thick finger down at the coloured lines on the paper. 'If they can't shift that lot, they'll have to turn all those eighty vehicles around, go back to Junction 13, down to Newbury, along the A4 to Hungerford and come back up to Junction 14. And those narrow roads, especially in Newbury, will be half-blocked by debris and knackered vehicles. It'll take them half a day!' He almost rubbed his hands in satisfaction.

They were standing in the early evening light behind the ancient turf ramparts at Liddington Castle. Behind them were scenes of intense activity, as a hundred men and women put up tents, moved vehicles and weapons and generally prepared for conflict. They had moved up earlier that day, leaving Cardiff as quickly as they could with all their available transport and were now ferrying up the last of the stores and ammunition from the stockpile near the railway at Swindon. As Ruddy Luddy was here with them, his fellow railway enthusiast Maldwyn was driving Ivor up during the evening, bringing the last of their reserves of ammunition and a back-up tanker full of diesel.

Over on the other side of the valley, a twin to their camp was being set up, with Beverley, John Lovatt, Robson and Bill Fleming in charge. With Brennan, were Casey, Jan Beelan and Mervyn. Even Mavis Strickland was there, having apparently shed her former pacifist views after Cambridge had been overrun.

Lance Prichard was in the air again and the little yellow Moth had not long ago flown up the funnel of hills that carried the motorway eastward below them. He had gained height as he went from his take-off point below the derelict Princess Margaret Hospital and was still climbing as he vanished over the Downs, aiming to see what the situation was at the ruined bridge.

'Is he going to be all right, Brennan?' Gwen asked anxiously, as the engine noise faded into the distance. She had volunteered her unskilled help in the ominously-named Casualty Clearing Station, one of the tents behind them.

'He'll be fine! I've told him to keep well up. They weren't expecting aircraft against them, so they'll have nothing useful to fire at him.' He said this with more conviction than he really felt, but there was little he could do other than reassure the woman and hope that Lance would be sensible.

The efficient Bruce Ludlow had trucked up ground sheets and sleeping bags to go with the dozen tents and now also brought up two vanloads of food and drink from the Swindon base. While they were waiting to hear from Lance, they sat on the dry earth and ate warm stew and hunks of bread, before dipping into urns of strong tea.

Once again, Brennan was struck by the incongruity of this familiar military scene, when in reality, his army consisted of almost a third of their whole community. They were equipped with radios, armoured cars, sophisticated weaponry and even an aircraft – in an empty country where most of the people were skeletons.

The mood passed and he restlessly paced up to the old earthworks that had been staring out over the Downs for the past two millennia. His VHF crackled and the voice of one of the two radio watchers at the Membury service station, six miles east, came through.

'We can see the plane coming back now. It should be over you in a couple of minutes.'

Brennan warned them to keep their eyes peeled down the road, in case any motorcycle outriders came through. 'And be ready for a swift getaway tomorrow, lads. You may not get much warning when they start coming.'

There was a murmur of anticipation amongst the troops as the Moth's engine was heard and it was watched intently as it glided down the valley and over the Marlborough interchange. Fifteen minutes later, there was a ragged cheer as Lance bumped up the track in a Toyota Land-Cruiser and jumped out to give Gwen a hug and claim a mess-tin of soup. He wandered over to Brennan, a lump of bread in the other hand.

'Phil Robson did a great job, Boss! He really knackered that bridge.' Between mouthfuls, Lance described the scene back along the M4.

'The first lot from the south are close up against the rubble, with the main column from Essex behind them. They've managed to unship that tracked field gun off its transporter and work it up to the front. Looks as if they're using it to drag the big lengths of broken concrete span aside with it, but I don't think it's powerful enough.'

'Are they likely to give up and go back through Newbury and Hungerford?'

The pilot shrugged. 'They'd have a hell of a job turning all that lot around on one carriageway. They're all nose to tail, running back about a mile. Must be over eighty vehicles, it would take them ages. I think they'll keep trying to move the obstruction.'

'How long have we got, I wonder? Can they work all night?' asked Mervyn.

'They won't have enough lights, surely,' cut in Casey. 'They daren't risk flattening their batteries, which must be one of their problems. And they can't use fuel all night, running their engines to keep charging.'

Lance scraped the last of his stew from the mess-tin. 'I'll get aloft and have another look first thing in the morning. There's no way that they can be on the move overnight. And why should they hurry, they don't know we're this near. I suppose they think we're in Bristol or Cardiff.'

He wandered off with Gwen to find some tea and give a more highly coloured version of his exploits to an eager audience in one of the tents. Brennan was drawn back to the grassy parapet as if it were a magnet and stared again up the valley, following the gently ascending ribbon of the motorway with the binoculars that hung around his neck. Maybe they fitted the image of a field marshal overseeing the field of battle, but otherwise Brennan didn't look like Rommel, as he was wearing a brown anorak over a green sweatshirt and creased jeans. A flat cap made him look more like a farmer going to the weekly mart, than a senior staff officer. However, everyone had a steel helmet filched from a dozen army depots, with strict instructions to put them on as soon as any shooting was likely.

The summer evening was drawing to a close when a belated ray of sunshine found a crack in the western clouds. The smoothly-contoured chalk downs were reddened by its rays, which also lit up the solitary tree that was silhouetted so prominently at the eastern end of the ridge.

Brennan listened to the subdued chatter and even some laughter from the camp behind him and worried again at the thought that the future and very lives of many of these younger people were in his hands. What if his strategy for tomorrow was wrong? He had been trained as a soldier, had gone through numerous courses on tactics at the Army Staff College, but in the final analysis, it was his judgement that mattered. And what if Gustaf Fischer, late of the German Army, was a better tactician?

As the evening closed in and Brennan still paced his barricades, he began to appreciate what Henry V must have gone through on the night before Agincourt.

Only the faintest greyness was visible in the east when Brennan went back to the earthworks with his field glasses. He had hardly slept all night and waited impatiently for the dawn. The wind had dropped and it remained dry. Swinging his glasses across to look at Bishopstone Down opposite, he was satisfied that not a glimmer of light could be seen. He had strictly banned any matches or torches, in case some probing motorcyclist had penetrated this far during the night.

As the light gradually increased, more people abandoned their sleeping bags and wandered out to see if anything was happening. All the 'troops', as he thought of them, were volunteers, men and women ranging between sixteen and sixty. The potential tragedy was that these were the most stable, energetic and well-adjusted members of the community, those left behind being older, less fit or mentally unsuitable. If this battle went badly, then the cream of a generation would be lost. Brennan tried to put such thoughts behind him as the countryside emerged from the gloom. It was now almost six o'clock and Lance appeared, yawning and stretching. They walked to the end of the embanked area and stared across the valley.

'This won't be the walkover we had at Newmarket, Lance,' said Brennan gravely. 'Unless we can knock our their heavy weapons at the start, we could take a lot of punishment.'

'I wish I could do more from the air,' replied Lance. 'But that little plane won't take any worthwhile bomb-load, even if we had them. And I'd have to go so low to hit anything, that they'd blow me out of the sky.'

'Lance, you've done more than your share already. We're all deeply in your debt, you know that.'

The younger man grinned sheepishly. 'I just happened to be the guy who could drive one of those things, that's all.' His voice dropped as he looked even more embarrassed. 'Look, boss, I'm sorry about that other business . . . you know, with Gwen. I just want you to know that I didn't make any moves until . . . well, until after Glastonbury.'

Brennan stared out over the earthworks. 'Don't worry about it, Lance. We've got far more urgent things on our minds now. You just be careful today, right?'

Awkwardly, Lance stuck out his hand and though surprised, Brennan gripped it firmly. 'No hard feelings, boss? I'll be on my way, then.'

As he walked off, Brennan wondered once more whether he would see him alive again. An hour later, the Tiger Moth buzzed past them, at first lower than their own positions, but rising as it vanished over the eastern horizon. Gwen came out with many others to see it pass and came to stand near Brennan afterwards.

'I'm staying right here until he gets back,' she said defiantly. They had not long to wait for within twenty minutes Lance zoomed back again and a few minutes later, he called up on his VHF from his airbase on the hard shoulder below the hospital.

'Not worth flogging back up the hill, as I'll be going off again a bit later.'

'What's the situation?' demanded Brennan, who stood in a circle of people all trying to hear both sides of the conversation.

'They're going hammer-and-tongs at the wreckage, as we guessed, rather than trying to bypass it. They must have used explosives during the night to break up some of the large lengths of concrete, as they've shifted quite a bit now.'

'How long d'you think they'll be?'

'A few hours yet. They've got that tracked gun dragging the big bits with a chain and hundreds of blokes are hawking debris by hand and stacking it to one side.'

'How many guns could you see?'

'That one big one, a couple more on armoured cars and two trailed behind trucks. I tried to get a closer look, but they started shooting at me, so I sheered off!'

'Shooting! Are you all right, Lance?'

'Sure, though there's a few holes in the wing fabric. Must get some Elastoplast stuck on 'em!'

He closed his trasmission and there was a babble of questions from those around Brennan.

'What was that about shooting?' demanded Gwen, grabbing his arm. 'Has he been shot? Tell me he hasn't been shot, Brennan!'

'He hasn't been shot, Gwen! Someone just loosed off a few and punctured the cloth on that mechanised kite.'

His matter-of-fact tone calmed her down and Brennan went back to his map, yet again checking distances from the blown bridge to their present position. There was nothing he could do until he knew that Fischer and his large force were on the move again. Surprise was Brennan's trump card, as it looked as if the continental force now well outnumbered them, given over eighty trucks full of men.

Brennan had planned well in advance and now heavy machine guns, rocket launchers and mortars were hidden in trenches and pits close along both sides of the motorway, with heavier armament lurking behind the crest of the hills. Their armoured vehicles were there as well, ready to charge down the wide, sloping fields when the moment was right. Everyone knew the part they had to play and if Brennan had been a religious man, all that now remained was for him to pray.

Once again, at about ten o'clock in the morning, the yellow Moth flew up the line of the motorway and lifted over the pass towards Membury, watched by a more subdued sea of faces on both hills. Tensely they waited for the little black VHF to crackle into life and soon Lance Prichard's voice came back over the fourteen miles.

'They're through, I can see two small vehicles like Land-Rovers on your side of the bridge, but stopped in the road.'

'What about the rest, can they get past?' snapped Brennan.

'Almost, I should think. They've put that howitzer thing back on the low-loader. Yes, a truck is edging through now, with a lot of guys pulling rubble from around its wheels. Jesus!'

Even above the noise of the plane's engine, Brennan could hear a burst of automatic fire.

'Get out of there Lance, you've seen enough! Get going, man!'

There was a change in the engine note, but Lance's voice came through again.

'No problem, I've climbed away to a couple of thousand feet. I'm coming back home. Just one last circuit high up.' There was a pause, then the pilot continued. 'They're in trouble further back. They're trying to tow-start some of the trucks – even pushing others with bumpers. Many of their vehicles must have duff batteries. If they stall during a fight, they'll be sitting ducks.'

Before Brennan could repeat his exhortation for Lance to clear away, there was a bang and the engine note changed again.

'Bloody hell, that was close! . . . no, it wasn't, it's a hit!'

Brennan shouted at him, but was frustrated by the one-way working of the radio, which had to be switched between each speaker. Lance kept his 'Transmit' buttton down and was still talking.

'The engine's packed up, they must have hit something vital like the magneto. Brennan, I'm turning away south, I've got a fair bit of height, I can glide a hell of a long way in this. I'll try to put her down in a field, then walk home. Give Gwen my love, tell her I'll see her back at the ranch. Out.'

The set went silent and there was no response to Brennan's urgent attempts to get him back on air. Gwen was staring at him, her eyes as round as saucers.

'He's going to die, isn't he?' she whispered.

He did his best to reassure her, but she seemed resigned to the loss of her latest lover. Liz came over and put an arm around her shoulders, giving Brennan an unfathomable look as she led the other girl back towards the tents.

Casey, Mervyn and Strickland pressed in on Brennan to hear the details of Lance's report. 'They'll be through anytime now, though squeezing all those trucks through a narrow gap will slow them down. Still, we'd better get everything ready.'

His first task was to speak to Beverley on the other side and put him firmly in the picture. Then he called up the two watchers in the Membury service station, who had a view down the motorway for over half a mile eastwards.

'Keep your eyes skinned from now on, lads. The moment you see anything coming in the distance, call me and then get out as fast as you can, understand? Burn rubber or they'll be on top of you!'

Desperately worried about Lance, he still tried to think of everything else that he had planned these past weeks. As much to assuage Gwen's fears as with any hope of success, he sent one of the youthful runners out in a small Suzuki 4x4 to look for the pilot. Brennan gave him one of the spare radios and told him to search around Marlborough and the Vale of Pewsey area. Brennan had no idea how far the Moth could glide, but if he could bring it down without killing himself, he could let them know his whereabouts on the VHF – if they were still alive to receive the message, he thought grimly.

Having done all the tasks he could think of, he did a round of the 'troops', giving encouragement and making sure they all knew what was expected of them. The vehicles were all manned, but their engines were shut down and the last exhortation Brennan made was for complete silence once the hostiles were in sight.

He went back to the irregular line of mounds that formed the front of the earthworks and for the hundredth time, swung his binoculars up to search the distant motorway where it rose up between the Downs. Almost an hour went by, an intolerable waiting time when the nerves of everyone could almost be heard twanging.

Then the radio sizzled into life, bringing a voice from Membury.

'Trucks and things coming in the far distance, sir.'

'Right, get off there, fast! Don't let them see you.'

The young men must have taken him at his word, as within five minutes, two figures on a big Kawasaki literally flew past them down below, doing at least eighty, weaving past the couple of wrecks that dotted the westbound lanes. The engine note died away beyond the interchange and stopped altogether as they reached the Moth's refuelling base, where six people were camped out on the hard shoulder. Silence fell again on the hilltop.

'It's got to be any time now,' muttered Brennan. He took off his cap and reached down for his steel helmet. As he put it on, dozens of others behind did the same. From the corner of his eye, he saw one middle-aged man furtively make the sign of the cross.

Another ten nerve-stretching minutes went by. Brennan had moved along the sloping bank of the Celtic fort to where a clump of rank couch-grass sprouted in a hummock on the top. He used this for cover, parting the coarse fronds to peer between them, in case some keen German with Zeiss binoculars was scanning the countryside from the turret of his armoured car.

His ears picked up the first sign of the enemy, a dull thrumming that was the combination of scores of motor engines coming in the distance. Then the first one appeared where the westbound carriageway sloped down between steep chalk banks.

'Here they come,' he murmured. Turning, he hissed at the nearest group of men. 'Remember, not a sound. Not even a cough or a fart, until the bridge goes up! Pass it on!'

Peering back at the road, he saw that the column was led by an armoured car, a British Army Scimitar like their own, with a small but effective Rarden gun poking from its turret. Then came a couple of old Ferrets, slowly escorting a line of trucks, two of which towed small field guns.

After a half dozen of these, a big low-loader, more used to lugging earth-moving vehicles around, carried a tracked vehicle like a small tank, with a large, stubby gun sprouting from its upper front. Even in his adrenaline-swamped state, Brennan's military curiosity forced him to whisper under his breath, 'Christ, an old M7 Priest – where the hell did they find that?'

This old veteran was the reason for the snail's pace of the hostile cavalcade, as the truck that was carrying it was making heavy weather of the weight and even going downhill as it was now, the driver seemed afraid that it would run away with him. Brennan was thankful for this extra bonus, as it gave him an added couple of minutes to complete his preparations. He quietly called Beverley on the other side to check that he had a good view of the column, and made sure that Phil Robson was in position, concealed with his detonating equipment in the fields below Bev. After a terse affirmative, the last seconds ticked away as the long line of vehicles crawled down the motorway. As in Newmarket, Brennan had last minute-qualms about visiting sudden destruction, injury and death on scarce remnants of the human race – but one look at the impressive array of weapons down below made it obvious that their adversaries were equally intent on annihilating them.

Brennan had arranged with Phil Robson to blow the bridge just as the leading vehicle passed under it, to wreck at least one without firing a shot – but their plan failed. As the Scimitar got within fifty yards of the overhanging span, the Land-Rover behind it stopped dead and from above, the frantic blaring of its horn could be heard. Vehicles behind stopped raggedly, some bumping into the one in front and several engines being stalled. As the Scimitar rapidly reversed back up to the Land-Rover, Brennan cursed their luck.

'They must have spotted the holes in the approach road!'

But even this had been anticipated in his planning with Robson and though baulked of dropping the bridge on top of the lead vehicle, Phil now pressed his switch and the whole of the eastern arc of Junction 15 erupted, followed by the surface of both approach roads. A rolling boom echoed up the valley and a vast cloud of dust and debris jetted into the air, some of it clattering on to the first few vehicles in the column.

Then, as the slight breeze carried the cloud westwards, all hell was let loose in the valley. Before the hostiles could recover from the shock of seeing their peaceful progress suddenly dislocated by what seemed like a volcano erupting in front of them, they were assaulted on both sides by concentrated fire from concealed positions in the fields just over the edge of the motorway.

Brennan's initial barrage came from mortars, which lobbed their missiles up and over the hedges into the trough formed by the steep banks that confined the M4 at this point – which was why he had chosen it for the ambush. Trapped in what was virtually a cutting through the chalk, Fischer's forces at first had no targets at which to fire and in the first minutes, a dozen of the trucks were hit and set on fire. But this time, there was not the disorderly retreat that had been seen near Cambridge – the Germans and their allies, after the first shock had passed, piled out of the trucks and ran for the shelter of the hard shoulder, under the overhang of the banks. Some stayed to unhitch their two light guns, swinging them round to face the unseen enemy on both sides.

From above, Brennan watched the first two minutes from the earthworks, while around him their armoured vehicles started up and began driving down the slopes, matched on the other side by Beverley's forces. Behind them, a pair of Saracen armoured troop carriers roared down, packed with men and women ready to drop into the undergrowth along the banks and use their small arms to fire into the death-trap of the motorway cutting.

Shoulder-held rocket launchers began adding to the barrage, as the armoured cars halted down in the fields and started firing into the massed traffic along the road. None of the gunners had ever fired in anger before and had only had a few practice shots out on common land near Cardiff, but at that short range, gun-laying meant little more than pointing the weapon in the right direction.

Brennan had seen enough after the first couple of minutes and ran for the remaining Saladin, a six-wheeled armoured car with a 76 millimetre gun in the turret, alongside a Browning machine gun. Casey was at the gun and a tough-looking girl from Swansea was driving. As they bumped down the long field with Brennan's helmeted head sticking above the turret, Casey peered along his guns and shouted up.

'We're not hitting the back end of the column, they're too far up the hill!' It was true, as the line of hostile vehicles was so long that the back end was beyond where Brennan had sited his ambush sites.

'They've got some armour up there, looks as if they're trying to bring it down,' yelled Casey again.

Another Scimitar armoured car and an armoured Land-Rover were pulling out of the back of the column and overtaking in the other lane.

They were obstructed by an old abandoned truck slewed across the road, but squeezed past it and came down the slope, firing to each side as they came.

'Get that one!' yelled Brennan and their driver turned them parallel to the hedge and raced up to close the gap. At five hundred yards, Casey yelled to her to stop and then started firing. He missed the Scimitar with two shots, but the third landed so close to the side of the Land-Rover that it bucked into the air and overturned. The Scimitar began firing back and two shells threw up gouts of white chalky earth twenty yards away, then it passed down towards the bridge.

Brennan's car kept going up along the hedges, so that they could reach the back of the queue of enemy trucks. Casey put a few shells into several trucks and raked them with the Browning. On the other side, two of Bev's Ferrets were doing the same thing and Brennan was relieved to see that two anti-tank guns were now deployed in the fields across the valley, and had started firing.

The hostiles had got over their first shock and were fighting back aggressively. All the foot-soldiers had scattered from the trucks and coaches and were hammering back with small arms fire, though they had few visible targets and had to shoot at the points from where fire was coming at them.

Brennan yelled at their driver to take them back down towards the wrecked interchange and as they bumped across the scrubby field, he saw that the tracked M7 with the big gun was lurching off its transporter. The crew were bravely – or rashly – driving it straight over the side to drop on to the road, having no time to do it in the proper way by fixing ramps at the rear end of the truck. For a moment, Brennan hoped it would overturn as it dropped several feet, but with a lurch it righted itself and turned crabwise around to bring its 105 millimetre gun to bear. It fired and a huge gout of earth erupted in the field above their Saladin, not forty yards away. It fired again and Brennan was appalled to see one of his armoured Land-Rovers suffer a direct hit and burst into flames.

Casey fired again and again, but failed to hit the M7, which now turned its attention to the earthworks on top of the hill, where one of their Saracens had stalled, with engine trouble. The biggest gun in the battle fired again and though it overshot the Saracen, there was a another fountain of earth from within the fortifications.

'Hit that bastard, Casey, for God's sake! Otherwise, it's going to screw us.'

Casey did his best but the tracked gun was now lumbering down the road and he missed it each time. Then salvation came from one of the small anti-tank guns on the Liddington side. Pulled down the field by the same old Forward Control 101 Land-Rover that they had taken to Traherne's farm, the two-pounder was set up by three young men and began rapid fire, all directed against the M7. With plenty of ammunition handed down from the 101, they soon got the range and though the mobile gun was still moving, one shot exploded in the left-hand track. It slewed the heavy machine around just as it was firing and the shell went into one of their own trucks and set it ablaze. Having no turret to traverse the gun, the M7 could now only fire straight ahead, as it depended on its tracks for aiming and was effectively paralysed.

The hostile Scimitar that had been in the lead, had now managed to scramble up the bank where there was a more gentle slope, just at the foot of the wrecked approach road. It gained the lower part of the field and like an angry bull, went roaring up towards the two anti-tank guns, bullets from its Browning machine gun rattling off the gun-shields. Brennan was a long way off, but yelled at their driver to close the distance. Casey fired as they went, though the bumps in the ground made his shots go wild.

'Only got two shells left, boss!' he yelled up. Fearful for the lives of the young gunners out in the field, Brennan suffered an agony of frustration, but Casey's next shot, though it missed the Scimitar, was so close that it attracted their attention. The turret slewed and the vehicle came around as they loosed off a shell that whistled a foot above the closed hatch above Brennan's head. He almost resigned himself to a terrible death if their next shot exploded in their cramped compartment, but Casey gave a yell of exultation. Squinting through the periscope, he saw that a shell from the anti-tank gun had hit the joint between the Scimitar's hull and turret, blowing the latter clean off. The armoured car careered on for a hundred yards, smoke coming from the interior, until it stopped and burst into flames.

Now all the fire-power of the ambush was concentrated on the column confined down on the motorway. A couple of rockets had finished off the partly-disabled M7 and only one of the wheeled guns was still firing. Some of the intact trucks were trying either to reverse back up the long hill or struggled to make a five-point turn from the queue to make a getaway. Ten of the trucks were on fire and most of the others in the lower half of the convoy were riddled with bullet-holes. Right at the tail-end of the line, one or two trucks which were beyond the fighting zone, had managed to turn round and were vanishing up the hill.

The lower end, where dust still hung over the collapsed bridge, was a scene of chaotic destruction. The trough-like cutting which carried the road was now hazy with smoke from explosives, gun-fire and burning vehicles. Most of Brennan's force had by now edged towards the banks lining the motorway and were firing down into the convoy and the scattered hostiles who were sheltering along the sides. They were firing back and one group had a mortar operating, but they were shooting blind into a force that was above them and mostly out of sight.

Brennan drove away from the wrecked Scimitar and descended to the rim of the main road, a few bullets clanging off the armour-plating. He intended to let Casey add his Browning's capability to the barrage, being out of ammunition for the main gun. However, his first look through his little periscope made his heart leap. Through the wreathing smoke and dust below, he saw a thin pole, probably a snapped-off radio aerial, poke up from the hatch of an armoured Land-Rover. There was a white shirt tied to it by the sleeves and it wagged slowly to and fro in the universal sign of surrender.

It took much yelling through Brennan's loud hailer to bring the conflict to a close. At first, the Germans kept up a ragged fire, which soon faded as they saw the shirt waving from one of their own vehicles. Brennan urgently radioed over to the other side to tell them of the capitulation, in case they'd not all seen the flag. There were still random shots rattling away along the banks, especially at the top end and he finally finished the matter by firing a couple of red flares from a Very pistol, arcing them high over the motorway.

At last there was comparative silence, broken only by the crackle of flames below, the occasional crack of exploding ammunition in burning trucks and the moans or occasional scream of a wounded person. As the smoke and stink of high explosive drifted past, Brennan climbed out of the Scimitar, keeping to the blind side in case someone decided to break the truce and take a shot at him. Casey followed him out. 'Don't trust the bastards, keep your head down,' he advised.

Crouching low, they ran to the edge of the bank and peered over through the weeds. The flag was now being held by a man who had left the Land-Rover and was walking with two others up the fast lane, shouting in German at those hiding along the edges. They were coming out at his command, hands held above their heads. Brennan, again in one of those incongruous flashbacks that sometimes plagued him, was reminded of old black-and-white propaganda films from World War II, where Germans were often depicted with their hands up and shouting 'Kamerad'. He switched on the loud hailer and stood up, much to Casey's alarm.

'Are you prepared to lay down your weapons?'

The man with the flag looked up to search for the voice. 'Yes, we surrender. Are you this man Brennan?' His voice was guttural, but his heavily-accented English was good.

'How the hell does he know your name?' muttered Casey.

'Yes, I am Brennan. We urgently need to treat the wounded, so send some of your men to do what they can for them until we get organised. You must move the rest of your men up the road, past these vehicles. Tell them to keep their hands up until they get there . . . OK?'

Brennan said 'men' automatically, then realised that unlike his troops, there was in fact no sign of a woman amongst the enemy.

The man shouted his assent and started leading the motley army uphill, still clutching his white flag. Brennan signalled to the hidden marksmen on his side to go down the bank and they began slithering and stumbling over the chalky white stones to the road below. He waved to Beverley, who he could see opposite and the same actions began over there. Very soon, about five hundred captives were sitting along the hard shoulder with their hands on their heads, faced by a line of men and women pointing rifles and machine pistols at them.

Brennan and Casey slithered down the bank and joined Beverley, Robson, Lovatt and Fleming from the other side. After detailing a dozen of their men and women to hurry along the road to seek out injured Germans, they advanced on the man with the flag.

'Are you Fischer?' snapped Brennan harshly. The other shook his head and pointed up towards Liddington. 'He's dead. He was in that armoured car. My name is Schultz – just a driver.'

Before he could reply, there was a crackling from Brennan's pocket and he pulled out the VHF.

'Brennan, it's Mervyn. There's trouble up here, we've taken casualties. Come up when you can.' The link was cut off and no one replied to Brennan's urgent call.

'Bev, there's some big trouble up at our camp, I'll have to go up there. How many casualties did we take?' He was almost afraid to hear the reply, but Beverley was unsure.

'We'll get on to that right now. I'll get vehicles around all the posts and use some of these trucks here as ambulances.'

Brennan set off at a trot with Casey and after scrambling back up the bank, he sent the other man to assess their casualties on this side. Already, the Forward Control and a couple of four-wheel drives were touring around, picking up the injured. Brennan climbed on to the plating of the waiting Scimitar and clung on as he yelled at the girl to go back up to the palisades. As they drove around the back of the earthworks, his heart sank when he saw that the tent that had been set up for casualties had disintegrated into shreds of fabric and that the adjacent one was also in tatters. A large hole in the ground and debris and soil scattered for many yards around told of the shell from the M7 that had scored a direct hit.

He leapt off the car and hurried over to where Mervyn and a small crowd of people were huddled over a row of bodies, covered with coats. The doctor turned to him, looking haggard and drained.

'Five dead – and six injured.' He hesitated, then put a hand on Brennan's shoulder and led him a few yards away. 'I'm afraid Liz was one of the wounded. She's pretty bad, I don't think she'll make it.'

Brennan felt a wave of sadness sweep over him. Not the same unbelievable, frantic horror that had gripped him when his wife died. This was a different emotion, one of regret for Liz, rather than himself – regret that her life was ending when it should have gone on far longer.

'Where is she?' he asked stonily.

'I sent them off in a truck down to the surgical unit. Two of them are really bad, as well as Liz. Gwen went with her – she's OK, apart from some scratches. Like a dozen more who've stayed up here.'

'I'll have to go down there, Mervyn. Can you cope for a bit?'

'Sure! I'm waiting for them to bring up more wounded from the fields, though I think we got off lightly considering what we were up against.'

Brennan climbed back into the Scimitar and his driver took him down the track to Badbury and then on to the motorway, as the western approach roads of the junction were intact. The surgical trailer was two miles further on, with three tents set up in a field alongside. Half a dozen women were looking after a row of wounded lying on ground sheets in one tent and an old military ambulance arrived just after them with more patients.

Gwen was standing outside the tent, her jeans and blouse spattered with earth and both arms showing many small cuts and bruises. Thankfully her beautiful face was unmarked, thought Brennan, inconsequentially.

'She's at the end of the tent, Brennan. The German doctor told me there's nothing he can do, she's had a lethal head injury.'

They went in past groaning men and one who would groan no more, to reach a still figure lying under a red blanket. Gwen had wrapped a white towel around her head and outwardly there was no sign of injury. Liz Peterson's face was calm and peaceful and she seemed to be asleep, rather than deeply unconcious. They squatted one each side and Brennan took her hand, which was cold and limp.

'Are we sure that nothing can be done?' he asked in a low voice.

Gwen shook her head, bits of earth falling from her bedraggled hair.

'The doctor said that even a neurosurgeon couldn't do anything. He's an expert, Brennan – and he's worth his weight in diamonds at the moment, the way he's working.'

They fell silent again and Brennan rubbed Liz's hand gently. Then he bent and kissed her gently on the cheek and stood up.

'I've got to get back, Gwen. We've won, but at a price.'

They looked down at the peaceful face of the dying nurse and Gwen's hand found his. 'I'm so sorry, Brennan.' She looked up at him, her eyes flooding with tears. 'We lost each other, now we've both lost someone else.'

He slipped an arm around her shoulders. 'Don't give up, love. Lance is a survivor, he may turn up yet.' With a last long look down at Liz, he said 'Stay with her, Gwen, until the end, will you?'

Then he loped out of the tent, the weight of the dead and wounded sitting heavily on his broad shoulders.

It was almost a week before a full council meeting was held in Cardiff Castle, as the 'army' had only arrived back two days before.

They began by standing in silence to remember those who had given their lives for the community. Thankfully, they were fewer than Brennan had feared, in part due to the skill of the medical team. Twelve had died and sixteen had serious injuries, but would recover. There had been many slight injuries, ranging from bullet grazes to embedded splinters, but considering the violence of the thirty-minute battle, they had got off lightly.

'What was the total casualties amongst the Jerries?' asked Mervyn bluntly. They had discovered that term 'Jerries' was far from accurate, as the hostiles had included Danes, Poles, Czechs and even Russians.

'Ninety-six dead and we've still got twenty-eight here in our sick-bay. I suspect that when they're recovered, most of those will want to stay with us!' He turned to the fair-headed man who sat at the table next to him.

'Now, what about you, Lazarus? Are you going to give us the details?'

Lance grinned at the allusion. 'I didn't come back from the dead, far from it. But it was a bloody long walk home.' He explained that when his plane was hit by automatic fire from the ground, his engine's electrics must have been mangled. As he was at two thousand feet, he was able to glide the little plane for almost three miles before he ran out of sky, as he put it. Unfortunately, all the fields at that point were badly overgrown with bushes, giving him a rough landing, so that the Moth finally tipped up on to its nose.

'I got a bash on the head and when I woke up, my radio was on the blink, so I couldn't tell you where I was.'

Gwen was sitting on the other side of the table and smiled at her lover, though she had heard his tale more than once before.

'I told you he'd turn up, like a bad penny,' Brennan growled at her, but grinned at Lance when he turned back to him. 'If we had any Victoria Crosses, we'd give you a couple, but you'll have to make do with an extra pint at the bar tonight.'

Mavis Strickland returned to more serious matters. 'They've now had two defeats at your hands, Brennan. Do you think they'll come back for more?'

He shrugged expressively. 'Who knows? But not for a long time, that's for sure.'

'What did you get out of that Schultz chap, the one with the white flag?' asked John Lovatt.

'He seemed bloody glad to be alive and equally glad that Gustaf Fischer was gone! He promised that they would slink back to the coast and behave themselves.'

'I think we'll be left alone until some ambitious bastard decides to have another go,' said Beverley. 'And hopefully, that may take years.'

'They won't have any significant weaponry or vehicles in the future,' explained Brennan. 'They must have cleaned out the eastern counties to get what they had and we've either taken or destroyed everything else in the south. We seized all his weapons and made sure Schultz only had those older trucks and coaches to carry his dead and wounded back home. What's left can rust on the motorway, unless there's anything useful we can salvage.'

The rest of the meeting was devoted to details of getting back to normal and planning for future food supplies, education and medical care. As they finished, Alfred Ashe stood and proposed a vote of thanks to Brennan, for hopefully giving them a generation of peace to enjoy.

'We made the right choice for our General Manager,' he said pompously. 'It proves the correctness of the democratic process!'

With a barely concealed grin, Brennan grabbed his papers from the table and hurried out, but he was caught up halfway across the castle grounds by Gwen.

'After that, you'll be stuck with this job for years, chum!' she said, with a return of her old gaiety.

'I told you he'd turn up, didn't I?' he countered.

She stopped and looked up at him. 'Nothing is for ever, Boss,' she murmured. 'Just you remember that, Arthur Brennan!'